A Winter Love Song

Rita Bradshaw was born in Northamptonshire, where she still lives today. At the age of sixteen she met her husband – whom she considers her soulmate – and they have two daughters, a son and six grandchildren. Much to her delight, Rita's first novel was accepted for publication and she has gone on to write many more successful novels since, including the number one bestseller *Dancing in the Moonlight*.

As a committed Christian and passionate animal-lover her life is full, but she loves walking her dog, reading, eating out and visiting the cinema and theatre, as well as being involved in her church and animal welfare.

RITA BRADSHAW

A Winter Love Song

PAN BOOKS

First published 2017 by Macmillan

This paperback edition first published 2017 by Pan Books
an imprint of Pan Macmillan
20 New Wharf Road, London N1 9RR
Associated companies throughout the world
www.panmacmillan.com

ISBN   978-1-5290-3234-5

A CIP catalogue record for this book is available from the British Library.

Typeset by Ellipsis, Glasgow
Printed and bound by CPI Group (UK) Ltd, Croydon, CR0 4YY

Visit www.panmacmillan.com to read more about all our books
and to buy them. You will also find features, author interviews and
news of any author events, and you can sign up for e-newsletters
so that you're always first to hear about our new releases.

This book is in memory of my wonderful, sweet, comical, beautiful and utterly loving furry baby, Meg. Seven and a half years weren't nearly long enough, precious little girl, and they've left me heartbroken, but they were perfection, and your devotion to me was so unique and so special it can never be replaced. You were so much more than a dog in your capacity for immense love and understanding, and that waggy little tail had a language all of its own. Muffin misses you, Dad misses you, and I physically ache all the time for you. You are loved beyond words, and you are more precious than silver and gold, as I told you every day of your life.

Acknowledgements

As ever, realms of research for this story, but special mention to:

Fairfield Folk by Frances Brown
Louisa's Fairground Life and Beyond by Louisa M. Prestney
Voices from the Fairground, Laisterdyke Local History Group
Jungle Warfare by J. P. Cross
Some Sunny Day: My Autobiography by Dame Vera Lynn
War Diary, Marshall Cavendish Books

Contents

Preface

He wasn't going to be able to fight his way out of this. He could read in their eyes that he was a goner, but he was damned if he'd make it easy for them. He didn't want to die, but if the price of staying alive meant beating that young lad to a pulp it was too high.

He watched them as they edged up the stairs, and strangely the crippling fear that had gripped him all night was gone. He'd brought this on himself, there was no one else to blame. He'd been such a fool.

It was the thought of leaving his little lass that was crucifying as he waited for them to make their move. He hadn't had the chance to say goodbye, to tell her he loved her and that she was his sun, moon and stars, and now it was too late. What would she think, what would she do . . . ?

And then they were on him and he could hear Mrs Walton in the background screaming and wailing like a banshee.

PART ONE

John

1928

Chapter One

'Now, Bonnie, I'm going to ask you something and I think you know what I'm going to say. Did you kick your grandma like she said?'

The small black-haired girl standing in front of the big thickset man whose upper arms were the width of her waist eyed him without fear. 'Aye, Da.'

John Lindsay closed his eyes for a moment. 'Why, hinny? Why did you do that?'

'Because she's cruel. She kicked one of Miss Nelly's dogs, the new one she's still training, just because it cocked its leg up the wagon steps. So I kicked *her*. It yelped, the poor thing, and it was limping when it ran off. Me grandma deserved it and I hate her.'

It wasn't the first time the child had expressed such sentiments. John crouched down in front of his daughter and if he had spoken what was in his heart he would have said he agreed with the child's summing-up of the woman who was the bane of his life. Instead he gently said, 'Two wrongs don't make a right, lass. You know that, don't you? And she's got a big bruise on her shin.'

Bonnie stared at her father. She wanted to say that she was glad about the bruise but she knew that would upset her da. But she didn't understand why he always stuck up for her grandma. Well, not always, she corrected herself. But a lot of the time. And yet her da didn't like her grandma any more than she did. She knew this to be true even though her da had never said such a thing, the same way as she knew her grandma hated her da even when she was being civil to him.

'I think you ought to go and say you're sorry, hinny, don't you?'

As soon as the words had left his lips John knew he should have put it differently rather than inviting her opinion.

Sure enough, Bonnie glared at him. 'No, I don't. She's nasty, spiteful, and she only kicked the dog because she'd had a barney with Franco earlier. I heard them when I got there but they stopped when they saw me. She was saying he'd stayed out half the night and she wasn't having him carrying on any more. What did she mean, carrying on?'

John stood up. He had a good idea what Margarita had been in a lather about. Franco had a roving eye and some of the silly young lassies who came to the fair didn't have the sense they were born with. 'That's not our business, Bonnie.'

'Well, that's why she kicked Miss Nelly's dog anyway.'

'Be that as it may, you can't go round kicking folk because they might behave differently to how you think they should. You're nearly ten years old, you're not a babby who doesn't know any better.'

'I don't kick everyone. I've only kicked me grandma.' Violet-blue eyes that were dark with righteous indignation declared more eloquently than words that Bonnie felt hard done by.

Realizing that he needed to take a different tack if some semblance of peace was going to be restored between the child and her grandmother, John scooped his daughter up into his arms. 'Say sorry to her for me, lass, all right? Your grandma's all upset and it'll make things better. I know you don't want to but do it for your old da, eh, hinny?'

Bonnie's body was as stiff as a board for another moment and then she relaxed, thin arms winding round his neck. Her voice soft against his bristled cheek, she whispered, 'All right, Da, but she's not upset, not like you mean. She's just angry that she got a taste of her own medicine for once.'

It was so on the ball that John had to bite his lip to stop from smiling. Cute as a cartload of monkeys, his bairn was, and with a way of cutting through all the flannel. 'That's a good lass.' He held her close for a moment before bending down and setting her on her feet. 'Go on, do it now. Better to get it over with.'

Bonnie gave him a wan smile. They were standing in a field that held the big tent with the platform inside

7

for the acrobats, jugglers and other acts, and this was surrounded by booths and stalls and smaller tents. A second field a short distance away was dotted with the wooden living wagons of the fairground community, smoke rising into the warm May air from a number of campfires and buzzing with the sounds of women talking, laughing and sometimes arguing; children playing, dogs barking, babies crying and horses whinnying. She began to make her way towards the wagons but had only gone a few steps when her father called after her, 'And say it like you mean it, mind.'

She stopped for a moment, her thin shoulders slumping, and then straightened and walked on, but not before a long and heartfelt sigh had caused her small chest to rise and fall.

Margarita Fellario watched her granddaughter coming towards her. She had seen her son-in-law pick the child up and then the way Bonnie had hugged her father, and it had done nothing to dampen her fury.

At fifty-four years of age Margarita looked much older, but then all the fair women did. It was a hard life. Besides looking after their children, doing all the washing by hand with water heated on open fires and emptied into big wooden barrels, cooking meals, gathering anything edible from the hedgerows and fields along with skinning and jointing any rabbits or game their menfolk trapped, and dragging supplies home from village shops, they were expected to make and sell baskets, wooden pegs and other items, mind the fairground stalls and turn their hand to anything and everything when the need arose.

Not that the menfolk weren't equally resilient in their efforts to make a living and feed their families, but always with the exception of bonding themselves to another in a job. Travellers had to be their own masters. To a man they had nothing but contempt for those who entered into a contract engaging themselves to an employer. Besides being showmen they were horse-dealers, and also adept at a number of rural crafts. Industry, cunning and thrift meant their pockets were rarely empty.

From spring to late autumn there was no life for Margarita and the fair community except that of the roads, and although the north-eastern winters meant they had to rest up for weeks at a time, no one was idle. Living wagons, swings, sideshows, stalls, carousels and other rides would be repainted, wheels checked and axles greased, and general maintenance carried out. Nevertheless, being anchored to one spot was irksome, and the winter they'd recently endured had been a particularly long and harsh one. Tempers had grown short and there had been several fights among the men, and a couple between the women too. Bonnie had suffered numerous lashings from Margarita's tongue as her grandmother had vented her frustration on the child, and their already thorny relationship had deteriorated further. It had been impossible for the fair to get on the road and secure their normal spot on Sunderland's town moor before

Christmas, as freezing blizzards scoured the country. The north had been cut off for weeks on end, and food supplies had been air-dropped into some villages buried in snow. Floods and gales had followed through January and February, only for the temperature to plummet again in March when more blizzards had racked Britain. Money had grown short, food had been rationed and but for the travellers' expertise in poaching – which was never talked about, along with the acquisition of a sheep or two that 'lost its way' into the camp – the community would have been in dire straits.

But now it was a lovely warm May, summer was just round the corner and everyone was happy again – everyone but her grandma, Bonnie thought bitterly as she approached the tall straight figure.

Her hands on her hips, Margarita waited until the child was standing in front of her before raising her black eyebrows. 'Well?' she said coldly. 'What have you got to say for yourself?'

Bonnie knew what was required of her but in spite of wanting to please her da, the words stuck in her throat. Not for the first time she asked herself how someone as nice as her mam had been – and everyone said she'd been beautiful and kind with never a cross word – could have come from the woman in front of her. Stammering slightly, not from fear but from resentment at what she'd been made to do, she said, 'I – I'm sorry for kicking you.'

'You look it.'

Bonnie's chin shot up. She knew what her grandma

was about, oh aye. She wanted to get her into more trouble. Miss Nelly had been talking to her da the other day and she'd said Margarita Fellario could make a saint swear. They hadn't known she was listening but she had thought then that Miss Nelly was right. Oh, how she hated her grandma.

Swallowing hard against the hot retort hovering on her tongue, Bonnie lowered her head so she didn't have to look at her grandma. 'Ignore her when she starts,' her da had said to Miss Nelly, but that was easier said than done.

'You're every inch your father's daughter, aren't you?' Margarita would have liked nothing more than to shake her granddaughter till her teeth rattled. 'You'll come to a bad end, m'girl – and look at me when I'm talking to you.'

There was a movement in the wagon behind and when a man's voice said, 'Let the child alone, Marge,' Bonnie looked up and saw Franco standing at the top of the wooden steps; his white shirt was unbuttoned to the waist showing his curly black chest hair and a gold medallion hanging from a chain round his neck.

Franco was the fair's fire-eater but he wasn't her granda. Her da had told her that her real granda had died before she was born, and her grandma had married Franco a little while later. He was her grandma's cousin, but most of the travellers were interrelated and in their particular community a good number had Spanish blood. Bonnie knew that her Spanish great-grandparents, along with several other families, had come to England in the middle of the last century, travelling up and down the north-east with their brightly painted, horse-drawn wagons, stalls and sideshows. She also knew it was because her own da was a Sunderland lad born and bred who had no travelling links that her grandma didn't like him. Miss Nelly had told her on the quiet that her grandma had wanted her mam to marry one of her Spanish relations, but her mam wouldn't have any of it once she'd met her da.

Franco now caught her eye and inclined his head towards the roughly hewn table at the bottom of the steps. 'You help your grandma with them baskets, girl, and work hard. You've gallivanted enough for one day.'

Franco knew she hadn't been gallivanting, Bonnie thought angrily. He'd seen what had happened with Miss Nelly's dog earlier and why she had kicked her grandma and then run off. But again, she said nothing, merely sitting down on the little stool next to her grandmother's chair.

'And that's it?' Margarita's voice was a low hiss. 'After what she's done to my leg? She wants a good whipping.'

'You know full well John wouldn't tolerate that, so let it lie, woman.'

'Let it lie! You're as bad as him. She's riding to hell in a handcart and neither of you can see it.'

Now the tone of Franco's voice changed, carrying a warning when he repeated softly, 'I said let it lie, so let it lie. I've had enough for one day, Marge. I mean it.'

Bonnie wondered if her grandmother was going to say more but after a moment Margarita flung herself down into her chair, her face stony, and Franco disappeared back into the wagon.

Reluctantly, Bonnie continued with the task she had left so abruptly earlier after the incident with the dog. She was making small round baskets, the size customers usually bought for their children, with short heathland rushes she had collected a few days before. They grew no more than a foot high and were perfect for the job. Her grandmother used the taller bullrushes for bigger containers that could be woven with the least amount of joining, and then there were the willows with their sallower wands for sturdier baskets. Margarita concocted colouring dyes for the baskets from the natural bounty in the countryside – blue from dogwood berries, yellow from peat or heather, brown from brambles, green from nettles or privet berries, and bright red from a plant she called ladies' bedstraw. Bonnie always thought her grandma looked like a witch when she was stirring her brews which often stank to high heaven, her face grim as she bent over her cauldron fixed above the fire.

She sighed silently. The sky was high and blue and the sunshine was warm on her face, and in the distance she could see a group of her friends sitting in a circle busy painting the wooden dolls and little boats and other toys the menfolk carved for the stalls. She wished she was with them but her grandma rarely allowed it. She sighed again. She didn't enjoy weaving the baskets – the rushes made her fingers sore and a couple of the dyes irritated her skin – but it was one of the many tasks she was expected to do and she did it without complaint. What she really loved were the times when she sang and danced in the big tent. She always got lots of coins in the box where visitors to the fair could show their appreciation, but although her grandma was all for it, her da didn't like her 'performing for her supper' as she had heard him put it.

But she *loved* singing – she'd sing every day if only she could, she thought longingly. Up on the platform she felt like a different person and she would have expected her da to understand this because he had a lovely singing voice too. He was billed as the fair's singing boxer, and his voice was as good as his boxing. None of the men who got in the ring with her da hoping to win the fight and the prize money ever succeeded, and when their time was up, her da would always act daft and serenade them out of the enclosure; everyone would laugh, even the men who walked away with a bloody nose.

'Stop your daydreaming, Bonita.'

Bonnie's reverie was interrupted by her grandmother's tight voice and she realized her hands were idle. Without a word she picked up the basket she was working on, but wished, with silent urgency, that something catastrophic would befall her grandma. Even calling her Bonita was meant to rile her – her grandma knew she didn't like the name and everyone else called her Bonnie.

*

John waited until he saw Bonnie sit down before he made his way over the field to where he'd promised to help Ferdinand, one of Louisa's uncles, mend a couple of the horses on the steam roundabout. They had got damaged the day before on the journey from Boldon to their present site in Washington. This location held fond memories for him. In the early days of his marriage to Louisa, Bonnie's mother, he had persuaded her to take a day off with him when the fair had stopped at Washington for a while. She had left her stall and he'd closed his boxing tent and they'd absconded with nothing more on their minds than enjoying a day in each other's company away from the close-knit fair community. He'd known he'd get some stick from Margarita for skiving off, as she'd no doubt put it, but he didn't care. He couldn't do anything right in his mother-in-law's eyes anyway.

John stopped and raised his eyes to the high blue sky, drinking in the heady scent of the May blossom which clothed the trees bordering the field.

That had been a grand day. They'd wandered along hand in hand on the north bank of the river, laughing and talking and so in love it hurt. Before they had retraced their steps in the evening they'd taken afternoon tea at Girdle Cake Cottage. The beautifully picturesque cottage was a popular place for refreshments and they had sat and watched the folk travelling upstream from Sunderland by boat to have their tea and then returning on the tide. He'd told Louisa this was their honeymoon and she had laughed and kissed him full on the lips, her dark brown eyes alight with love.

Louisa, oh, Louisa. For a moment the pain of her passing was as acute as on the day she had died, just nine months after Bonnie was born. She had been as right as rain one day, complaining of an excruciating pain in her stomach the next, and gone within seventy-two hours. Burst appendix, the doctor he had fetched to the site in the early hours had stated. It happened suddenly like that sometimes.

John shook his head at the memory of that nightmarish time. All he'd known was that he had lost his wife, his darling, his rock, and but for their daughter he would have walked down to the river and ended it there and then. But Bonnie had needed him. His Bonnie, bonny by name and bonny in appearance but a handful, oh, aye. John smiled to himself. Strong-willed and headstrong to a fault at times, but with a capacity for compassion and affection that covered a multitude of sins. He was fully aware that the stubborn and what Margarita labelled wilful side of his daughter's nature came from him, but he made no apology for being glad about how she was.

He narrowed the blue eyes his daughter had inherited. The world was a hard place right enough, it gave no quarter to the weak. He'd survived his early years in Sunderland's East End Orphan Asylum by his determination not to be crushed by the system, and he'd used that same resolve to persuade his Louisa to hold firm against her mother's objections and marry him. Best thing he'd ever done. And it was the same with the gaming. He knew in his bones that he just had to apply himself and one day he'd hit that running streak and make his fortune. There had been times in the past he'd been so close he could taste it.

He knew he had the gambling bug, as Louisa had called it. Even as a child in the orphanage he'd taken on the other lads for the coloured pebbles they'd played with in lieu of marbles, or the monkey nuts they were given on a Sunday afternoon. He supposed it was his way of fighting back against the Spartan discipline of the place where even names were replaced by numbers. They'd had no life of their own, ruled by regulations to the point where no one had dared to speak outside the designated times. Meals were taken in silence and woe betide a boy who dared to ask anyone to pass the salt. Then of course the orphanage uniform picked them out from other children at school and the bullies had had a field day with them.

But not with him. John's muscled chest swelled under his shirt as he drew in a large breath. No, not with him. He'd used his fists and his feet on the bullies no matter whether they were twice his size, even though he'd known he'd be knocked into next weekend on his return to the orphanage if it was reported. But it had worked. It hadn't taken long for the other lads to learn that he wasn't to be messed with. He never started a fight but by gum, he ended them.

He had told Louisa about some of the things that had cut deep in his boyhood, not least the stigma of having the word 'Asylum' emblazoned on his cap, and the indignity of being referred to as a number rather than a name. Afterwards he wished he hadn't because she had become upset. She had been curled up in his arms in their bed in the living wagon he had saved up for months to buy from another traveller who was having a bigger, custom-built one constructed to accommodate the needs of his growing family. He hadn't realized she was crying, not until he had felt her teardrops on his bare chest, and when he'd told her those days were in the past and he was the happiest man alive now, she'd sobbed that she was crying for the little boy he had been. He hadn't really understood that at the time, but once Bonnie had been born and his father's heart had kicked in, he'd known what Louisa had meant. The thought of his beautiful Bonnie being placed in some grim Victorian institution was insupportable.

Giving himself a mental shake, he muttered, 'Stop your daydreaming, man.' There was work to be done and Ferdinand was waiting for him. He liked Ferdinand, one of Louisa's uncles; he liked most of the fair community and he knew they liked him, despite Margarita's attitude. If it weren't for his mother-in-law, life would be pleasant enough for him and Bonnie. Maybe if Margarita had had more than one child she wouldn't have been so dominating with Louisa? He knew she was bitter about the fact that more babies hadn't come along, but then Margarita was bitter about so many things. And to marry a man like Franco after her first husband had died had been asking for trouble. More than ten years her junior and convinced he was God's gift to women – what had she been thinking of? You could hear the pair of them going at each other hammer and tongs some days, and ten to one it was over some lass or other.

John reached Ferdinand as the man was struggling to lift part of the roundabout into position, swearing and cursing with the effort. John grinned. 'Don't let them drum-banging hallelujahs hear you – they already think we're in league with old Nick as it is.' In Boldon, the Salvation Army had stationed themselves at the entrance to the fair, and men and women preachers had warned folk of the dangers therein, calling it a den of iniquity rife with immorality and drunkenness. Not that it had deterred the crowds one jot. The shooting galleries, coconut shies, gingerbread and toy stalls, china emporia, penny-trumpet booths and fried-fish vendors had worked their usual attraction, along with the rides and the entertainments in the various tents. The rides kept going from midday to midnight to the accompaniment of ear-piercing music, which was one reason Ferdinand was anxious to mend his steam roundabout before the afternoon was on them. No ride, no income.

Ferdinand snorted. Like most of the fair folk he had learned that it was better to work with the establishment than to antagonize it, but the Salvation Army got on his nerves in Boldon. He had nearly come to blows with one young zealot who made the mistake of referring to the showmen as Gypsies. Hereditary showmen were a race apart, different from Romanies and a cut above all other travellers on the road – at least, according to Ferdinand's proud reckoning. And the rest of the fair folk were in agreement.

Louisa had told John in the early days of their meeting that she, along with many others, could trace their respective families back more than a couple of hundred years, boasting of generations who had made their living at fairs, first in their homeland of Spain and then in Britain. He'd understood Louisa's pride in her heritage, and that of Ferdinand and the rest of them, but Margarita taking this pretension a step further and declaring that her daughter was ruining the pure bloodline by marrying him had sorely tried his tolerance.

He had confronted Margarita one day shortly before he and Louisa got wed. She had been turning wood shavings into artificial chrysanthemums which she then dyed and arranged in vases to sell on her stall, and she had looked down her aquiline nose at his approach. He had cast aside his hitherto softly-softly approach with Louisa's mother that day, fed up to the back teeth with the poisonous trickle of venom about him fed to her daughter at every opportunity, the latest being that any bairns of a union between them would be tainted. It had been a bitter and fierce encounter on both sides, but at the end of it Margarita had known she'd met her match. It had done nothing to improve relations between them but he had managed to convince her that if she didn't sheath her claws, once he and Louisa were wed he would see to it that they left the fair and set up home in a town. He had known he wouldn't do that – Louisa was a traveller to the core and every inch a product of her heritage – but fortunately Margarita had believed him, and hadn't wanted to lose her only child.

Once the roundabout was up and working again, the two men went their separate ways, but the incident with Bonnie and her grandmother, and his subsequent train of thought, had unsettled John. When Louisa had died he had been too grief-stricken for a long while to think about the future or what was best for their daughter. It had been enough to get through each day, and yes, he acknowledged now, he had been grateful to the fair folk for rallying round and helping him. There had always been someone willing to take care of the child when he was working. Let's face it, he thought ruefully, Bonnie was related to half of the fair community on Louisa's side in one way or other. And so he had stayed, telling himself the bairn needed her extended family especially now her mam was gone, but that one day, when she was older, he would make a life for the two of them somewhere else. But the years had gone by and he never had.

He walked over to his tent. He had made the boxing ring himself in sections so that it was easy to dismantle and reassemble when they moved. He was a good boxer, more than good. If he hadn't fallen in love with Louisa he knew he would have made a name for himself in boxing circles and likely earned a good living out of it. He was too long in the tooth now, but once he could have done it. He nodded at the thought. But a life on the road had been in Louisa's blood; he would never have asked her to give it up, whatever he had threatened to her mother.

John tied the entrance flap to one side before standing and looking at the ring; but he didn't really see it. There had to be better than a travelling life for his Bonnie. He would never have voiced the sentiment to a living soul – the fair folk would be mortally insulted, he knew that – but his bairn was as bright as a button with a mind that was razor sharp, whereas most of the travellers couldn't read or write. He had taught Bonnie her letters and the child had been reading at five years old. He had bought her children's adventure stories and the like at first, but then he had added history, geography and science books into the mix and she had devoured them all.

John frowned; he was between a rock and a hard place, as he put it. His bairn could go far, perhaps even become a teacher or work in an office when she was older, but to do anything like that she needed a better education than he could provide and that would take money, more than he could earn as a travelling boxer. And Bonnie herself worried him with this desire she had to sing and dance in the big tent. Her voice was beautiful, there was no doubt about that, and the bairn was in her element when she was performing, but he wanted more than a travelling life for her. It was grindingly exhausting for the women, and all she could expect was to marry within the community and drop one bairn after another until she was worn out before her time.

He flexed his great shoulders and hitched his moleskin trousers further up his waist. Gaming was the answer all right – if he could just get a big win all his troubles would be over. Bonnie was still young enough to adapt to a different way of going on but old enough that he could leave her by herself for a few hours if the need arose. He could see it all in his mind's eye – the two of them settled in a nice little house somewhere, but in a good area, safe and respectable where his lass could make nice friends and go to school regularly. He wouldn't tell a soul about it until it was done, and then Margarita and her venomous tongue could go and take a running jump.

But first he had to get Lady Luck to smile on him . . .

Chapter Two

The day had dragged for Bonnie, anchored as she was to her grandmother's side. Once the fair had opened at twelve o'clock Margarita had insisted her granddaughter remain with her on her stall. She knew from experience that she always sold more of her baskets and other wares when the child was with her. Mothers with children always smiled and talked to Bonnie, and invariably bought their offspring one of the little children's baskets filled with fresh flowers gathered from the fields and hedgerows when Bonnie said she had made them. Much as Margarita hated to admit it to herself, her granddaughter had a way with folk.

But now it was twilight, and the shows and booths and stalls that sprang into life at noon when the showmen unfurled their pictures and opened their tents always looked their best once darkness fell. Lamps flared and candles flickered on the fronts of shows, and smaller lights sparkled and twinkled along the rows of toy and gingerbread and sweet stalls, glimmering round the hot-potato and toffee-apple stands. Various booths were illuminated with hundreds of tiny lamps – sapphire and amber, emerald and ruby – arranged in the form of crowns, stars and feathers. These were Bonnie's favourites, and her grandmother had told her it was the way the booths were presented at fairs in the old country, as Margarita always referred to Spain in spite of having been born in the north-east of England and never having left its shores. The Spanish way of doing things was far superior to the English, Margarita said, and the showmen in 'her country' were artistes first and foremost.

Bonnie didn't know about that, but the fair at night thrilled her with its theatrical brilliance and she felt at those times it was the best place on earth. Pleasure-seekers who had been at work during the day flocked in and there was a different atmosphere once darkness bathed the scene. Any horse trading was done long before sunset, and the night was given over to locals who merely wanted to be taken out of their normally humdrum existence for a while.

Having been dismissed half an hour earlier by her grandma with the order, 'Get yourself off to bed and no dawdling, mind,' Bonnie had done exactly the opposite. She had worked hard for hours, first making the baskets and filling them with the flowers she'd gathered, and then helping mind the stall. Now it was her favourite part of the day when she was free to wander about the fair for a while as long as her grandma didn't see. Bonnie knew that most of the fair folk were in cahoots with her and didn't agree with how her grandma treated her; not that anyone would ever voice this – it was an unwritten rule among the community that no one interfered in anyone else's family by word or deed – but she knew nevertheless. Folk were always kinder to her somehow, as though to make up for how her grandma was. Like now, for instance.

Bonnie looked up into the smiling face of Pedro, the hurdy-gurdy man who had just thrust a couple of pennies into her hand and told her to buy herself a hot potato for her supper. She grinned her thanks, and then giggled as Mimi, his monkey, jumped on her shoulder and jabbered away in her ear. Mimi was dressed in a little flowered frock with matching pants; she had a wardrobe of such outfits, all made by Pedro's wife who was a dab hand with her needle and also a first-class crocheter. Her da had told her that folk came from miles around when they knew their fair was in town to buy the curtains, doilies, tray-cloths, table covers, bedspreads and other items Mrs Carlini produced. She'd make her wares to order when folk requested something specific, never working from patterns but from pictures people would give her. Such was her honest reputation, eager housewives were more than happy to pay in advance, knowing their order would be waiting for them to collect the next time the fair came. The bedspreads took 135 balls of mercerized cotton to make, and her da had said there were lots of shops who wanted Mrs Carlini's merchandise but she liked to deal direct with her customers.

Pedro's wife's stall was beautiful to see, and housewives had been known to nearly come to blows when two women had wanted the same item.

After leaving Pedro, Bonnie bought her potato and wandered into the big tent to eat it. Miss Nelly and her performing dogs were in the middle of their act, and Bonnie was relieved to see that the dog her grandma had kicked seemed none the worse for his fright.

Miss Nelly was so lovely with animals, Bonnie thought, licking the last of the butter from her fingers as she finished her supper. She was her favourite person in the whole wide world after her da. Her thick, sandy gold hair that she wrapped round her head in twisted coils was always shining, and she had the greenest of eyes with lashes so long they didn't seem real. When Miss Nelly was all dressed up in the clothes she wore to perform she could have been one of the good fairies from the story books her da had bought her – all floaty and sparkling and magical.

Bonnie half closed her eyes so that Miss Nelly's figure had a misty outline. It was better to wish for something when the real world was shut out a bit, she'd always found. She could give her whole attention to it then. Not that this wish had worked in the past, but she had to keep on trying. 'Let my da fall in love with Miss Nelly so he wants to marry her and she can be my mam,' she whispered, 'and I promise I'll never cheek me grandma again.'

She didn't ask for Miss Nelly to love her da; she had

seen the way Miss Nelly looked at him and it was different from how she looked at anyone else. Her big green eyes were soft and starry then, and her cheeks always took on a pink tinge. No, if her da would just look the side Miss Nelly was on, that would be all that was needed. She didn't dwell on the time her impatience had prompted her to help things along a little by pointing out to her da that Miss Nelly was sweet on him. Her da hadn't exactly shouted when he'd told her never to repeat such a thing again, but the tenor of his voice and the grimness in his face had brought tears to her eyes. He had taken her into his arms then, holding her close as he had muttered, 'All right, all right, don't take on. I know you don't mean nowt but it doesn't take much to set tongues wagging, lass.'

'I just meant . . .' Her voice had trailed away in a sob.

'I know, I know. You're fond of Miss Nelly, aren't you, but there are some things you're too young to understand, hinny. The way I felt about your mam . . .' He shook his head. 'Miss Nelly is a fine woman and a good friend to both of us, now isn't she? That's good enough, isn't it?'

It wasn't, but as she drew back and looked into her da's eyes she knew what he wanted her to say and her love for him, which was bigger than the desire for a mother, enabled her to lie with a sincerity that flowed with the smoothness of truth. They hadn't spoken of the matter again from that day to this, but that didn't mean she had given up on the dream. Her da was always saying it was good to have a pocketful of dreams; he had told her that from the time she was a toddler, saying how else were dreams going to come true if you didn't keep them safe? And she felt no qualms about holding on to this one.

Bonnie smoothed down the white pinafore she wore over her thick linen dress and left the tent, and as she did so Miss Nelly smiled at her to let her know she'd been aware of her presence. Once outside she stood for a few moments watching Ham Bastien's gallopers. No one within the fair community ever made the mistake of calling the gallopers a roundabout; it would have been more than their life was worth if Ham had heard them. Eighteen horses and eighteen magnificently painted ostriches made up the gallopers, and with the ornate carved heads of kings picked out in gold leaf on the rounding boards, the gleaming brass spiralled rods and the mighty beasts themselves, it was a majestic sight. Ham himself added to the grandeur, resplendent in a long red velvet frock coat, frilled shirt and black trousers with a top hat sitting on his curly black hair.

Her father had told her that the general Depression in the country, bringing as it did massive unemployment and a high cost of living, had hit some fairs hard. Folk didn't have much money in their pockets to spend on pleasure, but their fair, with rides like Ham's, stalls like Mrs Carlini's and the varied shows that went on in the big tent, hadn't really been affected. You only needed two or three outstanding rides and stalls and it drew the customers in, and then the lesser rides like Ferdinand's and the ordinary stalls and booths reaped the benefit from the crowds, he had explained. They were fortunate to be in the St Ignatius Fair in what were hard times for many travellers. Ham had also replaced his old organ with a new 89 Key Gaudin organ the year before. It had two extra keys that played a violin baritone but as it was bigger than the old one, Ham had been forced to cut the Gaudin down on either side to fit into the centre of the gallopers. Her da had helped Ham do the job and now Ham gave her free rides when the gallopers opened up each afternoon – when she could slip away from her grandma, that was.

Bonnie stood listening to the particularly sweet sound of the organ for a moment or two more, and she was just turning to make her way home to the wagon she shared with her da where she'd put herself to bed, when a large hand clamped itself on her shoulder, making her jump.

'What do you think you're doing gallivanting about at this time of night? Your grandma'll have your guts for garters if she catches you.'

That word again. Gallivanting. She didn't like it and she didn't like Franco either, Bonnie thought, as she stared up into the dark handsome face of her grandma's husband. Not that he was unkind to her – he wasn't, and there were times when he would actually take her side against her grandma – but she didn't like the way he was with Miss Nelly. Always laughing and joking and teasing her. She'd said that once to her da, hoping, she supposed if she was being honest with herself, that it might prompt him to look more closely at how pretty Miss Nelly was, but her da had just shrugged and said that was the way Franco was with everyone. Even in her child's mind she had known he meant it was how Franco was with the *lassies*, but it *was* different with Miss Nelly. She knew it was. She had seen how Franco had stared after Miss Nelly a number of times when she'd either ignored him or made it plain she didn't like his attentions; it was a hungry look, as though he'd seen something he wanted to eat.

Her thoughts made her voice tight when she said, 'I've just had a baked tattie I bought for my supper and I'm going home now.'

'Make sure you do.' Franco squeezed her shoulder before letting her go. 'You should've been in bed an hour ago.'

Huh! It was all right for him. He didn't have to sit with her grandma all day, did he! He wouldn't enjoy that any more than she did; in fact, sometimes she thought Franco didn't actually like her grandma one little bit. Her voice frostier still, she muttered, 'I was hungry. I didn't have any tea cos we were busy. Me grandma bought herself a bag of chitterlings but she didn't give me any.'

'Aye, well, likely she forgot.' Even to himself it sounded weak. He fished in his pocket for a coin and pressed it in Bonnie's hand. 'Get yourself a toffee apple to eat when you're in bed, all right? And straight home once you've bought it.'

Franco stood watching the child as she scampered off, and inwardly he was cursing his wife. She was a vicious so-an'-so, eating in front of the bairn and not giving her so much as a bite. Bonnie was her only grandchild and yet Marge had allowed the bad blood between herself and John to colour her view of the lassie. She was one on her own, his wife. How he had been persuaded to marry her, he didn't know. And then he shook his head at himself. Of course he knew. He'd had his fun with Marge the way he had with so many others, but he'd caught his toe with her. First she'd convinced him he'd got her pregnant, and then she had told him unless he married her without further ado she'd make his name mud in the family and the rest of the travelling community. And what had happened? Two weeks after they'd got wed, suddenly she wasn't pregnant any more. At first she had tried to soft-soap him that she'd lost the baby, but then in one of their rows the truth had come out. And there he was, saddled with a wife who had gradually got too old to give him bairns and, worse, who looked her age and more. And she was a shrew to boot. Aye, if ever a man had been taken for a fool, he had.

Frowning darkly, he made his way to the big tent where he was due to perform his fire-eating act once Nelly had finished her show with the dogs. He didn't enter the tent by the flap that opened at the back of the canvas structure for the performers; he wanted to watch Nelly first although he knew it would be sweet torture. He didn't think he had ever wanted any female as much as he wanted Nelly. She must be getting on for thirty but she didn't look a day over eighteen, possessing a fragile daintiness that set her apart from most of the fair women. But then she hadn't been born a traveller. She had arrived at the fair one summer's day not long after he and Margarita had got wed, driving a lorry that had been converted into her home, complete with stove, cooker, bedroom, cupboards, and oriel windows of diamond leaded glass. Outsiders were rarely allowed to join their community, but when she had shown Ham and the other elders her performing dogs they'd made an exception.

His hands thrust in his pockets, Franco stared at the object of his desire. He was used to lassies falling into his hands like ripe plums, but not Nelly. A woman of mystery, no one knew any more about her or her former life than the day she had arrived at the fair. Her voice was accentless and her speech and manner suggested she was a cut above, but as to her past life, no one had a clue.

The dog act coming to an end, Franco exited the tent and walked round to the back of it, entering the smaller structure which led into the main one. He nodded to José, his nephew, who he was training in his art and who was stationed waiting with the equipment, and then as Nelly emerged from the larger tent he smiled at her. 'Good crowd in tonight.'

She nodded, her answering smile polite but cool, and after clicking her fingers at the dogs, left the tent. His eyes followed her, his gaze fixed on the piled coils of her hair as he wondered how she would look stripped naked with her silken tresses falling down her slender back.

Feeling himself harden, he jerked his mind back to the matter in hand as José said, 'Uncle Franco? It's time.'

Aye, it was time all right, time he put a stop to this cat-and-mouse game between himself and Nelly – although she was no mouse and therein lay the trouble. He had never come across a woman like her before – beautiful, independent and seemingly needing no man in her life. But he was determined to have her.

He squared his shoulders, peeling off the shirt covering his spangly vest top and pulling free the band that held his thick black hair in a ponytail. The lassies seemed to like it loose, especially the young ones, and these days he found he was partial to girls in the springtime of life. The one he'd had the night before had been no more than fifteen or sixteen and a virgin to boot. She'd told him he looked like a pirate with his long hair and he had liked that. She had cried afterwards, saying she didn't want to be left with a bairn, and he'd spent some time petting her and reassuring her until she was smiling again. He'd walked her back to the gates of the big country house where she worked as a kitchen maid and where she assured him her pal, who worked with her in the kitchens, had promised to leave the scullery door unbolted so she could slip in late, and the cook – a tartar – would be none the wiser.

A kitchen maid . . . As Franco walked into the big tent with José following him he was remembering the girl's smooth, unlined face and shining eyes. Lassies were worked to death in service and the bloom of youth would soon fade. But not with Nelly. It was as though she'd drunk a magic elixir.

And then the crowd claimed his attention, full of bright eager faces, and after José had announced him the clapping went on and on, especially from a group of giggling lassies at the front of the staging. Flicking back his head so his hair rippled on his shoulders, Franco took the torch José had just lit, seeing the girls' eyes widen and their soft mouths form oohs of awe.

Putting everything else out of his mind, he began his act.

Chapter Three

It was now July and the fair had moved to Sunderland and was camped on the old town moor. Bonnie was sitting in bed staring at her father, and her eyes, always the window to her soul, were troubled. This was the fifth night in a row he had closed his tent early and left the fair for the town, and she knew why. Oh yes, she knew why, she thought bitterly, because hadn't her grandma caused such a ruckus when she'd hollered at him that everyone had heard them fighting like cat and dog? And she knew full well her grandma had done that on purpose to put her da in a bad light. Lots of men gambled, her grandma had screamed at him, and there was nowt wrong with a flutter now and again, but it was a sickness with him and one that would bring his daughter down too. That was when her da had gone barmy and there had been such an uproar that Ham and Franco had had to get between them.

Bonnie chewed on her thumbnail. It was nine o'clock and she had already been in bed half an hour. Since the barney between her da and grandma, her da had told her to keep away from Margarita and not to talk to her. Normally this would have filled her with joy, even though her da was insisting she was washed and ready for bed at eight-thirty prompt, which she thought was far too early, but with her da all upset and out of sorts, Bonnie's world was grey. Her voice small, she said, 'You . . . you look smart, Da.'

John had been about to pull his jacket on but now he paused and looked across the cramped space in the wagon at his daughter. Bonnie was sitting up in her bed which converted into a table during the day. It was positioned under a little arched window, one of four – two on each side of the wagon – and she had an open story book on her knees although she hadn't turned a page for some minutes.

He sighed. Damn Margarita. The bairn hadn't been the same since that old harridan had vented her last dose of venom, and he knew Bonnie was worried about him. If Margarita had but known it, the row had made him all the more determined to leave the fair at the first opportunity. He didn't want his little lassie within ten miles of her grandmother. The woman was poison, sheer poison. But first he had to get some money behind him, he knew that. The likelihood of finding work in the present climate was poor and he had no trade; his only hope was hitting a winning streak. When the fair had trundled into Sunderland, his old stamping ground, he had wasted no time in looking up a bloke he knew who could set him up with a few games where big money could be won – and lost. Aye, and lost.

Walking across to Bonnie, he crouched down at the side of the narrow bed and ruffled her hair. 'Listen to me, hinny,' he said softly, 'you forget about the shindy with your grandma, all right? She knows nowt about nowt, and what she doesn't know she makes up. What I'm about tonight, and what I've been about the other nights, is to make us some money so we can leave here and your grandma and set up on our own. I want you to have some proper schooling, better than I can teach you. You'd like that, wouldn't you?'

Bonnie's eyes were stretched wide. She could see her da was all fired up about this and she didn't want to disappoint him but . . . 'Leave the fair?' she gulped. 'Leave everyone?'

'And your grandma,' he reminded her.

'But can't we just not talk to her, like we're doing now? And she wouldn't talk to us. She pretends she doesn't see me the last two days since . . .' She swallowed hard. 'We don't have to go away, Da.'

'You can't have an education, not the sort I mean, while we travel, Bonnie. You see that, don't you? Think about when we stop somewhere for a while in the winter when the weather's bad and you've gone to a school for a few weeks. You've liked that, I know. Learning things, hearing about different places like when that teacher in Boldon or wherever it was told the class about Africa and India and other countries. You've got to think about the future, lass, and what you could accomplish if you have an education.'

'But—'

'You're bright, hinny. Brighter than most. And I'm not just saying that cos I'm your da. You don't want to waste what the good Lord's given you.'

'But He's given me my singing, Da. And that's what I want to do when I get bigger.' She'd like to do it now if her da wasn't so against her performing in the big tent. 'I can do that here, in the fair, and—'

'*No.*'

It was so definite it caused Bonnie to put her hand to her lips which had begun to tremble.

Seeing this, John said quickly, 'Don't cry, hinny. Come on, don't cry. We can talk about this tomorrow – now is not the time, with me having to go out. But I wanted you to understand that what I'm doing, I'm doing for us, lass. You and me. And I'd never stop you singing, hinny. I love to hear you sing, you know that. But not for money, not in the big tent. You sing for yourself, an' your old da, right? For pleasure. Like the birds when they welcome the sunrise every morning. Now give me a big smile so I know you're all right afore I go.'

Bonnie took the handkerchief he proffered, wiped her eyes and gave a wan smile. She could hardly believe her da had suggested they leave the fair. This was down to her grandma, she thought grimly. If she hadn't upset her da so badly he wouldn't be talking like this now.

'Now a few minutes reading and then you snuggle down and shut your eyes.' John leaned forward and held her close for a moment, kissing the top of her head before he stood to his feet. 'And like I said, we'll decide what we're going to do together, lass, so don't you go upsetting yourself while I'm gone. Promise?'

Bonnie nodded. Her small world had righted itself again. She would never want to leave the fair and everyone she knew and loved here, so she knew what she would decide.

Once her father had gone Bonnie read for a little while longer and then dutifully put the book away and slid down under the covers. Mrs Carlini had made the small bedspread especially for her and it had birds and flowers crocheted in an intricate design that was quite beautiful. As her fingers stroked over it, the sense of bewilderment and amazement that her da could ever think of leaving the fair swept over her anew.

But it wasn't what her da really wanted, she told herself comfortingly. She knew it wasn't. How could he want to leave the best place on earth?

The July evening was warm and noisy; the sound of music and folk screaming and laughing and shouting outside the wagon loud and raucous, but it acted like a lullaby on Bonnie's tired mind. It was what she had grown up with and meant safety and security and happiness.

Within a minute or two she was fast asleep.

*

John was kicking himself an hour or so later as he sat at the game he had been desperate to get into earlier in the week. He'd known at the heart of him that it had been risky to come here tonight, stupid even. Patrick Skelton was not a man to get on the wrong side of – he had his bony fingers in so many pies in the criminal underworld of Sunderland that he was known as Jack Horner. Not that anyone would have been foolish enough to call him that to his face.

He licked his lips nervously. They had gone dry after he had noticed two of Skelton's henchmen enter the room where the gambling school was operating. There were such places all over the town, some in houses, factories and steelworks, and others in backyards and even the collieries. Anywhere, in fact, where a group of men gathered together in their free time or during their tea and lunch breaks. But the serious gambling, such as this particular card game, took place under the cover of darkness with lookouts posted to keep watch for the police. You had to have a pound or two in your pocket for entrance into the gambling dens Skelton controlled; there was nothing tinpot about them.

John tried to concentrate on the cards in his hand but his eyes kept flickering to the two men standing impassively still. He knew them to be Skelton's bodyguards; he had seen them with their boss before. They looked what they were, brutish thugs who were handy with their fists and boots. Bullet-headed and broad-shouldered, they were built like brick outhouses and had as little feeling. He had a fair idea of why they'd turned up here. Someone had told Skelton he was playing.

The one window in the room was boarded up and the only exit was through the door against which the men were standing. An oil lamp hanging from a thick chain anchored in the ceiling cast its light directly into the middle of the long wooden table at which John and several other men were sitting, cards in hand. The room was ostensibly the office of the warehouse below them but hadn't been used as such in years. Patrick Skelton utilized the warehouse for storage, but what was in the crates and boxes that appeared and disappeared with regular predictability no one would have dreamed of enquiring. Neither would the word 'smuggling' be mentioned in Skelton's hearing.

John surreptitiously eased the collar of his shirt. He didn't think he was imagining the way the atmosphere in the room had changed since the two near the door had entered.

Looking at the cards in his hand, he groaned inwardly. He had lost four games in a row and this one would be the same. Why hadn't he done what he'd intended to do when he had pawned Louisa's jewellery, and handed the money straight to Skelton? But the thick gold earrings, bracelets and necklaces that had been Louisa's Spanish grandmother's, and which she'd inherited when she was twenty-one as was their custom, had fetched more than he'd expected, and the devilish inner voice that always came to tempt him had whispered that with such a stake he could win enough to pay his debts and retrieve the jewellery from hock. It was Bonnie's, after all, for when she was older.

He was a fool. His stomach turned over. And he'd been an even bigger fool to borrow money from Skelton's pal a couple of nights ago, but he'd hit a winning streak for the first time in months. Of course, now he could see it had been a set-up – the 'select' game for four players, the way he'd won six times on the trot before the stakes had been raised sky high, Skelton's lackey suggesting he'd lend him the wager and they could split the winnings between them . . . *stupid, stupid, stupid.* But to be fair, how could he possibly have known his benefactor was in Skelton's pocket? Although perhaps he should have smelt a rat. Skelton had been keen to get him on the payroll for a while, ever since he'd had too much to drink one time the year before when the fair had been in Sunderland and he'd told his fellow players about his plans to settle in the town in the future. Skelton had come to watch him at the fair after that and then offered him a job. He hadn't been too pleased when he'd refused.

John ran over the conversation he'd had with Skelton two nights ago as he glanced again at the two men. After the game had finished, Skelton had showed himself, paying off his stooge who'd immediately made himself scarce. 'It's me you owe now, John,' Skelton had murmured. 'But don't fret, I know a bright lad like you won't keep me waiting overly long.'

The soft voice had been mild, even amiable, as he'd

gone on. 'Course, there's more ways of settling this than you stomping up with the money. You're the best boxer I've seen in a while, lad. You could have been at the top of the game if you hadn't thrown in your lot with them fair folk years back. But then I understand a lady was involved, eh? Aye, we've all been young and had the sap running high. But things are different now, and at your age you can do better than having every bright spark who fancies himself as a hard 'un trying to knock ten bells out of you every day in the ring. And let's face it, you're not one of them travellers, John. You're an East End lad, born and bred, an' we breed 'em tough, an' I'd say you're tougher than most. I like a man who can take care of himself, and others, if you get my drift.'

He'd mumbled something about getting the money then, and Skelton's voice had changed, the pally note absent when he next spoke. 'Aye, well, if that's the way you want to play it, I'll give you a couple of days to come up with the readies, all right? But think on about what I've said. You're missing an opportunity here and I took you for an intelligent bloke. You could earn more working for me in a month than six grubbing an existence with them travellers.'

Skelton's tone had changed again, becoming nauseatingly benevolent when he continued. 'I understand you've got a bit bairn an' all, is that right? Aye, I've got a family meself so I know what it is to look to the future with them in mind. And these are hard times we're in, and they're only going to get harder by the day. My old mam, God rest her soul, used to say that the good Lord helps them that helps themselves, and she was right.'

Skelton had smiled, showing yellow pointed teeth. John had thought the man resembled nothing so much as a giant rat.

'Throw in your lot with me an' you'll be well looked after, lad. A house rent-free for you and the bairn and plenty of cash in your pocket, and that's just for starters. There's many a bloke who'd bite my hand off for half what I'm offering you, and that's a fact.'

He had thanked Skelton then, saying he appreciated the chance and that he would think about it, whilst knowing he had no intention of working for him. He hadn't met many men in his life he was afraid of – perhaps just the master at the orphanage and one of the teachers at school who'd been a sadistic brute and had had everyone quaking in their shoes – but there was something about Skelton that made his blood run cold, even when the man was being matey. Or perhaps especially then.

John surfaced from his thoughts to find the other players waiting for him to make his move. There was nothing else for it but to show his dud hand. Disgustedly he flung the cards down on the table and stood up. His money was gone, he still owed Skelton a small fortune, and there was no hope of retrieving Louisa's jewellery from the pawnbroker unless . . .

Knowing he had been backed into a corner by his own

crass stupidity and weakness, he made his way across the room. The two men stared at him impassively. He didn't prevaricate. 'I need to speak to Mr Skelton.'

'. . . So that's it in a nutshell, John. You show me what you're made of by doing this little job for me tonight, and if I'm satisfied, you're on the payroll. And we'll wipe the slate clean regarding what you owe me. But once you're in, you're in. There's no going back, not when you work for me. Understood?'

'Understood, Mr Skelton.'

'I've got plans for you, lad. I've been looking for a right-hand man for a while – I can't be everywhere at once. I had a good bloke seeing to things at the docks but he met with an accident. I dealt with the scum responsible –' Skelton's voice left John in no doubt as to what had befallen the unfortunates concerned – 'and the example I made of them will serve as a warning to others, but Stan still needs to be replaced. Stan had brains as well as brawn, like you, and he was loyal. You'll be loyal, won't you? Aye, course you will. You've got a bairn and you wouldn't want her to grow up without her da, would you now? So let's go and get this spot of business over and done with, and then we can talk some more over a bottle of the hard stuff.'

Skelton hadn't told him what the business was, merely that he happened to have a little job that needed taking care of and that would be right up his alley, but as John followed the narrow-shouldered, slight figure of his new boss with the two henchmen making up the rear, he found his guts had turned to water. It was a short walk from the East End pub where Skelton had been waiting for him to the dockside, and being a Saturday night the gin and pie shops were doing a roaring trade, as were the blowsy prostitutes waiting on every street corner. It was noticeable to John that not one of the women called out to them as they passed – one look at Skelton and they either turned away or lowered their eyes. The warm night was ripe with the stink of fish and other pungent smells but John was used to that; he'd been born in Low Street close to the docks, and filth and disease were no strangers to him.

A grimy East End twilight was falling as they walked along Thornhill Quay, passing a couple of fishermen's boats that had been pulled up out of the water. The terraced houses that bordered the rough cobbles leading to the side of the quay and the river were mostly three-storey, and in their heyday had been fine residences. Now they were tenement slums with whole families living in one room along with the rats and the bugs, and as many as thirty men, women and children sharing one outside privy and water tap.

It was a hell of a way to live, John thought, especially for some families who were decent enough but had found themselves poverty-stricken through no fault of their own. There were some who said that once you reached rock bottom the only way was up, but he hadn't seen much evidence of that in life.

'Now, lad, let me explain what I want you to do.' Skelton's eyes could have been chips of black ice. 'There's a bloke living on the second floor in a room at the back of the house who thinks he can take the mickey outta me by all accounts. Out of the goodness of me heart I put a bit of work his way, unloading some merchandise from this boat and that, you know how it is.'

John nodded. He knew how it was all right.

'And the next thing I hear is that this same bloke is after selling a few bottles of brandy cheap in the Golden Lion. I can't have that, lad, for two reasons. One, it'll be after giving the rest of 'em ideas, and two, no one does the dirty on Patrick Skelton and doesn't live to regret it. Now, you go up there and bring him down to me so we can take him somewhere nice and quiet and point out the folly of his ways, all right?'

It wasn't all right, it was far from all right. 'What – what are you going to do with him?'

'Me? Nowt.' The thin mouth smiled, showing the pointed yellow teeth. 'But you and them –' Patrick nodded to his two henchmen – 'are going to break every bone in his treacherous thieving body.'

John swallowed. 'But –'

'No buts.' Patrick stepped closer, so close John could smell his fetid breath when he softly said, 'You do exactly as you're told.'

He'd sold himself, soul, mind and body. 'What's his name?'

'Walton. Robert Walton.'

The front door to the house was ajar and even from outside the smell was foul. John walked into the dank hallway and in the fading light he saw great holes in the skirting boards where rats lurked. Striking a match, he saw lice crawling on the rotten walls and more bugs on the floor. He had thought his childhood days in this area had been bad enough, before his father was lost at sea and his mother and baby brother died of the fever, and he'd been carted off to the East End Orphan Asylum that had been founded for the children of seafarers, but this was a hundred times worse. His mother might have been poor, but she'd kept their two rooms in a house in Long Row as clean as carbolic soap and plenty of scrubbing allowed.

Gingerly he climbed the stairs that creaked and rocked ominously to the first floor. The landing was as filthy as the hall, and in the rooms above his head a baby was wailing and a man was shouting. His stomach churning, he stood for a moment in the semi-darkness. He didn't light another match; some things were best consigned to the shadows.

There were two rooms on the first floor and he forced himself to knock on the nearest door. He had to knock again before it opened a crack. A skinny young lad who couldn't have been more than fifteen or sixteen peered at him. 'Aye?'

'Does Robert Walton live here?'

'Who's asking?'

'That's neither here nor there. Does he live here?'

'No.'

Even before a voice from within the room called, 'Robert? Who's there?' John knew the boy was lying and his boot was already in the gap to prevent the door from closing when the lad tried to shut it. Thinking that there must be a father with the same Christian name, John said, 'I need to speak to your da, sonny.'

'Me da's dead.'

'Now don't give me that.'

'He is.'

It took little effort to shove the boy aside and fling the door wide open. He had been about to force his way into the room if necessary but now John stood on the threshold, the wind taken out of his sails. His voice quiet, he said, 'Mrs Walton?'

'Aye, I'm Mrs Walton.' A woman had risen from where she had been sitting in a battered armchair in front of the small fire in the tiny grate, and was now facing him. She had obviously been making toast when the knock had come at the door and still held the toasting fork in her hand with a slice of bread attached to it. In amazing contrast to what he'd seen of the rest of the house the room was spotlessly clean, but apart from the armchair and another hard-backed chair, the only furniture consisted of a rickety-looking construction of two platforms, one above the other and forming a unit, on which straw mattresses and thin grey blankets reposed. A black kettle and a saucepan and a few other utensils stood on a shelf fixed to the wall, and next to this was a framed certificate of honour stating that Mr Robert Walton had given his life for his country.

The woman saw John looking at this and her voice was quiet but proud when she said, 'My husband died in the war.'

'So you're Robert Walton?' John spoke to the boy, and when he nodded, added, 'It's just you and your mam?'

It was Mrs Walton who answered him. 'I've a daughter but she married a Newcastle man.' She spoke as though Newcastle was a hundred miles away but then it probably seemed like that to her. 'What can we do for you, Mr . . . ?'

John didn't reply to this. Looking at the boy again, he said, 'Did you do some work for Mr Skelton?'

He had his answer when the colour drained from the youth's thin face.

Hell's bells. Vitally conscious of the three men waiting in the street below, John said quietly, 'How old are you, laddie?'

Again it was the mother who replied, her voice now holding fear. 'He'll be seventeen come Christmas.'

He wouldn't see another Christmas if Skelton had anything to do with it. Coming to a decision, John stepped into the room and shut the door behind him. 'Listen to me. Skelton knows you took some stuff –' When the boy went to protest, John said urgently, 'He *knows*, so save your breath. He sent me to fetch you and he's waiting downstairs with a couple of bruisers. Is there another way out of here?'

Mrs Walton put her hand to her throat and sank back into the armchair as though her legs wouldn't hold her. 'Skelton?' she whispered. 'No, Rob. You told me you got some work from that innkeeper in town.'

'There *is* no work, Mam, and anything that comes up goes to married men with families. We were weeks behind with the rent and I thought . . .' He turned to John. 'I can't leave her.'

'Believe me, lad, you'll be leaving her one way or another,' John said grimly. 'This way you can come back when the dust settles or better still send for her to join you.'

Mrs Walton had grasped the severity of the situation. 'Our Phyllis would take me in, she's said before, but I've never wanted to leave me home – you know how it is.'

John stared into the lined face. He had no idea how old the woman was – probably umpteen years younger than she looked because poverty, disease, damp and mal-nutrition took a heavy toll on body and soul – but surely any time she had left to her would be better spent away from this pitiful room. Yet she clearly didn't see it that way. Turning to the boy, he said again, 'Is there another way out of here besides the stairs?'

'Only the roof. I've got a pal who lives in one of the rooms above in the attics and there's a little window that opens in the middle of the roof with the drainpipe run-ning below it. I could try and shinny up from there.'

'Do it. Get as far away from here as you can, and if your mam's going to your sister's in Newcastle I wouldn't show your face again round these parts. Skelton's got long fingers.'

'Why are you doing this? Helping us, I mean?'

John looked down into the young face. He must be getting on for a foot taller than the boy, whose legs were badly bowed; most of the East End bairns were bandy-legged to a greater or lesser extent. 'You haven't got time for questions. Say your goodbyes, lad.'

Mrs Walton's eyes were dry but her face was working as she embraced her son. 'Look after yourself, you hear me?'

'I'll be all right, Mam, an' I'll see you again, I promise.'

'I know you will, me bairn.' Mrs Walton held him close for a moment before pushing him away. 'Ta, lad,' she said softly to John who nodded awkwardly.

They opened the door and stepped onto the landing just as Skelton's men walked up the stairs. One of them started to say, 'Taking your time, aren't you? Mr Skelton thought –'

John never heard what Mr Skelton had thought because his fist, full into the other man's face, sent him crashing down the stairs, taking his companion with him.

'*Go! Now!*' Robert had frozen in fear and John pushed the boy so hard he nearly sent him sprawling. 'Get away from here.'

As Robert disappeared up the stairs, John turned to face Skelton's men. They had picked themselves up and were now coming for him, swearing and cursing. In the seconds before they reached him, regret raced through his mind, but then he was fighting for his life and the only things that were real were the fists and great hobnailed boots and searing pain . . .

Chapter Four

Nelly sat looking at her reflection in the mirror of her dressing table, and after a moment she wiped away the tears trickling down her cheeks. She wasn't ugly, she told herself – in fact, lots of men had told her she was beautiful – so why was it that the one person in the world she cared about seemed oblivious to her as a woman? 'A dear friend', John had called her that afternoon, and both his tone and the look on his face had stated plainly that that was all she could ever be to him, even before he had mumbled something about Louisa and how much he still missed her.

Was it possible to hate someone who had never done you any harm and who had been dead for nine years? And then she answered herself with a bitter little laugh. Oh yes, she was living proof of it.

Shutting her eyes tightly, she rocked back and forth a number of times before becoming still. Taking up her mother-of-pearl hairbrush, she brought it through the thick golden hair that reached to below her waist. It was engraved with the initials E. H., and was one of the few possessions that she had brought with her from her old life; it had been a gift from her maternal grandmother and as such was precious to her.

Eleanor Harper. Putting the brush back into the mother-of-pearl box in which it reposed with a comb and small hand mirror, she stared at it. She no longer thought of herself as Eleanor Harper, youngest daughter of Mr Lionel Harper, wealthy landowner who had a vast estate in Durham. She couldn't remember when she had first become aware that their magnificent house and manicured grounds, which took umpteen inside and out-side servants to tend to it, was the result of men toiling their lives away underground in her father's mine. And then there was the chemical works he owned, along with a paper mill and other business interests. But the realiza-tion had come after her mother had engaged a governess for her when she was eight years old. Miss Norton had only lasted eighteen months before her mother had discovered what she called the governess's 'subversive and wicked views', but the seeds had been sown and Nelly's eyes, even though they were still the eyes of a child, had been opened.

She ran her fingers over the smooth surface of the box as she let her mind wander back down the years. The fair was quiet now. It was past one o'clock in the morning, and the only sound was the occasional neigh from one of the horses outside, along with the mixed snores of her six dogs lying on their blankets at one end of the main living space.

She had been approaching her seventeenth birthday when her parents had announced their intention of sending her to the same exclusive finishing school her two sisters had attended. Her brother, Archibald, only son and heir, had been at university, her two sisters had been married off to suitable husbands of equal social standing, and suddenly it had dawned on her that as far as her parents were concerned, her life had been mapped out from the day she was born. She had looked at her family and realized that there was not one of them she liked or had anything in common with. The only person she had been close to had been her maternal grandmother who had died the year before. Grandmama had been something of a free spirit too. For the first time since her grandmother had died, it had occurred to Nelly that the reason the old lady had singled her out among her grandchildren for a small inheritance was because Grandmama had known the day would come when this particular granddaughter would rebel against her place in society. A suffragette in her youth, Grandmama had been full of the sort of radical ideas about independence for women that Miss Norton had had, and she couldn't be dismissed by the family like the unfortunate governess.

Nelly smiled now as she pictured her grandmother. The diminutive and genteel exterior had hidden a fierce Boadicea spirit. 'Decide what is worth fighting for in life,' her grandmother had said more than once. 'Unimportant issues you can let pass you by. And no matter what other compromises you feel called on to make, marry for love, Eleanor. I loved your dear grandfather with all my heart. I would have married him whatever his station in life, but it was most convenient he happened to be disgracefully wealthy,' she'd added with a twinkle in her eye. 'But even the most successful unions have their ups and downs, and you will find that love covers a multitude of sins.'

And so she'd chosen her first battle and refused to go away to finishing school. For the next twelve months until she was eighteen and could claim her inheritance according to her grandmother's will, she'd endured her parents' displeasure at what they called her ungratefulness. She'd confined herself to her suite of rooms as much as possible with just her beloved dogs as companions, only making an appearance for dinner or when she was required to attend a social function. Nine times out of ten these had been arranged by her parents with a view to finding their difficult youngest daughter a husband. But she had made plans.

Nelly sighed. Standing up, she walked to her bedroom door and looked out into the living area where the dogs were soundly sleeping, curled up together in a tangle of paws and heads. Once she was eighteen, she'd secretly commissioned the buying and conversion of her home. After going out on the road with the friendly car mechanic who had overseen the conversion, and who was tickled pink by the whole thing, she had bought her driving licence, packed a small suitcase, taken her dogs and told her parents she was leaving. Even now, she didn't allow herself to think of the things they had said in the terrible row that had followed, but she had left knowing she would never see them or her old home again.

And she had never regretted it. She let her gaze wander round the shadowed interior of her home. She had driven away from the family estate one sunny spring day not knowing where she was going, but only that she was free. From a little girl she had spent hours playing with her dogs and training them to do party tricks, but over the twelve months while she'd been biding her time, she had taken their training up several notches. Only one of the original dogs was left, an old white poodle by the name of Dora who was too ancient to do anything more than snooze the days away, and she was dreading having to say goodbye to her when the time came, as it surely must. Much as she loved her other dogs, Dora was special.

Her eyes filling with tears again, Nelly turned back into the bedroom. She had to pull herself together. She wasn't melancholy by nature; this was silly. Nothing had changed in the last twenty-four hours, not really. John was still her friend and he had never been anything more than that, so it wasn't as if she had lost anything, although somehow it felt that way. She was what she had always determined to be – self-governing and liberated and not beholden to anyone.

She still had most of her grandmother's legacy tucked safely away in a bank account, a nest egg for the future. Enough to buy a modest property somewhere with a little garden for the dogs. If any of the fair folk knew how much her grandmother had left her they'd consider her a rich woman, but compared to her family's wealth, the amount was tiny. But it was enough for her and her canine family. Yes, enough to be autonomous. And she was grateful for that, truly grateful, but somehow she had never envisaged ending her days as an old maid.

She pulled a face at herself for using a term she hated. That was society's label for single women, and as was so often the case, there wasn't an equally disparaging one for ageing single men.

She plumped down again on the little stool in front of the built-in dressing table, peering at herself as she checked for any wrinkles on her smooth clear skin. She was fortunate that she had inherited her mother and grandmother's youthful genes, but one day those insidious telltale signs would creep up on her. And she wouldn't mind that, not if John had fallen in love with her. She'd always believed that in time, once he had finished grieving . . .

Stop it. Suddenly Nelly was angry for the self-pity that had overwhelmed her in the last few hours.

She was lucky, she told herself firmly. In truth, she had led something of a charmed life over the years since leaving her parents' home, a life *she* had chosen and made happen. She had to count her blessings. That's what her grandmama would say, she could almost hear her. 'Count your blessings, Eleanor. Chin up, girl.'

Nelly gave a hiccup of a laugh that was more of a sob. She'd purposely determined to present herself as a woman with no past when she'd joined the showmen and their families. And such was their culture that they'd respected her right to privacy. Among the fair community she had no social position to live up to, and no one questioned her right to live as she pleased. She loved the variety and freedom of the travelling life – it was as though she'd been born to it – and whatever inconveniences there were she took in her stride.

Yes, she was lucky, she reiterated more strongly. And if it wasn't for this love for John, she would be truly happy. But she was done with crying for the moon; she had to face the fact that he would never want her and get on with her life. She closed her eyes, shutting out the sad-faced woman in the mirror. But oh, she didn't think she'd ever felt as unloved and unlovely as she did tonight, not even in her lonely childhood.

Bonnie knew something was different as soon as she opened her eyes. Her da always woke her with a hot mug of milky cocoa, made just the way she liked it with a creamy froth on the top. He'd draw back the curtains at the side of her bed, make a pronouncement about the state of the weather and grin at her, and then they'd have breakfast together once she was dressed. But today the wagon was quiet and still.

She slid out of bed, her stomach fluttering even as she told herself not to be silly. Her father slept at the rear of the wagon on a bed under the roof built over mirrored cupboards where they kept their clothes and other stuff, but now she could see that it didn't look as though it had been slept in. It was one of her jobs to tidy their beds each morning, putting her bedding away and then setting the table, after which she'd climb the little ladder to where her father slept and smooth the sheets and coverlet. But today it looked exactly as she'd left it the day before.

If the weather was fine, her da would have already lit the coals in their little cast-iron brazier outside and have the porridge simmering in the black cooking pot; otherwise, breakfast would be cooking on the wagon's tiny stove. Either way, it was nearly always ready for eating, but not today.

After poking her head out of the top half of the stable door of the wagon and trying in vain to catch sight of her da, Bonnie closed it again and quickly got dressed.

Where was he? she thought sickly. He must have had an accident in the town. He would never stay out all night, she knew that. Something was terribly amiss. He had been late home before, sometimes one or two in the morning, but never later than that.

She had rushed her dressing and realized with a little sound of irritation deep in her throat that she had put her apron on inside out. That righted, she opened the door of the wagon but then, in spite of her agitation, she stood at the top of the wooden steps for a moment. Who should she tell about her da? He might be back any minute and he wouldn't want her to cause a hoo-ha, especially after the barney with her grandma. Margarita would make the most of the fact that he was late back. Oh, she knew how her grandma's mind worked all right. But if her da had been able, he would have returned from the town. She knew that, *she knew it*. So this was serious.

Her heart thudding fit to burst and her head whirling, she stood for a few more moments, and then it came to her. Miss Nelly. She'd know what to do. And Miss Nelly didn't like her grandma any more than she did. Bonnie didn't consciously add here, *and Miss Nelly loves my da*, but the knowledge was the impetus that sent her flying to the lorry parked a little distance from the other wagons and living vans. And when Miss Nelly opened the door, it was the floodgate to Bonnie's tears.

Every minute of the last two weeks had crawled by, weighed down with the terrible heaviness of misery and anguish and the pain of not knowing. Bonnie took a gulp of air as she sat listlessly on the steps of the wagon, her sorrow so great she had to remind herself to breathe.

It was as though her da had vanished from the face of the earth. She had heard Ham say that very thing after one of the times he and a group of the travellers had returned from the town, their search fruitless once again. No one had seen hide nor hair of John since the night he'd gone missing, or if they had, they weren't admitting to it.

It had been Miss Nelly who had insisted on the police being notified of his disappearance, and this alone had been enough to terrify Bonnie. Travellers never involved the law, whatever the crisis, and the fact that Miss Nelly had gone against them all and fetched the police herself had convinced Bonnie something catastrophic had befallen her da. And then her grandma had found the empty jewellery box that should have held her mam's gold earrings and bracelets and necklaces. Bonnie's hands clenched into fists at her side. Her grandma shouldn't have been nosing about in her da's wagon to start with, and then she'd tried to suggest her da had taken the jewellery and run off to pastures new.

She'd gone for her grandma after that, biting and kicking and screaming, and it had been scant comfort that everyone had agreed that her da would never go off without her, because the alternative meant that someone had taken her mam's jewellery and killed her da for it. That's what the police had said.

Bonnie looked across the campsite where morning fires were already lit outside some of the wagons, even though there were remaining streaks of charcoal in the dawn sky. There was no sound emerging from her grandma's wagon as yet, though.

She had insisted on remaining in her da's wagon and had become hysterical when Ham and the others had tried to persuade her otherwise, so it had been agreed that the wagon would be moved next to her grandma's. It had been the last thing she'd wanted but she'd been forced to compromise.

She'd hoped Miss Nelly would suggest her da's wagon be placed next to her van, but she hadn't. Bonnie bit down on her bottom lip. She knew why, and it was all her grandma's fault. If Margarita hadn't accused her da of running off with her mam's jewellery, she wouldn't have shouted at her grandma that her da had told her he was trying to get enough money so they could live in a proper house and she could go to school. Her da would never leave her, she'd screamed at them all. He had plans for them both. It had been then that she'd become aware of Miss Nelly's face, and the only way she could describe her expression was that she looked as though she had been punched when she wasn't expecting it. And since then Miss Nelly hadn't been herself.

What was she going to do? It was a question she had been asking herself ever since that first morning when she had woken up and found her da wasn't back from the town, but as yet she had no answer. Every minute of every day she was silently praying for her da to come home, for him to come striding into the campsite saying it had all been a big mistake and here he was, right as rain, but . . . Bonnie raised her eyes to the fresh morning sky. Try as she might, she couldn't shake the feeling of sick dread that something terrible had happened to him. Everyone thought so – she could read it in their eyes, in their over-kind voices, in the way they were treating her as though she was poorly or something. Even her grandma wasn't going for her the way she usually did, although that was down to Franco more than anything. She'd heard him telling her grandma to lay off or he'd give her what for, and his voice had been grim.

'Bonnie?'

As she heard her name being called she realized Ham was making his way towards her, and she stood up and jumped down the last two steps to face him. She liked Ham – the leader of the travellers had always been nice to her – but she sensed immediately that she wasn't going to like what he had to say. 'My da? You've heard something about my da?'

'No, no, lass.' Ham watched the small body sag, and his voice was gentle when he said softly, 'But it's to do with your da I need to speak to you. We should have moved on from here a good few days ago, Bonnie. You know that, don't you? And we can't stay any longer. We've done everything we can to find him, and the law was here again yesterday and they've said they'll send word if they find out anything.'

Bonnie looked at him, horrified. 'We can't leave. Not without my da.'

'We have to, lass. And he'll know where to find us, now then.'

'But they'll stop looking for him, the police I mean. They won't bother if we go.' She knew the authorities had as little time for the fair folk as the travellers had for the law. When Miss Nelly had insisted on notifying them two weeks ago, she had heard some of the men muttering that it was pointless and that the law wouldn't worry themselves about a missing traveller. 'Good riddance to bad rubbish, that's how they'll see it,' one of the men had said. 'They might go through the motions but they won't lift a finger, you mark my words. And who wants them beggars sniffing about anyway?'

She did, Bonnie thought now. She wanted the beggars sniffing about if it meant them finding her da.

'Look, lass, it's the police themselves who'll get awkward if we stay any longer – me hands are tied. We have to move on, we've no choice. An' your da's a canny lad. Whatever's happened, he'll come out on top, don't you fret.'

Ham didn't really believe that. The child and the seasoned showman regarded each other. It was Ham's eyes that fell away from the sorrow in her deep blue ones and the grief that was evident in every line of her thin body.

Aiming to comfort her in his own way, he said gruffly, 'I'll get one of the men to see to your da's tent and load up, lass. He'll harness up Rosie an' drive your wagon for you till your da's back, all right?' Their horse Rosie was a placid, quiet animal who plodded uncomplainingly from camp to camp, pulling the living wagon and the cart that fixed behind it holding her da's tent and equipment. 'An' your granny'll take care of you in the meantime so you're not on your own, Bonnie.'

Her face said all too plainly what she thought of this last effort at reassurance, and now Ham hurried away without saying anything more. As he walked he was inwardly cursing John Lindsay, or to be more precise the gambling addiction that had probably done for him. Men were murdered and disposed of for a lot less than John had apparently had on him that night. One thing Ham was sure of was that John would never have abandoned his daughter of his own free will, so that left only one possible conclusion. *Damn fool*. Ham shook his head as he reached his own wagon. And now that poor little bairn was fatherless as well as motherless.

The fair had packed up and moved to Whitburn a few miles up the coast over the last forty-eight hours, a journey Bonnie had endured in deepest misery. Ham had permission for a month's extended stay there to take in the August Bank Holiday, and despite the Depression local communities made the best hay possible while the sun shone. To Bonnie the heatwave everyone was enjoying made her anguish and despair ten times worse. She didn't care that the roundabouts, chairoplanes, swing boats, coconut shies, shooting range and all the other various tents and booths were so much easier to dismantle and reassemble when the weather was kind; she felt as though it should be cold and rainy and bleak because that was how she was feeling inside. All the girls in their summer dresses and straw hats, the happy smiling faces and screams of laughter and enjoyment, mocked her grief and desperation. Life was going on as though her da had never existed and it petrified her, and added to everything else, her grandma was now officially in charge of her. Ham had made this decree on the day of the move and no one argued with his decisions, so that was that.

The only thing that brought Bonnie the faintest solace was her grandma telling her that over the next few weeks she was going to start singing and dancing regularly in the big tent. 'You need to earn your keep,' Margarita had stated coldly. 'There's Rosie's feed, and your food and other expenses. If you insist on keeping your da's wagon you'll have to start paying one of the men to drive it till you're old enough to handle Rosie, and there'll be repairs and such in the winter to see to. You can't expect me to pay. Do you understand, Bonita?'

Bonnie had understood and she preferred it that way; she didn't want to be beholden to her grandma for anything. She intended to keep her da's wagon ready for when he came home. And he *would*; she found she had to keep believing that because the alternative was unthinkable. Most of the time she could manage to hold on to her hope in the days, which were always busy; it was the nights that were a battle. Then the panic and terror and overwhelming sense of missing her da would cause her to cry herself to sleep. But at least Miss Nelly was speaking to her again.

Not that Miss Nelly had ever stopped, not really, Bonnie corrected herself as she sat in bed hugging her knees in the moonlight streaming through her little window. She had just been different. But then tonight, when Bonnie had been carrying a pail of water to where Rosie was tethered waiting for a drink, she'd seen Miss Nelly and told her how sorry she was that her old dog, Dora, had passed away that morning. She could tell Miss Nelly had been crying and she knew how much she'd loved Dora. Miss Nelly had hugged her and then they'd both cried together, although she wasn't really crying for the dog but for her da. And Miss Nelly had seemed to know this, because after they'd dried their eyes, she had said, 'Listen to me, Bonnie. If you need someone to talk to or help in any way, no matter what it is, my door is always open to you. Always. All right? Your father looked on me as his friend, just as I did – do – him,' she'd corrected quickly, 'so please don't hesitate to come to me. And always remember that your father loves you very much. Your grandmother might say all sorts of things but you know the truth, don't you?'

She had tried to answer Miss Nelly but her tears had choked her, and Miss Nelly's eyes had been wet when she had walked away. She would have run after her, Bonnie thought, because she had wanted to just talk about her da to someone who had cared about him, but Franco had come up to Miss Nelly and taken her arm, and for once Miss Nelly hadn't shaken him off. The two of them had walked away together, and so the moment had been lost.

She could go and talk to Miss Nelly now, though, when everyone was asleep and the fair was quiet. As the idea occurred to her, Bonnie sat up straighter. Miss Nelly wouldn't mind if she woke her up, but she might not even be asleep yet. They'd been late setting everything up for tomorrow after the move, and it had been past midnight before the last of the fair folk had turned in. It was probably only about one o'clock or thereabouts even now. And she did so want to speak to her. She hadn't realized how much she'd missed their old easy relationship until Miss Nelly had spoken to her earlier. Miss Nelly was linked in her mind with her da in a way no one else was.

Her mind made up, Bonnie slid out of bed. The day had been a hot one and the night was warm without a breath of wind. She didn't even bother to slip on a cardigan over her long cotton nightdress and left the wagon on bare feet, padding over thick tufty grass in the field outside as silently as a small ghost.

Nelly's fine motor van was often set some distance from the wagons and tethered horses, usually in a part of the area where the traction engines that hauled some of the loaded trucks and carts carrying the heavier rides were stationed. These engines, which also served as mobile power stations when the fair was open, generating electric current for the lights, were impressive beasts, and Bonnie, like all the fair children, had been brought up to show them due respect. They ate coal voraciously, but as each engine carried three hundred gallons of water in its tanks and managed a journey of fifteen miles before needing to stop at a watering-place, they weren't without their difficulties. In the middle of a dry summer, some villagers would try to prevent the showmen from sucking more water from their depleted ponds, but the present move had passed uneventfully. As Bonnie grew close to the powerful road locomotives with their rich midnight-blue paintwork lined out in gold, gleaming spir-alled brass rods supporting a canopy which read 'St Ignatius Fair' and massive wheels, she trod warily, as though they could suddenly wake up and leap at her. She had been brought up on stories of bairns being devoured under their terrible wheels, and, although she knew it was silly and fanciful, she couldn't rid herself of the notion that the engines were able to think and see.

Probably because she was concentrating on getting safely past the sleeping giants, she was up the steps of the vehicle and in the door before thinking about it. The dogs, who had all been snoozing outside under the van in the relative cool of the night, barely opened an eye, exhausted after enduring an unpleasantly hot day with their thick fur coats.

Bonnie had been in Miss Nelly's home a hundred times before, and even without the bright moonlight she would have been able to pick her way to the bedroom without mishap. She had been intending to knock on the door and wait for an answer, but as it was wide open she was in the doorway before she could knock.

Miss Nelly looked ethereal in the shaft of white moonlight slanting across the bed, her glorious hair fanned out against the pillow with one silken lock trail-ing across her bare up-tilted breasts. She was as naked as the day she'd been born, but it wasn't this that had Bonnie riveted in the doorway, her hand pressed to her lips to prevent any sound escaping. Franco was fast asleep too, one dark muscular arm draped across Miss Nelly's white belly and his black hair half covering his face as he lay on his side so his bottom was visible. He was as dark and big and hairy as the woman lying beside him was tiny and smooth-skinned, making the contrast all the more shocking to Bonnie's horrified gaze. She knew this was bad. She didn't understand the whys and wherefores, but she knew only married couples should share a bed and that things went on when they did, things that could produce a baby in due course. It was for this same reason that the travellers had strict rules about their daughters, once the girls reached a certain age, not being alone with a lad, and even when a lad had proposed to a lass, contact between them was supervised by the lass's parents until the couple were wed.

Numbly Bonnie backed away from the doorway, and when a few moments later she found herself walking back across the field with the living wagons, she had no memory of leaving Miss Nelly's home.

Once back in bed, she drew the sheets over her, covering her face in spite of the heat inside the wagon, but she couldn't shut out the picture imprinted on her mind. *Miss Nelly and Franco*. But Franco was married to her grandma, and Miss Nelly loved her da. Didn't she? But she couldn't, not if she was doing 'that' with Franco. No she couldn't, she *couldn't*.

She was consumed by a feeling compounded of intense pain and disappointment and a hundred other emotions besides, but by the time the dawn chorus heralded another day, Bonnie had settled several things in her mind, for good or ill. She was alone, really alone, and she had to face up to it. Nothing was as she had imagined, and she could put her trust in no one but herself. Until her da came home – she didn't allow herself to consider that he might not – she would manage by herself. She'd had her tenth birthday a few weeks ago, she wasn't a bit bairn any longer and she could do this. And she would, *she would*.

Her childhood was over.

PART TWO

Friendship

1933

Chapter Five

Bonnie stretched her toes, wiggling them in the warm soft grass. It was a beautiful moonlit night, with a gentle breeze blowing over the sleeping campsite. The day's toil was over, and all was peace and quiet. A hundred yards or so from the living wagons, the roundabouts, swing chairs and other rides, along with the stalls, booths and tents, were silhouetted against a glorious night sky. The day had been a hot one; the United Kingdom was in the grip of a heatwave with temperatures soaring to ninety degrees in the baking south and drought warnings in place, but here on the outskirts of Whitburn where the fair had arrived for the usual August Bank Holiday venue, a cool north-east breeze had kept the weather bearable.

Not that the heat had bothered her, Bonnie thought, lifting her face to the sky and shutting her eyes. After the harsh northern winters, the sun was always welcome. But their present location was a trial every year, reminding her of the first unbearably painful weeks after her father had gone missing. She'd long since given up hope that he would return and had accepted the unacceptable – that her lovely da had been murdered by person or persons unknown. And so she'd done the only thing she could and made the best of her changed circumstances that had become increasingly uncertain as the Depression deepened.

Money had become scarcer and scarcer for the average man and woman in the last few years, and although the crowds still came to the fair in the good weather, lots of people could do nothing but admire the bright lights and listen to the music, hungrily drinking in the elusive atmosphere of gaiety but never spending a penny, their pockets empty.

The last winter had been particularly hard. Bonnie sighed as she thought back to the endless weeks of biting cold and raw winds. But for Ham having had the foresight to buy a small copse of standing wood from a farmer in the autumn, the fair community would have been in dire straits. As it was, they'd parked their living wagons close by, and the men had felled the young trees, bringing the trunks and branches into the camp.

Every member of the fair family had done their bit. The men had sawed the bigger branches and trunks into neat logs to sack and sell; the younger lads had used bill-hooks to split a number of the logs in half for small fireplaces, and the girls had chopped others into kindling pieces with small hatchets. Even the very young toddlers had been expected to work at making the kindling into round bundles, packing the small pieces upright into a tin can which had been cut down and nailed by its base to a flat log. When the can was full, the youngsters twisted a length of wire round the sticks to hold them together, lifted the finished bundle out of its nest and added it to their steadily growing pile. And then the women and children had walked miles, going from door to door pushing a couple of handcarts piled high with sacks and bundles of wood. One of Ham's brothers had lost two fingers when the saw he'd been using had slipped, and little Ava, the only child of a young married couple, had been crushed to death when a stack of logs had fallen on her as she'd wandered too close. But the community had been able to eat each day and, come the spring, there had been enough money to buy fuel to get the fair on the road.

As the breeze ruffled her long black hair, Bonnie sighed again. She didn't want to go back into the wagon where Franco's guttural snores would be competing with her grandma's equally loud ones. Most nights, weather permitting, she would wait until the pair of them were asleep and then silently slide out of her narrow bed that served as a settee in the day and sit outside for hours, gazing at the stars and thinking.

She had turned fifteen at the end of June, an event that had passed by without comment, but she knew her grandma had remembered even though she hadn't spoken of it. Bonnie had overheard her talking to Franco about looking into a possible husband for her over the next twelve months.

Bonnie's full mouth tightened. Once it had become clear that her father wasn't coming back, her grandma had sold Rosie and her da's wagon to an engaged couple within the fair community who were getting wed shortly. She'd pocketed the money for herself, making it clear to Bonnie she wouldn't see a penny of it, while telling Ham and the others that she was keeping it safe for her grand-daughter. *Safe*. Bonnie's upper lip curled. It was as 'safe' as the money she earned singing in the big tent each evening which went straight into her grandma's cashbox. She'd protested more than once about the fact that she didn't even have a few pennies for herself, but as her grandma used her hands as well as her tongue in lashing out at her, Bonnie had learned to keep quiet. Many a time, sore and smarting from a beating, she had thought about running away, but where to? She didn't have a friend in the world outside the fair community and it was the only life she knew. The idea of leaving terrified her, or at least it had, when she was younger.

Bonnie brought her knees up and rested her chin on them, her arms clasped round her legs.

But maybe the alternative, that of staying and being married off to someone her grandma chose for her, was worse? She didn't want to be tied to a man and dropping one bairn after another, and in this respect she knew she was as different from her contemporaries as chalk from cheese. Perhaps it was because she had mixed blood, as her grandma never tired of reminding her, that she didn't quite fit into this life as she got older? But she knew one thing – the only time she was truly happy was when she was singing in the big tent. Then she became someone else entirely, and she knew her voice touched folk of all ages. Ham had billed her as the singing nightingale, and even in these hard times she drew more of a crowd than any of the other acts.

Bonnie stood to her feet. The soft night air held the tang of woodsmoke from the dying embers of the travellers' fires dotted about the campsite, the moon was riding high in a cloudless sky and the trees bordering the field were whispering ancient secrets to each other as the breeze ruffled their leaves. The thought of going into the claustrophobic confines of the wagon wasn't to be borne, and for more than one reason. In the last year or so, she had caught Franco looking at her in the same way he used to look at Nelly, and it made her feel sick. His eyes jerked away each time and his overall manner with her was normal; she might even have convinced herself she had imagined the greedy hunger in his face but for the number of occasions when he 'accidentally' brushed against her in passing or sidled into the big tent to watch her when she was performing.

She shivered, but not because she was cold. Perhaps it would have been different if Nelly hadn't left the fair shortly after her da had gone missing? She had felt a bit guilty about that in the following years, but after the night she had seen Nelly and Franco together, she hadn't been able to talk to Nelly in the same old way or even look her in the face. It had proved easier to avoid any contact. And then with the first chill of autumn, Nelly had upped and gone. She'd been relieved at first, still upset and angry at what she perceived as Nelly's betrayal of her father – she had to admit Franco's unfaithfulness had barely crossed her mind – but after a while the hurt had lessened and she'd found she missed the woman she'd hoped her da would one day marry.

Shrugging the memories away, Bonnie began to walk, her bare feet making no sound on the thick grass as once again she began to wrestle with thoughts of the future. She didn't want to marry anyone, she told herself fiercely, and no matter what her grandma said or did to persuade her otherwise, she wouldn't have it. Several of the lads in the fair communities had given her the eye in the last twelve months or so, but from a distance, careful to observe the unwritten code of conduct regarding young unmarried girls. Ham and the other men wouldn't tolerate a lad hanging around a lass unless the pair were officially engaged.

Exiting the field where the living wagons were parked and going into the dusty lane beyond, Bonnie sniffed appreciatively. There was the smell of the sea in the breeze now, and she could hear the waves crashing into Whitburn Bay. The year her da had gone missing, she had walked down into the bay on several nights, unbeknown to anyone else. She'd sat for hours weeping uncontrollably, begging God to send her father back to her.

The memory of that little girl, a lost child crying for the moon, brought a sudden flood of compassion into her breast as though it was for someone else, and it was, in a way, she conceded. Losing her father had changed her more than anyone knew. She'd been forced to grow up almost overnight, and she had lost something precious in the process – that belief in dreams her da had spoken of. The world was a harsh and cruel place and it crushed dreams to dust. She had long since stopped believing in miracles.

The thought saddened her, and then she made an impatient sound in her throat. This was her trouble, she admitted to herself irritably. Thinking too much. Her friends seemed to have nothing more on their minds than how soon they could marry a lad they had their eye on, and how grand a living van he could provide.

'And who are you off to meet in the middle of the night?'

She swung round with a startled scream to find Franco just behind her. He was barefooted like her and clad only in his trousers, his thick, curly chest hair accentuated by the moonlight gleaming on the gold medallion hanging from his neck.

Her first reaction was to appease him so he didn't carry tales to her grandma, and although her voice was indignant, it was also soft as she said, 'I'm not meeting anybody. I was hot and I wanted a walk, that's all.'

'Don't come that, not with me. Who is he? Is it Jed? He can't keep his eyes off you. Or Leo, maybe? Or is it someone from outside? Your mam was inclined that way, wasn't she? Is that it? You're seeing some lad or other from the town?'

'I told you. I just wanted a walk.'

'I'll break his neck, whoever it is.' He glanced around, as though someone was going to leap out from the hedgerow either side of the lane in which they were standing. 'I watched you sitting outside the wagon, biding your time, making sure no one was about, but you didn't know I was awake, did you? How many times have you done this? The truth, mind.'

The hot temper Bonnie had inherited from her father flared. Her voice still low but holding quite a different note, she glared at her grandmother's husband as she said, 'You're not my real granda, you can't tell me what to do.'

'No, you're right, I'm not your granda. I'm not related to you by blood at all.' It was clearly something he'd thought about before. 'Is that why you flaunt yourself at me while keeping me at arm's length? A little tease, that's what you are, but I don't mind that. A lass has the right to tantalize and play hard to get – all men like the thrill of the chase – but what I do mind is you carrying on with some lad or other on the sly. Now I'm asking you again, who is it?'

Bonnie had taken a step or two backwards as he had been speaking. Now fear of him was added to the anger, but it wasn't enough to stop her next words. 'I don't flaunt myself at you, I never have. Neither did Nelly and that's why you wanted her, isn't it? I didn't understand at the time but I do now. It was you who drove her away, after you'd –' she didn't know how to put it – 'after you made her . . .' She stopped again.

'What? What did you say?' Franco's eyes narrowed and now he grabbed her by the wrist, jerking her towards him. 'What have you heard about me and Nelly?'

'Nothing, I haven't heard anything.' She was struggling to free herself but with as little effect as a tiny fledgling sparrow in a cat's mouth. 'I saw you. I saw you myself.'

'You saw me? What did you see?'

'You were in her van, in bed with her. I saw you.'

Franco swore softly. 'You were spying on me?'

'No, I came to talk to her about my da. I didn't know you were there.'

'But you watched us?' He didn't deny it. In fact the idea of Bonnie watching him take Nelly had excited him. He'd only had Nelly the once and that still rankled. He'd taken a bottle of brandy round to her van that night, ostensibly to offer a shoulder for her to cry on after that old dog of hers had died, but he'd known the time was right. And she hadn't been used to hard liquor. It had been as easy as deflowering a bit lass half her age. He'd awoken after a couple of hours and made his way back to his own van, telling a furious Margarita who'd been waiting up for him that he'd taken a long walk. He had fully expected it to be the beginning of many such liaisons with Nelly, but she had had other ideas. She'd barely said two words to him before she'd left the fair a couple of months later.

Now he looked down into Bonnie's lovely face. He had always imagined there wasn't another female to compare with Nelly, but Madge's granddaughter had grown into a beauty with her long black hair and blue eyes and it had been a sweet torment over the last year or two living in such close proximity.

His voice thick, he whispered, 'Did you like watching us, Bonnie? Did it make you feel aroused, all hot and bothered inside? Did you wish it was you?'

Her guttural exclamation of distaste along with the look on her face left him in no doubt what she thought of that, and as she struggled harder, his fingers bruising the delicate skin of her wrist as he tightened his hold, she muttered, 'You're disgusting, repulsive, let go of me.'

'Oh, you want it all right, you're ripe for it, and you're going to give it to this lad, whoever he is. How many times have you met him like this? Has he had you already?'

As her free hand swung to slap his face, he caught it, pulling her hard against his chest so that her neck jolted painfully. Like most of the unmarried fair girls, Bonnie had only a rudimentary knowledge about the facts of life. Since living with her grandmother and Franco, she knew things went on in their marital bed now and again.

Things that involved grunts and groans and caused the wagon to creak in protest, but as her grandmother had never talked to her about the birds and bees, other snippets of information had been gleaned from her friends and these were sketchy at best. Apart from dire warnings that lads were only after one thing and woe betide a girl foolish enough to get too friendly with a member of the opposite sex, the travelling community considered it proper to keep their daughters in the dark about sexual relations until the wedding day, and even then some of the mothers evaded what they considered a highly embarrassing topic. This made for all kinds of wild imaginings among the girls, small threads of truth wound in with a great deal of conjecture.

Now Franco's mouth covered hers; one arm was wrapped round her slender waist like a vice and his other hand moved to grasp the hair at the back of her neck and keep her head still. Blind panic seized her. His tongue was choking her but her fists beating at his shoulders had no effect, and even when she kicked against his legs he didn't seem to feel it. Franco had always been proud of his muscled physique and worked hard each day to keep himself in shape, his body strong and powerful. Burgeoning on womanhood at fifteen, Bonnie was still slim and sylphlike, although since starting her monthlies the year before she had grown taller by some six inches, but this was no weapon against Franco's brute strength.

At one point she managed to wrench her mouth from his long enough to scream, but immediately he thrust her backwards so she lost her balance and fell over, the breath leaving her body and her head making thudding contact with the ground. And then he was straddling her, one hand across her mouth and the other yanking her clothes up over her thighs. She fought him as he ripped her knickers off, but it was the wild flailing of a desperate, frightened animal caught in a trap and knowing it was helpless. And then pain such as she had never experienced before rent her in two, burning, excruciating agony that was unbearable as she screamed silently against the cruel fingers clamped over her mouth and nose. She couldn't breathe as his body pounded her into the dust and she couldn't fight any more; hell had opened and swallowed her up, and the pain and terror and roaring darkness as she began to lose consciousness were taking her down into the depths.

It could only have been a matter of seconds before she came to. Franco was heaving himself off her, but even though his weight had lifted she couldn't move, lying limp and drained of life. He was breathing heavily as he did up his trousers, kneeling beside her, and then he stood up, flicking back his long black hair and offering her his hand to get up. Still she made no movement, tears rolling silently down her face although she was unaware of them. She was in a great deal of physical pain but her mind seemed to have closed down, her senses registering the call of an owl somewhere in the distance and the breeze rustling the leaves of the trees either side of the lane, but that was all.

He stood looking at her for a moment or two and it was this that made her pull down her clothes and roll onto her stomach, the dust and little stones rough on her face.

'Don't pretend you didn't want it. You're all the same, you lassies. Giving a man the come-on and then acting up after. It's part of the game you play, isn't it? But I'll treat you right, Bonnie. I want you to know that. Better than any young lad still wet behind the ears. Madge an' me haven't been seeing eye to eye for years, but you know that, same as everyone else. No one would blame me if I left her. We could run away together, join another fair, how about that? Somewhere down south if you like? You could have bairns, we could become a proper family. Madge has cheated me out of becoming a da but it's not too late – I'm in my prime and I'm ready to settle down. I'd never look at another lass, not if we got together.'

He waited, and when no answer was forthcoming from the crumpled figure on the ground he said impatiently, 'Come on, Bonnie, get up. Look, I could have been more gentle but it was you firing me up that made me act a bit rough. It'll be better next time, I promise you. And I meant what I said about us getting away. You'd like that, wouldn't you? Somewhere where your grandma would never find us.'

When he bent down and touched her it was the catalyst that brought life back into her limbs. She scrambled away on all fours before standing up some yards away from him, her fists clenched and her eyes wild. 'Don't you come near me. I hate you. I hate you.'

'Calm down. What's the matter?'

Even in Bonnie's dazed state she realized Franco seemed to have no real idea of what he had done, incredible though that was. He thought so much of himself that he couldn't imagine she'd meant what she said about finding him repulsive. As he took a step towards her, her voice rose. 'I'll scream and keep on screaming and I'll tell them what you've done.'

He hesitated. There had been a note in her voice that had finally got through to him. His face darkened and his tone was threatening when he said, 'Oh, aye, is that so? And how are you going to explain being out here then? I'll tell them you were meeting a lad and I'd got wind of it and followed to find you and him at it. No one will believe you, Bonnie. I'll say this lad scarpered when he saw me –'

'You come any nearer and I'll scream anyway.'

Franco raked back his hair again as he made a sound deep in his throat, but he must have decided she meant what she said because he didn't attempt to move closer. 'You'll come round.' The tone of his voice could almost have been called soothing. 'I'm offering to leave everyone and take you away to begin a new life – that's how much I care about you.'

'Care about me?' Her voice was so shrill a blackbird in one of the trees rose squawking from its roosting place. 'You forced me—'

'Forced you? We had a bit of a tussle, that's all, but you wanted me to do it. I know the signs, I've had enough lassies in my time. Look, it's no good talking now, not with you in this mood. Come morning you'll be in a different frame of mind and we'll make plans. It'll all come right, you'll see.'

He was mad. The whole world was mad.

After another moment he said, 'You coming back with me?' and when she continued to stand as if turned to stone, he added, 'No, perhaps best if we play it safe. You come when you're ready then.'

She watched him walk away but it wasn't until she was sure he was gone that she sank to the ground, her legs giving way. The storm of grief and shock and tears brought no relief, the numbness that had blanketed her mind was gone and now pain and horror were upper-most. It was a long, long time before she was able to pull herself to her feet again and she stood for some minutes, her eyes closed, trying to steady her shaking. Her torn knickers lay where Franco had flung them and she used them to wipe the blood and sticky mess from her legs, feeling as though she would never be clean again. She had to wash herself. She had to get rid of the smell and feel of him or else she would become inhinged, because she couldn't stand it.

Without thinking further she began to stumble along the lane towards the sound of the sea, whimpering as she went. Afterwards it frightened her that she had no re-collection of the next little while. It wasn't until she was waist deep in the icy waves that her mind became her own again.

There was no one about, the sea black and stretching endlessly in front of her, and she stood for an eternity, the spray covering her from head to foot before she bent down and took handfuls of sand to wash herself. She scrubbed herself raw but she couldn't feel it, not until she waded out of the freezing cold water and even then she welcomed it. Any last remnants of what had happened, of him, had been washed away from her body by the icy salty sea.

Shivering uncontrollably she began to walk back towards the campsite, but it wasn't until she had left the lane and entered the field where the living wagons were standing that she realized she knew exactly what she was going to do. Sometime during the hour or so she had been in the sea her brain had been working independently of herself, formulating a plan, and now all she had to do was obey the instructions in her head.

Chilled to the bone, the first thing she did, after establishing that Franco and her grandmother were asleep in their bed under the roof of the wagon, was to strip off her wet clothes and pull on dry ones. The wet ones she left where they fell – she would never wear them again. As silently as a ghost, she then pulled together her few personal belongings and another change of clothes, packing them in her father's old knapsack. This was the only thing she had left of him and she had insisted on keeping it when Margarita had sold the wagon and disposed of any contents the new owners didn't want.

The next thing she was about to do brought her heart thudding into her throat. The bed on which her grandmother and Franco was sleeping had ornate shelves underneath it with closed cupboards either side, and it was to the left of these that she crept. Praying the door wouldn't creak, she opened it with trembling fingers and took out her grandmother's big tin cashbox from behind a pile of blankets. Setting it on her own bed, she took a deep breath. Her grandmother kept the key to the cashbox on a small silver chain that clipped to her belt. It had never been discussed, but Bonnie knew this was to prevent Franco rifling it when he needed extra beer money. It was a bitter bone of contention between the two of them that Margarita saved what she could from any money she made on her stall, along with Bonnie's takings from her singing, and would never reveal what she put away from one month to the next. On more than one occasion when they barely had enough food to eat Franco had ranted and raved and threatened, but Margarita would not be swayed. Someone had to look to their old age, she always said, and as Franco didn't have a grain of sense it had to be her.

Bonnie stared at the narrow ladder that led to the bed above. Could she do this? Could she pluck the belt with the key from where it hung each night on a nail driven into the wood on her grandmother's side of the bed? What if she woke up? Worse, what if Franco woke up and tried to grab her? She knew if she ever felt his touch on her flesh again she would scream and keep on screaming. But the cashbox was going to be awkward to carry. It wouldn't fit easily into the knapsack and what if it proved too difficult to force open without the key?

She stood for a few moments more and then put one foot on the ladder. It didn't creak under her light weight the way it did when Margarita or Franco used it, and this gave her the courage she needed.

Franco was lying on his side, one arm flung across her grandma, in exactly the same position she had seen him in with Nelly, and although she couldn't determine much in the darkness, which was relieved only by a slanting shaft of moonlight through the lace curtains of the tiny window, his black bulk brought bile to her throat. His smell, a mixture of sweat and smoke and a musty odour, was stronger up here in the confined space, and she had to swallow hard several times to prevent herself from being sick. For a wild moment she seriously considered fetching her grandma's wicked-looking carving knife and plunging it into his chest while he slept. She stood on the ladder, trembling with the force of her hate and the pain caused by his brutality, fighting back the tears.

She wouldn't cry again, she told herself fiercely. Now was not the time to weaken. She had to do what she'd set out to do.

It took a few minutes but then she had control of herself once more. Slowly and carefully, she ascended to the top of the ladder. She knew where the belt would be, which was just as well or else she probably wouldn't have been able to distinguish it against the wood. As it was, she could just pick out its shape. Although the bed was little more than a large single, she found she still had to put one knee on the mattress in order to stretch across the sleeping occupants. Fortunately the flock mattress was old and lumpy and barely gave an iota, her slender frame making no impact.

When her fingers closed around the belt that her grandmother had curled into a ring and hooked on the nail, Bonnie's heart began to race, the blood pounding in her ears. Margarita and Franco were both snoring loudly, their mouths open, and the combined smell of their breath and the bed, and not least Franco, made Bonnie want to gag. Somehow she mastered the reflex, her stomach churning. And then she had lifted the belt from the nail. For a moment she couldn't believe she had done it. The key tinkled very faintly against the buckle as she drew back, easing herself fully onto the ladder and descending carefully. She sat down on her bed, her legs weak.

Her hands were shaking as she inserted the little key into the lock of the cashbox. Opening the lid, she found a number of notes along with several velvet pouches obviously containing coins. Her eyes opened wide. She had no idea how much money was here and she had no time to count it, but it was far more than she had imagined her grandmother had secreted away. But then for years her earnings had gone straight into the cashbox –

she hadn't seen a penny – and there had been her da's wagon and bits of furniture too. This wasn't stealing, it was claiming what was rightfully hers. Margarita had made her life a misery for as long as she could remember, and the last few years since her da had died had been much worse. And now this with Franco . . .

Her soft mouth hardened. She didn't care that her grandma and Franco would be left with nothing, in fact she was glad. She hoped what she had done ate them up, and that every day would be more miserable than the last for the pair of them as their mutual dislike and distrust of each other grew even stronger. And when a tiny thread of guilt at her thinking touched her mind, she straightened, as though throwing something off. No, she wouldn't feel guilty and she wouldn't leave so much as a penny in the cashbox, nor would she regret what she was doing in the future. And if any doubts ever crept into her mind, she would remind herself of the young girl standing in the sea, broken in mind and body and asking herself why she didn't just wade further into the water and let the elements take her to join her parents. But she hadn't given in to that temptation – she had chosen life, and she would not only survive, but also make a good future for herself. It was all up to her now.

Stuffing the notes and pouches into the knapsack, she fastened the straps before pulling on the shoes she wore when she sang. Her everyday black boots she left under her bed, along with her serviceable winter coat and hat that had long since seen better days. She wasn't going to take anything ugly into her new life, and as soon as she could she would buy herself a summer coat and bonnet, and maybe a couple of pretty frocks. Because she would need to look presentable to sing.

In spite of the pain between her legs, her aching head and her bruises, she felt a tiny frisson of excitement momentarily pierce the anguish. She was going to sing. She was going to become a proper singer, an artiste, or die in the attempt.

It was six o'clock in the morning when Bonnie got on the train. At the campsite the showmen and their families would be waking to a new day. Fires would be lit and smoke would be spiralling into the blue sky; children would be tumbling about playing, chunks of bread and jam clutched in their grubby hands, and the women would be seeing to breakfast while their menfolk busied themselves with the daily work needed to keep the fair running smoothly.

It was the only life she had ever known and yet she was leaving it without the slightest regret, which probably, she acknowledged, wouldn't have been the case even twenty-four hours before. But Franco's attack, coupled with the years of abuse meted out by her grandmother, had severed something deep inside. She wanted done with it all, and with everyone connected to what she was already terming her past life, even her childhood friends and folk like Mrs Carlini and Pedro and Ham. They had all known how cruelly she'd been treated since her da had died, but no one had stood up to Margarita. And she didn't care that that was the travellers' way – it was wrong, and that was the end of it.

It was only as the train began to steam out of the station that Bonnie realized how tense she was. Any moment she had half-expected Franco or her grandmother to appear and try to drag her back to the fair. But she was safe. She had escaped.

She sank back against the seat, suddenly feeling weak and slightly sick, and she must have looked peaky because an enormously fat woman who had boarded the train carrying two huge wicker baskets crammed with food leaned across and said, 'You all right, hinny?' Without waiting for a reply, she added, 'You had any breakfast?'

'No, I didn't have time.' Which was true enough.

'Ee, lass, no wonder you've come over queer. Here, get that down you.' So saying, she thrust a brown paper bag holding two great wedges of bread and a half-inch-thick slice of ham between them at Bonnie. 'I ate first thing but I always bring something along in case I get peckish. I'm going to see me old mam an' da and take 'em some bits to see 'em through for a week or two. One thing about marrying a farmer, you don't want for good grub. As you can see from the size of me.' She chuckled. 'I was a skinny little bit of nowt when I met my William, believe it or not.'

Bonnie felt acutely uncomfortable. 'I can't take your food. Although it's very kind of you—'

'Go on with you,' the farmer's wife interrupted. 'Do I look as if I'm wasting away? Get it down you, lass.'

Bonnie got it down her and felt the better for it. Her new friend continued to chat about the farm, her husband and bairns – five boys and three girls – and how she was trying to persuade her aged parents to leave the town and come and live with her on the farm. She asked for no more than a nod and a smile now and again which suited Bonnie. She couldn't have faced making conversation, nice though the woman was. She felt raw between her legs and ached all over, and her head was throbbing painfully, but it was the feeling of shame that had her clenching her hands and inwardly moaning. She should have stopped him. Somehow she should have been able to stop him, shouldn't she?

When the farmer's wife left the train a few stations later, it took all Bonnie's will to force her mind from the self-destructive cycle of recrimination and humiliation. She had to make plans, she told herself, and use this time on the journey south to get her story straight. With the right clothes and a new hairstyle she could pass for eighteen, and she had more than enough money to rent a room while she looked for work.

She had sat down under a giant oak in a grassy meadow once she had put some distance between herself and the campsite, and there, by the light of first dawn, she had counted the contents of the cashbox emptied into the knapsack. The size of Margarita's hoard was staggering. The notes, consisting of six large white five-pound notes and a number of ten-shilling and pound ones, had added up to forty-five pounds, and in addition to this the little velvet pouches had held guineas, sovereigns and half-sovereigns, as well as half-crowns, florins and smaller coins. Nearly sixty-five pounds altogether. A small fortune to Bonnie.

She had sat staring for some minutes at the money spread out on her lap, battling feelings of guilt before telling herself that the sale of her father's living wagon and dear old Rosie would have made up a good portion of the cash, and although she didn't know exactly what she herself had earned over the past few years, she knew it was a goodly amount. She had heard Ham refer to her as a 'little goldmine' to her grandma. No, she wouldn't let herself be beset by doubts. Not now, not ever.

As she made her plans to the accompanying drone of the train's wheels, she felt her eyes beginning to close. Settling in her seat with the knapsack clasped to her chest, a deep heaviness claimed her body and soul. Her last conscious thoughts were not of her grandma and the money, nor of Franco and what he had done to her, but of her father. What would her da say if he knew she intended to make her living singing? He had told her to sing out of joy and happiness, like the birds when they welcomed the sunrise. But even the birds had to eat.

She was going to leave the old Bonnie behind for good and become someone else, someone *she* wanted to be. And she *would* sing; wherever she could earn her living, she would sing. In public houses, in cafés, in clubs, it didn't matter where. As yet she had no idea how she was going to make this happen but again, it didn't matter. She had a head on her shoulders and she would learn, regardless that she had no one to advise or help her. She could do anything she put her mind to, she just had to believe . . .

Chapter Six

It was late afternoon when Bonnie stepped down from the train in London's King's Cross station clutching her knapsack and feeling very tiny and alone. The station was a hive of activity and the crowds were overwhelming; everyone seemed to know what they were doing and where they were going and moreover they were doing it very quickly. She exited the station simply by following her fellow passengers and doing what they did, having no real idea where she was, beyond that she had arrived in the capital and it seemed as far away from her grandmother as the moon.

The August evening was baking hot and devoid of any breeze; even the weather seemed different, along with the sights and smells of the big city. No one paid her any attention; she could have been invisible, which was comforting in a strange sort of way. She had been feeling as though she stuck out like a sore thumb but that clearly wasn't the case, and as she wandered along, her knapsack over her shoulder, she felt her confidence creep back.

In spite of her soreness and bruises she found she wanted to walk for a while after the long train journey, and the more she did, the hungrier she became. Apart from the farmer's wife's offering she had had nothing to eat or drink all day. She stopped at one of the street vendors' stalls which dotted the pavements here and there, buying herself a bag of chitterlings, a meat pie and a bottle of lemonade, which she consumed as she walked. Her earlier panic had subsided; she found she was actually enjoying the hustle and bustle and the noise and even the traffic which was so much more than she had encountered before. It all confirmed that she had escaped, that she was free; her back straightened and she felt altogether lighter as she walked on. Franco had hurt her but she wouldn't let him and her grandma win. She pushed the memory of what had happened to the back of her mind, telling herself she would deal with it when she felt better. For now the first priority was finding somewhere to stay.

She discovered she was walking along a street called the Marylebone Road and decided to turn off it into the grid of residential streets bordering it. In one of these, a long road of terraced houses where children were playing on the pavement and swinging from a rope they had thrown round a lamp post, she saw the sign 'Fairview Boarding House' and underneath, 'Vacancies within. No dogs, no Irish.'

Well, she hadn't got a dog and she wasn't Irish, Bonnie thought, a natural smile touching her lips for the first time that day. Although where this fair view was, she didn't know. The street was less than salubrious as far as she could see and the only view was of more terraces. She stood hesitating, wondering whether to walk on, but she was tired and within an hour or two it would start to get dark.

One of the boys swinging on the lamp post, a cheeky-faced urchin of indeterminate age, saw where she was looking: 'You thinking of lodging at Ma Nichols's?' he said chirpily, his broad cockney accent making him even more of a character. 'Me mum says Ma Nichols runs a good house, not like some round here.'

'Does she?' Bonnie smiled at the little lad who was filthy and wearing no shoes; she wondered what his own home was like. 'Thank you.'

He nodded at her, and when she still stood there, said, 'Aren't you going to knock then?'

The highly polished brass door knocker was in the shape of a goblin sitting on a toadstool. She'd no sooner rapped three times than the door opened and a small plump woman in a flowered overall peered at her. 'Yes, dear?'

'The sign says vacancies? I've come about a room.' Even standing on the doorstep she could smell lavender furniture polish and the lino in the hall was gleaming.

'Is that so? Well, you'd better come in a minute while we see what's what. I like to know a bit about someone who might live in my house before I let them have a room.' She stood aside for Bonnie to pass, saying, 'Go in the front room, dear. I'm Mrs Nichols by the way. Now sit down and tell me what a young woman like you is doing in the big city. That's a northern brogue, isn't it?'

The front room was as clean and neat as a new pin and the smell of furniture polish was even stronger, the highly starched white nets at the window and stiff upholstered suite immaculate. An embroidered fire screen depicting a picture of a thatched cottage and a garden full of flowers stood in the black leaded fireplace, and on the mantelpiece a large wooden clock ticked sedately. Bonnie had the feeling this room was rarely used. Gathering her thoughts together and mindful of the story she had decided on earlier, she cleared her throat. 'Aye, I'm from the north.' It would be useless to try and say otherwise. 'But I'm looking for work here and –'

'Looking for work? You mean you haven't got a job?'

'Oh, I can pay for a room,' Bonnie said hastily. 'I've been saving for years with the idea of coming to London and I've got plenty of money to keep me going until I find something.' It was true, in a way. It was just that her grandma had been holding on to what she had earned singing, along with the money from her da's wagon.

'And what sort of work are you looking for, Miss . . . ?'

'Cunningham. Bernice Cunningham. But everyone calls me Bonnie.' She'd thought it best to change her name but she hated the idea of losing Bonnie. 'And – and

I'm a singer.' It was the first time she had said it out loud and it brought a little thrill of pleasure that soon disappeared when she saw Mrs Nichols's face.

'Not another one thinking the streets are paved with gold.' Hilda Nichols sighed. 'I dare say you can sing, dear, but so can plenty of other girls just as pretty as you, and don't these club owners and the like know it. You'll find yourself on the casting couch quicker than you can say Jack Robinson.'

Bonnie had no idea what a casting couch was and it showed.

Mrs Nichols tutted. 'Oh, my word, as innocent as they come. They'll eat you alive, dear. Have you done any singing, professionally that is?'

'I've been with a touring company in the north.' At a pinch you could call the fair that.

'And how old are you if you don't mind me asking?'

She'd been expecting this. 'Eighteen,' she said firmly. Before leaving the train she had put her hair up in the same style she wore when she sang in the big tent, and she was tall for her age. She saw no reason why she couldn't pass for eighteen.

'Eighteen?' It was doubtful and Bonnie felt offended, regardless of the fact that Mrs Nichols had every right to be sceptical. 'Well, this touring company must have kept you wrapped up in cotton wool, dear, that's all I can say. You might look eighteen but you're not wise to the ways of the world, are you?'

'It was a family company.' Which again was true in a

way, she consoled herself, finding it was much easier to think up lies than actually voice them. 'They were protective of me.'

'And they told you that you could make your living singing in London, did they?'

'I've been earning my living singing for a long time and I was always very popular with the audiences.'

This had the ring of truth to it and Hilda's eyes narrowed. There was something she couldn't put her finger on here but the girl seemed nice enough and certainly respectable, as her puzzlement regarding the casting couch had proved. 'So you were a child performer?'

Bonnie nodded. 'I started very young.'

'And your parents approved of this? I presume they also performed in the company?'

'My da – my father did. My mother died shortly after I was born.'

'And your father is happy for you to leave and come to London by yourself?' Hilda's voice dripped disapproval.

'He died a little while ago and it wasn't the same once he was gone. I've got no brothers or sisters, just a grandma and some other more distant relatives. It seemed the right time to make the move. There's nothing to hold me in the north any more and I wanted to get away. To make a new start and see how I did here – or I thought I'd regret it in the years to come.'

'I see.' Hilda's intuition, which was finely honed after nearly thirty years of taking in lodgers, was telling her she hadn't heard the full story. She had been a young wife and mother of two small boys when her husband had come home from work one day complaining of feeling ill. He had gone upstairs to lie down for a while before the evening meal, and when she had gone to wake him half an hour later, she'd thought at first he was in a deep sleep. It was when she'd shaken his shoulder that she'd realized the truth. She had run screaming to her neighbour whose husband had fetched the doctor. A massive heart attack, the doctor had said. He wouldn't have known a thing. Which was a blessing surely? She had looked at the doctor in his three-piece suit and trilby hat and wondered what planet he was on. Nothing about being left a widow with two little ones under five and no income was a blessing. But that night, even through the shock and grief, she had vowed she would keep her home and that her sons would be clothed and fed, and by taking in lodgers and working eighteen-hour days for more than two decades she had accomplished just that. Both her boys were happily married, and shortly after the youngest had left home she'd finally paid the last instalment on the mortgage. So Hilda understood about making dreams come true. And when her home was bought and paid for she had scaled down the number of lodgers, reclaimed the front room and furnished it exactly how she wanted, and made sure once she'd had her tea at night that she put her feet up, had a glass of stout while listening to the wireless, and did nothing more that day. Her idea of bliss.

Now, looking at Bonnie, she came to a decision. The girl was keeping something back sure enough, but she seemed a nice young woman. Furthermore she would rather such an innocent lodged with her than with some of the types hereabout whose boarding houses were little more than brothels. They'd have such a pretty young thing on the game before the girl knew what was what.

Clearing her throat, Hilda said briskly, 'The room's at the top of the house on the second floor. The lady who occupied it until recently had been with me fifteen years but she's gone to live with her sister in Kent, after the sister's husband passed away. The other room on that landing is rented by Miss Parker, a schoolmistress. The bathroom's on the floor below. A young married couple have one of the rooms on that floor and I sleep in the other one, except, that is, for when my youngest son and his wife pay a visit. He moved to Southampton when he married her so she could be close to her parents.'

Hilda gave a sniff at this point and Bonnie got the impression she wasn't over-thrilled about the situation.

'It's twelve bob a week payable a month in advance, and that includes a cooked breakfast. I used to do an evening meal for my lodgers when I was younger but I like the evenings to myself now, and there's plenty of cafés round here. You'll have your own key but I don't keep a late house – I like my lodgers in by eleven at night unless you tell me otherwise. You can make yourself a hot drink in your room but I don't allow no alcohol on

my premises. And no visits from members of the opposite sex, no pets, no smoking.'

Bonnie blinked. Her head was spinning.

'Well, do you want to see the room?'

'What? Oh, yes. Yes, please.'

'Where's the rest of your luggage?'

This caught Bonnie off guard. Stuttering slightly, she
said, 'I – I'm having it sent on. When I'm settled. I did-
didn't want to have to lug it about while I looked for
somewhere to live.'

Hilda nodded, the while thinking, having it sent on my
backside! The girl had had a falling-out with someone or
she'd eat her hat. 'Come along then.'

Bonnie followed her new landlady out of the room
and into the hall. The stairs were steep, with just a narrow
piece of carpet in the middle of them, and the second
landing, like the first, consisted of highly polished floorboards, the smell of furniture polish tickling her nose.
They walked past one shut door to a second one, and
after inserting a key into the lock, Mrs Nichols opened it
and allowed Bonnie to enter in front of her.

The room wasn't large but neither was it small and like
the rest of the house she had seen thus far it was neat and
clean. Either side of a single bed with a bright patchwork
coverlet stood a mahogany wardrobe and a chest of
drawers, and above the bed an embroidered tract had the
words, 'When I lay me down to sleep, I pray the Lord my
soul to keep,' entwined with ivy leaves. A big rug made
from cuttings of material stood at the end of the bed on

the shining floorboards, and a small armchair was set at an angle to this next to a tiny black-leaded fireplace. Bonnie walked across to the window and saw a vast panorama of hundreds of rooftops beneath a darkening sky outside. For a moment she felt like a little bird that had made its way safely home to its nest.

Fighting a flood of emotion that had her wanting to cry, she said shakily, 'It's lovely, Mrs Nichols. Beautiful.'

Clearly gratified, Hilda smiled. 'I don't know about beautiful, dear, but you won't find bedbugs or any other type of creature in my house. Now here's your key –' she handed Bonnie the key to the bedroom door – 'and I'll give you one for the front door downstairs while I sort out a rent book. I bet you'd find a cup of tea welcome, eh? You come down to the kitchen at the end of the hall when you're ready, all right?' So saying, she bustled out of the room, shutting the door behind her.

Bonnie sat down on the bed, her knees suddenly weak. As if in a dream, she gazed about her. This was her little home and she had her own key to it. She opened her fingers and looked at the key in something approaching wonder. After what Franco had done to her it seemed strange that she could feel glad about anything, but she did. Her eyes were drawn to the curtains at the window, which were green and covered in hundreds of tiny flowers, like the meadows she had often walked in as a child with her da.

The tears had been held in all day and now, as she

buried her face in her hands, they were uncontrollable. She wanted her da, how she wanted her da. She would give the rest of her life for one day with him, to see his face and hear him laugh and know he would always look after her, that he loved her more than anyone else, that she was his darling.

It was some minutes before her grief subsided; grief for her father, grief for the young girl she had been before Franco had taken her, grief that life could never be the same again. She was sore in mind and body, exhausted and at the end of herself, but as she dried her face and redid her hair in order to go downstairs, she told herself she wouldn't always feel like this. Alone, lost, all at sea. And then her gaze moved round the room again, and the ember of gladness glowed faintly once more.

Her chin lifted. This wasn't the end of something, it was the beginning. Mrs Nichols had said there were lots of girls like her who could sing, and there might be, but they didn't want to succeed as a singer as much as she did. Furthermore she might not have known what a casting couch was, but she'd cottoned on to what Mrs Nichols meant after a time, and she would fight tooth and nail before she let any man do to her what Franco had done. She shuddered, her mouth tightening in disgust.

Her da had always said that she was like him in as much that she had a double portion of get-up-and-go. She inclined her head at the thought. It was up to her to use it now. And she would. No more crying or looking backwards. Life had to be lived looking forwards, it was the only way.

Chapter Seven

Over the following weeks as summer gave way to autumn Bonnie's resolve to find work as a singer was severely tested. She picked Hilda Nichols's brains for the location of any local pubs and clubs and halls which hired live entertainment for the enjoyment of their customers, and then widened her search to include areas as far flung as Kingston upon Thames to the south and Barnet to the north, but all to no avail. The fact that she couldn't read music was a handicap, even though she assured prospective employers that she could learn a tune after hearing it only once or twice, along with the words. Some rejections were couched more kindly than others but they all boiled down to the same thing; she had no proven experience of singing professionally, she spoke with a strong north-east accent, she was untrained, and – which she soon realized was the most important thing – she had no contacts within the industry and no one to vouch for her.

She left her lodgings each morning after one of Hilda's

generous fry-ups and returned late evening having spent the day trying her luck at any and every club, pub, theatre and hall she could find. She scoured the papers each night before going to bed, cutting out notices about venues and shows – those advertising for singers and even those that weren't – and then would present herself at the door of said establishments the next morning, but not once did she get as far as someone actually listening to her sing.

She was often frustrated, sometimes angry, once or twice unnerved when Mrs Nichols's casting couch was covertly suggested, and totally exhausted every night. But through it all she made herself count her blessings. First and foremost, Franco's attack hadn't resulted in a bairn, as the normal occurrence of her monthlies confirmed. But almost without her being aware of it, her horizons were broadening, her knowledge of the world outside that of the fair and the showmen was being developed, and – through disappointment after crushing disappointment – her inner self was being strengthened. After she had scoured the newspapers for advertisements, she read them from cover to cover, absorbing facts like a sponge. She was horrified to learn about the Nazis herding Jews into concentration camps in Germany, and the more she read about Adolf Hitler the more uneasy she felt; this was heightened when in October it was reported that the Nazi government had walked out of the Geneva Disarmament Conference and withdrawn from the League of Nations.

She discussed this over breakfast with Hilda, Selina Parker – who was fast becoming a close friend – and Verity and Larry McKenzie, the married couple who occupied a room on the floor below herself and Selina. Larry fancied himself as a political activist although Bonnie didn't see that he did anything but talk, since Verity wouldn't allow him to attend meetings or rallies and the like; he was scathing about the Nazis and their brutal rise to power.

'They're bullies,' he said earnestly, his eyes blinking like an overwrought owl's behind his round, metal-rimmed glasses. 'And everything that was predicted after Hitler became Chancellor is happening in front of our eyes. The persecution of the Jews and anyone who disagrees with it, the burning of all those so-called "un-German" books in May and the purging of the trade-union movement, banning all opposition parties and creating this Hitler Youth movement to brainwash the young, it's relentless. And what about the sterilization of "imperfect" Germans? How can anybody in their right mind agree with forcing those who are blind or deaf or physically deformed and so on to be sterilized? But it's happening, right now it's happening and the world is doing nothing about it. And this referendum next month to supposedly give the ordinary German man and woman the opportunity to approve Hitler's policies is a joke. All the other parties in Germany have been outlawed, for crying out loud. There'll only be the name of the Nazi Party on the ballot paper, and Hitler's Storm Troopers will make sure people are dragged to the polling stations if necessary. Hitler's crushing all resistance and rearming Germany, and you know what that means, don't you?'

Bonnie, Hilda and Selina stared at him, but Verity continued eating her breakfast. She had heard it all before, many times.

'War,' said Larry after a thespian pause.

'Don't say that.' Hilda's voice was sharp. She had lived through one war and seen the devastation it caused in families when their menfolk didn't come home.

Larry went a little red. 'Sorry, Mrs Nichols,' he said uncomfortably. 'I was just saying, that's all.'

'Well, don't.' Verity glared at her husband. 'Upsetting people when they're trying to eat their breakfast. And you don't know how things will turn out anyway. No one wants war, not even Hitler.'

There the conversation had ended, but in November when the Nazis won ninety-five per cent of the German vote, Bonnie thought about what Larry had said. Perhaps unsurprisingly though, not for long. She had come to the conclusion that the dream would have to wait for a while. She needed a job, any job. Her money was disappearing with alarming regularity. When she'd first arrived in London she'd bought a wardrobe of lovely clothes, knowing that she needed to be dressed well if she was going to have any chance at all at an interview or audition. On top of that expenditure, there was the rent for her room, an evening meal each day – after

Hilda Nichols's cooked breakfast each morning she had decided she could forgo lunch in the interest of economy – bus fares and the like as she travelled further and further afield in an effort to find a singing job, and, since the weather had worsened, coal for the little fireplace in her room. After seeing some of the other pretty young things she was competing against in the entertainment world, she had visited a hairdressing salon and had her long wavy hair cut into a shoulder-length, curly style that had immediately added two or three years to her age. The salon had also sold a selection of cosmetics, and the very nice girl who had cut her hair had shown her how to use the minimal amount to make the most of her clear translucent skin and big eyes. She had left the establishment clutching a bag holding creams and powders, lipstick and mascara as well as tweezers for tidying up her eyebrows, and feeling very much a modern miss.

But everything cost money, and she was finding life in the capital expensive. She had been hoping against hope that something in the entertainment industry would come her way but it was clearly not meant to be – yet.

After discussing her predicament with Selina, Bonnie knew the only sensible thing to do was to get herself a waitressing job or bar work because she couldn't face working in a factory and being shut in all day. She had come to this inescapable conclusion after lasting one day in a job at a pickling factory. The noise, the feeling of being hemmed in, the smell, and not least a foreman with roving hands, had made Bonnie sick to her stomach. She had arrived at the café where she was meeting Selina for their evening meal close to tears, but after a substantial plate of sausage and mash and a chat with her friend she'd felt better.

'You need a job where you're meeting people,' Selina had comforted her. 'Something with a bit more freedom to it than being confined to a conveyor belt from nine to five.'

Which was why, on a cold November morning with the smell of frost in the air, Bonnie left the house in Shouldham Street for a working men's club not far from Paddington station that had vacancies for barmaids. After the fiasco at the factory she felt more than a little nervous. She wanted the job and she needed to work, but if it was offered her she didn't want to fail again.

She had dressed carefully for the appointment she'd made the day before when she had called at the club. An elderly grey-haired woman had opened the door to her knock, and when Bonnie had explained she was answering the advertisement 'Barmaids wanted' in the previous evening's paper, the woman had nodded. 'There's only me here at the moment, ducks,' she'd said cheerily. 'I do a bit of cleaning most mornings. It's Ralph you want, he's the manager. I know he's told a couple of other girls to come along about ten tomorrow morning. Give us your name and I'll let him know you're coming an' all, all right?'

She had stuttered her new name, Bernice Cunningham, which still felt strange on her lips, and left. She had visited the club some weeks before looking for a singing job and on that occasion had seen a man called Dennis Heath who had the grand title of 'master of ceremonies'. He'd been very offhand with her and she was glad she wasn't seeing him again. In fact she nearly hadn't gone after the barmaid's job because she hadn't wanted to face him.

By the time she reached the club it was just before ten o'clock and several girls were waiting outside, eyeing each other up and down. One of them had been talking to another girl – a brassy blonde, Hilda would have labelled her – and it was she who turned and looked at Bonnie. 'You here for one of the barmaids' jobs too?' At Bonnie's nod, she added, 'Great. That's five of us after two jobs. Oh, well, better than odds of ten to one, I suppose.'

She smiled and Bonnie smiled back. None of the other girls spoke and after an awkward moment, Bonnie said, 'I'm Bonnie, by the way.'

'Betty.' Then the blonde giggled. 'Flippin' heck, Betty and Bonnie. Sounds like a double act, don't it! You're not from round these parts, are you?'

'I've recently moved from the north.'

Betty nodded. 'Thought that was a northern accent. I used to go out with a bloke whose family were from Newcastle. That where you're from?'

'No.' Feeling it would be rude not to elaborate, Bonnie added, 'Not as north as that.'

She was saved from further questions by the arrival of

a dapper little man whose grizzly grey hair stuck up straight from the crown of his head when he doffed his hat to them all. 'Ladies . . .' He grinned widely. 'What a bevy of beauties, if I may say so. A pity I haven't got work for five barmaids. Still, there it is. Come in, the lot of you.'

He unlocked the door to the club and stood aside for them to file past. A couple of the girls smiled at him as they did so and one, a small redhead with a definite wiggle to her hips, said cheekily, 'Ta, Mr Mercer, or do we call you Ralph?' as she fluttered her eyelashes.

'You can call me whatever you like, sweetheart, but if you want me to answer, it's Mr Mercer.' The tone was affable but Bonnie detected an edge to it, and Betty must have thought the same because once they were inside, she whispered, 'I reckon there's only four of us in the running now. He didn't like her coming on to him, did he?'

The club smelt strongly of smoke and stale beer but after the eye-watering smell of the pickling factory it was almost pleasant. The five girls followed the manager through a large room that had a bar rail down one side and a stage at the far end and was packed with tables and chairs, and out through a door into the back of the club where the manager's office was situated, along with the ladies' and gents' toilets. There was a row of hard-backed chairs along the wall of the corridor and Ralph Mercer pointed to them, saying, 'Sit yourselves down, ladies, and decide who's first and second and so on. I'll call you in one at a time.'

After he'd shut the door to his office, the redhead said, 'Well, I was here second after her.' She inclined her head at one of the girls who'd smiled at the manager as they'd come in. 'I suggest we go in the order we got here. Agreed?'

They all nodded.

Bonnie's heart sank. She was the last. That didn't bode well.

The first girl and the redhead were in the manager's office for no more than five minutes respectively and both left without a word to the others. Betty looked at Bonnie and the remaining girl, a tall individual with dark, bobbed hair. 'Neither of them have been offered a job,' she said definitely.

'Perhaps he's going to see us all and then let us know,' said the dark-haired girl in a bored voice. 'I don't care whether I get a job or not anyway. I'm getting married in the spring and my Hector don't agree with women working once they're wed.'

Betty stood up then as the door to the office opened and Ralph Mercer beckoned her forward as the third applicant.

Once they were alone, the girl continued, 'I was working at the Red Lion on the Bayswater Road till a few days ago, do you know it?'

Bonnie shook her head.

'It was nice there but my Hector got the idea the

barman was after me and waited for him after work and punched him on the nose. The owner wasn't too pleased and I was out on my ear.'

Bonnie didn't feel she'd like 'my Hector' over much.

'Still, like I say, I don't care. My Hector works at the docks and earns loads. He buys me whatever I want. Look –' She thrust out her left hand where an engagement ring sparkled. 'Nice, ain't it? An' Hector's already put a deposit on our house. He says he'd rather me stay at home and get me bottom drawer ready for when we get married than get another barmaid job.'

'What do *you* want?'

The girl stared at Bonnie as though she'd asked something ridiculous. 'Whatever Hector wants,' she said after a moment or two. 'If I don't get this I shan't bother to go after anything else.'

Bonnie gave up. For the next few minutes she listened to the girl rattle on about her wedding plans with 'my Hector' this and 'my Hector' that, and was inordinately glad when the door to the office opened again. Betty sailed out, giving Bonnie a broad wink and thumbs-up as she passed, and almost immediately 'my Hector' was called into the manager's office, only to emerge even faster than the first two applicants had done, grim-faced and with a heightened colour in her pale cheeks.

Mr Mercer was in the doorway and looked at the list in his hand. 'You must be Bernice Cunningham. Come in.'

The office was bigger than she had expected and had

three desks in it. Ralph Mercer sat himself down behind the largest one in the middle and pointed at the hard-backed chair set in front of it. 'Sit yourself down, Bernice.'

'I – I like to be called Bonnie,' she stammered as she did as she was told. 'No one calls me Bernice.'

'Right you are. Now, before we get going, tell me. Are you about to get married, Bonnie?'

Startled, she stared at him and a pair of keen blue eyes smiled back at her. Betty must have told him what the other girl had said. Unsure whether he meant the question seriously, she said, 'Absolutely not, Mr Mercer.'

'Well, that's a start.' He settled back in his chair. The office was lovely and warm from the heat given off by an electric fire and for the first time that morning Bonnie felt herself relaxing. 'Now, that's a northern accent if I'm not much mistaken. Your family moved down south, I take it?'

Bonnie gave him the limited version of the truth she'd told everyone since arriving in London, but without mentioning her desire to sing as she felt it could hamper her being offered the job, and insinuating that she had only just arrived in the capital.

Ralph Mercer listened without interrupting, but behind his expressionless face he was summing Bonnie up. After years in the pub and club trade he prided himself on being a shrewd judge of character. Hadn't he suspected his two previous barmaids were on the fiddle? That fool Dennis had taken them on when he was on holiday and as soon as he'd laid eyes on them his sixth sense had kicked in. Sure enough they'd had a scam going between them and had had their hands in the till until he had caught them at it and sacked them on the spot. They were lucky he hadn't called in the law; he would have done but for the fact that he knew one of them had an ailing mother and younger brothers and sisters to support and was the sole breadwinner in her house, the father having done a runner years before. Too soft, that was his trouble.

But this girl seemed honest enough although he'd bet his bottom dollar there was more to her than met the eye. Still, who didn't have skeletons in the cupboard? And she was dressed well and a bit more refined than Betty Preston who he had just taken on. They'd balance each other well.

He cleared his throat. 'Betty Preston tells me you really want this job, unlike Miss Madley. Is that true?'

Taken aback, Bonnie stared at him for a moment. How nice of Betty to put in a good word for her. Finding her voice, she said, 'Aye, yes, Mr Mercer. I do.'

'But you haven't worked behind a bar before?'

'No, but I'm a quick learner.'

'Good at adding up?'

This time she was ready. 'Definitely.'

'There's no standing on ceremony here so I warn you now. Old Ada comes in most mornings and does a couple of hours' cleaning, but when the club's busy you might be asked to clean the ladies' or mop up spills before someone slips and brains themselves, things like that. You've got to be prepared to muck in. There's a small kitchen at the rear where we make hot drinks but no food is prepared on the premises. Me missus brings that to sell to the customers – sandwiches, pork pies, scratchings and so on. We bring it out from the back as needed and the prices are on a blackboard behind the bar. There's a dance every Saturday and a couple of concerts in the week; always something going on so it's lively and there'll be times, lots of times, when you're fair rushed off your feet and on the go non-stop. It's always at the busiest times you'll get an awkward customer who's mouthy with it. Think you can handle that while still smiling? On the whole we have a nice enough bunch in but there's a couple of right so-an'-sos an' all. Same as anywhere.'

Bonnie nodded. 'That wouldn't throw me.'

'So, shall we give it a try? See if you suit?'

He was offering her the job. Eagerly she said, 'Yes. Oh, yes, please, Mr Mercer.'

'I pay one pound fifteen a week but you'll make a tidy bit in tips an' whatever you get, it's yours. Now I told your pal –' Bonnie rightly assumed he was referring to Betty – 'and I'm telling you, you play fair with me an' I'll play fair with you. I'm an easy-going fella on the whole, me missus'd tell you that, but cross me an' I'm like old Jumbo, I never forget.'

His eyes twinkled at her, and again Bonnie didn't know if she was supposed to smile. She decided not. 'My da used to say to deal with people as you'd like to be dealt with. He said spit into the wind and it's likely to come back on you.'

Ralph gave a guffaw of laughter. He liked this girl. Behind that pretty face she'd got some spirit and she'd need it on occasion, working behind the bar. But she'd do all right. 'We open at two in the afternoon but I like my bar staff half an hour before that. And I expect you to stay an' help clear up for as long as it takes after chucking-out time, all right? Tea-time you get a break out the back an' you can help yourself to whatever my Mary's brought in to sell. No charge. Perk of the job.'

He went on to explain a few more things but Bonnie was barely listening. She had been offered a job and, by the sound of it, so had Betty and she just knew they'd get on like a house on fire. She liked Mr Mercer too. Certainly he was nothing like the foreman in the pickling factory.

Things were changing at last. She felt it in her bones.

Betty was waiting for her when she left the club, smoking a cigarette in a nearby doorway. She came straight over, grinning, as she said, 'I can tell from your face he's taken you on. So, we'll be working together then, Betty and Bonnie, double trouble.' And she laughed at her own joke.

Bonnie giggled. There was something infectious about Betty's vivacity. 'Aye, I got it, thanks in part to you. He told me you said I really wanted the job, unlike that other girl.'

'I couldn't stand her.' Betty was obviously a girl of snap decisions. 'So, starting tomorrow same as me?' When Bonnie nodded, Betty added, 'Come on, let's go and have a cup of tea and a cream bun to celebrate.' She linked her arm through Bonnie's. 'We're going to have some fun, you an' me, Bonnie. You see if we don't. And with your looks we'll have the lads sniffing about and I'm quite happy to have the ones you don't want.'

Bonnie smiled but said nothing as they walked towards a café a few doors up from the club. She didn't want a lad, any lad. She would never want one. Just the thought of what had happened with Franco occurring again made her feel sick. She intended to become a singer and make that her life and if she needed to have singing lessons and learn to read music to make that a reality, that's exactly what she'd do. But lads, men . . . She shuddered inwardly. Never.

Chapter Eight

Over the next weeks as November turned into December and sleety icy rain became the order of the day, Bonnie found that Betty had been right. They did have fun. Her new friend had the happy gift of a sunny personality, and the knack of turning even the most frustrating situations into something to be laughed at. Life was never dull, and the mundane part of the job like washing up dirty glasses and crockery and clearing up last thing at night was enjoyable in Betty's company. Betty might be rough and ready, and certainly her language could turn as blue as any sailor's when she was provoked, but Bonnie didn't think she'd met anyone she liked as much as Betty in a long time. She looked forward to going to work each day, and her initial shyness at dealing with customers soon evaporated as she watched how Betty handled folk and took her lead from her new friend.

She introduced Selina to Betty the second Monday after beginning at the club. Monday was her and Betty's day off, and they met Selina out of work. The three girls had a meal together before going to the cinema to see the film *King Kong* in which the central character, a giant gorilla, falls in love with a human. The latest in special-effects technology had been brought to the screen, and there were screams from several ladies in the audience when the huge animal first appeared. She hadn't been sure how Selina and Betty would get on – they were certainly polar opposites, Selina being quiet and refined and very much a school-marm, and Betty . . . well, Betty was Betty, as Bonnie mused to herself. But the two hit it off immediately which was a relief. Suddenly Bonnie had two good friends, and for the first time since she had fled the north-east she felt happy.

Apart from the occasional lapse, Bonnie didn't allow herself to reflect on the life she'd left behind and more especially the circumstances of her departure. It was too raw, too painful. She told herself she was Bernice Cunningham now and that was that, but the past did surface now and again in sporadic nightmares that she could do nothing about. She would awake sweating and shaking, the feel of Franco's hands as he held her down and the crushing weight of his body as real as if it was happening over again. She'd lie wide-eyed and trembling until she had the terror under control and drifted off eventually into an uneasy slumber, but come morning her secret would be firmly locked away in the back of her mind. It was the only way she could cope. Fortunately her days were so busy and full she didn't have time to brood.

Ralph Mercer turned out to be a genuinely nice individual but the girls weren't so keen on Dennis Heath, his right-hand man. Betty said Dennis reminded her of a bad-tempered little cockerel, and Bonnie had to agree. He was always charm itself with the customers, standing on the stage on Saturday nights with his white gloves and patent pumps, clearly in his element calling out the names of the dances and cracking jokes, but he treated the two girls as skivvies and far beneath him. At times he was downright insulting.

Concert evenings were even worse. The committee would sit at their table with the entertainments secretary and Dennis was constantly trying to impress them. He'd invariably introduce each act by doing impressions of performers like George Robey or Al Jolson, and they were always so bad that Bonnie and Betty cringed. But Dennis was Ralph Mercer's brother-in-law and, as Betty remarked, blood's thicker than water.

As the days and weeks went by and Christmas approached, Bonnie learned that the working men's clubs were part of a network of entertainment that had been going since the end of the nineteenth century, and that there were hundreds of such places all over the country. The more she absorbed how they functioned, the more she began to understand that they could be springboards to greater things for all kinds of artistes. And the committee could be a help or a hindrance to the performers. It was the committee, sitting drinking at their table in front of the stage, who gauged the mood of an audience and who decided, courtesy of the strength of the applause, whether an act was worth an encore or not. Apart from an encore earning the performer an extra shilling and sixpence, it meant said act was worth noting, and the entertainments secretary would make sure they were booked again.

The entertainments secretary at Bonnie's club was a robust little man called Enoch Stewart with a wide smile and shrewd eyes. Like all the secretaries he was the equivalent of an agent and someone to be respected, but unlike Dennis Heath he didn't throw his weight about and the girls liked him. He was always visiting other clubs on the lookout for new acts, and once or twice Bonnie had thought of approaching him but always her courage had failed her. Enoch's day job was working in a factory as a glass-blower, but although his work as entertainments secretary was unpaid it was his driving passion, and his day job was very much second fiddle.

It was shortly before Christmas when she confided to Betty that she wanted to become a singer and it had been her main reason for coming to London. Betty was all agog, and immediately wanted to hear her. It was their day off and they were sitting in a little square of park eating a meat pie before they went to see Fred Astaire at the cinema. Bonnie looked around her, shaking her head. 'I couldn't, not here.'

'Course you can, there's no one about, and if you want to do that sort of thing you can't be shy,' said the ever practical Betty. 'Go on, Bonnie, sing us a song. I can't believe you haven't told me about this before.'

Bonnie shrugged. 'I tried for ages when I first came to London and got nowhere. I didn't even get one audition. Perhaps I'm no good.'

'How can you say that if no one even heard you?'

That was true. Bonnie knew she'd gone red. 'What shall I sing?' she asked uncomfortably, wishing she hadn't said anything.

'Don't mind. I know, "Smoke Gets in Your Eyes". I love that one. Do you know the words?'

It had been one of the hits of the year and Bonnie nodded. 'I only have to hear a song once and I remember the words and the tune. My da was the same. He had a lovely voice.' She had told Betty the same story she'd told everyone else since coming to the capital; that her mother had died when she was a baby and her father had brought her up, and it was his death that was the catalyst for making the move to London. Which was partly true.

'Go on then,' Betty said again. 'Look, I'll introduce you.' She jumped up from the bench and lifted her arm in an extravagant gesture much as Dennis did. And in an imitation of his ringing tones, she announced, 'Ladies and gentlemen, for your pleasure for one night only, the amazing, the beautiful, Miss Bernice Cunningham will sing "Smoke Gets in Your Eyes".'

Grinning, she pulled Bonnie to her feet and then sat down expectantly, her face bright.

Bonnie stood for a moment and then shut her eyes. Outside the small square London went about its business; the noise of traffic and people only slightly dampened by the trees and bushes surrounding the perimeter of the tiny oasis. When she had been living with the fair community after her father's disappearance she had sung most nights – her grandma had seen to that – but even during the day when she'd been doing other things she would sing for the sheer enjoyment of it. Since coming to London there had been little opportunity to practise, though, and for a second or two she was suddenly frightened she might be too rusty. She had never had any difficulty in deciding how to sing a song and bring out the emotion in the words – it was part of the feeling she experienced that she *was* the song, that was the only way she could describe it to herself. Now, after the first line or two, that familiar feeling took over and she sang as she had always sung, with her soul laid bare.

She didn't open her eyes until she had finished the last word, and when she did it was to see Betty sitting with her hand to her mouth while the tears rolled down her cheeks.

'I can't believe it.' Betty searched in her handbag for a handkerchief and dabbed at her eyes as she said, 'I flippin' can't believe it. That was . . .' She waved her hand helplessly. 'That was lovely. I mean, I *never* cry and here I am blubbing like a baby. You're ten times better than the singers we get at the club. Honestly, I mean it.'

Bonnie sat down beside her again. It was good to hear. She hadn't realized just how much the last months had knocked her confidence. 'You're not just saying that because you're my friend?'

'Er, excuse me, look at the state of me, woman.' Betty gave a watery grin. 'I'm a mess, and believe me, I'm pretty hard-boiled as you know.'

Bonnie did know. Betty had been brought up in the slums of the East End. Out of her nine siblings, three boys were in prison; two of her sisters, she'd frankly admitted to Bonnie, were on the game; and another sister was in effect a gangster's moll. Her father worked for someone about whom the family never asked questions, and her mother was as tough as they come but had a heart of gold, like her daughter. Bonnie had gone round to Betty's house for tea one day and hadn't stopped laughing from when she'd entered to when she left. They were what her da would have described as salt of the earth, even though the law would have had quite a different depiction of the Preston tribe.

Bonnie squeezed Betty's arm. 'Thanks. So you think I should follow my dreams then?' It was a rhetorical question. For just a minute or two she had been in a different place, a different world, somewhere where the past and future didn't matter and the present was magical. It was always like that when she sang and it was the only confirmation she needed that she had to press on. She had already decided to take singing lessons and learn how to read music, and seeing Betty's reaction had made her think she would do it sooner rather than later.

'No doubt about it. Your chance will come, Bonnie, and when it does you grab it with both hands, right?

You'll make it. With a voice like you've got, it's only a matter of time. You just need a break, that's all.'

Bonnie nodded. Put like that, it sounded simple. She just hoped she recognized a break when it presented itself!

Christmas Eve happened to be on a Sunday, and so the big Christmas concert at the club was being held the day before. Bonnie awoke that Saturday morning to a cold, overcast December day with the occasional desultory snowflake drifting aimlessly in the wind. She stood at her window for a while, looking out over the rooftops and thinking how different this Christmas would be to the year before and wondering if Ham had made provision for the fair community to get through the bad weather once again. Were little Ava's parents still grieving so bitterly for the child they'd lost, and had Mrs Carlini made another tiny fur coat out of rabbit skins for Mimi the monkey after the previous one had gone missing in the spring? The small animal felt the cold badly.

Mentally shaking herself, she turned from the window. She was so glad she had escaped, but she was no nearer to fulfilling the promise she had made herself on leaving the north-east. But she *would* succeed. She was only fifteen years old, even if everyone here thought she was eighteen. She had lots of time and she wouldn't give up.

There was an extra buzz in the air when she got to the club later on. The Christmas tree with its tinsel and glass baubles had gone up the week before, along with paper chains and big concertinaed balls for the ceiling, and even Dennis had been humming carols and was less snappy with the girls. The club would be closed until Wednesday as Ralph and Dennis and their wives were spending Christmas with family in Bath, but Bonnie's three days off were already booked up. Christmas Eve she'd been invited to spend with Betty and her family; Christmas Day she and Selina and Hilda were having together – Verity and Larry had already gone to stay with Verity's mother – and Boxing Day she'd agreed to accompany Selina on a visit to her elderly parents in Kensington.

Bonnie frowned to herself as she tidied her hair in the club's washroom. She was a little apprenhensive about Boxing Day. Selina seemed to have a strange relationship with her parents. She never talked about them, and was always quiet and withdrawn for a while when she had been to see them. Bonnie knew Selina was an only child and that her parents were well off but that was all. She'd been surprised at the invitation to go with her, and furthermore, she didn't think she had imagined the look of relief on Selina's face when she had agreed.

Bonnie had talked the matter over with Betty who had her own ideas about what was what. 'You can bet Selina's folks are the type who expected Selina to live with them indefinitely and take care of them in their old age. You see it time and time again with daughters, especially if the poor devil is the only one. I mean, why else would

Selina leave home and take a room somewhere else if not to get away from them? They're probably funny about her having a career an' all. You say she's not the same when she sees them so I bet there's plenty of argy-bargies. Perhaps she couldn't face that at Christmas and thinks if you go with her they'll behave themselves in front of a stranger.'

And Betty might be right, Bonnie thought, leaving the washroom and entering the main part of the club where a few of the regulars had already begun to arrive. Everyone was looking forward to the show later on. Enoch had booked a male tap dancer who also sang and did clog dancing, a child vocalist, two comics, a magician, and – as Betty put it – the star turn, a singer called Jenny Cook. Jenny had entertained the troops during the Great War and was fondly thought of, especially by ex-servicemen and their families. Enoch had been as pleased as punch to get her, but the cynical Betty had remarked that poor Jenny was well past her prime and should have been put out to pasture after the war.

'It'll be "It's a Long Way to Tipperary" and "Pack Up Your Troubles in Your Old Kitbag" again, you wait and see.' Betty had pulled a face. 'She only ever sings war songs. I mean, that was all right then, but the war's been over fifteen years, for goodness' sake. What about some nice modern ones? Songs like "Love is the Sweetest Thing" or "Stormy Weather"?'

'There's still a lot of people who like war songs,' Bonnie had protested, to which Betty had said, 'And there's a lot who are sick of them an' all,' and there the matter had been left.

Now, as Betty caught sight of her, she came hurrying over, her face alight. 'You'll never guess. Jenny Cook collapsed on stage last night and is in hospital. A heart attack.'

'That's awful.'

'For her, yes, but not for you. This is your chance, Bonnie. Enoch's tearing his hair out because he can't get anyone to stand in, not a singer anyway. An acrobat was free but he was so awful last time Enoch wouldn't book him again if he could pay him in washers. Broke his leg on stage apparently. There was a right do. Anyway, go and see Enoch. Tell him you can sing. Once he hears you, he'll love you.'

'Stand in for Jenny Cook, you mean? I couldn't, Betty. Everyone is expecting her and they'll have no truck with anyone else. Anyway, Enoch wouldn't want me.'

'Bonnie, it's Christmas and anyone decent is already booked up. Beggars can't be choosers.'

Betty had meant it as encouragement, Bonnie knew that, but she wished her friend had phrased it differently. Nevertheless, she felt a tingle of excitement – or was it panic – shoot down her spine. She stared at Betty and Betty stared back as a big grin spread across her face. 'You're going to do it, aren't you, I can tell. See Enoch, I mean. He's in the back and he's already had two stiff whiskies. Dennis didn't help when he offered to do

Jenny's slot with his impressions. I thought Enoch was going to blow his top. It was so funny.'

Nothing about this was funny. Bonnie looked down at her dress. 'I couldn't go on stage like this even if Enoch likes me.'

'You've got time to go home and change if you see him now. *Go on*, you've got nothing to lose.' Betty leaned closer and added in a whisper, 'And wouldn't it be one in the eye for Dennis if Enoch likes you and I know he will. Make sure you tell him you tried here before and Dennis wouldn't even hear you sing.'

She had more important things to think about than Dennis. 'What shall I sing?'

'That one you sang for me in the park, "Smoke Gets in Your Eyes". That was lovely.' So saying, Betty took Bonnie's arm and physically manhandled her towards the door that led to the back of the club. 'Go on, quick. He might be lucky and be able to book someone else if you dally.'

Bonnie found herself pushed into the corridor with the door shut firmly behind her. She stood for a moment and then walked slowly forward, stopping outside Ralph's office. Dennis and Enoch shared it when they were around, and as she stood there she could hear raised voices from within. Her heart in her mouth, she waited for a lull in what was clearly an argument and then knocked twice.

'Yes?' It was a bark, and when she opened the door Ralph and Dennis were sitting at their desks and Enoch was perched on the edge of Ralph's, his face red and angry. From what she'd heard when waiting outside, Dennis had been pressing his request to go on as Jenny's replacement and Enoch wasn't having any of it. His last distinguishable words had been, 'Over my dead body.'

'I can come back if it's not convenient.' It was a silly thing to say in the circumstances because if ever it wasn't convenient it was right now, but Ralph's voice was more controlled when he said, 'No, it's fine, Bonnie. What is it?'

'I – I heard about Jenny.' It was hard to get the words out with the three of them staring at her.

'Yes?'

'I – I can sing. What I mean is, I used to be a singer before I came to London. In the north. My family –' she took a deep breath, aware she was gabbling – 'my family were show people.' She had decided that was the best way to put it. 'But when my father died I decided to try my luck in the south.'

Dennis sat up straighter in his seat. 'As I remember it, you can't read music, you have no real experience of singing professionally on the club circuit and you are totally untrained. Is that right?'

Bonnie stared into the mean little eyes. Since she had started work at the club he had never mentioned that he remembered her talking to him about a singing job, and she had often wondered if he had recognized her. It was clear he had. Her chin rose a notch. 'You left out that I have no one to vouch for me and my accent is strong,' she said crisply, surprising herself as well as the three men. 'But I've been assured that when I sing no trace of my accent comes through unless it's a northern song and appropriate. I suppose that comes from my learning the words and music by hearing them, because, as you pointed out, I can't read music.'

'Now look here—'

Enoch interrupted Dennis with a sharp gesture of his hand as he said, 'How good are you?' his tone hopeful.

It wasn't the time for modesty and Bonnie knew it. Totally out of character, she said, 'Very good.'

'Is she?' Enoch looked at Dennis. 'Is she good?'

'I don't know.'

'Because . . .'

'For all the reasons I said, I considered her unsuitable.'

'So you never heard her?' Enoch's tone spoke volumes.

'No.' It was a sharp snap of a word.

These two really hated each other. Bonnie sensed that Enoch was willing her to be good if only so he could throw it in Dennis's face. Emboldened, she said, 'I can sing for you now if you like, Mr Stewart?'

'Let's put it this way, girl. If you're any good and you can get me out of the hole I'm in, I don't give a –' He stopped. 'I don't care that you can't read music and have had no formal training. Jenny Cook started like that, did you know?'

Bonnie shook her head.

'Well, she did.' He bounced his head in confirmation. 'And she went from strength to strength because in the end, talent outs. Come through to the club and I'll accompany you on the piano. What do you want to sing?'

Remembering Betty's reaction, Bonnie said, '"Smoke Gets in Your Eyes"?'

'Come on then.' He smiled at her, a real smile, and it helped enormously even as her heart plummeted to her shoes.

She hadn't reckoned on this, singing in the club itself. It wouldn't have been so daunting if customers hadn't already begun to arrive, but she couldn't very well refuse. She saw Dennis watching her and just knew he'd guessed how she felt, and again it put iron in her backbone.

Swinging round, she led the way back into the main room and walked up the steps to the stage where she stood by the piano. She saw that Betty was all agog but barely anyone else gave her a glance. Enoch joined her on the stage as Ralph and Dennis sat down at a table, and now a few of the regulars did glance their way, wondering what was going on.

Bonnie felt sick with nerves. At the very least, if all went well, this could be the means of getting established on the club circuit where a good living could be made, but as the clubs were a way into the music business and bigger things, it could mean much more.

'Ready?' Enoch had his hands on the keys and he smiled at her as he spoke, an encouraging smile. She had never needed it more.

Betty was beaming from her place behind the bar and

as Bonnie glanced her way, Betty raised both thumbs. Then Enoch played the first notes. All she had to do was sing, but could she? Her mouth was dry and her palms were sweating and she felt as though she might pass out.

She opened her mouth, shutting her eyes for the first few moments to capture that special feeling. The smoky club room, the murmur of conversation and clink of glasses, Dennis's glare from below and even Enoch sitting at the piano melted away and she sang as she had never sung before, not even in her most magical moments. She didn't look at anyone in particular as she sang but she was aware that the room had gone quiet. While she was singing it didn't even enter her head whether the silence was good or bad, but as soon as she'd finished and the stillness continued for an eternal moment she wanted to run away from all the upturned faces.

And then there was a roar of approval, people standing to their feet and clapping while some of the women, like Betty, dabbed at their eyes. Bonnie looked at Enoch and found he was staring at her, a mixture of amazement and excitement and sheer glee on his face. 'Blimey, gal, when you said you could sing you weren't joking.' He shook his head. 'What the hell were you doing working behind the bar? Why didn't you see me before? To think I could have let you slip through my fingers because of that daft so-an'-so,' he added, glancing at Dennis in disgust. 'Well, you're on tonight and in the New Year we'll see about getting you good material. I know a couple of music publishers in Denmark Street off Charing Cross Road. Do you know the "Tin Pan Alley"?'

Bonnie didn't have the faintest idea what he was talking about and it showed, as she shook her head dazedly.

Enoch grinned, nodding at the audience as folk sat down again and a few shouted, 'More!'

'Later,' he said to the room. 'She's on tonight so don't be greedy.' Turning back to Bonnie, he said, '"Tin Pan Alley" – that's what it's known as in the business – is where all the music publishers are based. If they think you can put a song over, I can get copies out of them. Public performances are what matter and we'll see about getting you on the circuit and well known as soon as possible. It'll be hard work, mind, but I've got contacts. One of my mates is a publishers' pianist and his job is to demonstrate songs to prospective professional customers – what he doesn't know about the business isn't worth knowing.'

Bonnie's head was spinning. She had the weird feeling that this was a dream and she would wake up in a minute in her little bed in Mrs Nichols's house. She glanced across at Betty who was grinning from ear to ear, and suddenly felt such a rush of love for this dear friend who couldn't be closer to her than a sister would have been.

'You'll go far, girl, I'm telling you.' Enoch was fairly bubbling with excitement at 'his' discovery. 'Come on, come into the office so we can talk properly.'

Bonnie followed Enoch, Ralph and a sullen Dennis into the office, stopping on the way only to hug Betty who had hurried out from behind the bar to congratulate her with a characteristic lack of envy. 'You were bloomin' marvellous,' she whispered. 'Even better than that day you sang to me.' She straightened to let Bonnie walk on as she added, 'I wish I could have seen Dennis's face when you started to sing. He looks like he's sucked a lemon right now,' and with that she danced joyfully back to her customers.

Once in the office, Enoch dragged Dennis's chair out from behind his desk for her to sit on, while he perched on the corner of Ralph's. Dennis stood behind her, leaning against the wall, his face as black as thunder, but for once Ralph ignored his brother-in-law.

'Now,' said Enoch. 'First things first. We need to get you something to wear for tonight.'

'I've got clothes back where I live.'

'Suitable to perform in?'

She nodded. 'Aye, yes. I bought them when I first came to London so they're fashionable and new. I always intended to become a singer so I thought I'd better kit myself out.'

'Good, good. Now your name's Bernice Cunningham, right? But you like to be known as Bonnie. Does that apply to your stage name? I like Bonnie but Cunningham's too long. We need something short and snappy. Bonnie . . . May. How about that? It's feminine and has a glamorous edge. What do you think, Ralph? A new rising star, the amazing Bonnie May?'

It was clear Dennis was going to have no say whatsoever.

Ralph nodded. 'Bonnie May. Rolls off the tongue and it would stand out on a bill. Would you be happy with that, Bonnie? It's important we get it right from day one.'

Everything was happening so fast she didn't know if she was on foot or horseback, but somehow she managed to say, 'That's fine. Yes, I like Bonnie May.'

Again Enoch said, 'Good, good. That's settled. Now I'll run you home in my car and you can change and do your make-up.' His eyes ran critically over her hair but he appeared to be satisfied when he said, 'Don't put your hair up, in case you were thinking of doing so. It looks nice as it is and it's a softer look for tonight's crowd. We want them to give you a chance.'

Every penny she had spent in that expensive hairdressing salon had been worth it, Bonnie thought gratefully, and at least she knew how to apply her make-up properly, thanks to the girl who'd cut and styled her hair. She only had one pair of stage shoes, high-heeled silver sandals, but she had practised walking in them on and off in the privacy of her room and could keep her balance now, which she hadn't been able to do at first.

'I'll get the missus to stand in behind the bar.' Ralph smiled at her as he spoke and didn't seem to mind that she had abandoned her post on what was probably the busiest night of the year. 'When Enoch brings you back you go straight to the dressing room, all right, Bonnie?'

This was a somewhat grand name for the small room situated between the ladies' and gents' toilets. It had a mirror taking up most of one wall and a number of chairs in front of a long counter where any performers could sit and titivate and have a drink and a cigarette if they were so inclined. Which most of them were.

Again Bonnie felt a sense of panic. The thought of sitting waiting in the dressing room with seasoned performers was daunting. She didn't let her consternation show, however, nodding brightly. 'Right, Mr Mercer.'

Enoch had slid off Ralph's desk and walked to the door and now she stood up and followed him, being careful not to meet Dennis's eyes. He was red in the face with suppressed anger. It wasn't often he was put in his place.

Bonnie was back in the club within the hour. The dress she had chosen to wear for her debut was a full-length evening gown in silver and black, sleeveless, but with large ruffs over the shoulders. The cut-away back – once considered so shocking – came with a small black fur cape, a style dictated more by climate than modesty now such dresses had lost the power to scandalize. The dress was at the forefront of fashion, like the other two she had purchased for stage wear when she had arrived in the capital, but this one in particular made her look more like her professed eighteen years, and she needed the confidence it gave her. Enoch had already warned her that she might get a little heckling from the crowd when it was announced she was replacing the beloved Jenny Cook but she was to ignore it and remain composed.

Her stomach turned over as she entered the celebrated dressing room where the other performers were already waiting. The child vocalist, a sweet-faced little girl in pretty pink with a look of the American four-year-old star Shirley Temple about her, was having her curls combed by her mother; the two male comics were deep in conversation, and the magician was inspecting the hind leg of one of his white rabbits as he said to the tap dancer, 'He was fine this morning but look at that. I reckon one of the other blighters has had a go at him.'

The tap dancer paid scant attention to the injured rabbit, glancing up at Bonnie and then rising to his feet as he did a double take. 'Hello . . .' It was drawled with definite interest. 'And who do we have here? If I'd seen you before I would have remembered. Frank's the name.'

She shook the proffered hand but it was Enoch who said, in a somewhat curt fashion, 'This is Bonnie May and she's new to the circuit so none of your flannel, Frank. Jenny Cook's been taken ill and Bonnie's going on instead.'

Frank gave a low whistle. 'Nothing like being dropped in the deep end. I hope she's good else they'll eat her alive, good will to all men or no.'

'Take no notice of him, sweetheart,' one of the comics cut in. 'They'll be content to just sit and look at such a pretty face, believe you me. You'll be all right – and you must be good else that beggar there wouldn't have hired you.' He grinned at Enoch. 'Hard as nails with a hide like an ancient rhinoceros, our Enoch.'

Enoch smiled, apparently unoffended. 'If by that you mean I pay you what you're worth, you're spot on, Maurice.' He pointed to a small table in the corner of the room on which reposed some bottles of beer and a couple of bottles of wine, an urn of tea, glasses and cups and saucers, and several plates of Mary's sandwiches. 'Help yourself to something to eat and drink, Bonnie. We'll be starting in a minute. You're on last so sit and relax. Read the paper or one of them magazines.' He nodded to a pile. 'I'll be back later before you go on.' So saying he left, and for a heart-fluttering moment Bonnie felt as though her last friend in the world had just disappeared.

She walked across and poured herself a cup of tea but she knew that if she tried to eat anything her nerves would choke her. She noticed that although the child vocalist and her mother and the magician were drinking tea, the other three men had beer glasses in front of them. The room was smoky and overly warm which didn't help her swimming head, but after a couple of sips of hot sweet tea she began to feel better.

She sat down by the mother and daughter, smiling as she said, 'How do you do? I don't suppose you're new to this like me?'

She knew immediately she'd said the wrong thing,

even before the mother said crisply, 'Gwendoline has been singing in public from the age of five. I'm surprised you haven't heard of her. She is extremely popular.'

'I'm sorry.' Her first blunder but no doubt not her last. 'I've only recently come to London after living in the country all my life. I hadn't even been to the cinema until a couple of months ago.' All of which was true enough if one stretched the truth a little.

The mother appeared mollified. 'Oh, I see. On a farm or something, was it?'

Bonnie nodded. The fair counted as a 'something'.

'Well, Gwendoline is eight now and in high demand. Aren't you, dear,' she added fondly to her offspring who was in the process of chomping her way through a ham sandwich. 'She could sing a song right through by the time she was two, but it's in the blood. Her father and uncles are all in the business to some extent, and her grandma had a lovely voice. I design and make all Gwendoline's dresses myself.'

She waited for Bonnie's murmur of congratulation which was duly given.

'She gets an encore every time, and we're booked up for weeks ahead. Her father taught her to step-dance, a second string to her bow, you know, and she took to that like a duck to water. There's nothing Gwendoline can't do.'

Bonnie looked at the little girl in her silk-and-satin dress with pink bows, and wondered when she ever got the chance to play and be a normal child. Betty had told her about some of the mothers who entered their children into every competition there was and pushed them onto the club circuit, regardless of whether the child wanted it or not. Apparently some of them could earn nearly as much in two nights as their fathers made in a week, and with the Depression biting, who was going to turn that down? A year ago the hunger marches and rioting had shocked the capital, and the Prime Minister, Ramsay MacDonald, had ordered an urgent review of the government's policies on unemployment, but every day in the club Bonnie heard men complaining that nothing had changed.

Gwendoline's mother continued to rattle on until Gwendoline was called to perform. The child was the first act, followed by one of the comics and then the magician. The tap dancer was next, and just before he left the room he gave a leery grin at Bonnie. 'Bonnie may, or Bonnie may not,' he said suggestively. 'Which is it then?'

'Shut your mouth, Frank.' The remaining comic leapt to her defence, and with a 'Huh!' of a laugh, Frank sauntered out of the room.

Bonnie had been sitting quietly pretending to read the magazines all evening, but the words had danced before her eyes and her stomach had been churning the whole time. The minutes had crept by with agonizing slowness as she had eavesdropped on the conversation of her fellow performers.

They had talked about different clubs, mostly in east

and north London and on the Essex fringe; about concert parties, pantomimes and revues; and about various entertainment secretaries – some honest and fair and others who apparently were willing to take a backhander, and had ruthlessly chewed over other artistes. It appeared that if an artiste had concerts at the weekends along with a cabaret somewhere, and was prepared to work at two places in the same night and also on weekdays when the opportunities arose, the financial rewards could be very tasty.

Public performances were what counted, and any artiste known to appear regularly in front of an audience was on the up and up, according to her companions. Most of what they discussed was like a foreign language to Bonnie; she hadn't heard of some of the people or places for a start, but she listened and tried to learn. Nor had she realized that children under fourteen were subject to strict controls and licensing regulations, and she was amazed that they apparently needed a licence to appear on public stages after a certain time at night. Certainly the fair folk hadn't availed themselves of such niceties.

This was a new world and a terribly confusing one, she told herself, trying to quell the blind panic as the comic left the room. And a world where everyone seemed to know everyone else – apart from her. She had never felt so completely out of her depth before, not even during the time when her father had disappeared or on the journey to London after Franco's attack. How could she succeed when she didn't have a clue who or what people were talking about? She'd been mad to think she had a chance. She should never have said anything to Enoch.

Her frantic thoughts were interrupted by the man in question popping his head round the door. He saw her white face and panic-stricken eyes and came fully into the room. 'Don't worry about Jenny Cook – they'll love you,' he said, putting her nerves down to the fact that she was replacing a club favourite. 'Now, we decided on "Smoke Gets in Your Eyes", "Stormy Weather", and an old favourite, "It Had to Be You". Right? Neville wondered what else you knew if they want an encore. He suggested "Just One More Chance". Happy with that?' Neville was the club's elderly pianist and an experienced old hand of the 'you-hum-it-and-I'll-play-it' school.

Bonnie nodded. Neville had been set to do Jenny's favourite numbers like "Till We Meet Again" and "Pack Up Your Troubles in Your Old Kitbag" but Bonnie had felt she couldn't compete with such an accomplished veteran by singing songs Jenny was known and loved for, and furthermore that it wouldn't be quite right, given the circumstances with Jenny ill in hospital. Enoch had agreed with her.

'Good. I'll be back in a couple of minutes and then you're on – and don't forget, I wouldn't have put you up there unless I knew you could handle it. You'll be marvellous and they'll love you. Everyone has to start somewhere, Bonnie – this is your moment. Believe that and you'll be all right.'

She thought of this a few minutes later as she stood on the stage while Enoch announced her after explaining that Jenny Cook had been taken ill and wouldn't be appearing tonight. Normally the master of ceremonies would have done this, and she wondered if Enoch didn't trust Dennis to try and pave her way.

Enoch certainly did his best, but along with the murmurs of disappointment and muttering from the assembled throng, one voice – louder than the rest – called out, ''Ere, Enoch, isn't that one of your barmaids? What're you trying to pull, palming us off with her? We paid good money for tonight and you know it.'

Enoch narrowed his eyes at the man in question. 'Bonnie *was* one of the barmaids here, but she auditioned for this spot and beat off the competition because she's damn good, all right? Pipe down, Jack Travis, and give the girl a chance before you ask for your money back, because I dare bet that's what you're leading up to.' And in an aside to the room, he added, 'Tight as a cockerel's backside and just as pretty,' causing a few titters here and there as he had intended.

The last remnant of Bonnie's precarious self-confidence drained out of her. The crowd weren't daft. They knew this talk of her beating the competition was so much wind. And Jack Travis was right, everyone *was* being palmed off. What had she been thinking of? She was going to make a prize fool of herself.

And then, as though this last thought had brought his face into focus, she saw Dennis sitting at the front of the room with Ralph and their respective wives. A smirk was twisting his mouth and smugness radiated from every line of his body. He was loving this. He wanted her to freeze with nerves and get booed off the stage so he could be proved right. Horrible man.

Her chin lifted. She was her father's daughter and she wasn't going to let a worm like Dennis have the satisfaction of watching her fail, not while she had breath in her body.

Enoch was whispering something about how she would be fine and not to take any notice when she turned to him with a brilliant smile that clearly took him back, before glancing at Neville and nodding. As Neville struck up the first notes of "Smoke Gets in Your Eyes", Enoch hurried off the stage and Bonnie turned to fully face the audience. She saw Betty at the back of the room, clutching a tea-towel and a glass and looking anxious, and just for a moment she thought, 'Oh, we're getting short of clean glasses again,' but then she put everything else but the song out of her mind. And she was singing this for her da. She didn't care about the rest of them, what they thought. Her da had believed dreams could come true and if it was only for tonight, this one night, hers had . . .

Three-quarters of an hour later the audience still wouldn't let her leave the stage. She had sung three encores and a couple of special requests and the atmosphere was such that Enoch was grinning from ear to ear and Ralph was looking as though Christmas had already arrived. Dennis and his wife had left after her second song and no one had so much as glanced at them. Every eye was trained on Bonnie.

After the first song there had been a moment of utter quiet as the last note died away, and then such tumultuous applause that Bonnie had actually jumped as she had come back to herself. The clapping and cheering had gone on and on, and when it had finally died down so she could sing again, Jack Travis had shouted, 'Money back? I'd've paid twice as much, gal,' and everyone had laughed; the feeling sweeping through the gathering was something special.

They liked her. Bonnie felt as though she was on the crest of a wave. They liked her, these forthright, tough, no-nonsense folk. Since she had been working at the club she had seen more than one performer receive short shrift from the customers who were as honest as they were merciless.

She was going to become a singer. The realization settled something fundamental. No, she *was* a singer. She had set her course tonight and whatever the future held, she wouldn't go back to pulling pints and selling sandwiches, not now she had tasted her destiny. No matter what the cost.

Chapter Nine

Bonnie was still on cloud nine when Christmas Eve dawned, and she spent a lovely – if noisy – time with Betty and her family. Her friend related all that had gone on at the club and Bonnie had to sing a medley of songs, starting with 'Smoke Gets in Your Eyes' after lunch, which made Betty's mother, who had imbibed liberally of liquid Christmas cheer, cry noisily. They all ate too much and Bonnie got home later that evening convinced she would never be able to eat the huge Christmas Day dinner she knew Hilda had in store for her and Selina.

She did, of course. And Christmas Day couldn't have been more different from the day before. The three women ate Hilda's superb lunch before opening the small gifts they'd bought each other, and then dozed the afternoon away in front of the fire. And later on, Bonnie and Selina went for a brisk walk in the thick London twilight to work up an appetite for the turkey-and-stuffing sandwiches and trifle Hilda had prepared. It was cosy and restful, but, unlike the day before, it failed to keep thoughts of the fair family at bay. She tried to concentrate on her success at the club and the encouraging things Enoch had said, but every now and again Pedro and Mrs Carlini and little Mimi and her childhood friends came to mind. She missed them. Not her grandma and Franco – she shuddered – never them, but the rest of the folk she had grown up with, who for so long had been the only community she'd known.

Later that night, curled up in bed, Bonnie gave herself a talking-to. She couldn't afford to let this feeling of melancholy take hold. There was no way she could go back to the fair – she had burned her bridges good and proper – but even if she could turn back time she wouldn't want to. When her father had disappeared everything had changed. Her life had been wretched, miserable, that's what she had to remember. Rose-coloured glasses were all very well but when she looked back at the last few years she had to see things clearly.

It was this festive season that was the trouble, she told herself after a while. It was sentimental, emphasizing, as it did, families getting together and everyone being lovey-dovey. But life with her grandma had never been that. She was free now, free to make the life she wanted, and if she made mistakes along the way then so be it.

She thought back to the applause at the club, the way the crowd wouldn't let her leave the stage and the lovely comments everyone had made. Enoch had been over the moon. She smiled in the darkness. He had told her he was going to see to it that her name became well known, and that he would use the contacts he had to push her up the ladder. He was a nice man, and his wife seemed a sweet, gentle soul. She felt sure she could trust them both to guide her as she ventured into a scary business she knew nothing about.

Along with the nasty people in the world – her legs instinctively pressed together even though she didn't allow Franco admittance into her mind – there were nice ones too. She mustn't let her past taint her future. She was going to be strong, that's what her da would have expected. He had been strong in so many ways . . .

She let memories fill her thoughts, memories of her da and the happy times they'd shared, of his booming laugh, his beautiful singing voice, his sense of fun and the way he used to carry her round the fair on his shoulders so she had felt like a princess. She missed him, oh, how she missed him, but he was with her mother now, that's what she had to believe.

She must have drifted off to sleep eventually, because when she next opened her eyes it was to the weak light of a cold winter morning through the thin curtains and the smell of smoked bacon pervading the house.

She lay snuggled under the covers for a few moments, thinking about the day ahead as the uneasy feelings she'd felt about Selina's parents came to the fore. Deciding that nothing would be accomplished by lying there brooding, she slid out of bed and got dressed with a swiftness fuelled by the icy room.

*

The December sky was low and heavy when Bonnie and Selina left Fairview later that morning. There had been a light sprinkling of snow during the night and the streets looked Christmassy as they walked arm in arm towards Kensington.

Selina had been quiet at breakfast and she wasn't particularly talkative now but Bonnie was content to stroll in silence. She emptied her mind of everything but the crisp air caressing her face with icy fingers, the cold wind ruffling her hair and the crunch of snow under her feet. She didn't want to think, but simply to be and enjoy the moment.

It took a while to reach the neat, tree-lined street of distinguished-looking three-storey terraced houses where Selina's parents lived. The street, along with the ones surrounding it, reeked of affluence; there were no snotty-nosed bairns throwing snowballs at each other or making slides in the snow *here*, Bonnie thought. Every front door was immaculately painted, every set of railings that separated the two yards of garden from the pavement gleamed ebony black, and Bonnie doubted that even the local birds would have the effrontery to mar the spotless surroundings.

Selina stopped outside a house halfway along the street. 'We're here,' she said flatly. 'This is my parents' house.'

'It's very nice,' Bonnie responded, not knowing quite what to say. It *was* nice, but soulless. She couldn't imagine people having real lives here somehow. There'd be no animated gossiping over the garden walls; no popping next door to borrow a bowl of sugar; no bairns swinging on the lamp posts or happily playing marbles in the gutter. Selina had told her that her father was a bank manager and Bonnie could see that a bank manager would live here.

'My mother's parents left the house to her when they died,' Selina continued in the same flat voice. 'There's a thatched cottage by the sea in Brighton too where we used to holiday each year. We'd often spend Christmas there.'

'That must have been wonderful.'

Selina made no reply to this. She stood for another moment staring at the house and then climbed the three steps leading to the front door and rang the bell. There was no knocker to spoil the pristine surface of the door.

Almost immediately it opened to reveal a tall, thin woman. At first Bonnie thought it was Selina's mother but her friend said, 'Hello, Mrs Eden. Merry Christmas.'

'Merry Christmas, Miss Selina. This must be your new friend that your father told me about. How do you do, Miss . . . Cunningham, isn't it?'

Selina's parents had a housekeeper? Feeling slightly over-awed, Bonnie followed Selina into the house after saying hello. Mrs Eden was imposing. Dressed all in black with her hair scraped back in a tight bun, she cut a severe figure. She looked as though she'd rarely smile and never laugh.

The hall was wide and partly panelled in wood, and the tiled floor was highly polished so that it squeaked as they walked towards what Mrs Eden referred to as the drawing room. The housekeeper knocked and opened the door, standing aside for the two girls to enter as she said, 'It's Miss Selina and Miss Cunningham, Mr Parker.'

'Thank you, Mrs Eden.'

Bonnie hadn't known what to expect. After all the vague misgivings she'd had about Selina's parents, nothing would have surprised her, but she found herself taken aback at the large, bright, beautiful room that was so welcoming. A seven-foot Christmas tree stood in one corner, decorated with tinsel and ribbons and baubles, and a roaring fire oozed warmth, which matched the wide smile on the face of the good-looking, middle-aged man coming towards them.

'Hello, hello, m'dears. Merry Christmas.'

He reached Selina first, bending as though to kiss her cheek and then straightening when Selina avoided the embrace, turning swiftly to Bonnie and saying, 'This is my friend, Bonnie Cunningham. Bonnie, my father and mother.'

A smartly dressed woman who looked to be in her early fifties had risen from the leather sofa where she had been sitting when they had entered the room, and now she joined her husband. The deep blue suit she was wearing was plain, but in a way that was both expensive and exclusive. Her fair hair was immaculate and her blue eyes exactly matched the colour of the suit. There was something about her that immediately made Bonnie feel gauche and ungainly.

Selina's mother smiled thinly, extending a pale hand as she said, 'How lovely to meet you, Bonnie. I may call you Bonnie? I can't remember the last time Selina brought a friend home to see us, can you, Llewellyn?' she added without looking at her husband. She gave a light, tinkling laugh. 'One could almost think our daughter is ashamed of her home.'

Bonnie's polite smile faded as she was ushered to one of the sofas dotting the room. She had been right, there was something wrong here. Something . . . unpleasant. For some reason she found she couldn't look at Selina beside her but she was aware that her friend's body was stiff.

Selina's father poured them both a sherry without asking if they wanted one, and as he passed Bonnie hers, he said, 'So, m'dear, are you a teacher like Selina here?'

Bonnie looked fully into his face as she took the glass. She supposed he was rather handsome as older men went. His silver hair was lovely and thick and his clear skin relatively unlined; he was tall and broad but not in a fat way and he exuded a warm charm, unlike his wife who seemed a cold fish. 'No, I'm a –' she had been going to say barmaid but that was behind her now, she was determined about that – 'a singer, Mr Parker.'

'Do call me Llewellyn, m'dear, and the wife's Felicity. We don't stand on ceremony here. So, a singer? Well, well, well. A singer. That's wonderful, wonderful.'

He was clearly a little flustered but trying to be nice and Bonnie found herself warming to him in a way she hadn't with Selina's mother. 'I used to be part of a family company of entertainers in the north,' she explained, keeping to the story she'd told everyone in London, 'but when my father died I decided to move here.'

'And your mother? Isn't she worried about you being here alone in the city? You're very young, after all.'

'My mother died when I was a baby.'

'Oh, I'm sorry, how sad.'

'It was very brave of you to come to London alone.' This was from Selina's mother, and said in a way that suggested foolhardiness or something worse.

Bonnie's chin lifted. 'Not really,' she said in the same cool tone the older woman had used. 'I am perfectly able to look after myself, Mrs Parker.'

It wasn't lost on any of those present that Bonnie hadn't called Selina's mother by her Christian name, and after a brief but pregnant pause it was Selina's father who again stepped into the breach and eased the moment by asking her which songs she preferred to sing. From there they got on to the different types of music that had emerged since the Great War, with Llewellyn – surprisingly – confessing a weakness for what he called symphonic jazz. 'I went to see Paul Whiteman and his orchestra a few years ago,' he said, pouring himself another sherry from the decanter on a small side table. 'He'd got Bix Beiderbecke, the trumpeter, you know?' – Bonnie didn't but she nodded her head as though she did – 'and trombonists Jack Teagarden and Tommy Dorsey, and a vocal group, the Rhythm Boys, who'd got that singer Bing Crosby among them. I was in New York visiting my brother and his family who emigrated to America twenty years ago. Wonderful night, it was. Quite wonderful.'

'Did you enjoy it too?' Bonnie said to Selina's mother, feeling a little awkward that she had bitten back earlier and that it was she and Selina's father who seemed to be doing all the talking.

'Oh, Felicity didn't accompany me that night, did you, dear?' Llewellyn smiled. 'The opera is more her cup of tea, or the ballet. No, I went with my two nieces, modern young things.'

Selina stood up abruptly, so abruptly she spilt some of her sherry which she'd barely sipped. 'Would you like to freshen up before lunch?' she asked Bonnie. 'Mrs Eden will be calling us through to the dining room in a minute, everything runs like clockwork here.'

'Uh yes, all right. Thank you, yes.' Flustered herself now, Bonnie followed Selina out of the room feeling somewhat awkward. Walking down the hall, Selina opened a door on the opposite side to the drawing room. 'Mother likes to call this the downstairs cloakroom,' she said, a touch of acid in her voice. 'And since coming back from that trip to America that my father spoke of, she's had a bathroom installed in each of the six bedrooms here. It's the American way, apparently. My uncle lives in a kind of a mansion in New York – it quite spoilt Mother's holiday.'

The cloakroom was as beautifully decorated as the

drawing room, a pile of neatly folded hand towels next to the wash basin along with an enormous vase of flowers. There were two cubicles inside, but as neither girl wanted to use them they merely washed their hands and tidied their hair.

Out of the blue, Selina said, 'You like my father, don't you?' She stared at Bonnie, her face closed and tight.

Bonnie blinked. It had been a statement rather than a question, but she answered as though it was the latter. 'Aye, yes, I do. He seems nice. Friendly.' Unlike her mother.

'Yes, he does, doesn't he? Everyone likes him. I think most people expect bank managers to be dour and stand-offish, and of course he isn't like that.'

'No.' Bonnie had the feeling she was treading on egg-shells without the slightest inkling of why. And then to her amazement – and relief – a gong sounded in the hall outside.

'The ceremonial call.' Selina grimaced. 'Even when it's just the two of them Mother insists on Mrs Eden using the gong. "Standards, Selina."' She gave a good imitation of her mother's well-bred voice. 'Oh, how I hate that gong. It personifies everything that's wrong in this house – immaculate and clean and shining on the outside but rotten inside.'

Bonnie stared at her friend, her eyes wide, but she had no chance to comment before Selina grabbed her arm and opened the door into the hall.

The dining-room table was a picture of snowy white

tablecloth and napkins, glittering crystal glasses and silver crockery, with another bowl of fresh flowers in red and white in the centre. The first course was a thin soup which was nothing like Bonnie was used to and which she didn't particularly like, followed by a fish course that the fair folk would have described as a fancy bit of nothing, but when the main course was served by Mrs Eden, Bonnie was relieved to see it wasn't turkey. Two turkey dinners in two days was quite enough. And the beef joint was beautifully cooked, as were the accompanying vegetables.

Selina's father had poured each of them a glass of wine once they had sat down at the table, but Bonnie hadn't touched hers. She wasn't used to alcohol and the glass of sherry had gone to her head as it was. Selina, she noticed, had drunk two glasses of wine by the time pudding was served, however; a definite flush to her friend's cheeks and a brightness to her eyes indicating that she might be a little tiddly.

The pudding, a lemon soufflé, was as light as air, and Bonnie accepted a second helping, although Selina appeared to have eaten next to nothing.

Llewellyn had kept up an easy, non-demanding and amusing conversation throughout lunch, and although Selina and her mother had said little, Bonnie thought she would have enjoyed herself if it wasn't for her concern for her friend, especially after her last comment in the cloakroom. There had been real bitterness in what Selina had said, but along with that had been something Bonnie recognized as pain and anguish.

She would have to talk to Selina on the way home, she decided, and risk being told it was none of her business. Bonnie glanced speculatively at Selina under her eyelashes. She knew her friend had been relieved when she had said she would come with her today, which in itself was odd. Admittedly her mother was cold and uppity, but her father was lovely and he made up for her mother, surely? What she would give for her own da to be alive and wanting her to visit him at Christmas.

After lunch was finished, and at her mother's suggestion, Selina showed Bonnie round the house. The bedrooms were coldly beautiful, each one decorated in a different colour, but Selina only paused outside her father's room saying, 'That's Father's. He and Mother sleep separately,' but without opening the door.

It was as they were preparing to leave that it happened. Selina had excused herself to go and have a word with Mrs Eden before they departed and thank her for the lovely meal. A moment or two after she'd left the room, Llewellyn got up, muttering something about fetching a fresh bottle of brandy from the cellar. Bonnie saw Felicity glance at him sharply; no doubt Selina's mother thought her husband was merry enough. He had been drinking steadily all afternoon although to be fair it hadn't really seemed to affect him, beyond a slight slurring to some of his words.

Bonnie felt uncomfortable about being left with

Selina's mother, and after trying to make conversation which was met with little encouragement, she gave up. A minute or two ticked by with excruciating slowness, before she stood to her feet. 'I'll just pop to the cloak-room before I leave, Mrs Parker.' There was no way on earth she could call this woman Felicity. She had to be the coldest fish Bonnie had ever met.

She was about to enter the cloakroom when she was sure she heard Selina's voice coming from the dining room at the end of the hall. The kitchen was situated at the back of the house via a corridor and you had to pass the dining room to enter it.

Bonnie paused, listening hard, and distinctly heard Selina say, 'You were waiting for me, weren't you, for when I left Mrs Eden? Let go of me. I don't want to talk to you.'

She heard the mumble of Llewellyn's voice but couldn't make out what he said, and then Selina's voice came again, more frantic. 'No, I mean it. Get off me or I'll scream.'

Bonnie didn't think about her next action. She fairly flew to the dining room, flinging open the door which was slightly ajar to find Selina pressed against the wall by her father, who had one hand under her buttocks and the other at the back of her head, holding her hair as he attempted to kiss her. Without pausing, Bonnie grabbed the nearest thing to hand, which happened to be one of the ornate brass candlesticks entwined with holly that stood at either end of the table, and brought it down with all her might, aiming for the back of Llewellyn's head.

But for the fact that he had begun to turn she might well have crushed his skull; as it was, the candlestick hit his shoulder and the shriek he gave as he collapsed to the floor could have woken the dead. As Mrs Eden, closely followed by Selina's mother, came rushing into the room, Bonnie took her friend in her arms and turned to face them.

'What on earth . . .' Felicity Parker stared at her husband grovelling and moaning on the floor. 'What's happened here?'

'I hit him.' Bonnie's voice was shaking but clear. 'With the candlestick.'

'You hit Llewellyn?' Her gaze moved from her husband to the two girls and then back to her husband. 'Are you mad, girl?' Mrs Eden had knelt beside her employer, helping him to sit up and then supporting him as he leaned against her, holding his shoulder, his face ashen and his eyes closed.

'He was trying to – to kiss Selina.'

'A father tries to kiss his daughter and you attack him with a candlestick? I repeat, are you mad, girl?'

'Don't, Mother.' Selina spoke for the first time, straightening up as Bonnie released her. 'Just don't, not today.'

'Don't what?' Mrs Parker said imperiously.

'Don't pretend, not any more. This is the last time I

shall come to this house or set eyes on the pair of you, so let's have it out in the open.'

'You're as mad as your friend.' Mrs Parker's mouth was a tight line and her eyes were blazing. 'I have no idea what you are talking about, but I'll have the police on this girl here. She needs locking away, she's not safe, and I'll tell them so.'

'Do. You do that. But you won't, will you? No, you won't, because you can't risk them believing me over him, not now Bonnie will say what she saw. It's suited you to close your eyes to what was happening in this house for years, from when I was a child, in fact. A child, Mother. I tried to tell you but you made me feel . . . wicked. And so I believed it was my fault, because why else would a father think he could do that to his own flesh and blood? But you knew, you knew, Mother, and because you didn't want him in your bed you let him come to mine.'

Mrs Eden gasped, but her next words made Bonnie's hands clench into fists. 'Oh, Miss Selina, how can you suggest . . . To say such a thing about your father. You must be ill, unhinged. Your father is a wonderful man.'

Llewellyn whimpered, tears of pain coursing down his contorted face. 'Get me a doctor, Mrs Eden.'

Bonnie was feeling sick, hardly able to take in what she was hearing. Selina's father had done *that* to her? He was her father, her *father*. But she didn't doubt it was true. She had heard what was in Selina's voice when her father had got hold of her, and it had curdled her stomach.

Aware that her friend was trembling from head to foot, Bonnie took hold of her arm. 'You need to sit down.'

'No, I need to leave this house.'

'Come on then.'

Selina's mother made no attempt to detain them as they left the room but Bonnie noticed that she didn't kneel down by her husband as Mrs Eden had, or offer him any words of sympathy.

Once in the hall, Bonnie rushed around collecting their handbags and coats and hats while Selina leaned against the wall, looking as though she was going to faint. Bonnie virtually dressed her friend, putting Selina's arms through the sleeves of her coat and then doing up the buttons before setting her hat on her head. Once they were both ready, Bonnie led Selina to the front door, opening it and then helping her down the steps into the street. It was snowing again, fat, feathery flakes that were settling fast, and as they began to walk Bonnie kept tight hold of Selina.

They had reached the end of the street before Selina broke the silence. 'It started when I was eight years old.'

'Selina, you don't have to say anything –'

'No, I want to tell you. To tell someone. I can't go on any longer if I don't. Someone – someone who will believe me.'

Bonnie pressed Selina's arm through hers. 'Of course I

believe you. Even if I hadn't seen what I saw today I would have believed you, and it's your mother and father who are wicked. Not you. You know that, don't you?'

Selina began to cry, loud, guttural, painful sobs that seemed to be torn out of her, and they stood in the gathering winter twilight, the snow falling more and more thickly as Bonnie held her close. The streets were deserted in this select part of London, only the occasional motor car passing them, and as Bonnie murmured words of comfort, much as a mother might to soothe a heartbroken child, she felt engulfed in sorrow and grief for her friend. She had thought the worst thing on earth had happened when Franco raped her, but now she knew it was nothing compared to what Selina must have gone through. And her father had appeared so lovely, so funny and warm and charming. She had liked him, she had actually *liked* him.

And then, as though Selina had read her mind, her friend choked out, 'How would anyone have believed me when he appears so nice? And he *is* like that, Bonnie, that's the thing. It really isn't an act. Before he – before I was eight years old I truly thought he was the most marvellous person in the world. I utterly adored him, worshipped him. Mother – well, you've seen how she is, but Father was always there for me, drying my tears when I hurt myself, spending time taking me to the park and visiting places, reading me stories and playing with me. He was my world. And then, when I was eight, things began to change. When he came to my room to read my bedtime story he would sit me on his knee and – and fondle and touch me in a way that worried me, but always saying how much he loved me and that I was his precious darling, his princess.'

They had begun to walk again, arm in arm, but Selina kept her gaze looking ahead and Bonnie did the same.

'I was eleven when – when *it* happened. Mother was out at the opera with some friends and it was Mrs Eden's day off and she was visiting her sister. He had insisted he sit with me while I had my bath and then he began to dry me . . . I tried to stop him, I said he was hurting me and I pushed him and cried and –' She took a hard breath. 'And afterwards he said it was because he loved me so much and that I loved him and it was our special secret. I mustn't tell anyone because if I did they would say I was bad and making it up and they would lock me away for ever.'

'Oh, Selina.' Tears were running down Bonnie's face but she made no attempt to brush them away.

'The next day Mrs Eden must have told Mother about the blood on the bath towels because she came and sat me down and told me about monthlies, you know. I didn't have a clue what she was talking about, I knew nothing about the way a woman's body works. When she mentioned the bath towels I tried to tell her what had happened the night before. I was so sore, so in pain. She – she slapped me. Right across the face. She said if I ever made up anything like that again she would see to it I was put in a place where other mad, wicked people were sent. And so I learned to put up with it. He didn't come to my room every night, not even every week. Sometimes it was two weeks or more before he would visit me, but every single night from when I was eleven I lived in terror that the door would open and there he would be, tiptoeing across the room. I knew that Mother knew. And she knew that I knew.'

Selina stopped, and now her voice took on a bewildered tone as she stared at Bonnie with tears spurting from her eyes. 'But in the day, when he was my father rather than the person at night, I – I loved him, Bonnie. He was always buying me presents and beautiful clothes and taking me to nice places that he thought I might like. It was as though I imagined the other times, like they were nightmares I thought were real. And I wanted them to be just nightmares so much, so very much.'

Selina took a deep breath. 'One night when I was fifteen I wedged a chair against the handle of my bedroom door. I don't know why I hadn't thought of it before – probably because his power was absolute as far as I was concerned. It was a few days later before he came. He tried the door for a while, and I lay with my heart beating so furiously it filled my ears, and then he went away. He came back again of course, again and again, but the chair was always there. And do you know, when Mother came one morning before I was up and the chair was still there, she didn't ask me about it.'

Selina lifted up her head to the snowflakes as she repeated, 'She didn't ask. He still tried to waylay me now and again if the house was empty, always at night, never in the day. In the day he was Father. Just once I wasn't quick enough to evade him but I fought back that night. I scratched and kicked and bit, and afterwards he sat and cried because I said I hated him. It wasn't long after that I got my teaching qualification and could leave once I got a job.'

'But you still visit occasionally.'

'They're my parents,' said Selina simply. 'But I've only ever been back to see them in the day. And till today he hasn't – He's been Father. But he drank a lot, didn't he, perhaps that was why . . .'

They began walking again as Selina said, 'I always knew one day it would be the finish, that I would never see them again, and this will sound strange . . .' She paused. 'It *is* strange, I know, in view of all I've told you about what's happened, but I feel . . . lost.'

'Selina.' Bonnie took both her arms and turned her friend to face her. 'His control over you was broken today and that's a good thing. Whatever you felt about the daytime father, the night one was a monster. You would never have been free to really live your life while he was part of it. You do see that, don't you? The break had to come sooner or later.'

'I feel so ashamed, so . . . unclean.' Selina fell against her, sobbing again. 'I let him do those things.'

'No, it was him. You told me he was your world and he betrayed that simple innocent trust in the worst way possible. You have been sinned against, you're not the sinner, Selina. You were a child and you loved your da, your father.' She hugged her hard. 'Now it's time to make your own life and you will, I know you will. You're a strong woman.'

'I wish that was true.' Selina's voice was full of despair.

'It is. Think what you've come through. If that's not strength, I don't know what is. You're amazing, Selina Parker.'

'So are you.' Selina wiped her eyes and managed a wan smile. 'To think you hit him with a candlestick. I can't believe it.'

'Neither can I.' And that was true. What if she'd brought the candlestick down on his head as she'd intended? Bonnie shuddered. She might be standing here knowing she had killed a man. Not that he didn't deserve it for what he'd inflicted on Selina for umpteen years, but still . . . 'He won't forget today in a hurry, that's for sure, and to be honest I don't feel a shred of sympathy for him. Do you?'

The question was more than just about Llewellyn's smashed shoulder and Selina knew it. She stared into her friend's face for several long moments, and as Bonnie stared back she saw something lift from Selina's countenance. It was like the sun breaking through the clouds. 'No, I don't,' Selina said softly. 'I'm free, aren't I? I'm really free . . .'

PART THREE

Nelly

1936

Chapter Ten

The small slight woman with thick gold hair cut in a fashionable bob paused in the foyer of the theatre. She was oblivious to the glances that came her way – interested, covert glances from members of the opposite sex, and mostly disapproving ones from their female partners. It might be the age of liberation for women, you could almost hear the bristling matrons thinking, but 'nice' girls still didn't go to the theatre or into bars on their own. This was what came from giving women the vote – it had opened Pandora's box.

Nelly made her way to the ticket booth, bought a seat in the front row of the circle and went straight upstairs. Once seated she didn't look around her; not from embarrassment at being unaccompanied but because her thoughts filled her mind to the exclusion of anything else and they were all about Bonnie.

Could it be *her* Bonnie who was appearing here with the travelling troupe? She asked herself this for the umpteenth time since she had passed the theatre the day before and seen the picture of the girl next to the words 'Bonnie May'. The name had caught her eye first – Bonnie was unusual – and then the picture on the poster. The artist's sketch wasn't particularly good but it had been enough like John's daughter to rouse her interest.

Nelly bit down on her bottom lip, a mixture of excitement and apprehension causing her stomach to flutter. If this girl *was* Bonnie, and of course she might not be, should she try and make herself known to her? After all, she and Bonnie hadn't been on good terms when she had left the fair. Well, no, that wasn't quite fair. They had been speaking but there had been a coldness between them for which she blamed herself entirely. She knew she hadn't been the same when she had discovered that John always intended to take Bonnie and leave the fair for a new life. Leave *her*. Looking back, she had realized that Bonnie had never needed her more than in those first days after her father had gone missing, and she'd let the child down badly. It was her deepest regret. And then of course there had been Franco. She must have gone mad for a while back then.

Nelly moved restlessly in her seat as the memory of the one night she'd spent with Bonnie's step-grandfather intruded. She had been so ashamed, so desperate when she had left the fair but that was still no excuse for going without saying goodbye to Bonnie. Of course she couldn't have explained the circumstances, and at the time that had seemed sufficient excuse for stealing away like a thief in the night. Now she wasn't so sure.

And even if this Bonnie May *was* John's daughter, would the girl want to acknowledge her? She would be fully in her rights to pretend she didn't remember a woman from her past who had turned her back on her when the chips were down.

No, she hadn't exactly turned her back on the child, Nelly told herself wretchedly, before admitting in the same breath – well, as good as. Yes, as good as. She had known what Margarita was like and she should have protected Bonnie from her grandmother. She had often wished she could go back to the fair and see Bonnie, but of course that had been out of the question.

Self-recriminations continued until the lights went down and the band in the orchestra pit struck up a fanfare to introduce the compere, a dapper little man in top hat and tails. The variety show was typical of its type but Nelly couldn't have told anyone afterwards what she had watched. Her whole being was waiting for the girl who was due to sing before the star of the show, a cockney comedian.

Nelly stayed in her seat during the interval, pretending to read her programme over and over again so she didn't have to make conversation with anyone, and then the lights dimmed once more and the second half of the show began. Her heart was pounding and she felt physically sick as the act before Bonnie May left the stage, and then the compere was saying, 'And now a real treat, ladies and gentlemen. This little lady is making quite a name for herself, in the best possible way, of course.' He waited for the laughter to subside and Nelly wondered what everyone would say if she stood up and shouted for him to get on with it. He waffled on a bit more and then announced, with ringing splendour, 'And here she is, so please give your best Manchester welcome to the singing nightingale, Bonnie May.'

Nelly leaned forward in her seat as the raven-haired girl in a simple white full-length gown walked onto the stage. As she gazed down at the beautiful face with the huge eyes she knew were violet-blue, her heart somersaulted and tried to jump out of her chest. It was her, it was John's daughter. What should she do?

'There's a lady outside says she knows you, Bonnie.'

Bonnie glanced up as Stuart, the compere, popped his head round the dressing-room door after knocking. The dressing room was squalid to say the least, and in the last two and a half years Bonnie had discovered that the modest but adequate accommodation in the working men's clubs was often superior to the theatres. The digs they were all put up in could vary too, and the present one in Manchester was 'cabbage and cat's pee' as Mabel, the conjurer's assistant and wife, described it. Bonnie had often thought that Mabel and Betty were twin spirits.

'A lady?' She was sure she didn't know anyone in Manchester. Since her debut that first Christmas she had never had to return to bar work, but she did have to travel far afield on occasion, as was the case with the present tour of theatres in York, Leeds, Manchester and

Sheffield. She much preferred to stay in London; she could sleep in her own bed and go out with Betty and Selina when she had any free time. Selina had really come out of her shell in the last couple of years or so, throwing off the school-marm persona that she wore in the day and partying with Betty most nights. Bonnie didn't know if that was a good thing or not, but she was so busy she didn't have time to brood about it, although Selina's frantic nightlife worried her.

Besides the bread-and-butter engagements at working men's clubs, Bonnie also regularly performed in carabets and private and public dances, as well as singing at firms' dinners and anything from twenty-first birthdays to weddings. Enoch had impressed on her that she had to work the circuit and get her name well established, and she followed his advice to the letter. She trusted him, and had become good friends with him and his wife, a calm, sweet woman who was the perfect foil to her dynamic, restless husband. The pair had never been blessed with children, and had taken Bonnie under their wing.

When it was possible, Bonnie had got into the habit of having Sunday lunch with Enoch and Gladys. Gladys always cooked an enormous roast and her Yorkshire pudding was second to none. Once the meal was over and she had helped with the dishes, Bonnie would wander down the little garden and find Enoch in his shed. The first time she'd entered his holy of holies she'd been amazed. A glass-blower by day and entertainments secretary by night, she wouldn't have expected Enoch to have time for hobbies but his shed proved otherwise. Apart from being a self-taught carpenter and making fine pieces of furniture for friends and family, Enoch was a dab hand at mending shoes for all and sundry on his three-footed iron shoe last.

Bonnie had never seen one before and had been fascinated the first time she'd watched him at work, cutting the leather and hammering away on one of Gladys's shoes, holding the nails in his mouth and working the edges of the leather with black heelball, a stiff wax that gave a professional-looking finish. As Enoch worked, he chatted about show business, regaling her with stories of some of the personalities he'd encountered, explaining the many pitfalls that were out there, telling her how things were done and – just as importantly – not done, and providing a huge wealth of information that was invaluable to someone like her, someone just starting out and who was as green as the hills.

She thought of Enoch now. '"I tell you one thing,"' he had warned her several times during their Sunday afternoon chinwags, '"and that's if you make it – and I'd bet my right arm you will go to the very top of the tree – you'll find yourself with friends you never knew you had. They'll be coming out of the woodwork, gal, I can guarantee it. And when that starts to happen make sure you don't get taken in. Remember that, if you forget everything else I tell you.'

Was this lady who was waiting for her one of Enoch's

'woodwork' friends? Bonnie glanced round the dressing room she shared with another of the acts, identical twins called Milly and Molly who danced rather better than they sang. They always had to double up in the theatres – sometimes it was three acts to a dressing room. Only Bart, the star, could command his own room. Everyone was presently waiting for Bart to finish so they could join him on stage and take a collective bow before going off to their respective lodgings, or – in the case of Bart who was a heavy drinker along with one or two of the other male performers – to the nearest bar.

Aware that Stuart was waiting for her answer, Bonnie found her mind racing. Should she ask this person, whoever she was, to come into the dressing room so she could talk to her with other people present, or would it be better to see her outside in the corridor? She didn't know why but she felt strange about this. She'd had other folk ask to meet her – it happened to all the artistes quite often – but somehow this felt different. And why ask to see her before the final curtain had come down? After all, Bart was the draw. He had regularly been featured on the radio and was very popular with the audiences.

The decision was taken out of her hands in the next moment. A burst of cheering and clapping filtered through from the main theatre, indicating that Bart was drawing to a close, and immediately Stuart said, 'That's it, ladies. On stage, please.'

As they filed out of the room after the compere, Bonnie saw a figure standing at the far end of the corridor with one of the two doormen. She paused, intending to call that she would be returning in a few moments if the lady wanted to wait, but the words died in her throat. She recognized Nelly instantly. As Milly and Molly followed Stuart to the door leading to the back of the stage, Bonnie froze.

'Nelly?' The words were a whisper at first, and then more strongly she said, 'Nelly? Is that really you?'

They covered the distance between them in a moment, and as Nelly took Bonnie's outstretched hands, she was half-crying, half-laughing as she said, 'I didn't know if you would want to see me.'

'Not want to see you? Of course I want to see you. Oh, Nelly, I can't believe it.'

'Bonnie, this is all very touching but your friend will have to wait.' Stuart had come up behind her and now took her arm. 'Come on, the others are waiting.'

'Stay here.' Bonnie was terrified Nelly would disappear again. 'You will, won't you? I won't be long.' And to the doorman she added, 'This lady is an old friend and she can wait in my dressing room. You don't need to stay.'

The next instant Stuart had whisked her away to join the others waiting in the wings, before he went on stage. The audience were still clapping and cheering a smiling Bart. As Bonnie listened to Stuart reeling off his slick spiel before the curtain went up and they all moved forward to line up with Bart, nothing registered. *Nelly*. Of all people, Nelly. And she hadn't realized until the moment she had seen Nelly's face how much it meant to see her again. Nelly had searched her out. As this fact dawned on her, she felt euphoric. Nelly had cared enough to do that.

She fairly flew back to the dressing room, ridiculously worried that Nelly might have gone when she opened the door but of course she hadn't. This time they hugged, and when they drew apart as the twins came back they were both a little tearful.

'I can't believe you're here,' Bonnie said again, a catch in her voice. 'I never expected to see you again.'

'And I couldn't believe the famous Bonnie May on the poster outside was my Bonnie,' said Nelly, wiping her eyes with a handkerchief. 'When did you leave the fair? Did your grandmother leave too?'

Although Milly and Molly were changing, Bonnie knew their ears were flapping. 'Look, let me get out of my dress into my ordinary things and we'll go somewhere for a cup of coffee,' Bonnie said quickly. 'We can catch up then.'

Nelly took the hint. Once Bonnie had changed and removed her stage make-up, she told the twins to let their landlady know she would be late back to the lodgings and the two of them left the theatre by the stage door. The August night was muggy without a breath of wind, and as they stepped into the street, Nelly said, 'Why don't you come home with me for a bit? We could have a pot of tea and a slice of cake and take our time having a chat. I only live a couple of streets away, it's not far. And . . .' She hesitated. 'It will be more private. I – I need to explain why I left the fair so suddenly.'

'You don't need to.' Bonnie felt embarrassed. There had been a note in Nelly's voice she couldn't describe to herself but it had made her uncomfortable.

'Yes, I do.' Nelly slipped her arm through Bonnie's as they began to walk, and changed the subject by saying, 'Oh my goodness, you are all grown up and taller than me now. Whenever I thought of you I pictured you as a little girl, not as an elegant young lady. When did you begin to sing professionally?'

It was a moment before Bonnie answered. 'About two and a half years ago.' When Nelly had taken her arm she had noticed a wedding ring on the third finger of her left hand. So Nelly was married now, but then why wouldn't she be? She was a beautiful woman, inside and out. Of course someone would have snatched her up. Carefully, so that Nelly didn't think she minded, she said, 'I see you're married? Are you sure your husband won't object to you bringing a stranger home unannounced?'

'What?' Nelly faltered and then regained her pace.

'I'm sorry.' Bonnie wasn't quite sure what she was apologizing for but Nelly seemed flustered. 'I couldn't help but see your wedding ring.'

'Oh, oh, I see.' After a split second of hesitation, Nelly continued. 'That's part of what I want to talk to you about but we're nearly there now.'

Nelly *did* think she minded about her being married. Bonnie deliberated whether to say more but decided against it. Nelly had always known that she would have liked her da to marry her, just as she had always known that Nelly was in love with him. With the benefit of hindsight she'd often thought that her da's rejection of Nelly had been the cause of her succumbing to Franco's advances that night when she'd found them together. That and losing her little dog. Franco would certainly have made the most of a momentary weakness on Nelly's part. Bonnie's lip curled. In the last years since becoming a singer she'd come across other men like Franco, predatory opportunists, and she had nothing but contempt for them.

The street they now turned into was pleasant, certainly more pleasant than the one in which her lodgings were situated. There were large cherry trees between the lamp posts either side of it for one thing, and it was wider, with good pavements. The terraced houses were substantial with a well-kept air, and a few yards of front garden divided from the pavement with waist-high railings.

Nelly stopped in front of a house with window boxes under the ground-floor windows and a blue front door, opening the little gate that was painted the same colour. Some of the front gardens had been paved and others had bushes or a patch of lawn, but this one was crammed with brightly coloured flowers, the scent of which hung in the warm night air.

They had walked in silence for the last minute or two since Bonnie had mentioned the wedding ring. Now Nelly's voice was warm as she said, 'Welcome to my little home, Bonnie. It's not a mansion but it's mine and I love it,' and so saying she opened the front door, calling as she did so, 'Hello, I'm back.'

Instead of the husband Bonnie expected to see, a young girl of maybe fourteen or fifteen appeared from the front room, smiling widely. 'Did you have a nice time, Mrs Harper?' she asked with an interested glance at Bonnie which Nelly ignored.

'Lovely, thank you, Cecilia.' Nelly got out her purse and gave the girl some coins as she said, 'Thank you for holding the fort. Tell your mother I'll see her tomorrow for the church jumble sale.'

'Righto, Mrs Harper, and thank you but you didn't need to give me any money, not after getting them choc-olates and magazines,' the girl said, deftly pocketing the coins nevertheless, and closing the front door behind her as she left.

Feeling more bewildered by the moment, Bonnie didn't object when Nelly turned to her, saying, 'There's someone I want you to meet before we talk. It will be easier that way. Do you mind following me upstairs?'

The stairs led up from the side of the hall, and like the hall they were fully carpeted. Nelly led the way, and as she reached the first landing, she said, 'There are two bedrooms and a bathroom on this floor,' before continu-ing to the second floor of the house. 'These used to be two attic rooms but I had them converted into a bedroom and another bathroom before I moved in,' she added, quietly opening the first door and beckoning Bonnie in.

Bonnie stopped just inside the room, gazing about her in wonder, but it wasn't the tasteful decor or largeness of the bedroom that caused her mouth to open slightly, nor the shelves crammed with books and toys. It was the young child curled up fast asleep in the single bed who looked to be about seven years old. He had a mass of short curly hair falling across his brow, brown curls that glinted golden in the light of the bedside lamp positioned on a small cupboard, and his lips were a full rosebud shape, like Nelly's.

'Thomas, my son,' said Nelly, her voice a soft murmur that throbbed with love.

Chapter Eleven

Bonnie was too taken aback to speak as she stared at Nelly's son, although she told herself in the next moment she shouldn't be surprised. Nelly was a beautiful woman; why shouldn't she have married and created a new life for herself away from the fair? There had been nothing left for her there except memories of the man who hadn't wanted her love.

Pulling herself together, she whispered, 'He's beautiful, Nelly. Absolutely beautiful.'

'He's my world, my universe.'

A hundred and one questions were clamouring in Bonnie's mind but she didn't voice any of them, not even when they left the bedroom a few moments later.

She followed Nelly downstairs without speaking, and Nelly led the way to the back of house and into the kitchen. This room, like the rest of the house Bonnie had seen thus far, was nothing like the dark and somewhat dingy interiors she was used to. It fairly glowed with colour and light.

Instead of the traditional black-leaded range and heavy cumbersome furniture, the kitchen was light and modern, with bright tiles, pale sunshine-yellow walls, a gleaming gas stove and – something Hilda would have loved – a refrigerator. White-painted chairs were tucked under a kitchen table on which reposed an enormous vase of sweet-smelling flowers that filled the room with their fragrance. Two ancient dogs were curled up on a thick rug that had a pair of small armchairs positioned either side of it, and they stood up creakily and pushed their noses into Nelly's hand as she bent to pet them, before resuming their places. 'The last two from my time at the fair,' said Nelly softly. 'All the others have gone now.'

She straightened. 'I had the house decorated exactly as I wanted before we moved in and I still love it.' And then, as though Bonnie had queried the 'we', Nelly clarified, 'I mean Thomas and me.' She swallowed. 'There's no Mr Harper, Bonnie. There never was, not in the sense of a husband, I mean. Harper is my family name. I was born Eleanor Harper, so it seemed less complicated to revert to that when I left the fair, rather than Nelly Bell. I knew I would be forced to tell a string of lies in the days and months ahead to protect my baby, so any I didn't need to tell was all to the good. As far as the rest of the world is concerned, I'm a widow. Thomas has been told that his father died in a motor-car accident shortly after he was born.'

Nelly had been expecting a baby when she left the fair? Is that was she was saying?

'I bought this house with funds left to me by my grandmother,' Nelly continued. 'She was a very modern woman for her time, but I think even she would have had to take a deep breath at my circumstances.' She hesitated. 'Are you very shocked?'

Immensely. 'No, of course not.'

'Oh, Bonnie, you're very sweet but a poor liar. Please, try not to think too badly of me. Sit down and I'll put the kettle on and then we can talk properly. I – I want to tell you all of it, it will be a relief. I've never been able to share it with anyone before.'

Bonnie was glad to sit. Nelly's revelation had knocked her sideways. An illegitimate child was a huge disgrace whatever way you looked at it, and yet Nelly seemed so happy and settled, and she clearly adored her son.

Nelly plumped down beside her at the kitchen table a moment or two later. 'Can I start at the beginning?' she asked quietly. 'I'm not going to offer any excuses but I want you, of all people, to understand. I – I'm not a bad woman, Bonnie.'

'Oh, Nelly, I know that.' Impulsively Bonnie took her hand. 'And you don't have to explain anything.'

'I do.' Nelly extricated her hand and stood up, beginning to pace back and forth. 'You know, of course, that I loved your father. From the first moment I laid eyes on him I loved him and that has never changed. When I discovered that he had always intended to leave the fair with you and that he had never contemplated my being part of your lives, well . . .'

'I know, I know.' It was painful, even now, to hear the hurt and sadness in Nelly's voice.

'I think I went a bit mad. That is the only excuse I can give for what I did, Bonnie. I – I allowed a man into my bed, someone who had been after me for years. You know him.'

'Franco.' Bonnie tried to keep her voice expressionless. 'I know, Nelly. I came to your wagon one night and you were sleeping and he was beside you.'

'Oh, Bonnie, I'm so sorry.' Nelly stopped her pacing and sat down, and now it was she who took Bonnie's hand. 'You saw us? That must have been devastating for you. What can I say? It was just the once, Bonnie, I swear it. The next day I made it clear it was a huge mistake and that it would never be repeated. How much of a mistake I didn't realize then.' And then Nelly shook her head. 'No, I can't in all honesty put it like that, not when it gave me my Thomas. Franco is his father, Bonnie. I have only ever slept with a man once in my life, can you believe that? What are the odds of falling for a baby the first time? But it happened to me, and I suppose there are others it's happened to.'

Bonnie felt sick. She remembered Franco's hot breath on her face, his hands holding her down, the way he had hammered into her body . . .

Nelly was wrapped up in her story, oblivious to Bonnie's turmoil. 'When I knew I was expecting a child I was distraught. I didn't want Franco to know anything about it. He – he disgusts me. How I could have done what I did . . .' She gulped hard.

'You were hurting,' Bonnie said quietly, trying to put her own memories to one side. 'He took advantage of that.'

Nelly nodded. 'Thank you. Anyway, I knew I had to get away so I left the fair without saying goodbye to anyone. I wanted to tell you, I did truly, but I was ashamed and desperate and not thinking straight –'

'It's all right, really.' Nelly's voice had broken on the last words, and Bonnie put her other hand over Nelly's, pressing it. 'I know that after the night I saw Franco in your wagon I avoided you. It's not your fault.'

'Bonnie, I was a full-grown woman. You were a child,' said Nelly wretchedly. 'I just made one mistake after another, I know that. Anyway, I got as far away from the fair as I could and ended up in Manchester. I called myself Mrs Harper, saw a doctor and sorted my affairs. By the time Thomas was born I had the house ready and brought him home. And so my life really began.' Nelly smiled mistily. 'I never dreamed how much I would love him. I was terrified before he was born, thinking I'd see Franco in the child, that I wouldn't be able to take to it, that I wouldn't cope on my own, oh, all sorts of things. But he's mine, Bonnie. All mine. That's the way I see it. And it was my fault as much as Franco's. I should never have succumbed to his advances. He's not a bad man, I suppose, just a wayward one where women are concerned. Not that I would ever want Thomas to know the truth,' she added quickly. 'As far as he is concerned, his father is dead.'

Bonnie stared at her old friend as the realization dawned that she would never be able to tell her what Franco had done. Her throat constricted. If she had been able to confide in anyone, it would have been Nelly. She had thought many times about divulging her past and the real reason why she had left the north to Selina, but somehow, each time she had come close to telling her, she hadn't been able to follow through. Perhaps it was because after what Selina had suffered for so long, Franco's brutal treatment of her seemed almost trivial? Not to her, but it might appear that way to Selina. But no, that wasn't the real reason. If she talked about it, if she voiced it, it would mean that night would come with her into this new life, that was the way she felt. Stupid, perhaps, but she couldn't help it.

One thing was for sure – the fact that Franco was Thomas's father made it impossible for Nelly to know about the rape. It wouldn't be fair. She didn't want to be responsible for Nelly knowing that the man who was the father of her son was capable of raping a child, because that was what she had been when he had forced himself on her.

Rightly or wrongly, she must not share her secret. She had to keep it buried, locked away. And maybe that was for the best anyway? She had already decided that when she had considered confiding in Selina, so nothing had changed. She was Bonnie May now, a different person.

'Are we still friends, now you know it all?'

Bonnie came out of her dark thoughts to find Nelly staring at her uncertainly, and immediately cleared her expression. 'Of course we are.' She pressed Nelly's hand again. 'How could we be anything else? I'm proud to have you as my friend, Nelly, and I think it's wonderful how you've made a home for your son without anyone to help you.'

'Thank you. It's more than I deserve.' Nelly's bottom lip wobbled. 'And we'll keep in contact now we've found each other? I would love that.'

'Absolutely, Nelly. I promise.'

The shiny little kettle was beginning to sing on the hob and Nelly stood up, giving Bonnie a hug before walking to the stove. With her back to the room she busied herself mashing the tea as she said, 'Now that's enough about me, tell me about you. I'm amazed you left the fair. I never imagined your grandmother would let you leave, for one thing. I know your father always thought she had her eye on you as a meal ticket and he was determined that wouldn't happen. He told me many times he wanted you to sing for pleasure, not because you had to. Has – has there ever been any news about John?'

'Not that I know of, no, Nelly. I'm sorry.'

Nelly didn't turn round but Bonnie saw her shoulders slump before she straightened. 'Of course not, I didn't expect there would be. He would never have left you willingly and so the alternative . . . But I suppose everyone lives in hope in those circumstances when they care about someone.'

Hope had died in Bonnie a long, long time ago, but now she said softly, 'He thought a tremendous lot of you, Nelly, but he just couldn't forget my mother.'

'I know, I know. Really. I do, and I'm all right about it.'

Injecting a lighter note into her voice, Bonnie said, 'I actually left the fair in much the same way you did, Nelly. I disappeared in the middle of the night without a word to anyone. Although in my case it was with the contents of my grandma's cashbox.'

'You didn't!' Nelly swung round, giggling. 'Oh, good for you, Bonnie. She was a perfectly dreadful woman. I loathed her.'

'I made my way south to London and worked as a barmaid in a working men's club for a while after I couldn't get a job as a singer, and then the first Christmas after I'd left the fair I got my break. I had to say I was older than I was, of course, and I changed my name, but it's all worked out all right.'

'I'll say. Look at you touring and everything.' Nelly placed a steaming cup of tea and the sugar bowl and milk jug in front of her. 'So, we both have told our quota of lies,' she said wryly, 'although yours are teeny compared to mine.'

Bonnie smiled, taking a sip of tea so that she didn't

have to comment. How ironic that the reason for them both leaving the fair boiled down to one man.

'I'll always love your father, you know,' said Nelly pensively after a while. 'I understood about how he loved your mother – I loved him in that way after all – but I could have made him happy nonetheless if he'd given me the chance. And love begets love if it's allowed to.'

'I wanted you as my mother.' Bonnie smiled. 'I used to pray every night for my da to fall in love with you so we could become a family. It was all I ever wanted as a child.'

Nelly smiled back and then sighed. 'Ah, well, what will be, will be. Now you're all grown up, perhaps you could be Thomas's auntie instead? He'd love that. His school friends all have grandparents and aunties and uncles, and he does feel hard done by sometimes. A famous auntie would more than make up for my lack in providing him with a ready-made family.'

'That'd be lovely.' Bonnie grinned. 'Although I don't know about the famous. I'm not there yet.'

'You will be.' Nelly spoke with conviction. 'Your voice is wonderful, Bonnie. It's got an extra something that's hard to describe but it's there and it's real.'

'Nelly, do you mind if I ask you about your family, the Harpers? You said Thomas would like grandparents and I just wondered what happened to your parents and how you came to be living with the fair folk. You never spoke like the rest of us and my da always used to say you were a cut above.'

'Did he?' Nelly grimaced. 'Perhaps that was another reason he couldn't see us together. Well, it was like this . . .'

As Nelly told of her childhood and youth, Bonnie listened without interrupting, and when Nelly came to a close there was silence in the room before Bonnie drew in a long breath. 'Oh, Nelly, Nelly. I'm so sorry that my father was such a fool as not to see what he had within his grasp.' Rejected by her parents and family all her life, and then only to escape them and fall deeply in love with someone who rejected her again. Poor Nelly. No wonder she'd loved her canine family so much.

And then Bonnie had to amend the last thoughts when Nelly said softly, 'I don't regret loving your father. Truly, I really don't. And I'm so happy now. I've been given the greatest gift I could ever have in Thomas, and I have my own home, enough money to live comfortably, my dogs, friends . . . I'm blessed, and I thank God each night for it.' She smiled. 'And now I have you too, don't I?'

The question was gentle but none the less urgent for it.

'Always. I promise.'

'Then I am fully content. Will you be able to come back tomorrow and meet Thomas properly?'

'In the morning. I have to be at the theatre soon after midday to get ready for the matinee.'

'Morning is perfect. It's the summer holidays so there's no school for Thomas which he thinks is absolutely marvellous. We'll have an early lunch before you have to leave. At least you'll only be a stone's throw from the theatre. Oh, Bonnie. To think I only caught sight of your name on the poster by chance.'

The two women stared at each other, realizing how easily they might have missed this precious reunion. It didn't bear thinking about.

Chapter Twelve

The tour stayed another ten days in Manchester and Bonnie joined Nelly and Thomas every morning and had lunch with them before she had to leave for the theatre. Thomas turned out to be a charming little boy with exquisite manners that hid a predisposition to shyness. But Bonnie liked that. It made the child nothing like his father. In fact she could see little of Franco in the boy, except for his appearance. His curly hair, the shape of his nose, the colour of his eyes were all Franco's, but softened by his mother's genes. The golden tints to his hair and his pale skin and heart-shaped face came from Nelly, and the combination of both parents had produced a breathtakingly handsome little boy. He was clearly delighted to have an auntie of his very own, and by the time the tour left Manchester Bonnie was completely under his spell.

He cried on her last morning, holding tight to her hand with his small ones. In fact, the three of them cried. It was seeing his mother's tears that dried up Thomas's.

'Don't cry, Mummy,' he said, letting go of Bonnie's hand and putting his arms round his mother's legs. 'We'll see Auntie Bonnie again soon, after all. We'll go to the park this afternoon and feed the ducks. You like that, don't you.'

Bonnie had noticed his devotion to Nelly before; in some ways the child was like a little old man. Even at his young age he clearly felt he was the man of the house and it was his job to look after his mother and protect her. It was beautiful to see, and again Bonnie reflected that in nature the boy was nothing like the selfish, swaggering, egotistical man who had sired him. Nelly had said Thomas was all hers, and she was right. She held out her arms to him. Can I have a hug?' she said softly. 'And don't forget, I'm going to send you postcards from every place I go to from now on. You and Mummy must come to London one day and I'll show you the sights.'

'The Tower of London?' Thomas said eagerly. 'Where they used to torture and behead people? That's where I want to see first.'

Both women smiled. For such a sweet little soul Thomas could be as ghoulish and macabre as the next boy.

The two women embraced on the doorstep and Nelly whispered, 'I'm sorry I wasn't there for you when you needed me most, Bonnie. No, don't say anything because we both know it's true, but I'll never let you down again. Anything, any time, you only have to ask.'

'Thank you, and the same goes for me. Anything, any time.'

Bonnie walked along the street wishing she could stay with Nelly and Thomas for ever, but of course that was impossible. And she didn't really want that anyway; it was just so hard to say goodbye after finding Nelly again.

She turned at the corner to see Nelly and Thomas standing on the doorstep. They were both waving. A huge lump in her throat, Bonnie waved back. If things had gone differently Nelly could have been her stepmother and Thomas her half-brother. But then he wouldn't *be* Thomas, not with a different father. She nipped down on her bottom lip, fighting the tears. Oh, she knew what she meant. It would have been everything she'd ever wanted, to have Nelly as a mother and Thomas as a brother, for them all to be a family with her da. She gave one last wave to them but they were blurry through her tears, and then she turned the corner.

She felt very small and very alone as she walked on, wiping her eyes with her handkerchief. And then she told herself not to be so silly. Everything was just the same as before she had met Nelly again, except that now she had both Nelly and Thomas in her life which was wonderful. And it was no good crying for the moon. Her da was gone, her childhood was over and she had set her course for a different life than that of being a wife and mother. This yearning she'd always had to be part of a proper family, a loving, warm, *real* family, was one dream that had to be packaged away for good. But she had Nelly and Thomas now, and that was an unexpected bonus she could never have imagined. She was lucky.

She nodded to the thought as she reached the stage door of the theatre, her eyes dry now and her mouth firm. She *was*, she was lucky, and she wasn't going to waste one more tear on what could have been. She had come a long way and she intended to go further still, and if this ache deep down inside her was the price she had to pay for the solitary path she had chosen, so be it. 'No more bellyaching, lass,' as her da used to say when she was whining for something.

She pushed open the door and entered the theatre. It welcomed her with its familiar smell of greasepaint, mustiness, stale smoke and the distinct but indecipherable odour all theatres had. She breathed it in, as other people would inhale the sweet perfume of orange blossom on a summer's day, and her world righted itself.

It was a few months before Nelly and Thomas came to visit, and this was solely because Bonnie was so busy when the tour ended and she was back in London. The day after she got home from the north Enoch had fixed up a cabaret spot for her in a cricket club that was also used for concerts and events. He'd also arranged for Art Franklin, a prominent and extremely influential local bandleader, to come along to the club on the night to hear Bonnie sing, although he kept this from her, knowing it would be likely to send her into a tizzy.

Art was thirty years old and a giant of a man at six foot five inches, his shock of jet-black hair and piercing dark eyes causing female hearts to flutter wherever he went. He'd begun his career as a trumpet player when he was sixteen, and two years later had formed his own band. This proved so successful that within a few years – finding himself in the position of having to refuse more work than he accepted – he set up an agency to supply bands for engagements within the entertainment business, whilst still keeping his own band intact. Art was both an excellent musician and an astute businessman, but he had a reputation for being something of a Lothario, a fact which seemed to make the ladies even more besotted as each one dreamed of being 'the one'.

Bonnie had been hoping for a few days' rest when she got home from the tour; she was physically exhausted and still recovering from the lingering effects of a stomach upset caused by one landlady's undercooked chicken dinner. But Enoch had booked the date and so she attended, transforming into Bonnie May the moment she stepped onto the stage and putting everything else aside.

Enoch was waiting for her when she had finally managed to make her last curtsy, after three encores, and he was grinning from ear to ear. 'You knocked 'em dead, gal, as always,' he said, taking her arm. 'And you knocked someone else dead an' all. Art Franklin wants to meet you.'

She knew who he was – everyone knew who Art Franklin was – but she had never seen him, let alone met him.

As Enoch hurried her along through the club and out into the car park, Bonnie stopped dead. 'Enoch, where is Mr Franklin?'

Enoch stared at her. 'He's waiting in his car, of course.'

'I'm not getting into a car with Art Franklin.' She had heard enough about him to know that Hilda's casting couch was alive and well in Art Franklin's world.

'Don't be daft, course you are.'

As he made to take her arm again, she stepped back.

'Enoch, I am *not* getting into a car with Art Franklin. Unless –' a thought had occurred – 'are you accompanying me?'

'He'll want to talk to you privately.'

She bet he would. 'Unless you stay with me I'm not putting myself in that position.'

'Bonnie, Art Franklin, the king of the local bandleaders, is going to offer you a job. At this stage in your career you do not look a gift horse in the mouth.'

If the gift horse had wandering hands and thought he was God's gift to womankind, that's exactly what she was going to do. 'Enoch,' she said, in the same tone he had used, 'I see no reason why any conversation with Mr Franklin cannot take place outside his car and with you present.'

'Quite right.'

The deep, slightly husky voice caught them both unawares, causing Bonnie to gasp and Enoch to give a stifled groan. The next moment a tall, a *very* tall figure emerged from the shadows at the side of the eight-foot wall enclosing the car park.

Art Franklin hadn't been sitting in his car. He had been standing smoking a cigarette in the cool of what had been a warm September day. The realization hit Bonnie at the same time as she looked up – and up – into a darkly handsome face, the mouth of which, she saw to her chagrin, was twitching with barely concealed amusement.

'Art Franklin, Miss May. How do you do?' A large hand reached out, and as Bonnie proffered hers it was engulfed in a hard warm grip for a moment. 'As I'm sure Enoch has already explained, I liked what I heard tonight. I have a vacancy for a vocalist with my band and the job is yours if you want it. You'll be working most nights a week, sometimes every night, and I expect total commitment from everyone who works for me and that will include you. Unless you are at death's door you will be expected to sing – whatever your personal circumstances, whatever the weather, no matter if little green men land in a spaceship in your garden. Do I make myself clear?'

His eyes seemed to bore into her soul; she didn't think she had ever met anyone with quite such a penetrating gaze. His mouth, though, was still on the verge of laughter, and it was this that put iron in her backbone. She didn't know if he expected her to fall on his neck in gratitude or grovel or stammer out an apology for what he had overheard, but the fact that he seemed to be silently mocking her did away with all those options. Her voice so crisp it surprised even herself, she said, 'I don't have a garden, Mr Franklin.'

She heard Enoch groan again beside her. Clearly he thought she had ruined whatever chance she'd had, but Art Franklin stared at her for a moment before throwing back his head and laughing out loud. 'No, I'm sure you don't, Miss May,' he said wryly in the next breath. 'I can offer you five pounds a week, take it or leave it.'

'I'll take it, Mr Franklin, and – and thank you.' She was secretly over-awed at the amount. Everyone in the business knew that if you earned five pounds a week you'd made it big time. And this was five pounds *every* week, guaranteed.

'Now, Enoch tells me you're pally with Julian Wood, Miss May?'

Bonnie nodded. Through Enoch she had been introduced to all of the people in the publishers' offices and most of them had been friendly enough, but Julian was a particular friend. He worked on what Enoch called the 'exploitation' side of the music-publishing house of Norman Mortimer. This meant Julian would try to match the right song with the right artiste, and since Bonnie had met him he'd kept his eyes and ears open for songs he thought would suit her as well as offering encouragement and advice. Listening to the wireless was becoming very popular and to get on the radio was a wonderful opportunity for any burgeoning artiste; Julian had told Enoch and Bonnie many times that her voice was perfect for it.

Then, if your luck held, he'd added, the next step was making records. Bonnie hadn't dared to hope for that. It seemed like reaching for the moon.

'Julian's one of the best in the business. I've got some radio broadcasts lined up in the near future so I think we'll go along and see Julian together, Miss May. I'm sure I hardly need to mention that once you're signed to me I don't want you broadcasting with anyone else.'

Bonnie tried not to look as amazed as she felt. Did he really think that was an option, that bandleaders were lining up for her to sing with them? 'Of course, Mr Franklin,' she said, in what she hoped was a businesslike tone.

'Good, good.' He half-turned and then swung back to face her. 'What's your telephone number, Miss May?' he asked as he fished a notebook and pen out of his pocket.

'Telephone number?'

'You do have a telephone?'

Why on earth would she have one? No ordinary person had a telephone, for goodness' sake.

'You don't have a telephone,' he drawled in a resigned, I-should-have-known sort of way.

'I live in lodgings, Mr Franklin, and—'

He was no longer listening to her. Looking at Enoch, he said, 'Get a telephone installed at her place, Enoch, and bill me, all right? Then let me know the number.' Turning back to Bonnie, he added, 'It's a necessity, not a luxury, Miss May. There will be times when I call you at extremely short notice to sing with one of the agency bands if a vocalist is taken ill or if our own band's schedule changes. You live in lodgings, you say? What is the address?'

She told him, her head spinning.

'And is there usually someone available to take a message if you are out?'

'My landlady, Mrs Nichols.'

He wrote swiftly and then snapped the notebook shut. Looking directly at her, he suddenly smiled. 'Don't look so tragic, Miss May. Whatever you might have heard, I promise I don't make a habit of eating my vocalists for breakfast. Your honour is quite safe.'

Bonnie felt the colour flood her cheeks. She wanted to come back at him with some witty, light retort but it was beyond her. The overall quality of his clothes, his sophisticated manner, the hard planes and angles of his face were intimidating enough, and she had just caught sight of what was an expensive and clearly newish vehicle in the car park which just *had* to be Art Franklin's. Deciding that silence was the best way to hold on to what remained of her dignity, she simply inclined her head in what she hoped was a decorous manner.

Art shook her hand, and then Enoch's, and the two men exchanged pleasantries before he strode off towards his car.

'Phew.' Enoch breathed out and shook his head as they watched Art drive away. 'I thought you'd blown it then, gal. Art's used to telling people to jump and them asking how high.'

'Is he indeed?' It didn't endear her towards her new boss. 'What a charming attribute.'

'Oh, come on, Bonnie. Get off your high horse. Art's a great fella to have backing you.'

'I know, I know.' Feeling ashamed that she hadn't thanked Enoch, she said quickly, 'I appreciate the chance you've made possible, Enoch, I really do. I'm not ungrateful, truly. It's just that . . .'

What was it exactly? She wasn't sure. Certainly Art's reputation with the ladies was a factor, but then in this business no bandleader would want to give the impression of being cool and unavailable to their admirers, the ones that weren't married, that is. And even some of the married ones. But it was more than that. It was the man himself. He was so self-assured, so poised, so . . . *male*. He had charisma, that was the word, she told herself. And she didn't like it. Or him. But then she didn't have to. She only had to work for him.

She smiled at Enoch, slipping her arm through his as they walked back into the club. 'You really are my fairy godfather,' she said warmly, eliciting a chuckle in response.

'Gal, I've been called many things in my time but a fairy isn't one of 'em.'

Chapter Thirteen

That had been four months ago, and since then Bonnie had hardly paused to take breath.

The telephone had been duly installed in Hilda's hall amid much excitement. It was big and black with two parts, one for your ear and one to speak into. The dial was on the base and when you picked up the telephone to make a call, you spoke directly to the operator and gave them your number. Hilda was terrified of it, but the other occupants of Fairview, including Bonnie, thought it was wonderful. It took Hilda a good few days before she dared answer it when it rang, and Art complained to Bonnie that her landlady nearly deafened him, she shouted so loudly into the receiver.

The first time Bonnie was due to broadcast she felt ill with nerves. She was just a little nobody from a north-east fair, she told herself beforehand – unhelpfully. She had been fooling herself and everyone else thus far, but now someone would tumble to the fact that she wasn't good enough for all this. The band were waiting for her when she reached the studio, her knees shaking, and once inside, the morning became a jumble of microphones, red lights, song sheets, instruments, other band members, Art and the studio clock.

Somehow she got through, and it was never so bad again. By the sixth or seventh broadcast, she had begun to relax and actually enjoy it, although never as much as singing at Art's nightclub in Regent Street. True, the club hours could be gruelling, but she was doing what she loved and it made all the difference. She wasn't frightened of hard work – in fact she thrived on it – but by the time Christmas approached she was ready for a break. Nelly and Thomas were coming to stay and Bonnie was longing to see them again. Verity and Larry wouldn't be around because they were visiting Verity's mother, but the rest of the Fairview household would be there, and Selina's boyfriend, Cyril Preston – Betty's brother – was joining them for Christmas Day dinner. Cyril was the only one of Betty's brothers who had 'gone straight' as Betty put it and never been in trouble with the law. He had been working at the docks since leaving school fifteen years ago and had a little place of his own, a two-up, two-down terraced house not far from where his parents lived. The big, muscled, blunt and loud-mouthed docker and the middle-class school-marm made an unlikely pair in some respects, Bonnie considered, but since they had started courting a couple of months ago, Selina had changed. The somewhat wild partying side of her friend that had worried Bonnie when she'd had time to think about it had disappeared, and Selina appeared quieter and more content. Added to that, Cyril clearly worshipped the ground she walked on.

The only fly in the ointment, as far as Selina was concerned, was that Cyril knew nothing about her father's treatment of her. He knew she had fallen out with her parents some years ago and there was no possibility of a reconciliation, but that was all. Selina wanted to tell him, she'd confided in tears to Bonnie just nights ago, but she was terrified she'd lose him if he knew the truth.

'He treats me like a princess,' Selina had whispered when she'd come to Bonnie's room once the rest of the household were asleep. 'He's so respectful, it was only on our third date that he even kissed me goodnight, and he never, you know, tries anything. Betty's told me he's had umpteen girlfriends but once they get serious about him he gives them the old heave-ho, and she's sure he's sown his wild oats in – in the fullest sense of the word. But he's already talking about our future as though he sees us staying together.'

'Do you *have* to tell him about your father?' Bonnie had whispered back. Betty had told her that when she and Selina had been out on the town there had been lots of blokes who had shown an interest in getting to know Selina better, but she had cold-shouldered all of them. And then Cyril had been at his mother's house one day when Betty had brought Selina home for a cuppa, and that had been that. Betty said she'd never seen two people fall for each other so fast.

'I do if he's serious about us, you know, marriage and everything. How could I not? He'd have the right to know, wouldn't he? If you were me you'd tell him, I know you would.'

Yes, she would. She couldn't deny it, but she wasn't Selina and it didn't seem fair that her friend might lose the only man she'd ever cared about because of her father's wickedness. She had prevaricated by saying, 'How do you think Cyril would take it if he knew the truth?'

'He – he thinks I'm pure, untouched. He knows I've never had a boyfriend before. Oh, Bonnie, I'm so frightened, I don't know what to do.'

'You don't have to do anything for now,' Bonnie said practically. 'You've said yourself he's had loads of girl-friends but once they want him to put a ring on their finger he backs off. He might be the sort who will never settle down with one woman, Selina. I'm not saying he doesn't think the world of you but old habits die hard, and some men can never make that commitment, no matter how in love they are. See what happens, take it a day at a time. You'll know if the moment comes to tell him but it might never happen.'

'You're so wise. I'm years older than you and yet I haven't got half of your discernment about things.'

She'd nearly told Selina about Franco then. Told her that this supposed wisdom her friend had credited her with was only skin deep, that it came from fear and mistrust of the male sex. Just the thought of intimacy with a man caused her skin to crawl. But this was about Selina, not her. She had passed the moment off and a little while later Selina had trotted back to her room in a calmer state of mind. She, however, had been left feeling totally at odds with herself and it had taken her hours to fall asleep; even then her slumber had been populated with menacing shadows and half-formed creatures with hard grasping hands.

But now it was Christmas Eve. Nelly and Thomas were due to arrive later that morning. Verity and Larry had kindly offered them the use of their room because they would be staying with her mother, which had suited everyone perfectly. Everything had fallen into place for a lovely Christmas.

Bonnie had awoken early and lay watching the cold light of dawn slowly envelop the darkness outside her window. She had bought Thomas a sackful of presents and thoroughly enjoyed herself in the process, and after a while she slid out of bed and put on her thick dressing gown and bootee slippers and finished wrapping the last of them. In spite of the smouldering remains of the fire in her little grate the bedroom was icy cold, and she reminded herself to light a good fire in Verity and Larry's room once breakfast was over. She wanted it to be welcoming.

She *so* wanted little Thomas to have a good Christmas, and with that in mind she wasn't sorry that Verity and Larry had already departed for her mother's. Hilda had shouted at him a few days ago, and since then things had been a little tense. It had been Larry's fault though.

Every morning for the past year he'd subjected them all to reports on the fast deteriorating state of the world in general, and Hitler's part in the decline in particular.

It had been the law banning Jews from employing women under thirty-five in Germany in January; Spain's new left-wing government coming to power in February; Hitler and the Nazis defying the treaties of Versailles and Locarno in March when the stomp of the jackboot announced that they had entered the cities of the Rhineland; and the goverment reintroducing military service in Vienna in April in violation of peace treaties, because they were terrified Germany was going to invade in the coming months. And so the year had continued. Mussolini had proclaimed his Fascist empire from the Palazzo Venezia in Rome in May; and civil war had finally exploded in Spain in July with terrible atrocities being committed by both sides. But it was the Berlin Olympic Games in August that had caused Larry to have an apoplectic fit most days, according to the letters Selina had written to Bonnie, letters that had made Bonnie glad she had been away on tour and out of the house.

'Honestly, Bonnie, Larry's driving us all mad,' Selina had written. 'Going on about how the Germans have only one aim with the Games, to glorify the Nazi regime of Hitler. No one doubts that Larry's right. It's so obvious, isn't it – even the poster depicts an Aryan hero. And the way they're treating Jesse Owens from the United States, who is the undisputed star of the Games but also very much non-Ayran and very black, is awful,

just awful. Hitler refusing to shake his hand or acknowledge him and Goebbels publicly declaring Owens and
all the other American blacks 'black mercenaries', it's
disgusting. But it's all Larry can talk about, that and the
fact that Hitler and his Nazis are getting away with
literal murder and no countries are standing up to them.
He keeps saying we're all going to reap what we've sown
and war is inevitable. He really is the most depressing
person in the world, I don't know how Verity puts up
with him. Mrs Nichols is absolutely sick of Larry. She
calls him the master of pessimism now.'

No, all things considered she hadn't been sorry to
have missed August in London, Bonnie decided as she
finished wrapping the last present – a fine kite that
Thomas could take to the park with his mother – and
got dressed to go downstairs.

It was odd, she mused as she tidied her hair, considering what a fiercely political animal Larry was, that he
hadn't taken such an avid interest in the constitutional
drama that had been played out in Royal circles at the
beginning of the month, as the female occupants of
the house had done. She and the others had been enthral-
led by the secret love story between the King and the
American, Wallis Simpson, once the news of their affair
had become public. And when he had renounced the
throne a couple of weeks ago, saying he couldn't be King
without the help and support of the woman he loved,
well, they'd all been in tears.

But not Larry. He had merely remarked that the new

King, George VI, would be a better bet than his brother when the country went to war anyway. George had seen action in the Battle of Jutland in the last war, Larry told them, and then had served with the RAF. He knew what war was like first hand. He wouldn't be afraid of taking Hitler on.

It had been the last straw for the long-suffering Hilda. 'When?' she'd yelled at him over the breakfast table, making them all jump out of their skins. '*When?* Oh, it's "when" now, is it? Not even "if" any more. Well, that's it. This is *my* house and *my* kitchen and I forbid you, *forbid* you, do you hear, to mention the word "war" again in my hearing. *Do you hear me, Larry McKenzie?*'

It was highly likely the whole street could hear her.

They'd all slunk out of the kitchen that morning, and since then Larry had kept a low profile, hiding behind his morning newspaper as though it was a shield protecting him from Hilda's wrath. He still commented on the occasional snippet – he couldn't seem to help himself – but it was in an aside to Verity now and the 'w' word was never uttered. It *was* a relief to eat breakfast without their resident prophet of doom going on and on, as Selina remarked to Bonnie, but the atmosphere in the kitchen was distinctly frosty now. In spite of how Verity felt about her husband's obsession with Hitler and his constant harping on about a war, she had come down on Larry's side and was consequently very cool with Hilda. She'd told Bonnie and Selina that she was waiting for an apology from the lady in question. Bonnie had said nothing at the time, but privately she'd thought that there was as much chance of that as hell freezing over.

But things might be better after Christmas. Hilda had baked a Christmas cake for Verity's mother and it had clearly been offered in the nature of a peace offering. And Verity had hugged Hilda and wished her a merry Christmas before she and Larry had left the day before. Bonnie grinned as a thought hit; they really were like a family at Fairview and what family didn't have a squabble now and again?

She was now earning well in excess of the five pounds that Art had originally mentioned, sometimes double that amount, and she knew Art found it odd that she had no wish to rent a little flat somewhere, but she would hate to leave everyone at Fairview. She always did the Saturday-night broadcasts with the band, but after she had been with them for a week or two, Art had begun taking her to his Sunday concerts too, to give her a little more exposure and experience. She hadn't expected to get paid extra for this – Art had warned her when he had taken her on that she would be expected to work as and when he demanded – but practically from the first week she had found extra in her wage packet. When she had thanked him, he had smiled the smile that crinkled the skin round his eyes and sent women into a swoon. 'You play fair with me and I play fair with you,' he said easily. 'That's the way it is. Any of my musicians would tell you the same. And I like your work ethos, Bonnie.'

It had been praise indeed from a man who was renowned in the business for calling a spade a spade. And from that moment on Bonnie had found herself relaxing more around Art. He was friendly but businesslike and he maintained the same amiable attitude with her as he did with his other band members. They might flirt a little with her and tease her on occasion, but Art never did. He also gave her complete freedom of choice over what she sang, which Enoch assured her was rare in the business. She had found as soon as she started broadcasting with Art that she was sent lots of songs by hopeful composers and musicians who wanted to make a name for themselves, as well as the established ones, but as she had a very clear understanding of what suited her voice and what she liked to sing, Art didn't interfere.

She was happy. As she opened her bedroom door, she smiled to herself. Really happy. In a way that she hadn't been since the day she had woken up and found her father gone. She could picture the years ahead now, years of doing what she loved and building up her reputation as a singer. Everything looked rosy. And she was going to make a record with Art in the New Year. She had hardly been able to believe that when he had told her the previous night at the club, just before the taxi had arrived to take her home. Art always insisted on booking a taxi for her no matter where the band was playing, and he always paid for it too. She couldn't fault him on his generosity.

'Bit of news to mull over, Bonnie,' Art had drawled in his lazy, nonchalant way as he'd helped her on with her coat. 'We're going to be cutting a record on the first Monday in January with the Crown label. Their policy is to have a well-known published song on one side of the record, and an unpublished number on the other. They've given us a few songs of the latter from their stock to consider.' He'd handed her a sheaf of song sheets as he'd spoken. 'Look through these tonight and come up with a couple of favourites. We'll discuss them with the lads before the concert tomorrow and then have a few run-throughs before the New Year, so you can familiarize yourself with the melody and so on. But I know with you the words are more important, right? You need to feel the connection with the song.'

She had gazed at him in shock. A record. They were going to make a *record*. He'd smiled at her expression before bundling her out of the door and into the waiting taxi, and she'd sat in a daze all the way home.

But she knew precisely which song she was going to suggest, Bonnie told herself as she walked down Hilda's steep stairs to the kitchen. It was called 'A Song at Sunrise' and immediately the title had made her think of her father, and how he had told her to sing for pleasure like the birds when they welcomed the sunrise and a new day. The words were tender and poignant, telling the story of young love lost before being found again in the twilight years. The song had touched her deeply and she knew she could sing it with the emotion to touch her listeners too. No other song would do for her debut into records, she'd make that clear to Art and the others, and Enoch when she saw him on Boxing Day. He and Gladys had invited her and Nelly and Thomas to spend the day with them, bless them. She knew Gladys had bought a beautifully painted wooden train set for Thomas. She had been as enchanted with the tiny steam engine and carriages, small stationmaster's house with a picket fence and little figures, and even a miniature signal box, as Gladys had been. Enoch had set the train up on its track to show her before he had packed it away in its box ready for Gladys to gift-wrap it, and both women had noticed that he had played with it for some minutes, ostensibly to make sure it worked properly, before handing it over.

She was *so* lucky. Bonnie paused before she opened the kitchen door, her heart flooding with gladness. Her career was on the up and up, she had good friends here in London and now she had Nelly back in her life and dear little Thomas too. It was the icing on the cake. There had been times when she had almost felt her father was an ethereal figure and she was in danger of losing the clarity of her memories of him, but when she had met Nelly again he had suddenly become real once more. And that was so precious.

The future was rosy, and like Hilda, she didn't think for a moment that what was happening in Germany and other countries like Spain and Italy would impinge on Britain. It was horrible and she felt sorry for the innocent victims of the Nazis, but it was so far away, after all. The government were adamant that Hitler didn't want war and she believed them. The Great War had been terrible enough but lessons had been learned, and who in their right mind would want a repeat of that? No, Larry was a gloom merchant just as Hilda said. He always looked on the dark side and because he fancied himself as something of an astute political analyst, it didn't help matters.

Everything would settle down in time and all would be well. She wouldn't believe anything else, because the alternative was too frightening. She brushed off the brief sense of foreboding that had come with that thought, recaptured the happiness of minutes before, and entered the kitchen humming the latest hit song, 'The Way You Look Tonight' to herself.

PART FOUR

Art

1938

Chapter Fourteen

Art Franklin sat staring in disgust at the newspaper he had just flung down. The headline on the front page read: 'Peace for our time', a direct quote from Neville Chamberlain, the Prime Minister, on his return from Munich the day before.

'"Peace for our time,"' Art muttered, standing up and walking over to the French doors that were open to the pocket-sized London garden of his Kingston-upon-Thames cottage. Did Chamberlain really believe that handing the Nazis Czechoslovakia on a plate was going to appease Hitler's deranged quest for power? It was a sell-out to Hitler's subversion and threats of war, and every man and woman with a grain of intelligence knew it.

Art looked up into the cherry tree in the centre of his courtyard garden where a blackbird was singing its heart out to the morning sky. Today, the first of October, German troops were already marching into Czechoslovakia under the terms of the agreement Chamberlain had signed, and the Czechs, poor beggars, could do nothing about it. They'd been hung out to dry, that was the truth of it, and he, for one, was ashamed to be British. This day would go down in history as one to mark Britain's shame, he was sure of that, and one which the Prime Minister and the rest of the government would live to regret. It was the beginning of the end. Chamberlain had rolled over and shown his soft underbelly, and Hitler and his sabre-rattling chums would pierce it through sooner or later. Hell, what a mess.

Art finished the last drops of the mug of coffee he had in his hand, wondering how on earth Chamberlain and others could ignore the threat of Hitler's fast-expanding empire, an empire built on death and destruction and unspeakable atrocities. But then as the Prime Minister himself had broadcast, he was a man of peace to the depths of his soul, and armed conflict between nations was a nightmare to him.

Art grunted in frustration at the man's stupidity. To have such views was one thing if you were an ordinary Joe Bloggs in the street, quite another if you were the Prime Minister and aired them openly to all and sundry. Hitler must think all his Christmases had come at once. And look at the way the Duke and Duchess of Windsor had cosied up to the Führer when they were in Berlin last year – it had made sickening reading. Apparently the pair had declared themselves charmed by Hitler and delighted by Nazi Germany. It would be laughable if it wasn't so damn dangerous.

The blackbird took off into the high blue sky and as Art watched it go, he wondered how much longer the skies around Britain would merely have birds and friendly aircraft to contend with. War was coming. It could be weeks, months, even a year or two, but it was coming. And this war wouldn't be like the last one, hell, no. The Nazis would make sure of that. What could you expect from an enemy that already interned their own people in death camps for daring to speak out against Hitler, and took children away from parents if they weren't sufficiently rigorous in drilling Nazism into their little ones? His guts twisted. International tension was escalating and it would only get worse.

'I'm ready to dish up your breakfast, Mr Franklin.'

His elderly housekeeper had come up behind him and now Art turned, smiling at the little woman who had faithfully looked after his house and himself ever since he had moved to Kingston upon Thames eight years ago. Annie was a superb cook and meticulous about keeping the house as neat as a new pin, and – more importantly – at seventy years of age had no romantic inclinations in his direction. He had interviewed several women before finding Annie, and more than one of them had fluttered their eyelashes at him. Annie was a widow with three grown-up children who had families of their own and whom she visited regularly on her days off as they all lived in London. From the day she had moved into his home he knew he had found himself a gem and paid her accordingly. For Annie's part, she was devoted to him and utterly loyal. He had never brought any of his women friends to the house; he preferred to keep his love life and his home totally separate, which he supposed said a lot about his capacity to let even the women he slept with into his life. And then Bonnie had come on the scene.

He followed Annie into the small blue-and-white dining room at the front of the house and sat down at a table set for one. He had often wondered if Bonnie had an inkling of how he felt about her, but every time the thought came he told himself the same answer. Of course she didn't. They had built up a good working relationship over the last couple of years and there were times she was as relaxed and chatty with him as she was with his band members, but he knew her ease with him and the others came from the knowledge that he'd always made it plain that work and play were separate. And he did believe in that rule; he'd seen more splits in bands because one of the musicians had started a love affair with the female vocalist which had then turned sour than he'd had hot dinners. But that didn't stop him loving her, aching for her, going crazy sometimes as he tossed and turned the night away.

'Here we are.' Annie bustled into the room with his usual plate of eggs, bacon and sausages and a fresh pot of coffee. Ever since he had gone over to America ten years ago for a few weeks to see how things were done there, he'd developed a taste for coffee over tea. He'd enjoyed his time in the States, the highlight being when he'd been taken to the Cotton Club in Harlem by a black musician friend to hear Duke Ellington and his band play. Ellington's trademark 'jungle sound' created by growling brass, tom-toms and 'wa-wa' mutes had inspired him, and he had never approached the music his own band played in quite the same way again. It had changed him, that trip, and caused him to challenge the commonly held belief that jazz came in two versions, black and white. And what was wrong in incorporating some blues into the equation? He'd met Ma Rainey, a rumbustious character known in America as 'the mother of the blues', and other leading blues singers, and their searingly emotional impact when they sang had touched the core of him.

Bonnie sang like that.

He took a mouthful of bacon, reflecting ruefully that it was rare a minute or so went by without her intruding into his thoughts. And the galling thing was, he was sure once she finished work she never gave him a thought. In the early days he had attempted to scratch the itch of her by dating other women, but that hadn't helped. One day he had woken up in a hotel room with a woman he had met the night before at one of his concerts, and told himself enough was enough. He'd had plenty of women in his time but not under false pretences, not pretending they were someone else. They deserved more than that. And so he'd gone on the wagon, so to speak.

He smiled to himself at the analogy. Certainly it would have been a damn sight easier if his problem *had* been alcohol, rather than a girl/woman who could be shy and bold, vulnerable and fearless, diffident and confident all at the same time. She'd turned his life upside down and inside out and she didn't even know it. Damn it, she didn't know it. Which was just as well. He didn't like to think about what might have happened in her past to cause Bonnie to keep the male sex at a distance the way she did, but it was more than a natural girlish modesty, that was for sure. He wouldn't have said she was particularly self-effacing in the normal run of things, but should a man, any man, try to get a little too friendly then there was a definite shrinking back on her part. At first he had been relieved it wasn't just him she found . . . He had been going to say repellent but perhaps that was too strong. Anyway, certainly off-putting, he thought irritably. But relief had been replaced with frustration and then pain and dejection before he had come to terms with the situation.

If he wanted to keep Bonnie in his life, and he did, for as long as was humanly possible, then he had to play a part. The part of a non-threatening, caring but not too caring big brother. And gradually, as months had passed, it had worked. And if nothing else their careers had soared because of it. The number of nights he spent working on musical arrangements for the band and even composing some of his own stuff, often into the early hours, to dull the burning in his loins and lustful thoughts he found hard to control, had paid off. Their broadcasts attracted huge audiences now and their records sold well;

they were up there with the biggest bands in the business like Bert Ambrose, Billy Cotton and others.

And this in a time that was strange for the dance-band world as a whole, Art reflected sombrely, sitting back in his chair and pushing his empty plate away as he lit a cigarette. Some bandleaders were having a tough time economically, and he knew that many musicians were being asked to take cuts in their salaries. It was generally acknowledged that the record industry in particular had plunged into a state of depression, but as yet it hadn't really touched him and he was grateful. He was still able to pay his musicians top whack, and Bonnie's weekly pay packet had risen to thirty pounds, partly because she was worth it but also, he admitted to himself, because he didn't want her to be enticed away by someone else. It haunted him, that possibility.

He stretched his long legs out under the table, staring somewhat morosely across the room. He was quite aware that he'd schemed to make Bonnie feel indebted to him over the time he had known her, manipulating circumstances to his own advantage now and again, and he had no intention of feeling guilty about it. Bonnie had, after all, benefited from everything he had done.

Quite soon after she had begun working with the band, he had taken her to his bank and arranged for her to set up an account of her own. The bank manager, a personal friend, had agreed to advise Bonnie on financial matters himself, should the need arise in the future.

He had also encouraged her to learn to drive, feeling

that a motor car of her own would make her less vulnerable than using taxis or buses. He had recommended a local driving school and also taken her out in his own car a few times when she was finding some particular aspect hard to grasp. It had been a sweet torture, having her so close, but it had helped cement their friendship. And when she had passed her test, it had been he who had driven her around to various car showrooms and garages until she'd found exactly what she was looking for – a smart midnight-blue Austin that she had paid for outright.

That had been a good day. His expression softened. Bonnie had been so excited about the car that she had let her guard down and agreed to have dinner with him to celebrate, and he had taken her to a chic little restaurant where he'd played the role of amusing dinner companion. He'd delivered her back to the wretched boarding house she insisted on living in, although she could well afford to rent or even buy a flat of her own now, without so much as a goodnight kiss; his reward being when she'd shyly told him she'd had a wonderful time and had reached up and touched the side of his face for an instant before darting into the house. The gesture had been nothing, not really, except that it was the first time that he could recall her voluntarily touching him. Ridiculous, but like a schoolboy he had felt he never wanted to wash his face again.

Damn it, he was the world's biggest fool. He drew

deeply on his cigarette before rising abruptly from the table and walking through to the garden once more.

Here he was, a man at the top of his career who could bed any number of women, and he was as celibate as a monk in a monastery. What the hell was he doing?

He flung himself down on a garden chair set under the cherry tree and scowled up into its branches. He was lusting after a woman who was oblivious to him in a romantic sense. And then he caught at the thought. But that summed it up, didn't it? That was the rub. It wasn't lust he felt for Bonnie. He knew all about that carnal urge – it had first stirred when he was a callow youth still wet behind the ears – but the emotion he felt for Bonnie was something much more than lust. Love. He stubbed out the remains of the cigarette under his heel, grinding it to little pieces as though he could extinguish his feelings for her in the same way. And he would if he could. He had seen first hand what love could do to a man. His mother had run off with her fancy man when he was nine years old and it had broken his father, but in the six years it had taken for his father to drink himself to death, he wouldn't hear a word said against her.

Art shook his head. She had left them both without a word, a note, anything, disappearing into the blue yonder with a used-car salesman of all things. It had been his father's mates who told him what had been going on under his nose while he'd worked all hours at the docks to give her the easy life and nice clothes she wanted. But his father had died with her name on his lips. Art had vowed then that he would never let any woman make a monkey out of him, and he hadn't. Not until he had stood in a dark car park one night two years ago and heard an indignant female voice declare that she had no intention of getting into a car with him. He'd been a goner right then, he just hadn't known it.

'Mr Franklin, there's a Mr Odell on the telephone for you.' Annie interrupted his thoughts, standing in the doorway to the French doors as she dusted her floury hands on her apron.

Looked like there was a pie for lunch, Art thought hopefully. Annie had such a light touch with pastry it melted in the mouth. He stood up and followed her into the hall where the telephone resided, and as he walked he felt a frisson of excitement in the pit of his stomach. He had been waiting for this call for a few days. Odell was on the television side of show business, and although reception was confined to a limited area in the south-east of England it was still a good media to break into. He had been negotiating the possibility of mounting a stage show on television with Odell. A stage show was nothing new to him; most big dance bands had been doing it as part of their livelihood for a long time. He had a small file of top-class dancers, jugglers, magicians and other visual acts that he'd used before and although the band was the main turn and paid accordingly, he knew the other acts would leap at the chance to perform on television, unable, as they were, to make the transition to radio as musicians had.

He picked up the telephone as his heart beat loud in his ears. James Odell had other dance bands he'd used in the last year or two for fairly lavish productions; whether he would be prepared to give him a chance he wasn't sure, but he wanted this. It was a natural progression after all, and television was the future. He could see it snowballing in the next years, although if Hitler provoked a war, as he was sure he would, that would put a spanner in the works.

'Art?' James's lazy voice gave nothing away. 'Beautiful morning, isn't it? How are you?'

'Good, good. And you?'

They went through the social niceties, Art aiming to keep his impatience out of his voice, and then James drawled, 'So, that little thing we discussed recently? How soon can you pull a show together for me?'

Art's heart leapt. 'Today too soon?' he joked carefully.

James laughed. 'A little. What about a fortnight from now? Two half-an-hour shows in the same week? Can you handle that?'

'With bells on.'

'Great. Look, I'm at Alexandra Palace this afternoon. Call in, would you, and we'll go through the formalities. And you'd use that vocalist you favour, Bonnie May, wouldn't you? I feel the cameras would like her.'

'Sure thing, James.'

'See you later then, about three? Good man. Bye, Art.'

Art put down the telephone, a big grin on his face. Wait till he told Bonnie and the rest of the band. Once they had a foot in the door of television there'd be no stopping them, he felt it in his bones. He knew what his public wanted – it had been one of his strengths from the early days. He'd always believed in paying top dollar to get the best people, and television was where it would pay off big time.

He imagined the look on Bonnie's face when she knew she was going to be on television and his grin widened. If he was a fool then he was a successful fool, and that was something . . .

Chapter Fifteen

Bonnie looked at herself in the mirror of the dressing room and had to laugh. The thick, dark, revolting make-up that was necessary for television was truly horrible, and the vivid yellow cocktail dress she was wearing which would appear white on the screen was a pretty vile colour too. The first time she had been made up by one of the make-up artists at the television studio some months ago she had been horrified, convinced her appearance had to be some cruel practical joke in spite of the girl insisting everyone had to have the same, but when she had seen Art and the others she had relaxed. They looked like weird clowns too. And she had had enough to think about that day without worrying about her appearance, the barrage of instructions she'd received from the studio manager ringing in her ears. She had to stick to her chalk mark on the floor and not wander about; she had to remember to sing to the camera as though it was the audience; if she forgot her words – heaven forbid – she mustn't, on any account, freeze but

243

just carry on and ad lib; the performance went out live of course and thousands of people would be seeing it. The directions that went with appearing on television had been endless, and so very different from anything she had experienced before. But she had got through.

She slid off the make-up stool after thanking the girl who had caked the thick foundation and powder on, her eyes already feeling gritty under their heavy layer of shadow and mascara. She didn't like it, but at least she was used to it now, and once she was on stage and singing nothing else mattered. That hadn't changed. And this was the last television show for some time as the band was off on tour to Holland in a few days at the beginning of February. Unlike Art and the rest of the band she had never been abroad before, and the prospect both excited and worried her. But at least she would be away from England for three months. It was silly perhaps, but since Art had first told her they were going to do a television performance, she had been worried that her grandmother might find her, and a sense of foreboding had dogged her days and nights. Try as she might, she couldn't throw it off.

She took a deep breath and prepared herself for this last show. It had been different when she had performed in the London clubs and concerts or on tour, and even radio hadn't concerned her in the same way. You could remain anonymous with the radio broadcasts. Oh, your voice was well known of course, but people couldn't see you, they didn't know what you looked like. She had liked that. And she knew that when Art had told her about the television opportunity he hadn't got the re-action he'd wanted. She had stared at him, the colour draining from her face, before asking in a small voice if she *had* to sing with the band.

Poor Art. Bonnie smiled ruefully. She had taken the wind out of his sails good and proper that day, and although he had tried to be patient and understanding at what he had put down to nerves, she knew he had been cross with her. Anyone in his position would have been. So she had done the television appearances, telling her-self that of course her grandmother wouldn't see her and neither would anyone who knew Margarita. Not that it was her grandmother who was the problem, not really, much as she disliked her. It was the thought of coming face to face with Franco that made her feel sick.

Art was waiting for her in the corridor outside the female dressing room as he had from that first appear-ance back in October, and not for the first time she wondered how he could still manage to look so hand-some plastered in a make-up that was almost mauve in natural light. The heavy foundation made his white teeth look even whiter as he smiled. 'Last one for a while,' he said softly. 'Looking forward to the tour?'

'Of course.' She smiled back. Art was like all the other members of the band – he treated her as though she was a little sister he had to look out for, and at first she had appreciated this. She still did, of *course* she did, she told herself firmly. She'd discovered that musicians were a friendly, gregarious sort of people who, although they took their music deathly seriously, were always ready for a joke and a bit of fun. But Art . . . He never chaffed her like the others. They would pull her leg and wind her up on occasion, but Art, although friendly and kind, always seemed to keep her at arm's length. And that was fine, just fine. It was what she wanted, especially knowing of his reputation with the ladies. Or it was what she *had* wanted.

No, she still did want that, she reaffirmed in her mind as they walked along the corridor together. Anything else would be impossible. Art would never settle down with one woman, she knew that. Oh, what was she thinking? She glanced at him out of the corner of her eye as he opened the door into the recording studio and stood aside for her to precede him. She didn't want a relationship with Art or any man, a relationship that would inevitably include *that*. Or did she?

She stitched a smile on her face as one or two of the band called out to her.

The trouble was that being around him made her feel as though she didn't know which end was up most of the time, and it wasn't exactly comfortable. And now they were going on tour for three months, which meant close proximity practically every waking moment.

She took her place at the microphone, checking the chalk marks on the floor as she did so and then glancing at the cameramen who gave her the thumbs-up sign. She was starting the show with 'The Folks who Live on the

Hill', followed by 'September in the Rain' before the other acts Art had hired came on, with 'Blue Moon' in between the magician and two male tap dancers. The comedian was the last of the turns, and then she would finish the show with 'A Song at Sunrise' which seemed to have become the band's signature tune.

As always, before the actual moment when she started to sing, her stomach was inhabited by a host of butterflies while the studio manager called out instructions, technicians did their last checks and everyone settled into place. Then the band struck up behind her, she opened her mouth and the words flowed effortlessly from her lips as she inhabited the song.

It was raining when Bonnie and some fellow performers left Alexandra Palace later that night, an icy, chilling rain that was verging on sleet. Bonnie was deep in conversation with one of the female dancers who also originated from the north-east, and they were reminiscing about the Winter Garden at the rear of the museum and library building in Sunderland's Mowbray Park. Bonnie's father had taken her there as a little girl one day, and she had been fascinated by the huge conservatory full of tropical plants and flowers with an aviary and a pond teeming with goldfish. It was a precious memory.

Art and a couple of the boys from the band had been waylaid by a group of giggling young women who were asking for autographs, a regular occurrence these days. Bonnie had her own admirers too who sent letters and flowers and sometimes made themselves known at Art's nightclub or on tour, but clearly the bad weather had put all but the most ardent fans off tonight. And then, with her mind half on what Peggy, the dancer, was saying, she heard her name called from somewhere behind her.

She turned, expecting it to be one of the bunch of people around Art who had spoken, only to stand transfixed as she watched two figures approaching her. Like a mouse before a snake she was frozen at the inevitability of what was about to happen.

Margarita's face was wearing an expression that could only be described as triumphant, but Franco, a step or two behind her, was deadpan. Bonnie didn't speak, not even when they stopped a couple of feet away and stared at her, not until Margarita, her dark eyes burning with venom, said, 'Still bold as brass, I see, you dirty little thief. Risen high, haven't you, but them as rise have further to fall.'

'Hello, Grandmother.'

The coolness of her voice surprised even herself, but then hadn't she been waiting for this day? After the first glance when she had taken in Franco behind Margarita, she hadn't looked at him again. But instead of falling to pieces as she had imagined would happen if she ever saw him again, a welcome numbness had put iron in her backbone. She despised and hated this man, and the feelings she had for her grandmother were just as fierce. In their different ways the pair of them had used her and robbed her of her childhood but she was no longer a child and she wasn't afraid of her grandmother any more.

'Don't you dare come the fine lady with me, girl. I know who and what you are.'

Peggy was standing open-mouthed beside her and one or two other people had drawn closer, sensing something was going on, but it was Art, who had turned towards her when Margarita had called her name, who now took control. He had reached them in a few strides and at a glance had taken in the confrontation. He took hold of Bonnie's arm as he cast a glance at Peggy and the others, saying, 'Show's over folks, goodnight,' and to Margarita and Franco, 'Follow me, please.'

Bonnie let him lead her down the steep slope away from Alexandra Palace and she was aware that Margarita and Franco had fallen into step behind them, probably too surprised to do anything else. Art at his most commanding was formidable. She kept the numbness wrapped round her like a cloak and concentrated on the physical action of walking, and it was a minute or two later when Margarita said behind them, 'What's going on? I want to talk to my granddaughter.'

'All in good time.' Art didn't lessen his pace or turn round, and no one spoke again until he led them through the doors of a public house a little while later.

Again Margarita said, 'What's going on?' but Art didn't reply. Bonnie knew where she was – a crowd of them often came to this pub for a meal after rehearsals and the landlord was friendly and obliging, always providing sandwiches if the kitchen wasn't open for hot meals. It was near closing time but Art walked over to the bar, still keeping her within the crook of his arm and not looking to see if the other two followed.

The landlord smiled at Art and then leaned closer as Art said quietly, 'I need somewhere private for a spot of business for a few minutes, Bruce. Your dining room empty yet?'

'Sorry, Art, got a few late eaters today. Tell you what, use the function room upstairs. Switch on the light to the left of the door as you go in, mate.' Bruce had a lot of time for Art Franklin. Not only was his band the best in the country, as far as Bruce was concerned, but Art had no side to him, not like some he could mention. He had all sorts calling in his pub from the Palace and some of them fancied themselves rotten once they'd been on the television, but not Art. And he tipped well. 'Want some drinks sending up?'

'No, thanks.' Art slipped a folded note across the counter of the bar, which, although he protested, Bruce deftly pocketed.

'Follow me,' Art said over his shoulder to Margarita and Franco as he and Bonnie walked out of the bar into a long narrow corridor. The gents' and ladies' toilets along with the kitchen were off this, but Art made for the wide staircase at the far end that led up to an uncarpeted landing. He opened the door in front of them and switched on the light to reveal a long wide room complete with a small stage at one end and a number of tables and chairs stacked along the far wall. It smelt strongly of smoke and stale beer and was reminiscent of many pub function rooms that Bonnie had sung in when she was getting started in the business.

Art let Margarita and Franco walk past him into the room before he shut the door, and his impassive face revealed nothing of his thoughts. So this old harridan was Bonnie's grandmother? Well, well, well. And a nasty bit of work if he judged correctly. Who was the bloke, the grandfather? Whoever he was, he hadn't so much as opened his mouth.

Margarita was fully aware of who Art Franklin was – most people were even if they weren't particularly inclined to that sort of music – but she wasn't about to give him the satisfaction of admitting it. Taking an aggressive stance, her chin jutting forward and her hands on her hips, she hissed, 'An' who are you when you're at home, may I ask?'

'Yes, you may ask.' Art's voice was calm, unconcerned. The woman was spoiling for a fight but he'd met her type before and she didn't intimidate him in the slightest. 'Art Franklin's the name, Mrs . . . ?'

'Well, Mr Art Franklin, this is between me an' my granddaughter, all right?' Swinging round to Bonnie, she said, 'And you, disappearing in the middle of the night with every penny I had, you're nothing but a common little thief. What would all your fine friends say if they knew the truth, eh? About how you got started? Stealing from your own flesh and blood?'

Any fear that Bonnie might have felt was swept aside by the evident pleasure, if not joy, that was written on her grandmother's face. She was an evil woman, she always had been – bitter, twisted, and filled with a malevolence that tainted the very air around her. Art still held her arm, and now she extricated herself from his grasp, walking forward a step as she said, 'I stole nothing from you. I took only what was rightfully mine and you know it.'

'Do you hear her?' Margarita appealed to Franco who still hadn't said a word and looked as though he wished himself anywhere but here. 'Can you believe the nerve of her? Running off with the contents of my cashbox and not a shred of shame. Brazen, she is. But that's what comes from mixing pure blood with the scum of the streets.'

'If you're referring to my father there was never a finer man than him and I'm proud to have his blood running through my veins. But if we're talking scum, what about what you've lived with for years? You know what he is. I see, now I'm grown up, that you've always known but you chose to turn a blind eye or put up with it, both probably, whereas my father never looked at another woman once he had met my mother. This pure-blood idea that you used as a weapon to try and make me feel inferior when I was a child is rubbish. My father knew that and so do I. As for you –' she took another step forward and Margarita was forced to take a step backwards

– 'you're as dirty and filthy-minded as him. You're two of a kind.'

'Don't you dare talk to me like that. And you needn't think carrying on like this will stop me claiming what's mine. I'll go to the law when I leave here, you just wait, and then this fine life you're living will be over. Mud sticks, madam. Remember that. Mud sticks.'

'Do that, go to the police, I want you to.' And as Art said, 'Bonnie,' she looked at him as she repeated, 'I want her to.' Her eyes on the furious face of her grandmother once more, Bonnie's voice had lost its shrill tone and was weighted with intent when she said, 'I shall tell them how you took the money from my da's wagon and horse and all my earnings over the years and barely gave me enough to eat, how you used to hit me for the slightest thing and make my life a living hell. It was because of you my da felt he had to get enough money to leave the fair; you drove him to it with your spite and venom and his blood is on your head, you wicked old woman, you.'

'Are you going to let her talk to me like that?' Margarita's face was scarlet with rage as she glared at Franco. 'Say something.' And when he just shook his head and said in a pleading voice, 'Madge, leave it, let's go,' Margarita looked as though she was going to explode with rage. A sound came from her throat like the snarl of a dog and sheer hatred coated every word as she ground out, 'You, all wind and water as usual. I might have known I couldn't expect any help from you. Useless you are, good to neither man nor beast. But you'll do as you're told over this, by all that's holy you will. You'll back me for once in your life.'

Bonnie was conscious of thinking that something fundamental had happened between her grandmother and Franco in the years since she'd last seen them. The balance of power had changed. Before she left the fair it had always been Franco who had the last word, who was the master in their relationship. But not now. This was on the perimeter of her mind as she said, 'Let him do that, yes, let him do that. And I shall tell my side of the story there too. Have you ever wondered what made me leave that night, *have you*? Or perhaps you didn't want to think about it too much because I know you'd seen the way he used to look at me, like he'd looked at Nelly and others. I was barely fifteen, a child still, but it made no difference to him.'

She heard an intake of breath from Art standing slightly behind her and the look on his face must have been enough to alarm Franco because he sprang across the room with an agility that belied his bulk, taking them all by surprise, and was out of the door before anyone could stop him. As Art went to follow, Bonnie caught hold of his arm. 'No, let him go, he's not worth it. Please, Art.' And as he tried to shake her off, she said again, her voice breaking, 'Please, Art.'

Margarita's gaze snaked back and forth between them for a moment, but she clearly had a mind for her safety when she took in Art's murderous expression. She edged past them but once on the landing couldn't resist her parting shot. 'I'll have my day with you, girl. You see if I don't. You'll get what's coming to you as God is my witness.'

As Art made a movement towards her, Bonnie still clinging onto his arm, Margarita disappeared down the stairs after her errant husband, leaving a faint lavender smell behind her.

'She's gone, Bonnie. They both have.'

The numbness had long since evaporated and now Bonnie's legs gave way. Art caught her and supported her weight while he half-carried her across the room to where the tables and chairs were, pulling a chair out and sitting her down on it. The tears were oozing from her eyes now that reaction had set in and she was trembling uncontrollably.

'Sit here, don't move.'

As she nodded her compliance to the order, Art was out of the room like a shot, returning quicker than she would have thought possible with a glass of brandy in one hand.

'Drink it down, all of it,' he said, holding it to her lips.

Again she obeyed without protest, gasping and choking as the neat liquor hit the back of her throat.

'All of it,' he encouraged, keeping the glass to her mouth until it was empty. 'That's it, good girl. You're all right.'

And the brandy helped, burning a fire down into her innards and clearing the faintness that had threatened to take her over. She sat with her hands to her face, and as the shaking and tears eased, a sense of shame and embarrassment crept over her. What must Art be thinking? She wanted the ground to open and swallow her. And her grandmother, she was so vile. And Franco . . . She shuddered, nausea rising in her throat before she willed it away.

He must have noticed her shiver because the next moment he had put his coat over her shoulders, crouching down beside her as he said softly, 'You're all right, don't worry. Just breathe deeply and take your time. You're in shock but you're safe. Bruce is bringing up some coffee in a few minutes.'

She couldn't look at him or speak, and it wasn't until Bruce had been and gone that she nerved herself to straighten in the chair and meet his gaze. And that was nearly her undoing. She had prepared herself for distaste and disgust, for impassivity or coldness, but not for the softness in his face that made him look like someone else entirely. And his voice reflected the same emotion when he murmured, 'Feeling better? Here, drink some coffee or you'll be tipsy after all that brandy.'

Bonnie did feel light-headed and she wasn't sure if it was the brandy or the scene she'd just endured. She took a deep breath before she whispered, 'What must you think of me?'

For a moment Art was tempted to tell her but now was not the time. She didn't need a declaration of undying love, he thought wryly. That would put the tin lid on her precarious self-control. Gently, he said, 'The same as I have always done, that you are one amazing lady. There's two spoonfuls of sugar in this coffee for shock, so get it down you.'

'That – that was my grandmother and her husband. He – he isn't my natural grandfather, he's her second husband.'

'Bonnie, drink the coffee. You don't have to tell me anything unless you want to, all right?' Much as he had wanted to get hold of the man who was apparently Bonnie's step-grandfather, Art acknowledged to himself now that it was probably just as well she had prevented it. If he'd got it right and the dirty swine had done what he suspected, from what Bonnie had said, then he would have wanted to hurt him – badly. And a charge of grievous bodily harm or even murder and the ensuing publicity that would have inevitably embroiled Bonnie too was not what she needed. Not what either of them needed.

Bonnie took a sip of the coffee and he saw that her hand was still shaking. No, he reiterated grimly. It was definitely as well he hadn't got hold of the man.

'I – I want to tell you,' she said after a moment, putting down the coffee cup. 'I want to explain. My grandmother won't let this drop, not now she's found me. She'll want her pound of flesh, and it's important you understand the truth.' Even as she spoke she wondered why it was *so* important Art understood. Of course he was her boss, and if the papers got hold of it and she was cast in a bad light it would reflect on Art and the band, but it was more than that.

Clearing her mind of everything but the story she needed to tell, she said slowly, 'It started when my father went missing. No, even before that, I suppose. I knew my grandmother hated my father from when I can first remember. My mother was her only child and she, my grandmother, was possessive of her to the point of obsession . . .'

Art didn't interrupt as Bonnie's story unfolded. It was clear she was keeping nothing back which he was glad about in one way. He'd spent many a sleepless night wondering about her background and feeling frustrated about the mystery surrounding her, but when she reached the night she had left the fair and the reason for it, his hands bunched into fists and he bitterly regretted not beating Franco into a pulp when he had the chance.

Bonnie didn't look at him the whole time she spoke, her gaze concentrated on her hands clasped together in her lap, but her voice didn't falter and he was amazed at her strength. He had known she was remarkable, but not *how* remarkable, he told himself wretchedly, wishing he could take her into his arms and tell her how much he loved her, that she was his sun, moon and stars, that he adored her, worshipped her. But of course that was further away than ever now he knew the reason she shied away from any physical contact with the male sex.

It was five minutes before she came to the end of her story and she had told him everything – about her struggles when she had first come to the capital; Enoch and Gladys's parental love that had been balm to her soul; her doubts and fears that she was as good a singer as everyone said; even the fact that her reason for continuing to stay at Fairview was because the people there provided the family unit she craved. The only part of her past she kept to herself was the role Franco had played in Nelly's life and the fact that he was Thomas's father; it wasn't her story to tell and would have felt like a betrayal of her friend.

The room was very quiet when she finished speaking. She raised her head to look at Art and his eyes were waiting for her. 'Are you very shocked?'

'If you mean, do I want to kill that so-an'-so with my bare hands, then yes. Am I in awe of your bravery and strength, then yes again. And let me make one thing plain before anything blows up with your grandmother – we fight her together, all right? You're not alone, Bonnie. You have friends, good friends, and I hope you count me among that number? Good. I can't change the past for you but I can sure as hell see to it that the future is different. My protection is there for you, always. Whatever the circumstances, whatever the situation, Art Franklin is on your side.'

He wanted to say so much more but forced himself to smile, and his reward was when she smiled weakly in return. 'Thank you.' It was a whisper. 'I've never told anyone about – about him before.'

'Then I'm honoured you trust me enough.' Even

though her revelation was going to cause him agony of mind when he thought about what she had gone through. 'Are –' this was difficult for him to say and he felt as though his guts were being ripped out at the thought – 'are you still frightened of him?'

'I have been. For years, ever since I ran away, I have been. But not now, no.' She had looked at Franco today and seen a somewhat pathetic figure, she thought with some amazement. He had aged considerably and was losing his hair, and the muscled body he had always been so proud of was turning to fat. He still made her flesh creep, but then maybe that was inevitable. But frightened of him, no. A weight somewhere had lifted, and she voiced this, saying, 'For five years he's been there at the back of my mind, a threat, haunting me, I suppose, but seeing him today, that's changed.'

'Five years . . .'

Art was staring at her oddly, and she said, 'What?'

'It's just occurred to me you're not twenty-three after all. You're three years younger.' And that made him even older than her, twelve years older to be exact. Funny but nine years older hadn't seemed so bad.

Bonnie was staring at him with some concern. 'Is that a problem? It's not like anyone else needs to know, is it?'

'No, no, of course not.' Pull yourself together, man. Twelve years, nine years, it made no odds. He had no chance with her anyway. He handed her the coffee cup she'd put down half full. 'Drink up. I'd better be getting you home or that landlady of yours will have my guts for garters, especially if you walk in with the smell of brandy on your breath.'

In spite of herself Bonnie had to smile. Hilda was a thorn in Art's flesh on several counts. She still avoided picking up the telephone for as long as she could, hoping it would simply stop ringing, and when she did answer it she bellowed down the line with enough force, so Art complained, to burst his eardrums. She liked Bonnie home as soon as the clubs closed, and worried so much if Bonnie drove herself once it was dark that Bonnie had felt duty bound to avoid doing so as much as possible. But perhaps the greatest nail in her landlady's coffin, as far as Art was concerned, was Hilda's absolute distrust of any males within the world of show business, and musicians in particular. She had made her feelings very plain about this the first time Art had called at the house, and in the two years since had not mellowed an iota.

'She makes me feel like one of those dastardly moustachioed villians of the silent films,' Art had said recently, having delivered Bonnie home in the early hours after a band member's birthday party. Hilda had still been up. She had flung open the front door before Bonnie could even get her key in the lock, glowering at Art as she had said a curt, 'Goodnight, Mr Franklin,' and promptly shut the door in his face.

Bonnie had giggled as he'd continued. 'You know the sort, the ones who tie helpless females to the railway lines as the train is approaching. I mean, you're a grown woman, for goodness' sake, and she's not even your mother.'

'It's nothing personal,' Bonnie had tried to assure him. 'She'd be the same with any man. She cares about me, that's all, bless her.'

'I'd like to "bless her",' Art had grumbled, but said no more on the subject that day. In truth he was torn. He would have liked Bonnie to have her own place, with Hilda out of the picture, but on the other hand he knew that the older woman's concern for Bonnie was genuine and at least her protectiveness kept the other wolves away. It would be a brave man indeed who knowingly incurred Hilda's wrath.

They left the function room a few minutes later and outwardly Bonnie was composed, but once in the darkness of the street she had to will herself not to glance around. Art must have guessed how she felt anyway, because his voice held the soft note again when he said, 'They've gone, Bonnie, I promise.'

For now at least, he added silently to himself. But that vicious old crone would be back, as sure as eggs were eggs, with her degenerate sicko of a husband in tow, no doubt. Hell, what a pair. The grandmother had been after money, no doubt about that, and from what she'd said she would be quite happy to blackmail Bonnie into paying her if she could. Whether the woman would actually go to the police in view of what Bonnie had said, he wasn't sure. In one way it didn't matter, because he was damned if he was going to stand by and let that pair have any presence in Bonnie's life. He hadn't had umpteen years on the nightclub scene without coming face to face with the darker side of London life, and he counted more than one gangster among his friends. Speak as you find, he'd always determined, and what a man did when he left his nightclub was none of his business. But these people could put the fear of God into worse than Bonnie's grandmother and the sleazeball she'd married, and he knew they'd be willing to help him. You didn't argue with the people he'd got in mind, not unless you wanted to end up in the Thames with your feet tied to a block of concrete. Come to think of it, he hoped the husband *did* argue . . .

His car was still parked outside the Palace and as they walked he took her arm again, tucking it in his, and feeling as giddy as a schoolboy when she seemed content to leave it there. It was nothing, the action of a friend, that was all, but it was more than he had felt able to attempt before and, as such, meant the world.

Damn it, Art, he thought ruefully as he walked with Bonnie beside him, you've got it bad . . .

Chapter Sixteen

'Don't lie to me, Franco.'

Margarita hadn't known which way Franco had turned when she emerged from the pub, but she had taken a guess and gone right, running as fast as her arthritic knees permitted. It hadn't been long before she had seen him in the distance, walking with the slightly hunched-over stance he had these days since the accident. He'd crawled under a cart to mend the wheel and the whole thing had collapsed on him, trapping him by the lower torso and top of his legs and crushing bones in the process. He was in constant pain, she knew that, and sometimes she awoke in the night to hear him snivelling beside her, but she felt not the slightest shred of pity.

She had caught up with him at the end of a row of shops, dark and deserted at this time of night, pulling him into an empty doorway so violently she'd almost caused him to stumble and fall.

Now she said again, her eyes slits and her voice venomous, 'Don't lie to me. You had her, didn't you, same as that floozie Nelly and countless others. Sweet-talking them out of their drawers and having your fun, you filthy dirty so-an'-so. I should have castrated you years ago, cut it off when you were asleep and thrown it in the muck where it belongs. But you've had your come-uppance an' not before time. The great lover unable to get it up and peeing himself like a bairn.' After the accident Franco had seen more than one doctor but none of them had been able to help him.

'Shut up.'

'Shut up,' she mimicked. 'Is that all you can say? You're pathetic, you know that, don't you? Not a man any more, not anything. You sit around all day, blubbering and carrying on. You disgust me. But you're going to back me in this, Franco. You owe me that. She's earning a fortune – she must be, what with being on the television and all – and how would it look to her adoring public if it came out that she had cast off her poor old starving grandma without a penny to her name? Not only that, but she'd stolen from her to get started. No, whatever else she is, Bonnie's not daft, and neither is that fancy man she's got with her. They'll stomp up plenty for us to keep quiet, you mark my words.'

Franco looked at the woman in front of him and such was his expression that he could have been surveying something putrid. He had disliked her almost as soon as they had been wed, and over the years dislike had turned to loathing and loathing to a deep, dark hatred, but it had been since the accident that he had thought about killing her, his wife. *Wife*. A bolt of revulsion shot through him. He had thrown his life away the day she had trapped him into marriage, he'd known that soon enough, but since the accident he had realized he was living with something that was pure evil. How else could you explain the glee, the sheer pleasure she took in his misfortune? The first time he had wet himself she had stood and laughed, and then verbally stripped him of anything that remained of his manhood.

'You might find you've taken on more than you can chew with Art Franklin.'

'Oh, I expected you to take that tack, that don't surprise me. But like I said, you'll back me in this. Since your accident it's been me that puts food on the table, remember that. If it wasn't for the bit I get on my stall we'd starve. And there's that little madam, dressed up to the nines and rolling in money. I'd given up thinking we'd find where she'd scarpered to, and who would have thought it'd be the other end of the country? But though the mills of God might grind slowly, they grind exceedingly fair.'

She was always doing that, quoting bits of the Bible to suit herself, though he had never met a less religious woman than Madge. But then they said the Devil knew the Bible inside out and could use it better than any parson when it suited, so perhaps it wasn't surprising. If ever the Devil had an advocate on earth, it was Madge.

Margarita had paused, waiting for a response, and when none was forthcoming she stepped closer so he could smell her sour breath as she said, 'I'll make her squirm, you see if I don't. She won't get the better of me. I just thank the good Lord she was brazen enough to go on the television and my cousin saw her.'

A branch of the Spanish part of the family had worked a fair in the south for as long as Margarita's had in the north, but in the last few years the fair had been struggling and they had taken the decision to close. The cousin's husband had always been a shrewd customer and having seen the way the wind was blowing, had made arrangements in advance for his family's well-being. As they'd had winter quarters in London most of their lives and the fair had moved round the southern end of the country in the summertime, they'd already had a small two-up, two-down terraced house in the East End, and during the winter they'd just about got by living on their summer takings and earning a few bob here and there with manual work. For two or three years before the fair had disbanded, the cousin's husband, along with his three grown-up sons, had worked at the docks in the winter, getting friendly with one or two of the gaffers who had a sideline in 'acquiring' stuff that regularly fell off the backs of lorries, or in this case, ships. By the time the fair had actually folded, the four men were well in with the people who mattered. So much so that the cousin's husband had been able to move his family to a comfortable semi-detached house in the suburbs complete with an indoor bathroom and modern fitted kitchen, and provide his wife with luxuries like a refrigerator in the kitchen and a television set in the sitting room.

This must have been on Margarita's mind, for now she said, 'There's Maria, in a house fit for a princess and never really done a hard day's work in her life, not like me. Even when the fair was going, her Juan never expected her to do anything but cook and clean and look after their bairns. Well, I want a nice place – I don't intend to end my days trying to scratch in the dirt like a chicken and living hand to mouth. Our fair's going the same way as Maria's and it won't get better, not with all this talk of war with the Germans. And I'll wait for ever for you to do anything. I learned a long time ago that if I want something doing I have to do it meself. Useless as a sack of spuds, you are, and you can't even do the job of keeping me warm in bed no more.'

Always she came back to that, goading him, sticking the knife in. Franco ground his teeth. 'What are you going to do?'

'What am I going to do? Go back to Maria's and have a couple of drinks, and let the wonderful Bonnie May stew for a day or two. Bonnie May! Stupid name. And her and her fancy man are stupid too if they think I'll let this drop. You, an' all. I'm not frightened of Art Franklin even if you are.'

'I didn't say I was frightened of him.'

'No, but you are, aren't you? When that cart took care of your wedding tackle it took the last of your gumption an' all. Scared to death back there you were, shaking in your boots. You wait till I tell Maria and Juan what a useless so-an'-so you were. Never so much as opened your mouth. Come on.'

Margarita turned and stepped out of the doorway, pulling her black felt hat more firmly on her head as an icy gust of wind blew along the street. She began walking and didn't bother to look back and see if Franco was following. She knew he would be. He did as he was told these days.

They had caught a bus that dropped them in Alexandra Park Road, so now, as they reached a main thoroughfare and Margarita stepped onto the kerb and hailed a taxi, she was aware of Franco's look of surprise. 'We're going to come into money,' she said shortly. 'This is the way I intend to go on from now.'

He made no reply to this and neither of them spoke on the way to Maria's house in Enfield. Maria was waiting up for them but Juan had gone to bed. Franco had the feeling that Juan liked Margarita as little as he did. He left the two women jabbering away over a couple of bottles of stout and went upstairs to the spare room that he and Margarita were sleeping in. As he sat down on his side of the bed he was aware of the canvas tarpaulin under the sheet. Margarita had taken fiendish pleasure in telling Maria and Juan why it was needed after they had first arrived at the house, while he had inwardly writhed with humiliation and shame.

He got undressed slowly. He did everything slowly these days, the pain that was with him day and night particularly acute after the walking he had done that day. After a while he heard Maria come upstairs and use the bathroom before walking along the landing past their room to the one at the front of the house that she and Juan shared. He knew what Margarita was up to downstairs. No doubt she'd made some excuse to Maria about needing to sit a while before she came to bed, but she would have made sure Maria poured her another stout before her cousin had left her. She had said earlier that the money she earned fed them, but most of it went on drink these days. He used to drink his fair share before the accident, it was true; being three sheets to the wind had helped him endure sharing a bed with Madge if nothing else. He remembered the first night he'd returned home from the hospital when she'd sat supping and he'd asked her to pour him a beer. She had stared at him with disdain and told him that when he was earning again he could have luxuries like that, but not until then. They had both known he'd never work again. Since then he had begged her once or twice, when the pain was nigh unbearable, telling her he needed something to dull the agony that his pills weren't touching, but he'd quickly come to understand that not only did his pleading do no good but she actually enjoyed it.

He slid down under the blankets and thick eiderdown and lay waiting for her. He knew exactly what she would do. In the four days since they had been here each night was the same. She would drink Maria's stout – only that day he had heard Juan mutter to his wife about hiding the bottles from the kitchen cupboard so he was clearly sick of Madge taking liberties – and then come upstairs to the bedroom, whereupon she would get undressed and put her dressing gown on to go to the bathroom for a bath. She'd been pea-green with envy about Maria's bathroom, using copious amounts of her cousin's lavender bath salts each night and staying in the bath until the water was all but cold. Juan wasn't overjoyed about this either, making pointed remarks at breakfast each morning about the lack of hot water in the tank. Not that Madge took any notice.

Sure enough, a little while later the bedroom door opened and Margarita came in. Wafts of stout-laden breath and the creaking of the bed told him she was getting undressed. He feigned sleep and waited until she had walked along to the bathroom before he sat up, wincing at the gnawing pain in his lower torso as he listened to the sound of the bath being run. Once it stopped, he gave her another five minutes before sliding out of bed. He knew precisely what he was going to do. This had been brewing for weeks, months, years, but it was seeing Bonnie again that told him the time was right. He wasn't going to let Madge spoil the new life Bonnie had made for herself, and she would. Oh yes, he knew his wife well enough to realize that even if Bonnie gave her all the money she had and kept paying, eventually Madge would find a way to bring her granddaughter down. It was unnatural the way Madge had always been with her; even when Bonnie was a babe in arms, his wife had appeared to dislike her, and once John had gone she had made that child suffer. But then so had he.

Franco shut his eyes tightly for a moment, shaking his head. He still didn't know what had come over him that night when he had taken her so brutally, but it had been the cause of him drinking more and more heavily in the years since. When he had woken up the next morning and she'd been gone, the guilt had made him feel for a time as though he was going mad. He had never forced a woman in his life, he'd never had to. Even the ones he'd had to wait for, like Nelly. He wasn't a bad man, or he hadn't thought he was.

It took him a few moments to straighten up and it felt as though little red-hot pokers were piercing his innards. He walked soundlessly across the room, his bare feet making no sound on the carpet either in the bedroom or on the landing outside. That was another thing that had caused Madge to writhe in envy, the fact that Maria had fitted carpets all over the house, even in her kitchen. It didn't matter that Juan was in effect a villian and counted members of London's criminal underworld among his friends – Maria had a home to be proud of and that was that.

The bathroom door was shut, the signal that someone was inside as there was no bolt on the door. As he opened it he said softly, 'It's me, Madge, I need the lavatory,' because the last thing he wanted her to do was to call out.

'Oh, for goodness' sake! Can't I have two minutes to meself? That's not too much to ask, is it?'

He shut the door carefully and walked across to the lavatory, but instead of raising the seat he drew the lid down and sat on it as he said, 'We need to talk.'

She stared at him, clearly taken aback. She had slid further down in the bath as he had entered and put the flannel across her breasts, for all the world like a shy young bride, but there was nothing virginal about Madge, he thought. She had been over forty when he had married her and certainly her first husband had had the best of her. Now, at sixty-five, she looked ten years older in her face at least, but that was what bitterness and hatred could do. He'd often mused that it was acid running through her veins rather than blood.

She recovered almost immediately, her voice waspish as she said, 'Talk? What would I want to talk to you for? I'm not about to change my mind about Bonnie if that's what you're after.'

'That's as may be, but nevertheless, we *will* talk.'

Margarita's eyes narrowed. He was acting different, more like the old Franco who played the big man. Well, she wasn't having that. She'd got him where she wanted him since the accident and she didn't intend to go back to the way things had been before. Her lip curling, she mimicked, '"Nevertheless, we *will* talk." Hark at you. Pity you didn't show a bit more gumption earlier, that's all I can say.'

'There's all kinds of evil in the world. Did you know

that, Madge? Oh yes, all kinds. There's the power sort, like this bloke Hitler and his Nazis, and then there's folk who just enjoy seeing others in pain, get pleasure from it, you know? And yet again them that twist the truth and gossip and scheme to bring people down so they feel bigger. I could go on. But evil stems from one source when you narrow it down, no matter how it manifests, and that's a black heart.'

'You gone barmy or something?'

He carried on in the same quiet, conversational voice as though she hadn't spoken. 'And your heart is black, Madge. Black as sin, stinking and fetid and rotten. I should have left you years ago, once I realized what you are, but you're clever, I give you that. You got a ring on your finger before you showed your true colours. You robbed me of what I thought I was going to have – a proper marriage, bairns – and you've gone on robbing me.'

'Oh, give it a rest, you spineless beggar. Feeling sorry for yourself, are you?'

'A bit. Aye, a bit. But if truth be told I feel more sorry for Bonnie and I tell you now, you're not going to bleed her like you've bled me through the years.'

There was a swoosh of water as Margarita reacted to the name as though she had been prodded with a sharp blade. 'I'll do what I want as regards that one and you can't stop me.' She glared at him, her dark eyes deadly. 'And if you don't want any of the money, that suits me down to the ground.'

'No, it's not money I want, Madge.'

He got up. For a moment she thought he was leaving, and by the time she realized his intention it was too late.

It was an uneven struggle from the start. She was scrawny and thin and Franco weighed twice as much, his powerful shoulders and thick arms holding her under the water without too much trouble. It was over quicker than he had envisaged; in fact, he continued to press the body down for a good thirty seconds after she appeared dead, expecting her to rear up or thrash about if he let her go.

When he straightened, he stood for a minute more looking down at the figure in the water. Her face had been contorted, her eyes wide and desperate as she had died, but now it was smoothed out, a few tendrils of hair from the bun she wore on the top of her head floating lazily as the water became still.

He left the bathroom as quietly as he had entered it, but once on the landing he paused. How many bottles of stout had Madge consumed? If this could look like an accident because she'd gone to sleep whilst drunk and incapable, all the better. He didn't care about himself, his life wasn't worth living anyway, but if the police caught on to the fact that Madge had been murdered the resulting publicity would be bound to embroil Bonnie sooner or later.

As he walked down the stairs he was aware of not feeling a shred of guilt or remorse about what he had done, and he wondered if that was normal. But then murdering your wife wasn't normal, was it? He smiled a small smile. In the past when Madge had been particularly obnoxious and he had imagined doing away with her, he had always thought it would give him pleasure, or if not pleasure, then satisfaction. But he had felt nothing as he had drowned her and he still felt nothing. It was a job that had had to be done, that was all.

Once in the sitting room, he saw that Madge must have cleared up after her, and sure enough he found a glass in the sink and five empty stout bottles in the kitchen bin. Of course, one or even two of those could be Maria's. He stood for a moment, contemplating, before opening the cupboard that held Maria and Juan's stock of alcohol. Juan drank whisky, but alongside a couple of bottles of fine malt stood a dozen or more bottles of stout.

The first one tasted like the nectar of the gods. He had thought about merely tipping them down the sink but then why waste good stout? And if ever he had needed a drink it was tonight. His insides were giving him gyp.

The second bottle tasted just as good, and by the fifth Franco was aware of feeling a trifle light-headed. Of course it had been a long time since he'd had a drink, he told himself. Madge had seen to that. But the pain felt better for it. He might even be able to get a good night's sleep.

He put the empty bottles in the bin with the others before retracing his steps to the bedroom, and once in bed, settled himself comfortably under the covers. He'd done what he could to cover his tracks but the law had a way of sniffing out subterfuge and he'd never been a good liar. He had no idea what the morning would bring but for now he was warm and relaxed, the pain dulled to the point where he barely noticed it. It was enough. He was at peace.

Chapter Seventeen

Maria's screams the next morning brought Franco out of the best night's sleep he'd had since the accident, and for a moment his mind was so befuddled he couldn't remember where he was – instead of the confines of the bed under the wagon's roof he was in a large room. Then the events of the night before flooded in. He struggled out of bed – lying still in one position all night had made him even stiffer than normal – and without bothering to pull his dressing gown over his pyjamas, and bent almost double, he walked across the room and flung open the door. Juan had come running from his room and they almost collided on the landing.

Maria was standing in the bathroom doorway with her back to them, still screaming, and it was Juan who shouted, 'What the hell?' as he reached his wife, swinging her round and bundling her along the landing. 'Stay there.' As Franco joined him, they both stared at the body in the bath. Juan swore, loud and long, before gingerly feeling the water. 'It's stone cold.' He looked at Franco. 'Has she been here all night?'

'She must have been. I heard her come upstairs at some point after Maria and then go into the bathroom but I must have fallen asleep.'

'Looks like she did an' all,' Juan said grimly.

Maria's voice came from behind them, choked with tears. 'Is – is she . . .'

'As a dodo.' Juan raked back his hair. 'Damn it, I don't need this. I don't want the law sniffing about.' Turning to his wife, he growled, 'I told you to move them bottles of stout, didn't I, but no, you said. Looks inhospitable, you said. How many did she guzzle to get in such a state that this happened? What did she have before you came up?'

Through fresh sobs, Maria gasped, 'Two, same as me. An' I – I gave her another one as I came up. She said – she said she wanted to sit a while.'

'I bet she did.' Juan was livid. 'Go down and check the bottles. See if she helped herself once you were out of the way.' Her face streaming with tears, Maria disappeared down the stairs, and as she did so, Juan repeated, 'I don't need this. I'm sorry, Franco, but I really don't need this. I've got a couple of . . . delicate deals on the go at the moment, and the coppers with their hobnailed boots all over the place might put the wind up certain people. Know what I mean? I don't want to appear insensitive but she's gone, hasn't she? We can't do anything for her.'

He waited for a reaction and Franco obliged. 'You're

saying what, exactly?' he murmured, trying to hide his elation. Never in his wildest dreams . . .

'I'm saying that what is done is done. Bringing in the coppers won't help her and certainly won't help me. You're her next of kin and it's not as if she's got any kids or anything, is it. I know there's the granddaughter but she'd fallen out with her.'

Maria had returned, stopping halfway up the stairs as she said, 'There's another few bottles been drunk as well as what she had when I was with her.'

'Why did you leave her down there? You know what she's like.'

'It's not my fault.' Maria's face crumpled at her husband's rebuke. 'How did I know she was going to drink so much? She hasn't before.'

'Yes, well, it only takes once, doesn't it, as we know now. Damn it, Maria, I told you not to write and tell her when you saw her granddaughter on the television. Let sleeping dogs lie, I said. Don't interfere. But no, you wouldn't be told and now look.'

'It's not Maria's fault, Juan.' As Maria plumped down on one of the treads and began to sob again, Franco felt compelled to speak up on her behalf. 'Let's face it, Madge was old enough to know what she was doing.'

'Maybe, maybe.' Juan looked at his wife and his voice was softer when he said, 'Go down and make us all a cup of tea and put a drop of whisky in it. We need something to steady our nerves. Hell, what a mess.' He took a few cautious steps into the bathroom, pulled the plug to let the water out and then shot back to Franco as though he was afraid the body was going to sit up and object. 'Come on,' he said, pushing Franco fully onto the landing and shutting the bathroom door. 'Let's go and have a cup of tea and decide what to do.'

Maria was sniffing and dabbing her eyes as they sat down at the kitchen table, and no one spoke until they had taken a sip of the hot tea liberally laced with whisky. Then Maria turned to Franco, her voice trembling as she said, 'I'm so sorry, I had no idea she would drink so much, else I wouldn't have left her down here.'

Again Franco said, 'It's not your fault. Really, Maria, it isn't. She's . . . she's had a growing problem with the drink but none of us could have foreseen this. And you know as well as I do that you can't tell Madge what to do. If she wanted a bath last night, she would have had it come hell or high water, regardless of how drunk she was. And an accident is an accident. It's no one's fault.'

'Thank you.' Maria's eyes filled up again. 'She *was* very determined, wasn't she?'

Juan had obviously been feeling bad about his previous attitude to his wife because now he said, 'Of course it's not your fault, love. No one's saying that. But this couldn't have come at a worse time for me.' He hesitated. 'How do you feel about not reporting this, Franco? I mean, she's gone. Nothing can bring her back, can it?'

Franco took a big gulp of tea, relishing the taste of the whisky. 'No, nothing can bring her back.'

Maria looked at her husband. 'But – but there's the

body. We can't leave her up there.' She shivered. 'And what is Franco going to say to people about her dying? He can't just go home without her, can he? What are folk going to say?'

'I dunno, let me think.' He passed Maria his empty cup. 'Pour me another and no whisky this time. I need a clear head and you must have used half a bottle between the three of us.'

Maria poured Franco another cup too, and when she gestured at the whisky bottle, he nodded. He couldn't have described to anyone what he was feeling this morning but he was sure it wasn't how you were supposed to feel if you'd murdered your wife. Serenity was totally out of place in this scenario surely? He took the cup from Maria with a nod of thanks, noticing that she added a good dollop of whisky to her cup again too. Poor Maria.

It was a few minutes later and no one had spoken when Juan moved his chair back a little, stretching his legs as he said, 'I know how this could be resolved with the least amount of bother but it depends on you, Franco. You're her husband after all and I can't force you to do what I'm suggesting.'

'Which is?'

Juan didn't answer this immediately. What he did say was, 'Like I said before, having the coppers involved could prove awkward for me. Some of my business associates would be unhappy if I brought attention to myself in that way.'

'I understand.'

'And it's not our way, is it? The travellers' way, I mean. We sort out our own problems.'

Franco didn't think it beneficial to point out that Juan was no longer part of that life, merely nodding in response.

'Margarita's death is tragic and I'm sorry for your loss but nothing we do or don't do now can bring her back. We're travellers –' again Franco noted how Juan was labouring the point – 'and the rules that most of them out there live by don't apply to us. Now, I know that ideally you'd want a proper funeral for her but just listen to me for a minute, all right? See what you think.'

Again Franco nodded. He had gone to sleep wondering if his next night would be spent in a police cell – anything was better than that.

'What I'm proposing is this. I know a few people –' Franco just bet Juan did – 'and a certain associate of mine has a contact who works in a crematorium not too many miles from here. Probably better you don't know which one in view of what I'm going to suggest. I know this person has done the odd favour or two for my colleague for the right price and he can keep his mouth shut. If I have a word with my man and explain our current predicament, I'm sure he could arrange for the bo– for Margarita to be collected and taken there. When the . . . job's done, we can have the ashes back and you'll have something to take home with you to the others. Of course it won't be entirely her ashes – she'd have to go in with a bona-fide cremation, in the same coffin, I mean. But –' he paused as Maria gave a strangled sob – 'it'd be the best we could do in the circumstances. And she would be treated with respect, don't worry about that.'

Franco wondered how dumping Margarita's body on top of another corpse and burning her without so much as a by-your-leave could be termed as treating her with respect, but he wasn't about to argue.

'Once you get back up north, the story'll be that she died suddenly – a heart attack or something – which is partly true, and as you were staying with family and it's a long way from the north-east, it was decided by all of us the best thing to do was to have a cremation here, so you could take her home and have a wake when you scatter her ashes with friends and family in the north. I'll get a death certificate for you to take back that'll look authentic –' another contact, Franco presumed – 'and I'll give you enough readies for a wake that'll keep everyone happy. What do you think?'

Franco thought Juan was a genius. Warning himself that he was supposed to be the grieving husband, he said hesitantly, 'I don't want to put you in a difficult position, Juan. That's the last thing I want but I don't know whether this is right.'

'Look at it this way, Franco. Margarita will still have a send-off once you're back up north and no one there will be any the wiser. She's dead – I hate to be blunt but she is – and does it really matter about the actual funeral? Not to her, does it?'

'If you put it like that, then no, I suppose not.'

'And this way it's best for everyone. Think of all the palaver if the law got involved – there'd be the coroner's inquest for a start and I wouldn't trust any of them blighters as far as I could throw 'em. They trust travellers even less. They'll be poking their noses into this and that and putting words in your mouth. Margarita herself wouldn't want that, now, would she? Of course she wouldn't. Far better we sort this ourselves, like our kind always does. What do you say, eh? Let's keep it in the family, private like.'

'I say do what you think best, Juan. I meant it when I said I don't want to put you in a difficult position. You and Maria had us to stay out of the goodness of your hearts and now it's brought all this trouble on your heads. I feel bad about that. And as you say, nothing can bring her back.'

Juan let out a long slow breath of relief. He liked Franco as much as he had disliked Margarita, and the poor devil must have had a hell of a life at times. Margarita might have been Maria's cousin, and he knew he shouldn't speak ill of the dead, but she'd had a tongue on her, that one. He couldn't have put up with her for two minutes. 'Have another drink, Franco,' he said genially, 'and I'll go and make a couple of calls. We'll all feel better when she's – when it's clear upstairs.'

'What about Bonnie?' Maria said suddenly. 'You saw her yesterday, didn't you? So she knows her grandmother's here in London. Did you say you were staying with us? Does she know where we live? Will she come calling?'

'You were never mentioned. And frankly, the way Madge went for her I wouldn't be surprised if Bonnie never wants to see her again.'

'Margarita told me the girl stole off her and she was going to get the money back with interest.' She poured Franco a third cup of tea as she spoke and added more whisky. 'Won't Bonnie think it strange that Margarita lets it drop?'

Franco worded his reply carefully. 'The thing is, Maria, this stealing business wasn't entirely true. I'm not saying Bonnie didn't run off with a wad of cash, but a good part of it was what Madge was holding for the girl, from the sale of her father's wagon and horse. And to be honest, Bonnie earned more than me an' Madge put together, right from when John went missing. She was a huge draw even then, and Madge took every penny of her earnings. I suppose Bonnie felt she was entitled to the money. Of course, Madge didn't see it that way.'

Juan's voice was very dry when he said, 'No, she wouldn't.'

'But Bonnie made it clear she didn't intend to give Madge anything so I would imagine she'll assume her grandmother has given up if she hears nothing from her.'

There was silence for a moment, and then Juan said, 'I don't like loose ends, Franco. Look, once you're home, write to the girl. I can find out where she's living before you leave. Tell her Margarita's dead. You needn't be specific. If there's such bad feeling between them I doubt she'd want to know anyway. Wish her well or something and that can be the end of it.'

It was exactly what he had intended to do and he had been wondering how to accomplish it. 'I'll do that, Juan.' The whisky had covered the ache in his lower stomach like a warm blanket, and Franco could have sat in Maria's kitchen for ever. It was sleeting outside and the wind was whipping the bare branches of the trees in the garden into a frenzied dance, but inside it was cosy and snug.

As Juan disappeared to make his telephone calls, Maria got up from the table saying something about breakfast and that they all still had to eat, but Franco continued to sit quietly, mulling over in his mind how he would word his letter to Bonnie. He would tell her about Madge of course, he told himself, but he would start by begging her to forgive him for what he had done to her the night she ran away. He would make no excuses. How could he? There were none. But he would tell her that that night and the wrong he'd done her had haunted him ever since and would to his dying day.

He drained his tea, sitting back in his chair again as his thoughts meandered on. And his dying day would be soon. He didn't want to carry on as he was, less than a man and in the sort of pain he wouldn't wish on his worst enemy. A bottle of whisky and a good few of his pills would do the job, but only after he was back home and had written the letter to Bonnie. Tied up the loose ends, as Juan had put it.

He had never imagined he would depart this world without leaving part of himself behind in the form of sons and daughters, but getting hooked up with Madge had killed that dream. That was what he'd hated her for the most. Just one child would have done, a little lad perhaps who would have grown up big and strong, or a daughter he could have loved and spoiled. But he was as barren as any woman who was unable to bear young. All the seed he had expended when he was young and virile, all the women he'd had and nothing to show for it, not really. Nothing that mattered. A useless life.

Juan walked back into the kitchen, sniffing the aroma of the bacon Maria was beginning to fry before he said, 'All done. Someone'll be round later this morning. Maria, why don't you go shopping with Franco once we've eaten? Get yourselves a spot of lunch somewhere before you come back, maybe go to the pictures. The New Victoria cinema's showing a James Cagney film. You'd like that, Franco. And things'll be tidy when you come back.'

Tidy. He was talking about disposing of Madge with as much feeling as you would a piece of rubbish, but then why wouldn't he? He hadn't liked her, no one liked Madge. Even Maria – after her initial shock and tears – was cooking bacon sandwiches and had brightened up at the thought of a shopping trip and lunch out, followed by the cinema.

'Though the mills of God might grind slowly, they grind exceedingly fair.' Madge's quote of the day before came back to him, and now when he nodded it wasn't so much in answer to what Juan had said but to her voice in his mind.

Chapter Eighteen

'Try and relax, Bonnie. We leave for Holland tomorrow, and there's no chance your grandmother and her husband will turn up there. In fact, I'd be surprised if you hear from them again. And if you do, then I'll deal with it.' Art's voice was reassuringly calm, but inwardly he was more than a little frustrated. He had fully expected Margarita Fellario to contact Bonnie within a day or two of their meeting outside Alexandra Palace, but that was a week ago and they hadn't heard a word. He had explained the situation to a couple of the heavies who frequented the nightclub, and they were more than willing to muscle in on his behalf and frighten the living daylights out of the pair, but until Margarita made contact again they had no idea where she was staying. And what really made his blood boil was that he knew Bonnie was looking over her shoulder day and night – she was as jumpy as a cat on a hot tin roof.

Bonnie forced a smile. 'I'm all right, Art. Truly I am.' It didn't sound convincing, even to her, but in truth she was grateful Art was putting her tenseness solely down to the most obvious cause. She *was* jittery about her grandmother and Franco, of course she was – their showing up had brought to the surface horrors she preferred to keep buried – but it was Art himself who was the major problem and she would rather die than let him know it. Her grandmother's sudden appearance and all that had resulted from it, not least her telling Art her life story and his understanding and acceptance, had surprised her into admitting something to herself she had refused to recognize for months now. She was head over heels in love with perhaps the most unsuitable man on the planet; unsuitable for her, that was. She was sure there were many women who could cope with his womanizing and well-documented aversion to remaining faithful for more than five minutes, but she wasn't one of them. Furthermore, and this was the most humiliating part, Art had never, by word or deed, indicated that he was the least bit interested in her in a romantic way.

'If this is you when you're all right, I'd hate to see you when you're not.' He sighed, shaking his head. 'You've hardly touched your food.'

'Oh, I'm sorry.' Bonnie hastily took a bite of the fillet steak on her plate. 'It's lovely, honestly, but I suppose I'm too excited about tomorrow to have much of an appetite.' Art had picked her up early that morning for a meeting with the rest of the band to discuss the final details concerning their trip to Holland, and then insisted he take her to lunch.

'Bonnie, I wasn't born yesterday.'

'Yes, all right, I suppose I am a bit on edge about my grandmother and – and him.' Try as she might, she couldn't prevent hot colour staining her cheekbones. She bitterly regretted confiding in Art about the rape once she'd had time to think about it. She'd waited for years to unburden herself to someone and then it had had to be him – what had she been thinking of? But that was it, she hadn't been thinking. Not really.

'I know.' Art let his hand rest briefly on hers for a moment, but only a moment. He knew she didn't want to talk again about what had happened to her, and he respected that, but the urge to reassure her was strong. 'I promise you they won't get within six foot of you again, I mean that. And you know my word is my bond.'

Bonnie smiled again, more naturally this time. 'Yes, I know that.' And she did. She had come to understand in the last years that show business was a sycophantic world where people gushed and enthused and said what others wanted to hear rather than the truth, but Art wasn't like that.

She ate another mouthful of food although it was an effort. He was a complex man, that was for sure. And a mass of contradictions. But she would trust him with her life. She gave a wry, silent 'Huh!' to herself at the thought. But it was true.

'How about the lemon soufflé for dessert? You liked that the last time we came here.'

She felt a frisson of pleasure that he had remembered,

before she warned herself that that was part of his charm. He would be the same with any woman; it didn't mean anything. Suddenly she had the desire to get back to Fairview and her little room. 'Would you mind terribly if we skipped dessert? I've still got to finish my packing and I've promised Betty and Selina we'll have a girls' night tonight before I leave.'

'Of course.' He held up his hand for the waiter and immediately the man was at his side. It was always like that with Art. As the waiter went off to fetch the bill, Art said pleasantly, 'How are the wedding arrangements coming along?'

Selina's Cyril had finally popped the question and the couple were getting married in the summer. Betty and Bonnie were going to be bridesmaids, something both of them had privately admitted they weren't particularly looking forward to once they'd realized Selina had chosen salmon pink for their dresses, which Hilda was making on her Singer sewing machine. But it was Selina's big day and both would have endured far worse to make her happy, especially because at first it had looked as though the wedding wouldn't happen. When Cyril had proposed, Selina had finally told him about her father's abuse and he had disappeared to goodness knows where for a few days, leaving Selina sure she had lost him for ever. On his return he had told Selina he had needed time to come to terms with it, and although Betty and Bonnie had wanted to strangle him for putting Selina through days of misery, she had welcomed him back with open arms.

Such is the power of love, Bonnie thought, gazing at Art as he paid the bill the waiter had just brought to the table. And she supposed Cyril had been honest about his initial shock and confusion, but Art wouldn't have acted like that in the same circumstances, not if he had loved the woman in question. He was made of sterner stuff. She knew she was just a colleague and friend to him, but look at how wonderful he had been the night she had told him about Franco. But then perhaps that was the point? Art didn't love her and so his reaction hadn't been as extreme because his heart wasn't affected. Men had a thing about being the first with the woman they loved enough to marry; that's what all the romance novels and magazines said, anyway.

As the waiter disappeared, Art said, 'Bonnie?' and she realized he was still waiting for an answer to his question about the wedding, and this was what they talked about as they left the restaurant and walked to Art's car parked a short distance away. Her car was already locked up in a garage she had rented for the next three months while she was away. When she had said the night before that she would catch the Tube to meet up today, Art wouldn't hear of it. The IRA had bombed the Tottenham Court Road and Leicester Square stations a couple of days ago, and he had forbidden her to even think of using the underground.

They chatted about the coming tour on the way back

to Fairview; light, inconsequential talk. Bonnie knew that Art was trying to keep her mind off her grandmother and Franco. What he didn't realize was that being so close to him in the luxurious confines of his car with the faint lemony smell of his aftershave teasing her senses was causing her more of a problem. And that was putting it mildly.

Telling herself she was a grown woman and not a silly schoolgirl in the middle of her first crush on a boy enabled her to say goodbye fairly composedly once they reached Shouldham Street, and she even managed a cool smile as she climbed out of the car.

'Get a good night's sleep,' Art warned her when they were standing on the pavement. He always insisted she remain in the car until he had opened her door for her and helped her out. She knew it was merely evidence of the good manners which were an integral part of him, but it was nevertheless very nice to be treated with such consideration. 'It'll be the last time you sleep in your own bed for a while and you know what some digs are like. Believe me, they're no better abroad than they are here. Worse, in fact.'

'I still can't believe I'm going to sing in Holland. Sometimes I have to pinch myself to make sure this is all real.'

Art smiled, but his voice was serious when he said, 'Start valuing yourself a little more, Bonnie. There are lots of female vocalists out there but only one or two with the quality to their voices that you have. It's something no amount of technique and practice can achieve, believe me. You open your mouth and start to sing and time stands still. You make a man forget his troubles, forget the world can be a dark place – hell, you make him forget his own name . . .'

She stared at him, the husky timbre to his voice and his ebony eyes holding her transfixed as the moment went on and on.

It was her name being called behind her that broke the spell, causing Art to swear under his breath before he raised his voice and said, 'Good afternoon, Mrs Nichols. And what a fetching sight you make framed in the doorway like that.' He had long since given up trying to win Hilda over, and now treated her with a mixture of amused irritation and indulgent sarcasm.

Bonnie giggled. She couldn't help it, even though she knew it would earn her a black mark in Hilda's copybook. Turning, she said over her shoulder to Art, 'I'll see you tomorrow,' and then followed a bristling Hilda into the house. It was only then she noticed Hilda was holding an envelope.

'This came for you shortly after you'd left this morning,' Hilda said, trying – and failing – to hide her curiosity. It was rare for Bonnie to receive mail. Any letters or postcards from the band's fans went to Art's nightclub or the television and radio studios, and Bonnie had been zealous in guarding her privacy since her arrival in London. Very few people were aware of her address. Nelly was an exception, of course, but this wasn't Nelly's elegant, flowing script; it was a large, rather childish scrawl. 'The postmark's the north-east,' Hilda added as Bonnie took the letter from her.

'Thanks.' Bonnie had no intention of opening the envelope in front of Hilda, fond of her as she was. Stuffing it in her pocket, she said, 'I'm going to finish my packing before Selina comes home and Betty gets here.' She had already paid Hilda the three months' rent for her room while she was in Holland.

Bonnie ran lightly up the stairs, but once in her room she stood with her back to the door and pulled the envelope out of her pocket. She stared at it for some moments, her hand trembling, before throwing it on her bed. Then she took off her hat and coat, stoked up the little fire she had left burning in the grate and added more coal to the flickering flames, before retrieving the letter and sitting down in the armchair. Kicking off her shoes, she rested her feet on the small fender which was faintly warm and again she stared at the envelope, turning it over in her fingers.

How long she sat nerving herself to tear it open she wasn't sure, but suddenly she was angry with herself. 'Don't be such a coward,' she said out loud. 'Open the flippin' thing and be done with it.'

The envelope contained one sheet of paper, and as she smoothed it out her eyes went to the signature at the bottom of the page. 'Franco.' For a moment she felt sick, letting it drop into her lap as though touching it contaminated her. Her heart was thudding at twice its normal rate now and she had to take a few deep breaths before she could bear to pick the letter up again. Even then she shut her eyes tightly for a good ten seconds before opening them and beginning to read:

Dear Bonnie,

I know I am the last person you want to hear from. I'm sorry, I'm heart sorry for what I did. Please believe me. I don't know what came over me that night, and if I could go back in time and change things, I would willingly give my life to do so. The fault was mine and mine alone, and I betrayed the trust of the innocent girl you were then in the worst possible way. Perhaps it might make it easier to put the past behind you if you know that by the time you read this letter, I will have ended my life. I'm in constant pain after an accident and don't want to go on any longer. But that is by the by. Your grandmother is dead, Bonnie.

She dropped the letter again, gasping, as the blood thundered in her ears. And then obeying an inner voice that seemed to be working independently of her and was saying, 'Pick it up, read it, read it to the end,' her fingers closed over the sheet of paper once more. Telling herself she couldn't cry yet, that she mustn't fall apart, she read:

She died the night we saw you. She drank too much, she was gloating over how she was going to bleed you dry, but fate had other ideas. The death certificate says

heart attack, but it was her wickedness and cruelty
and spite that did for her in the end. And I'm glad
she's dead because the world's a better place without
her in it. I wanted you to know that she had gone,
Bonnie. That we've both gone by now. That's all really,
except to say that your da would be proud of you,
lass. Forgive me.

    Franco.

And then the tears came.

It was half an hour later when Hilda came to see if
Bonnie wanted a cup of tea and found her red-eyed and
weeping and quite beside herself, the letter still clutched
in her hand.

Hilda led her down to the kitchen and made a strong
brew, spooning in plenty of sugar and standing over her
while she drank it, much as Art had stood over her the
week before. And somehow Bonnie felt it seemed right to
show her the letter and then tell her story again for the
second time.

Hilda said nothing until Bonnie came to the part
about the rape, and then she used a word that shocked
them both, before again becoming silent and letting
Bonnie finish. Hilda's eyes were wet when she put her
arms round the girl she had come to think of as a
daughter, saying, 'I'm glad you've told me, lovey. I always
knew there was something. And I must say, him, that Art

Franklin, has gone up in my estimation a bit for how he handled that pair. Wicked so-an'-sos, both of them.'

Bonnie took a deep breath. She felt better for telling Hilda, and she felt calmer now, as though she had come through a storm that had threatened to overwhelm her.

'I agree with you about my grandmother being wicked,' she said slowly. 'There was nothing good in her, not a thing, but Franco wasn't all bad. When I was a little girl, after my father had gone, he used to protect me from her at times and make sure I had enough to eat, things like that.' She had forgotten that in the intervening years, it had only been that last terrible night she had remembered. 'He could be kind.'

'You're not making excuses for him, are you? He wanted stringing up for what he did.'

'No, I'm not making excuses.' And she wasn't, not really, but the letter had changed something although she wasn't yet quite sure what.

'Good. Cos in my book a man who uses brute strength to get what he wants from a woman, let alone a slip of a girl, is worse than an animal.' And then Hilda's tone changed, becoming soft as she said, 'I'm glad you told me, lovey. And as much as you can, you want to put it behind you now. One day you'll meet someone you can love, and when you do, don't you let the past spoil the present and the future. I know that's easy for me to say but it's right, Bonnie. Some people get stuck in the past and it don't do them no good.'

'I know.' For a moment Bonnie wondered whether to

confess how she felt about Art, and then decided Hilda had had enough shocks for one day. Art would be a bridge too far. Besides, there was nothing to tell and never would be.

She finished the last of her tea and stood up. 'I'd better go and make myself presentable – Betty and Selina will be here soon.'

'Yes, you do that. And have fun tonight, Bonnie. Let your hair down.'

Bonnie stared at her landlady in amazement. Never in her wildest imaginings would she have dreamed of such words coming out of Hilda's mouth. It was always, 'You be careful and only one drink, mind' or 'You watch yourself and don't go talking to strangers', as though she was ten years old. Smiling, she said, 'Who are you and what have you done with my landlady, Hilda Nichols?'

'Oh, go on with you.' Hilda smiled back and then they both laughed, and as Bonnie left the kitchen and walked upstairs she was conscious of thinking that she felt altogether different from an hour ago. Then she had felt as though the end of the world had come, and strangely – and it *was* strange, she emphasized to herself wryly, in view of the past – part of that had been because her grandma was dead. They had always hated each other and their last meeting had been as vitriolic as ever, but her grandma had been her mam's mother, her own flesh and blood, family. For a while up there, knowing she had gone, she had felt more alone than she could bear.

Stupid. As she reached the top of the stairs she nodded

to the voice in her mind, and then said it out loud, 'Stupid. You're stupid, Bonnie Lindsay.' And it *was* stupid to be so maudlin and illogical. She had Hilda and Selina and Betty, Enoch and his wife, Nelly and dear little Thomas and all her other friends besides. They were her family. And her career was going from strength to strength, she was healthy and young and enjoying life, and had a bank balance she could only have dreamed of when she had first come to London. What more could she want?

And when her mind suggested the answer, she said sharply, 'No more of that.' She and Art had the next three months packed in a coach with the rest of the band as they travelled from venue to venue, and of necessity a tour meant everyone lived in each other's pockets. She had to get her thinking straight about him or else she'd never last the course without going stark staring mad.

She walked into her room, stuffing the letter into her handbag and resolving to show it to Art the next day so his mind would be at rest about her grandmother and Franco. And then the whole embarrassing scenario could be put behind them and never mentioned again. With any luck he would forget all about it.

She walked to the window and looked out at the view that never ceased to thrill her, the endless sky above hundreds of rooftops stretching on and on, while here was she, safe and secure in her tiny home. She knew Art couldn't understand why she didn't want a bigger place, a flat or even a little house of her own, and her feelings were too complex to explain, even to herself. But this room was the foundation of the new life she had built for herself and it was precious.

She smiled wryly. The psychiatrists would have a field day with her, no doubt, especially if she admitted that most of the time she played a part, pretending to be the self-assured, successful singer and a modern miss to boot. She didn't feel like that inside. Sometimes she felt like a little girl crying for her da, lost and alone and frightened and trying to make sense of a world in which there was no sense.

She took a deep breath, shaking her head at herself. But she didn't feel like that all the time, and with each year that passed she felt herself growing stronger, which was a blessing. Hilda was right, she had to look to the future. The past was the past and no amount of wishing could change it. She had muddled through this far, after all, and not made too bad a job of things, everything considered. It was seeing her grandmother and Franco again that had thrown her, and now this letter. If she believed Franco, and there was no reason not to, then they were both dead and gone and the threat of them was gone too. When she had time to take that in then perhaps she would feel differently, and this irrational sense of loss would fade away. She hoped so. Oh, she did so hope so.

Chapter Nineteen

Art Franklin stood on the bridge looking down into the icy cold mass of the river Thames, and his thoughts were as dark as the swiftly flowing water beneath him. It had been over eighty years ago when the great stink of the sewage-filled river had finally penetrated even the Houses of Parliament, forcing MPs to take the link between disease and water contamination seriously and begin to do something about it, but how was the world going to clean up the stink of Hitler and his murdering Nazis? In the last months since war on Germany had been declared, the initial grim satisfaction and relief that the shilly-shallying was at last over and the die had been cast, had given way to the reality that the world was being changed for ever, and not for the best. Psychopaths like Hitler and Mussolini were in charge and forcing the pace, and weak-kneed fools like Chamberlain were no match for them. How Chamberlain was still Prime Minister he didn't know; the country needed a man of war to take on those swines.

Lifting his head, he stared into the darkness that was hiding London. Since the blackout had come into play barely a chink of light escaped closed curtains and blinds, but he knew the buildings were there just the same. And so did the Germans, no doubt. Sooner or later this phoney war, as people had taken to calling it, was going to erupt. It was only a matter of time. But he was grateful for the normality of the last few months, he didn't deny it, especially because once it became obvious that Britain wasn't going to be subjected to the predicted immediate bombing and mayhem, entertainments of all kinds had boomed. Evidence of the nation's 'eat, drink and be merry, for tomorrow we die' type of thinking, he supposed. And on the back of that he had planned a new tour for the band after the one to Holland had been so successful.

Art dug his hands deeper into the pockets of his overcoat; the night was freezing. It was the first of March today, but the bitterly cold winter they'd endured showed no signs of letting up just yet.

Yes, he thought, he'd been both surprised and glad that the recent tour around the country had gone ahead; not least because it had given him what he really craved – more quality time with Bonnie. Sooner or later the war would impact on Britain beyond the inconvenience of food rationing and fumbling your way through the streets after dark by the faint light of a little torch with two layers of newspaper between the bulb and the glass. A touring band was probably one of the most enclosed, intimate circles in the world, and he had made every minute count. He'd seen to it that he and Bonnie had sat together in the coach as they travelled the country, and stayed under the same roof at the various digs, and he had done so quite unashamedly, sensing that time was short. Not that it had done him any good.

He pulled the collar of his coat up and adjusted his muffler before beginning to walk. It was three o'clock in the morning but he'd been tramping the streets for hours, unable to sleep.

No, it hadn't done him any good, beyond making him something of a laughing stock with the boys in the band. Why was it everyone else seemed to know how he felt about Bonnie, besides the lady in question? He scowled to himself. They'd sit for hours in the coach talking about everything under the sun, eat and drink together, see the occasional film and visit museums and art galleries when time permitted, but still she persisted in treating him like a benevolent, kindly uncle. They had got closer, there was no doubt about that, but it had been such a sweet torture at times that he'd spent half the nights on tour lying in a cold bath for a while before he could go to bed and trust that his body would let him sleep.

He ran his hand over his face with a groan. He felt as though he had been treading on eggshells for months and it was playing havoc with his equilibrium. If it hadn't been for what she had endured in her past, he would have declared himself months ago, but he couldn't risk spoiling the friendship they had – that's what he'd thought. But enough was enough. He couldn't go on like this any longer. And after this morning, he wouldn't have to.

He and the boys in the band had known from the onset of the war that they would be called up sooner or later, and for a while now he'd thought that rather than waiting for the government to pick them off individually one by one, they'd all stand a better chance of remaining together as a band if they volunteered en masse. And the others agreed. So in a few hours they were meeting outside the local army recruitment office to offer themselves for king and country, in the hope that as they were musicians they would be able to play their music as well as fight if need be in this damn war.

But first he was going to see Bonnie and tell her he loved her. If she was shocked and repulsed, then at least he wouldn't have to see her every day while he came to terms with it. But if there was a spark there, just the faintest spark, then absence might make the heart grow fonder. Certainly it might prompt her to see him as a man, rather than a cross between a benign Santa Claus figure and an androgynous elderly uncle.

A cat darted across the path in front of him, its green eyes glowing in the blackness as it briefly glanced his way. He stopped, disconcerted. Was a black cat a symbol of bad luck or good fortune? He was blowed if he could remember. And then he shook his head at himself. Whatever, it was merely superstition. What was the matter with him? This was what she had reduced him to.

*

It was six o'clock when he came across a little café that was just opening not far from Paddington station. He went in and had two cups of strong tea and a bacon sandwich to calm his nerves, the phrase 'the condemned man ate a hearty breakfast' coming to mind as he ate.

By the time he reached the house in Shouldham Street, the charcoal sky had streaks of pink and silver running into the retreating darkness and the morning smelt fresh and clean with the frost that had fallen during the night hours. It was going to be a beautiful day.

He paused on the doorstep of Fairview, running his hand over the stubble on his chin. He should have gone home and shaved, changed his clothes, spruced himself up a bit, especially in view of what he was going to say to her. Still, it was too late now. He was here. It had taken him months to find the courage for what he was about to do and he wasn't going to risk losing it now. Of course, it didn't help that he was going to have to face the dragon that guarded the castle and fair lady before he could speak to Bonnie.

As expected, it was Hilda who answered his knock on the door. Before he could say anything, she eyed him up and down. 'You look rough.'

'Thank you.'

'Well, I'm just saying, that's all.'

'Of course you were.' Dratted woman. 'I need a word with Bonnie.'

'She's not down yet.'

There was no way he was going to go away and have

to come back. Holding on to his patience by the skin of his teeth, he said, 'Could you tell her I'm here, please?'

She looked at him for a moment more and he wouldn't have been surprised if she had shut the door in his face. Instead she stepped back into the hall. 'You'd better come through to the front room and I'll make you a cup of tea when I've told her you're waiting.'

It was said in the manner of a great concession and Art replied meekly, 'Thank you, Mrs Nichols,' as he followed her into the house.

Nothing had changed in Hilda's front room since the day Bonnie had stepped into it when she had first arrived in London. The stiff white nets at the window in their starched folds, the even stiffer three-piece suite, and the wooden clock on the mantelpiece ticking the minutes away were all the same. Art sat down in a chair gingerly, feeling he had been given admittance to the holy of holies, which in a way he had.

Hilda looked at him perched on the edge of the armchair and her voice softened as she said, 'You've been good to Bonnie, all things considered.'

It was on the tip of Art's tongue to ask her what were the things she had considered, but he restrained himself. 'It's easy to be good to Bonnie, she's a wonderful girl.'

'Yes, she is.' There was a pregnant pause before Hilda said, 'You like her, don't you?'

Her meaning was clear, and for a moment Art wondered if the whole world knew how he felt. It would seem so, damn it. 'Is it so obvious?'

'Not really.' There was another pause. 'I liked the way you dealt with that old witch of a grandmother of hers, and him, that dirty old man she was married to.'

Bonnie had told him she had confided in Hilda, but only in her. Art looked at the little woman in front of him. She'd said he had been good to Bonnie, but so had she. Bonnie had been such an innocent when she had arrived in London, and but for Hilda she might have been taken advantage of in all sorts of ways, especially after what had happened in the north-east and her being so young and beautiful. Clearing his throat, he said, 'I would do anything for Bonnie, Mrs Nichols. Anything.'

Hilda stared at him for a good ten seconds, and she must have been satisfied with what she read in his face because she said shortly, 'Call me Hilda. I'll go and put the kettle on.'

She shut the door of the front room behind her, and after a moment Art sat back in his chair. How long had the shrewd old woman known he loved Bonnie? But it didn't matter. Against all the odds this was an auspicious start and he wasn't about to look a gift horse in the mouth. The last champion to his cause he would have expected was Bonnie's landlady.

It was two or three minutes later when the door opened and he looked up, thinking it was Hilda. Instead Bonnie said, 'What is it, Art? Is something wrong?' as she walked into the room, her face anxious. 'What are you doing here so early?'

He stood up, his heart threatening to jump out of his

chest. 'No, no, nothing's wrong. Sorry, I should have said . . .' He had never felt so nervous in his life. Facing the Nazis would be nothing compared to this.

'Are you sick?'

'No. Yes. What I mean is, only if you count heart sickness.' Damn, he hadn't meant to say that. He had been going to be so calm and inoffensive. He knew he could come across as pushy and forceful and he didn't want to bully or intimidate her. Taking a deep breath, he said quietly, 'I – I need to talk to you, Bonnie. The boys and I are joining up today as you know –' and when she would have spoken, he held up his hand – 'I know, I know you don't agree, but for the reasons we've discussed I'm sure it's the right thing to do. A musician's biggest dread is not being allowed to perform and this way we've got a chance of keeping a working band together. But that's not why I'm here. At least, not solely. What I mean is . . .'

He stared helplessly at her, and now it was Bonnie who said softly, 'Sit down, Art.' When he sat on the sofa, she joined him rather than taking a chair. 'Are you worried you or one or more of the others might fail the medical?' A couple of the band members were heavy smokers and drinkers and had coughs like a traction engine starting up. 'Is that it?' She hoped that did happen, in Art's case at least. Since he'd begun to talk about joining up she had prayed every night he would fail his medical. Nothing serious, she'd qualified to the Almighty, just something like flat feet or poor eyesight. She knew it was wrong, with so many brave men going away to war and leaving wives and families, but she didn't care.

Inwardly Art groaned. She really didn't have any idea what he was going to say or how he felt about her. And a few years back if anyone had told him he would be in this ridiculous position, he would have laughed in their face. But he wasn't laughing now. For a second he contemplated making some excuse or other and beating a hasty retreat while he still had some pride left, but only for a second. What did pride matter? She'd taken that, along with what was left of his ego, months ago.

'Bonnie,' he began, and then stood to his feet, pulling her up with him. He couldn't do this sitting down. 'This is nothing to do with medicals or the band or anything else except me and you. And I'm not expecting anything, not a thing because I know you don't feel the same way, but I have to tell you how *I* feel before I join up.'

He was holding her elbows and he felt how she had begun to tremble although she made no effort to break free. Her eyes were wide but her face was still and he couldn't read a thing from her expression.

He knew he was making a dog's dinner of it; the carefully rehearsed speech he'd gone over and over in his mind had flown out the window. Casting caution to the wind, he said softly, 'I love you, Bonnie. I've loved you from the first moment I set eyes on you when you were so determined you weren't going to get in my car. I fought it at first, mainly because I didn't believe in "for ever", or because I didn't *want* to believe in it, but that's another story. I'm not going to make any excuses for the sort of man I was before I met you, but I'm not proud of it. All I can say is, I love you. Totally, absolutely, and definitely for ever. That's it, that's what I came to say.'

She still hadn't moved. But for her trembling, he would have imagined she had turned to stone. Now he said, 'I've frightened you. I'm sorry, that's the last thing I wanted to do. I would rather die than cause you one moment of distress. But I had to tell you, even though I know—'

'I love you too.'

It was the faintest of whispers and for a moment Art thought he had imagined it. Bending his head, he said, 'What did you say?'

For an answer, Bonnie put her lips to his, wrapping her arms round his neck and pressing herself against him. 'I love you,' she murmured. 'I love you, I love you, I love you.' And then her words were smothered as he responded to her mouth, crushing her against his chest in an agony of wild joy mixed with disbelief.

It was a full five minutes later before Hilda, wise woman that she was, quietly opened the door, a tray with two cups of tea in her hand. For a moment she surveyed the couple sitting closely together on the sofa, so wrapped up in each other that they were oblivious to her presence. Then, just as silently, she closed the door again.

*

They were married in the middle of July and by then the phoney war was well and truly over. The Dutch and Belgians had fallen to the Nazis in May, and in June Allied forces had been evacuated from Dunkirk in a heroic operation by a huge fleet of destroyers, ferries, fishing vessels and even river cruisers. These had braved the German bombs and machine guns raking the Dunkirk beaches and harbour to save the British Expeditionary Force, along with vast numbers of French and Belgian troops, from total annihilation by a merciless enemy. The Nazi swastika was now flying from the Eiffel Tower and the Arc de Triomphe, and Mussolini had declared war on the Allies. Neville Chamberlain, totally discredited, had resigned against a backdrop of mounting military catastrophe in May, handing over control of the country to Winston Churchill, who had declared he had nothing to offer but blood, toil, tears and sweat in a rousing speech about ultimate victory for Britain.

But on a sunny July day in London at Marylebone register office, Bonnie and Art weren't thinking of the recent developments in the war, dire though they were. This was their day, and Hitler and his horde of murdering Nazis had no place in it.

Art looked very dashing in his uniform, and Bonnie was just beautiful in a delicate lacy white dress that fell below the knee and a matching jacket. She had white orchids, specially ordered from a florist in the West End, entwined through her dark hair and she carried a bouquet of the sweet-smelling flowers tied with dusky pink ribbons. Enoch was giving her away, and as Bonnie entered the room on his arm to see Art waiting for her surrounded by all their friends, she thought she would burst with happiness.

Art turned as she approached and his heart was in his eyes, causing Hilda, Annie and Gladys, who were sitting in the front row, to reach for their handkerchiefs. Nelly and Thomas, Betty and her family along with Selina and Cyril, Verity and Larry, all the band members and their wives or girlfriends, and a whole host of other friends and colleagues were packed into the relatively small room. Even Julian Wood from Norman Mortimer, and Ralph Mercer with his wife Mary, were there. Art had been liberal in his invitations, saying that as he and Bonnie had no close family he wanted all their friends to share their happiness. After the ceremony everyone was going back to Art's nightclub where somehow – and Bonnie didn't ask how – a spread had been laid on that defied ration books. She knew Art had bought in a crate or two of champagne, and as one bottle cost five pounds she didn't like to think what he had spent thus far. But he was happy, in fact he was like an exuberant schoolboy, and so she hadn't said one word about the expense.

They held hands tightly as they said their vows, made all the more poignant by the troubled times they lived in, and as the smiling registrar pronounced them husband and wife, Art whisked her off her feet and twirled her round and round to ribald cheers and shouts from the assembled throng.

The rest of the day passed in a blissful blur for Bonnie, but then at last they were on the train for a four-day honeymoon in a hotel in Brighton, confetti and rice littering the carriage from the enthusiastic send-off by their friends at the station. The other band members only had a twenty-four-hour leave but Art had five days, although that seemed pitifully short as Bonnie snuggled into his side on the journey.

'Hey, penny for them.' Art lifted her chin so she met his gaze. 'You've gone quiet on me. Not regretting the fact that you're Mrs Franklin already, are you?' He kissed the tip of her nose, his eyes smiling.

'I was just thinking how little time we've got before you have to be back at the base,' she admitted, a catch in her voice.

'I know, sweetheart.' He kissed her again. 'But you're going to be busy in your own right making a name for yourself without the band. You won't have time to brood while I'm gone, you'll see, and once the war is over we'll start proper married life and produce our own little crop of baby Franklins.'

Bonnie smiled, as she was meant to, but in truth she was finding her changed circumstances stressful. Her time singing with Art and the band was over, she knew that, and because of the war the whole pattern of broadcasting was changing. For security and other reasons, direct transmissions from clubs and hotels had ceased and everything was different. Fortunately the records she had made with Art and the band had got her name known to some extent, and she had done the occasional radio variety show in the last months and other work. Enoch had told her there had been several enquiries from the variety circuits about whether she would be interested in doing solo spots, something he was keen for her to do. When Art and the band had joined up, it had seemed the obvious thing for Enoch to become her permanent agent, and she knew Art's mind was more at rest knowing Enoch was on board. She had already made two records as a solo artiste which had been quite well received, and this had boosted her confidence to some extent. Nevertheless, when Enoch had told her a few days ago that he had got her a spot at a prestigious Birmingham theatre on her return from honeymoon, she had felt panicked. With Art and the band behind her the weight of the performance hadn't been all on her; now it would be and it was more than a little sobering to think she might fall flat on her face, metaphorically speaking. But she had begun singing as a solo artiste, she reminded herself now, and she could do so again. This was a new period in her life and she had to embrace it whether she liked it or not, as people all over Britain were having to do. The entertainment business was doing its best to keep people's spirits up and she could do her bit for the war effort by taking folk out of themselves for a while; it was as simple as that.

More at peace, she glanced at the gold band resting on the third finger of her left hand next to Art's sapphire-and-diamond engagement ring. He had chosen sapphires to match her eyes, he'd told her when he had presented her with the ring, and the diamond because she was a diamond among women, unique and incomparable. He said such beautiful things, things that were all at odds with the tough, hard-bitten front he presented to the rest of the world.

A soft, warm twilight was falling by the time the taxi they had caught from the station deposited them at their hotel. At reception they gave in their ration books so that the coupons for their food could be taken out during their stay, and a smart bellboy who didn't look much older than Thomas showed them up to the bridal suite. Once they had unpacked, they went downstairs for dinner and Bonnie was glad it had been something of a rush. She was feeling shy, and a little apprehensive of what lay in store that night. It was silly, she told herself, and she *knew* it was silly, but memories of how much it had hurt when Franco had had his way with her kept intruding. But Art wouldn't hurt her, and even if there was any pain it would be worth it to belong to him, body, soul and spirit. He had been so patient waiting for their wedding night before making love to her, and it had been his decision rather than hers.

'You're going to be my wife and the mother of my children,' he had told her tenderly when she had broached the matter two months before on his brief return home for a forty-eight-hour leave. 'You're different to the others and I'm doing this right. I can't explain it but it's the foundation of the marriage I want us to have together. You know I've had women in the past, Bonnie, and I can't change that, but with you . . . it has to be perfect.'

She hadn't argued with him because he had told her what had happened between his parents, and although he hadn't gone into details she had sensed how much his mother's desertion of him and his father had hurt him, but the word 'perfect' had scared her. He'd had many women, beautiful, wordly, experienced women who knew how to please a man in bed, whereas she . . . She was just an ordinary little northern lass under the skin. But she *did* love him, and perhaps her love would guide her? She was so frightened of disappointing him that she hadn't slept properly for the last week or so.

She forced down the food without really tasting it and drank two glasses of the wine Art had ordered with the meal, hoping it would give her Dutch courage. If Art noticed her brittle laugh and the fact that she dropped her knife and fork twice, he didn't comment on it. He lingered over their coffee which Bonnie found excruciating. It wasn't exactly romantic, she thought, but she just wanted to get on with it now, for better or worse.

They held hands on their way back to the room, and once inside he drew her into his arms and began to kiss her, slowly and leisurely but in a way that caused an ache deep in the core of her long before he began to undress her. She didn't know what she had expected, but it wasn't the unhurried, sweet, wildly erotic and tender exploring of every inch of her once they were both naked, an exploration that had her moaning for him long before he actually took her. And when he did, when the world splintered and shattered and was nothing but sheer endless hot ripples of pleasure, his cry of exultation was echoed in her.

It took them a while to come back to earth, and even then Art held her and stroked her and whispered endless endearments as she nestled against him, expelling with his love the dark ghosts of the past and all the heartache and regrets and pain that went with them.

She was still wrapped in his arms as she drifted off to sleep, her head resting on the hairy pillow of his chest where the steady slow beat of his heart was like the most exquisite lullaby. *Four days*, she thought, before the heavy blanket of sleep finally overcame her. *It wasn't enough. Four lifetimes wouldn't be enough. Oh, God, keep him safe in this war. Keep us both safe. Give us time, God. Give us time.*

PART FIVE

Bombs, Backbone and Burma

1943

Chapter Twenty

'Blimey, gal, that one was a mite too close for comfort.'

Enoch was clearly rattled, and as Bonnie nodded, she had to admit the explosion somewhere in the area outside the theatre had been particularly loud. Enoch had wanted her to leave the theatre once the raid had started, and take refuge underground in the Tube station a short distance away. Most of the audience had gone there or to other places of relative safety, but for once Bonnie had refused to budge from her dressing room. She simply couldn't face hours of being packed sardine-like in a shelter tonight. It wasn't bravery, but a combination of weariness and fatalism.

She had only arrived back in London a couple of days ago after touring the provinces for three months, and these tours were always exhausting. As normal now she had topped the bill, and she and the other performers would do the show in the late afternoon and evening, after going to service camps, munitions factories, works canteens and hospitals in the district earlier in the day.

She would rise at six o'clock most mornings and rarely fell into bed in her digs before midnight, but the fan letters that now came in their hundreds left her in no doubt that she was fulfilling her wish to contribute to the war effort. And even now she was home again, almost every hour of every day was accounted for. Besides variety appearances, she would be recording, doing radio shows and charity performances, and still fitting in visits to hospitals, airfields and army camps when she could. But she welcomed the non-stop busyness. It meant she had less time to worry about Art. Whenever she visited hospitals to entertain the wounded, be they air force, navy or army, it was as though she was singing to Art.

He had been in the Dieppe raid the year before, although thankfully she hadn't been aware of that until it was over and he'd had some leave. It had been the biggest Allied assault on Hitler's Fortress Europe of the war, involving several thousand British, Canadian, American and Free French troops. Casualties on both sides had been heavy, and Art had told her about the furious air battles that had taken place as the Germans had tried to break up the Allied aerial umbrella over the land and sea forces.

'I don't know if Churchill intended a full-scale invasion,' Art had told her the first night he was home, as they'd sat in the little courtyard garden in late-September sunshine. 'But if he did, it failed. We lost so many men, Bonnie.' He shook his head. 'Of course, the powers on high are claiming it was a planned reconnaissance intended to gain vital experience in mounting an amphibious attack against coastal positions with large numbers of troops and heavy equipment, and if that's true, I'm glad I didn't have to make such a decision. To my mind it smacks of what the old Zulu chiefs used to do. They would sacrifice the lives of their young braves to work out where the enemy fire power was and how to mount an attack that would succeed.'

Bonnie had put her hand over his but had said nothing. What could she say? Two members of the band had been killed in Dieppe, and a third – jaunty little Anthony who was a terrific piano player – had been taken prisoner by the Germans.

They had made the most of that leave, sensing that there wouldn't be another for a long time, and they'd been right. Art had been sent to Sicily and hadn't been home since.

Now, as another explosion made the windows vibrate, Bonnie saw Enoch flinch. She reached across and offered her Thermos flask. 'Have some coffee. It'll calm you.'

Enoch shook his head as he accepted the Thermos. 'You're one on your own, I'll give you that. Don't you have any nerves like the rest of us?'

'Of course I do.' And she did; sometimes she was petrified, especially when she witnessed the aftermath of what a bomb could do to human flesh, but she had driven her car all through the Blitz because it was hopeless to rely on buses to get to a performance on time, and after that she had become almost resigned to the idea that if a bomb had your name on it, it would get you somehow. There she'd been, driving her faithful work-horse around with a metal plate over her headlights with a small slit in it so that other drivers could see the car in the distance, more than once with shrapnel pinging on the metalwork and her little tin helmet on her head in case a shard pierced the roof of the car, and she had got through unscathed. Whereas poor Betty and her family had all been killed when their Anderson shelter received a direct hit. Selina and Cyril had been at his mother's earlier that evening, and but for the fact that they'd gone home early because Selina was feeling unwell, they would have lost their lives too. Both of her friends at the same time, it didn't bear thinking about. She still found it hard to accept that Betty was gone – big, warm, funny Betty who'd had a heart as generous as her frame.

Enoch took a little hip flask out of his jacket and tipped a measure of brandy into the cup, offering it to Bonnie who shook her head. 'I like to keep my wits about me when I'm driving.' Owing to the fact that she was an entertainer and had to get to theatres or hospitals or other venues she got extra petrol rations. Enoch, along with most people she knew, had given up using his car, and so she drove them both everywhere. She also received extra coupons for her stage costumes because she worked in the West End frequently, and as yet she had not been reduced to drawing lines up the backs of her legs with an eyebrow pencil but could still afford stockings. Even with the coupons there was always a shortage of fabric for her costumes, though, as silk was almost impossible to source, and but for Hilda and her little sewing machine – as good as any Bond Street dressmaker – she would have struggled more than she did. Apart from altering old dresses and transforming them by adding or removing bits, Hilda could take a piece of material that was pretty ordinary and make it into something any couturier would be proud of.

Enoch downed his coffee and looked at her morosely. 'Damn Nazis,' he muttered irritably. 'But I tell you, gal, you've got more backbone than me – more than most folk, truth be told,' he said in a tone that made it less of a compliment and more of a criticism.

Bonnie had to smile. Poor Enoch, he'd never got used to the bombs and she supposed she had, to some extent. Sometimes during a show when the alert sounded most of the audience still remained in their seats, depending on where the venue was, and at those times she would just carry on singing. On her most recent tour when she had been singing her signature number, 'A Song at Sunrise', and a particularly loud blast had brought dust and debris falling from the ceiling of the old theatre, some wit in the audience had called out, 'And tempest at twilight, eh, girl?' and everyone had laughed, her included. Everyone but Enoch that was, who'd turned a whiter shade of pale at the piano.

Once the air raid was over, Bonnie drove Enoch home to where Gladys was anxiously waiting. As they'd surmised, the raid had been a bad one. The streets were chaotic, full of firemen, hosepipes, burning buildings and rubble. The wardens and police were directing people here, there and everywhere, and the air was chokingly thick with black smoke and dust. It was a common sight but gut-wrenching nevertheless, especially when they passed a woman sitting in the gutter cradling a young child in her arms, an air-raid warden crouching beside her.

Enoch swore softly, shaking his head but saying nothing, and they drove the rest of the way in a heavy silence.

Once she had dropped off Enoch, Bonnie negotiated her way home which took longer than normal due to this recent raid blocking several roads and causing mayhem. Home was now Art's beautiful little cottage in Kingston upon Thames. She had finally bitten the bullet and on her marriage left her precious little nest in the eaves of Fairview. It had seemed the logical next step and meant Annie wasn't on her own, now Art was away fighting, besides which Bonnie felt closer to Art there. The small courtyard garden was a constant delight and refuge when she managed to steal the odd hour or two out of her ridiculously busy schedule.

Hilda had totally understood when Bonnie had said she was moving out. Furthermore, Hilda and Art's housekeeper had got on like a house on fire when they'd met at the wedding, and when Bonnie was away from home Hilda often joined Annie for their evening meal or Annie went to eat with her new friend. The pair were close in age and were like two fussy mother hens with Bonnie, which she rather enjoyed. Nelly and Thomas had come to stay for a few days once or twice when Bonnie hadn't been off round the country touring, and these occasions always eased the ache in Bonnie's heart that was family-shaped. Knowing how Nelly had loved her father, how she still loved him even though he had been gone for so long, brought him closer to Bonnie in a strange sort of way. It wasn't that they talked about him much, although they reminisced about the old times now and again, it was more that her memories of him sprang to life when she was with Nelly and she could picture him with more clarity in her mind's eye. He had been a special man, a wonderful man, and while she and Nelly were alive he wasn't lost and forgotten in the endless corridors of time.

Once she had parked the car outside the house in Kingston upon Thames she sat for a moment after turning off the ignition. She felt immensely sad tonight; whether it was seeing that mother holding her child amid all the devastation, or that she was missing Art, or she was just exhausted and had used up all her reserves over the last weeks, she didn't know. The terrible things they were hearing about daily, the scarred and shattered city she was living in, the destruction she saw all over the country on her tours felt too much tonight somehow. She felt tiny and alone, a little piece of flotsam and jetsam in a world where bad seemed to be winning and good was being ground into dust. And she knew tomorrow she would take up the reins again, that she would put on her

Bonnie May face and sing the simple, hope-filled, emotional and nostalgic songs that seemed to bring comfort to so many people if her fan letters and popularity could be believed, but right at this moment she was just Bonnie Lindsay, a little girl crying for her da and wishing she could go back in time to the golden days she hadn't really appreciated when she'd been living them.

The front door to the cottage opened and she looked up, quickly clearing her expression and expecting to see Annie in the doorway. But it wasn't Annie's wrinkled little face looking at her. It was Art. Big, rugged, handsome Art, leaning heavily on a stick but with a smile as wide as the Cheshire cat's on his face. Bonnie was out of the car like a homing pigeon, leaving the door wide open as she flew into his arms.

The world had righted itself again.

After they'd made love in their big double bed, they talked until dawn. It appeared Art had been wounded when the Allies had captured Messina in Sicily and had been shipped home to recover. A kind officer had given him leave for twenty-four hours, but then he had to report to a military hospital-cum-convalescence home in Surrey to get fully fit before he rejoined his unit.

It was as pink was entering the night sky that Bonnie broached something she'd been thinking about for a while. It had become more and more apparent since the war began that the boys fighting in the services felt a connection with the sentimental songs she liked to sing.

Vera Lynn was hugely popular, and although Bonnie knew she couldn't compete with the 'Forces Sweetheart', her songs were of the same ilk as the tender, sweet songs Vera sang so touchingly. The men wanted to hear words that spoke of home, loved ones and a brighter future when they were far away, and Bonnie knew her strength had always been in the fact that once she began to sing such songs, she believed every word. And because she believed, her listeners believed too.

Art nodded as she spoke. 'Couldn't agree more,' he drawled in his easy way. 'I wouldn't have wished this war on us, but your voice and delivery and the type of ballads you sing are perfect for the days we live in. The razzle-dazzle numbers of the twenties wouldn't have been for you. Not that you couldn't have sung them,' he added hastily, as though it had been a criticism, 'but they wouldn't have been right.'

'I get loads of letters from servicemen,' Bonnie went on carefully, knowing that when she got to the crux of what she was trying to say Art wouldn't like it at all, 'and they emphasize how important the radio link is to wherever they are, but it's not like actually *going* there, is it? Singing in person, I mean.'

She felt Art stiffen. 'You're working yourself to death with the constant visits to hospitals and airfields and army camps and the rest of it, besides recording and doing variety shows. Annie's been worried about you for months, between you and me. If anyone is doing their bit for the war effort, you are, Bonnie.'

'Perhaps.' She raised herself on one elbow and stared at him in the dawning light. 'But you know as well as I do the lift it gives to the boys far away from their loved ones when an actress or singer or comedian goes out to where they are. That's what I want to do, Art. I'm not decrying what I've done to date and Annie's right, it *is* hard work and also worthwhile and all the rest of it, but I just feel the time is right for me to go out of my comfort zone and entertain the troops overseas for a season. Other entertainers do it, so why not me?'

'It's too dangerous.'

'Art, it's no more dangerous than London. Well, it might be a little, but I got through the Blitz, didn't I? And that night in May a couple of years ago was like Dante's Inferno when the Germans tried to bomb London out of existence. But we survived.'

'I know, I know, but it's not like knowingly walking into the front line. That's a different kettle of fish entirely.'

'I want to do it, Art. I've already made enquiries about joining ENSA, and I've got an appointment with Basil Dean at his office in Drury Lane next week.'

'What's Enoch's take on this?'

'I haven't discussed it with him yet. I intended to write to you first.'

'Well, that's something, I suppose.'

'Don't go all grumpy on me.' She dropped a kiss on his mouth. 'I don't suppose Gracie Fields and George Formby and all the others were breaking their necks to do troop concerts in the midst of muck and bullets; they do it because they feel it's their patriotic duty and it'll do some good, boost morale and so on.'

'Then let them go on doing what they do and you stay here and work the home front.'

'Art, you don't really mean that.'

'The hell I don't.' There was silence for a few moments and then Art groaned, rolling over and sitting on the edge of the bed before standing up and limping over to the window where he moved the blackout blind to one side.

Bonnie joined him, putting her arms round his waist as she rested her chin on his back and murmured, 'You'll have the warden shouting the odds. He's a bulldog of a man.'

He didn't say anything for a full minute. Then he let the blind fall back into place and turned round, pulling her against him. 'Are you set on this?'

She nodded. 'I feel I have to, Art. I really do.'

'Have you thought as far as where you would go?'

'Well, there seems to be no shortage of entertainment for the troops in Italy and the Middle East, but at one of the hospitals I visited a few weeks ago, a soldier told me he thinks Burma's been more or less forgotten. He was shipped home with terrible injuries –' she didn't go into the nature of them which had been on her mind ever since – 'and he said if ever there's a place and men who need encouragement, it's Burma.'

'Did he?' said Art grimly, wishing he could get his hands on the unfortunate soldier for a few minutes.

'But of course I'd discuss this with Mr Dean next week.'

'The Japanese are devils, Bonnie. They have no respect for soldiers or civilians alike, including women.'

'I shan't come into contact with the Japanese.'

'And you'd be in the jungle. You've no idea what that's like, have you? We're talking a heat and humidity you can't imagine, bugs of every description, poisonous snakes, scorpions and hornets, wild animals and danger everywhere. That's not even taking into account the lack of sanitation and privacy you'd experience, and the food. Meat goes bad the same day it's prepared, and cooked rice turns sour in hours. I know. A friend of mine was in the tropics for a while some years back, and he came home a shell of a man with rampant malaria and lung rot.'

Bonnie stared at him. 'All that just confirms that if ever the troops need a boost, it's the ones in Burma.'

'Stubborn as hell,' he muttered, before kissing her long and hard.

The kiss led on to other things and they didn't speak about Burma again until Art was ready to leave. An army Jeep had come to pick him up and take him back to base before he would be transferred to the hospital in Surrey, where Bonnie would be able to visit him.

As they stood on the doorstep, Art drew her into his arms. 'About Burma.' He moved a tendril of hair from her brow. 'I'm not going to pretend I want you to go, but if you feel you have to, then I won't try and persuade you otherwise. But I want two promises from you, all right? One, Enoch goes with you to Burma. If he can't, or won't, then you knock this idea on the head, Bonnie. I don't want you going out there without him.'

She stared at him. 'I'm hardly of an age when I need a chaperone, Art.'

'And that's just the sort of comment that makes me even more set on Enoch going with you.'

'Oh, for goodness' sake.'

'I mean it. Now promise me.'

She nodded sulkily. Even if Enoch couldn't go she would need an accompanist so it wasn't as if she would be on her own. But she couldn't argue with him, not when he was off to the hospital. His leg had looked awful when she'd examined it although he assured her the doctors had said he would make a full recovery in time. But then that was a mixed blessing. A full recovery meant he would go back to the fighting. 'What's the second promise?'

'That you look after yourself, my love. I shall be suffering the torments of the damned if this trip comes off. Just remember that, and take care.'

'Oh, Art.' For a moment, but only for a moment, Bonnie was tempted to say she wouldn't go. Instead she kissed him hard on the lips, oblivious to the driver of the Jeep who was a pal of Art's. 'I love you so much.'

'And I love you, impossible though you are at times.

I could have fallen for any number of women, docile, amenable, sensible women, but who took my heart? A lion-hearted beauty who's as determined as me, and that's saying something.'

'So you don't mind?' she whispered sweetly, kissing his chin. 'About me going to Burma?'

'I mind like hell, let's get that straight, and no amount of soft soap with those baby-blue eyes of yours will make me say different.'

She kissed him again. He was going to have a further operation in the next few days when he was in the hospital to remove more shrapnel from his leg, and then some weeks of remedial exercise, so for a short while at least she would know where he was and that he was safe. Worrying about him the way she did, she could completely understand why he didn't want her to go to Burma. And she didn't want to cause him concern – that was the last thing in the world she wanted – but she had to go. Just talking about it with him over the last few hours had cemented the desire even more firmly in her mind, but what she was going to do if Enoch wouldn't play ball, she wasn't sure. She didn't want to break her promise to Art but . . .

She kissed him again and watched as he hobbled to the Jeep.

She'd cross her bridges when she came to them.

Chapter Twenty-One

To Bonnie's relief and secret surprise, Enoch was fully on board for a trip to Burma. The only fly in the ointment as far as he was concerned was that it meant turning down work for the months they would be away. The fact that they would be flying halfway round the world into enemy-occupied Burmese jungle populated by wild animals and snakes and deadly insects, not to mention the Japanese, was of much less consideration to him than the loss of income. The basic ENSA salary fluctuated between ten and twenty pounds a week which, as Enoch put it, was chicken feed compared to what Bonnie normally earned. However, he manfully agreed to go against all his instincts as an agent and set about clearing a block of weeks from April to July in the following year.

So it was, not long after the most spectacular and daring operation of the Burma campaign in March 1944, when a large Allied force was landed two hundred miles behind Japanese lines, that Bonnie said goodbye to a tearful Annie and joined Enoch in the taxi waiting to take them to the train station from where they would go to the coast. According to the newspapers over the last two or three weeks the reinforcements to back the 'Forgotten Army' – General Slim's 14th Army – meant that at last the tide was turning in Burma, although it was going to be a slow and painful process. The British and the Americans working together had delivered a coup that the Japanese hadn't been expecting, but no one doubted the truth voiced by one old General that when rats are threatened and cornered, they come out fighting all the more viciously.

Art had continued to be full of misgivings about the trip, emphasizing the dangers whenever he wrote to her. And Bonnie tried to reassure him in her letters and promised every time she wrote that she wouldn't take any unnecessary risks.

His recovery in the hospital in England had gone well, and he had rejoined his regiment towards the end of the previous year. Bonnie had been hoping he would remain in Surrey for Christmas but it wasn't to be. His regiment had been seconded to Italy in the aftermath of the country's military about-face, when Italy had declared war on Germany – her previous ally – in October, thereby suffering a wave of atrocities at the hands of the retreating Germans.

The newspapers had reported that Naples had been subjected to a five-day reign of terror as retreating German soldiers took revenge on their Italian 'betrayers', murdering civilians at random and looting and blowing up buildings. Hospitals had been attacked, water mains and sewers dynamited, and any resistance put down with a savagery hitherto unprecented. Meanwhile, tens of thousands of disarmed Italian soldiers had been crammed into sealed trains under guard and taken to Germany as slave labour.

Art had written of the grief of Neapolitan mothers mourning for their sons, killed during guerrilla battles with the Nazis, and Bonnie could tell their despair had affected him greatly. Much as they both wanted children, they had agreed that to bring little ones into a world that was so volatile and uncertain was out of the question, and Bonnie had been glad that she had no sons who would be called upon to fight. It was bad enough that Art was in the thick of it; what she would have felt if their children were in the firing line didn't bear thinking about. Thomas would be fifteen soon, and Bonnie knew Nelly was desperate for the war to be over before there was any chance he would be expected to fight.

But for now she was thinking solely about the forthcoming trip, and flippant as it might be, her main concern centred on what clothes to take with her, bearing in mind they were going to be in the middle of the Burmese jungle. She would be wearing her ENSA uniform, an unembellished military-looking outfit that didn't have a whiff of show business about it, but when she performed she wanted to be able to bring a touch of glamour to the proceedings. It was all part of the show and, for men living hand to mouth in the most appalling conditions, even more important, she felt. Basil Dean had warned her to travel light, so eventually she decided on a close-fitting red dress that moulded to her curves and flared out from knee to ankle, and a more demure midnight-blue one, packing them carefully into her trunk amid layers of tissue paper.

Enoch smiled at her as she plumped down beside him in the taxi. He had seen to most of the practical arrangements for the trip and had been like a fussy old woman for weeks, worrying about this and that and fretting that he had forgotten something important, but this morning he seemed bright and perky.

'Well, gal, this is it. We're off.'

Bonnie beamed at him. 'I'm so glad you're coming with me, Enoch. It makes all the difference to how I feel about everything.'

Enoch patted her hand. He wouldn't have let her go without him. No one would take care of her the way he would – except Art, of course – but in truth he'd had the skits for the last few days since the newspapers had reported the death of Orde Wingate, the hero of Burma, in an aircraft crash. The unorthodox general had been the leader of the Chindits and they'd wreaked havoc behind the Japanese lines; if they couldn't provide *him* with a good pilot and aeroplane, what chance did he and Bonnie have? He'd asked himself this in his more panicky moments, before trying to reason that accidents could happen to anyone and it had just been bad luck. Nevertheless, the enormity of all the travelling they were embarking on had hit home in the last week, not that he had mentioned his concerns to Gladys or Bonnie. Funnily enough though, this morning he felt better. Whether it was because they were actually on their way, he didn't know, but a feeling of 'in for a penny, in for a pound' had quietened his nerves, for which he was grateful.

For the umpteenth time since he'd opened his eyes that morning he went through the travel arrangements in his mind. They were flying to Gibraltar for the first step of the journey, but because they couldn't fly a more direct route across occupied France he'd been told the flight would take seven hours across the Atlantic. After an overnight stop the next port of call was North Africa, and then Cairo where they would stay for three days while Bonnie did a couple of performances to entertain troops who'd just returned from fighting in Italy. After a few radio broadcasts they were flying across the Suez Canal, then Transjordan and Iraq, before stopping at Basra. Names of countries and places Enoch had never thought to see went through his mind as he ticked off the route – Bahrain, Dubai, Karachi, Bombay, Calcutta, Chittagong and then finally Burma. And on most of the stops Bonnie would be doing open-air camp shows, as well as visiting hospitals, making radio broadcasts, signing records and pictures and doing any impromptu visits for places like orphanages and displacement camps that they found time for.

Bonnie was wearing her ENSA uniform, and he glanced at her feet which were encased in sensible brogues.

She saw his look and lifted one of her feet as she said, 'See, I did what you told me and wore good solid shoes, even if they are spectacularly ugly.'

'Believe me, you'll need them. It's going to be military aircraft and army trucks from now on.'

'I don't mind.'

'I'll remind you of that in a few days when we've been bumped and jolted from pillar to post and we ache all over.'

Now it was Bonnie who patted his hand. 'Don't worry, we'll be fine,' she said happily, glad the months of waiting were over and she was finally about to do what her heart had been yearning for. 'You'll see.'

They left England's shores in a Sunderland flying boat, and within a very short time it became apparent that poor Enoch was going to suffer with air-sickness. This, along with the change in climate, prickly heat and the hectic schedule, played havoc with Enoch's equilibrium over the next seven days before they reached Burma. Bonnie on the other hand felt reasonably well, apart from itching all over from an attack by bedbugs in the first hotel they'd slept at, in Gibraltar. Mosquitoes were proving to be a constant aggravation and she made sure she slept under a net. She felt terribly sorry for Enoch and tried to smooth his way as much as possible – making him sleep in where he could, if it wasn't essential he accompanied her, and making sure that he didn't become dehydrated and so on, but at no point did she regret the trip.

She knew she was meant to be doing this, and it wasn't only a sense of patriotic duty, as she had said to Art months ago. From the first time Burma had been mentioned, something had happened – a feeling, a conviction, a certainty, call it what you will – and from that point on the pull had been irresistible.

She hadn't tried to explain it to anyone because she didn't understand it herself, but it was real and the driving force in this whole undertaking. Whatever was thrown at her, she would deal with it and get on with her job, she was determined about that.

She glanced at Enoch now. They were staying in the Officers' Club at Chittagong which was by no means as grand as it sounded. There was no running water for a start, but at least Bonnie had been able to fill an old tin bath with enough tepid water for a soak of sorts which had been wonderful, although as soon as she had dried herself and got dressed the heat and humidity had made her clothes damp on her back.

They had been in Chittagong for a day or two and Enoch was feeling a lot better for the break from flying. They had done a round of concerts and hospital visits, travelling from venue to venue in an army truck with a driver and NCO, while another soldier drove a lorry holding Enoch's piano, the microphones and other equipment. Enoch had to plug the amplification system in wherever he could, often into the headlights of vehicles, for the larger concerts. It was difficult because the size of audience could range from a few dozen men in one place to several thousand in another, and they never really knew what they were going into. But Enoch coped manfully with these inconveniences now he was on terra firma.

Bonnie watched him down his third gin and tonic before she said, 'So, we're off into the proper jungle tomorrow. No more civilization.'

'Is that what it's been thus far?' Enoch grimaced. They had been told that day that the next leg of the journey was into the hottest and most humid part of Burma along the Bazar–Teknaf Highway to Bawli Bazar. There would be nowhere to stay in some places but grass huts with mats to sleep on and no toilets apart from buckets, just dirt floors and life at its rawest. 'Make sure you wrap your mosquito nets round you at night,' one friendly officer had warned them both. 'And if there is any way you can sleep raised up off the ground, take it. The creepy-crawlies just love soft pink flesh.' He had grinned at them and Bonnie had laughed, but Enoch hadn't found it funny. 'Don't worry,' the officer had added, glancing at Enoch's grim face. 'The boys'll make sure you're all right, even if you sleep in one of the string hammocks the natives use. They're damn uncomfortable and your back'll be killing you in the morning, but it's better than a scorpion or snake bite.'

Thinking about this previous conversation, Bonnie said, 'Don't worry, Enoch, worse things happen at sea.'

'I've always thought that saying ridiculous but never more so than this evening.' Enoch stretched his legs, flexing his ankles which were swollen with the heat as he thought longingly about Gladys and their little house. It had been cold and rainy when they had left England's shores, and he knew he would never complain about the weather at home again. This combination of heat and humidity was beyond anything he had known before, verging on the unbearable, and the thought of it getting even worse was frightening. It was draining, sapping you of energy and killing your appetite. He'd already had to tighten his belt by a couple of holes.

This thought cheered him. Gladys had been on about his beer gut for years but it was disappearing fast. He'd go home a new man. If he survived, that was, which at times over the last week he'd doubted. But however much he grumbled about the hardships, he could see that Bonnie was doing something good for the boys. They were with her every inch of the way during the concerts, singing along with the songs and clearly enjoying them-selves, but it was when she visited the hospitals – mostly under canvas and basic, to say the least – that he found himself with a lump in his throat. There were so many really young servicemen, some still in their teens, and when Bonnie sat by their beds and talked softly with them their guard would come down and they would cry, unburdening themselves in a way they couldn't do with their comrades. Bonnie would comfort them and let them talk about their families back home and their mothers and wives and girlfriends. No matter if the smell of sweat and gangrene and bodily fluids and disinfectant was overpowering, she never flinched or let them see she was struggling.

He reached over now, patting her arm as he said, 'You're a good girl – you know that, don't you? – and I'm proud to be with you out here, I am straight. Take no notice of me when I bellyache about this and that, gal. I don't mean it. I'm glad we came, to tell you the truth.'

There were times the next day when Bonnie wondered if Enoch regretted those words. They set off along the Bazar–Teknaf Highway, which in effect was a dirt track, at seven o'clock in the morning and arrived at their destination at six in the evening, stopping twice for Bonnie to do a show en route. They were close to the front now, and at the last stop the soldiers had waited patiently for hours in the unrelenting heat to hear her sing.

Bonnie found it humbling and touching to see the rows of men, most of them looking exhausted and gaunt, come alive as she sang, and she knew she would never get such appreciative audiences in the rest of her life. One of the boys presented her with a bouquet of jungle flowers after the performance, and she had a hard job to keep back the tears. He looked no more than seventeen or eighteen, had already seen sights that would haunt the strongest man, and yet he was sweet-faced and gentle and thrilled to bits he'd had the honour of being the one to give her the flowers. She had wanted to gather him up in her arms and whisk him back to England and to his mother, who, he whispered shyly so no one else could hear, had played 'A Song at Sunrise' when it had first come out all day every day until his father had threatened to break the gramophone. He rolled his eyes and grinned at her and she had smiled back, wondering if he would be one of the lucky ones who survived the war. She hoped so. Oh, she did so hope so. She had kissed his cheek and all his pals had whooped and cheered as he'd returned, red-faced and suddenly jaunty, to his seat. So young, nothing more than a baby really.

That night they slept under canvas with the cries of jackals puncturing the jungle night and a mouse-sized spider frightening Enoch to death as it ran over his boot just as he was about to take them off for bed. He slept with them on after that.

The next morning they were up at the crack of dawn again to visit a hospital, and so the pattern was set. Travelling dirt tracks in a jungle land; hearing the sound of elephants and jackals and other wild animals; constant swarms of mosquitoes day and night, and insects the size of which would have done credit to any horror film. Bonnie did shows in tents, bamboo huts and out in the open, and found she had been wildly optimistic to think she could wear her evening frocks. It was long khaki trousers and buttoned-up shirts with long sleeves in view of the mosquitoes, and make-up wasn't an option with the oven-hot heat and humidity. They washed at night and in the morning by the simple process of pouring a bucket of tepid water – the water was always tepid due to the conditions – over their heads, and ate what was given to them, often not enquiring too closely what was in the inevitable stews or rice-based dishes. Enoch swore on his life he had seen a claw in one of the vast metal feeding troughs the cooks used, and it was more than likely.

The days and weeks became something of a blur as they travelled from one camp to another in a state of constant exhaustion, the odd venue more memorable, like the show Bonnie performed at an airport where they were housed in proper beds overnight, or the one at the other end of the spectrum when a concert was interrupted in the depths of the jungle by an irritable bull elephant making his presence known. Some of the roads they travelled were difficult and dangerous and others just plain bumpy and uncomfortable, but it was towards the end of the tour at Dimapur, near the Japanese border, at the height of the Kohima battle that something happened which was to change Bonnie's life in a way she could never have foreseen.

They had arrived at Dimapur late one evening and gone straight to sleep in a kind of shed where a sheet had been fixed between Enoch's bunk and Bonnie's, presumably for modesty. The next morning Bonnie had visited two hospitals to chat to the patients, but at the third one, after lunch, she was due to do a show. This meant the doctors and male nurses – she hadn't seen one female nurse to date – would move the patients into the largest ward so there wasn't an inch of elbow room left after the piano had been dragged in. So many bodies in such a confined space, along with the smells that went with them and the heat, meant these occasions really were a labour of love. But this hospital, like the two in the morning, was housing men injured from the raging Kohima battle and all the patients were severely wounded but incredibly brave. The fact that they wanted to hear her sing was humbling, but it also brought up feelings that tore her apart when she let herself dwell on them. That one madman's quest for power could start a rippling effect that resulted in such horror was terrifying, and she constantly had to check the depression that could have gripped her if she had let it, and tell herself she would think about it all when she wasn't so exhausted.

She started the concert with 'A Song at Sunrise' and as she sang you could have heard a pin drop in the packed tent. Some of the men shut their eyes as tears welled up, but others were openly crying, and when she finished the song the burst of applause actually made her jump. She continued with other popular numbers, including 'You'll Never Know' and 'My Heart and I', as well as songs relevant to the war like 'We'll Meet Again' and 'The White Cliffs of Dover', finishing with 'This is the Army, Mr Jones' which always lightened the atmosphere.

Once the performance had finished and she'd had a drink of boiled water in which a few desultory tea leaves floated, she asked the officer who was escorting them if there were any patients whose injuries meant they couldn't be moved but who would like her to sing to them. These were normally the men who had little chance of survival, in spite of the new wonder drug – a yellow powder put directly onto the wounds and called penicillin – that was bringing others back from the brink of certain death.

The officer looked at the fresh-faced young girl in front of him who didn't look a day over eighteen, although he had been told she was several years older, and said very gently, 'There are a few but you would find their injuries very upsetting, Miss May. Perhaps it would be better—'

'I want to see them if they are willing.'

'I'm sure they would be willing and it would do them the world of good to hear you sing. It brings them closer to home for a little while. You know?'

Yes, Bonnie said. She knew.

Leaving Enoch to a second cup of the boiled water that passed as tea, the officer having said the tent with the very badly injured wouldn't accommodate a piano, Bonnie followed her escort out into the blazing heat, which was only slightly hotter than inside the tents. How the injured must long for a cool breeze or a drink of cold water, she thought as she walked. The unimaginable heat must mock them, reminding them every moment that they were in a foreign land and far from home.

When she walked into the tent it was the stench of gangrene and putrefying flesh that first hit her and it took all of her control to show no reaction. There were four beds in it. Two of the occupants were lying completely still, one so badly burned it was impossible to know how old he was, but the other two men moved their heads when the officer said, 'Miss May wanted to sing for you.'

She had managed to stitch the customary smile on her face along with showing no shock or horror, but as her gaze met that of the man in the last bed she knew her expression had frozen. The blood pounded in her ears, she felt sick and dazed and dizzy, and then the dirt floor rushed up to meet her as she fell.

Chapter Twenty-Two

He had heard she was coming to the camp, of course. The doctors and nurses had been full of it over the last day or two in an effort to jolly everyone along, but he'd thought being in the 'no-hopers' ward, as the men called it, she wouldn't see him. He'd suffered the torments of the damned over it, part of him desperately wanting to look at her face once more before he died, and the other part dreading what would happen if she realized he was still alive. If she recognized him.

John Lindsay lay back on the hard plank bed, his head spinning. And she had recognized him, all right. It had been a moment or two since the officer had carried her unconscious body out of the tent, muttering something about the heat and exhaustion. Would she come back when she came round? And what would he say to her if she did? How could he explain why he had let her think he was dead? He'd known it was cruel, but it had been for her that he had continued to be 'dead' when he'd remembered who he was. And he could have been dead, would have been but for Skelton calling his gorillas away when he saw a couple of coppers walking down the road.

It had been Robert who'd saved him, Robert and a pal of his. Apparently they'd got him away in a handcart and Robert had pushed the thing for days on end, putting as much distance between Sunderland and Skelton as he could. He himself had been unconscious for more than three days, according to Robert, and when he'd come round he couldn't remember who he was or anything about his past life. Skelton's thugs had done a good job on his head with their hobnailed boots.

Robert had told him the little he knew, emphasizing that they would be dead men if they went back, and so once he was physically able, the two of them had signed on as members of a crew on a boat leaving for the West Indies. He had chosen the name Abe Turner for himself – it was as good as any other – and he was still known by it today.

He and Robert had been away for over twelve months when he had begun to have the occasional fleeting flashback to his past life. Faces, a name, the image of a place or building had come and gone before he could pin them down to mean something. And then one morning, for no apparent reason, he had woken up and his mind was his own again. He had a bairn, a little lassie. He remembered it all. And his heart had wept.

It had been a shock to find out what sort of man he was, a man who could take the jewellery his wife had left for their daughter and pawn it, whose obsession with gambling had eventually reduced him to agreeing to be one of Skelton's lackeys. Not only that, but in crossing the gangster the way he had, he'd put a price on his head. He couldn't go home, and Bonnie's best chance in life would be without a millstone round her neck like him. It had been a bitter pill to swallow, and for a long time he had sought solace in the bottle. He'd had nothing but contempt for himself, and but for Robert sticking by him there was no doubt he would have drunk himself to death or ended it all by jumping off one of the boats into the deep dark waters of the ocean.

But then had come the war. They had been in Portsmouth looking to board another ship when it had happened, and – having had enough of the sea by then – he had volunteered to become a soldier and Robert had followed his lead. And eventually, after other bloody battles, they had ended up in this malignant, foul place. How he hated the jungle.

He shut his eyes, the pain from the stump of his leg that had been amputated a few days before and the agony from the deep wound in his stomach, which had laid bare his insides, nothing to the torment of seeing Bonnie again.

When they had been told they were being shipped to Burma, he had been blissfully unaware of what that meant, but within minutes of landing on Burmese soil he'd found out. The jungle was like nothing else on earth – the permanent semi-twilight – gloomy even when sunshine dappled the jungle floor with shadows; the constant dampness – rain or sweat – of stifling, windless heat; the dirty clothes on smelly bodies; the heavy backpacks and loaded and cocked weapons they were forced to carry, it all drained a man quicker than the most ferocious fighting. Tensed reflexes, inaccurate maps, constant vigilance, tired limbs, sore shoulders where equipment straps bit in, a chafed crutch and the desperate craving for a cigarette to quell the nerves for a while. And a cold beer. Hell, he would have given his right arm for a cold beer many times. As it was, it was his right leg that had been separated from his body, he thought grimly.

But it was perhaps the constant expectancy of death from behind the impenetrable screen of green in the jungle that got to you the most. He nodded to himself. In the heart of the jungle he and his fellow soldiers had found the fight against the Japanese almost incidental. The real fight was against the enervating climate, the demanding terrain, the fitfulness of sleep, the lack of hot meals, the disease and the accidents every day because of the many natural hazards. The insects and wild animals were bad enough, but one of his pals had had a leech go inside his penis, blocking the passage. And in spite of all the doctors had done, the poor beggar had died screaming. But then there were so many ways to die in the jungle and none of them pleasant, especially if the enemy had anything to do with it.

He and Robert had only been in Burma for a week or so when they were out on patrol one day and saw what looked like one of their soldiers embracing a tree. They had gone to see what the trouble was and found that the Japanese had nailed the man to the tree by his hands and feet. He was dead, but he hadn't died easy. It had been their first encounter with the unique cruelty of the Japanese but not their last. It had made them very careful but also determined always to have a grenade by them so that if it came to it they'd choose to go while taking as many of the enemy with them as possible.

It hadn't been long after that when their patrol had entered a village close to a Japanese administrative area. They'd found a Nepali living there, and he had reported to the CO that the Japanese had looted his village, killed his wife and stolen his cattle to eat. They had also taken away his son and two daughters and he believed them to be dead also. The CO had ordered them to take the Japanese compound and once they had killed the enemy they had discovered the two young girls in the house. Both had been repeatedly raped but were still alive, as was the son who couldn't have been more than twelve or thirteen and who the Japanese had used as a servant to fetch water and cook food.

They had taken the children – the girls were even younger than the son – back to their father, along with several of the cattle that hadn't yet been slaughtered, and left what medical supplies they could spare with the family for the girls. He had found it hard to sleep that night. War was one thing, but the rape and buggery of children? Who – *what* – could do that?

John rubbed his hand across his face, aware he was fighting against thinking about what he would say when Bonnie came back. *If* she came back. But she would, he knew she would. His lass had never been one to shy away from conflict. Did she hate him? He wouldn't blame her if she did.

He groaned, forcing his mind to replay the lecture on jungle craft that they'd had on their first day in Burma, a lecture that had become the mantra by which they lived – or died. He could recite it off by heart and he did it now, dulling his brain to any other thought.

The ability of a soldier to live and fight in the jungle; to be able to move from point to point and arrive at his objective fit to fight; to use ground and vegetation to the best advantage; to be able to melt into the jungle either by freezing or intelligent use of camouflage; to recognize and be able to eat native foods . . .

There was more, much more, but John found he wasn't winning. Bonnie wouldn't be denied. It was after the war had started that he had discovered the Bonnie May who sang on the radio and made records was his Bonnie. He had seen a signed photograph she had sent to one of his comrades, and he hadn't been able to believe his eyes. Everything in him had wanted to write to her, but what could he say? 'This is your da, Bonnie. The one who deserted you and ran off with your mother's jewellery and then fell foul of a gangster who controlled a large part of Sunderland's underworld. Oh yes, and my name's Abe Turner now.' She would have thought he had contacted her because she was well off and famous, anybody would.

One of the nurses had heard him groan and now appeared at his side with a syringe, injecting him with whatever it contained even as he asked how the pain was. John didn't object. He knew what being in this ward meant. The Grim Reaper was waiting. And if he could have died without Bonnie knowing about his other life he would have been content to go. He had always hoped she had imagined he'd met with an accident and knew that he had been meaning to come home that night, even though the jewellery was missing. That she hadn't doubted his love for her. That her memories of him were good ones.

But now . . .

Hell, he would rather be waiting to face a Japanese soldier than Bonnie right now. They might be cruel so-and-sos and barely human as far as he was concerned, but anything would be better than having to look into her eyes again and see himself reflected as the scum he was. His fingers pulled at the sheet covering his body, the stitching already rotten. Everything went mouldy or rotted in the jungle. Rust appeared overnight and mildew could grow on leather between dusk and dawn when it rained.

A movement brought his head turning to the entrance

of the tent and there she was. And the next moment she had knelt down beside him, taking his hand and murmuring, 'Da, Da, Da,' through her tears.

He tried to speak but the lump in his throat was choking him. He felt helpless and weak and consumed by shame, totally undone by the love he could see shining out of her face. He didn't deserve this, he told himself as her arms went gently round his neck and he felt her tears on his face. She should hate him for leaving her and letting her think he was dead. He hated himself.

It was a little while before either of them spoke, and the officer who had escorted Bonnie back to the tent had left, but not without casting a quizzical glance John's way. He was clearly as puzzled as the other conscious occupant of the ward who, having had half of his jaw blown away, wasn't in a position to ask any questions but had raised himself on one elbow and was staring at them.

'I'm sorry, lass. I'm so, so sorry.' John had kept his eyes shut and now, when she straightened and moved slightly to sit down very carefully on his bed, he opened them to find the love was still there in her face.

Bonnie stared at her father. For a long time after he had disappeared she'd had dreams in which he appeared. She had run to him and been whisked up into his arms, and she had laughed and cried and he had told her it was all a terrible mistake and of course he wasn't dead. And she had been so glad, so happy. And then as time had gone on, even when she had dreamed the dream she'd known it was only that, a dream, but she had tried to stay asleep so she could make the most of seeing him again. And eventually the dreams had stopped. But he was here. He was alive. The impossible had become possible. She took one of his hands and stroked the big, gnarled knuckles that she remembered from childhood. 'I love you,' she whispered.

'And I love you, me bairn. I always have, you must believe that. After your mam passed away you were the only thing that mattered to me and that's never changed.'

'I can't believe you're alive.' But even as she said it she wondered for how long. He looked so ill. In all the dreams he had been strong and big and brawny. 'Da, what happened?' She had to ask, she had to know why he had left her. She would have staked her life on the fact that only death could separate them. 'Tell me everything.'

And he told her, beginning from the night he had kissed her and settled her in bed before walking out of her life. And as Bonnie listened, the terrible hurt she'd felt when she had come round in the officers' mess and known he was alive and hadn't tried to find her melted away. She could see how it had happened and understood he had thought he was doing the best thing for her, but he had been wrong, so wrong. She wouldn't tell him that now. Maybe one day in the future if God spared him.

She stayed quietly by his side, telling him all about her life and Art, her grandma and Franco, Nelly and Thomas, missing out any bits that might distress him and painting a deliberately rosy picture of how life had been after he had gone. 'When you're well enough to come home, you'll live with me and Art,' she declared firmly. And when he made some protest, she said, 'Please, Da. I can't lose you again,' and he became silent.

He slept for a little while once or twice, the morphine in his system making him drowsy, and she remained holding his hand tightly, praying for all she was worth that he would get better. He had to.

Enoch came to find her during one of these periods, and when she explained the situation he promised he would go and find the commanding officer and make sure she became next of kin on any paperwork, and that the army was aware John had a home to go to when he was discharged. 'That's the most we can do,' he whispered as she stared at him with tragic eyes at the thought of leaving. 'You understand that, don't you? You can't stay here with him, Bonnie. I can give you twenty-four hours and you can miss tomorrow's engagements, but after that we'll have to continue the programme.'

'I can't leave him here, Enoch.'

'You've no choice, I'm afraid. He's too ill to be moved – all the men in here are – and the CO wouldn't let you stay. My hands are tied, I'm sorry. But once we're back in England I promise you we'll move heaven and earth to have him shipped back home, all right?'

'But what if he doesn't make it? He's so ill.'

'If he is anything like you, he will make it. And don't

forget he has something to fight for now he's found you. It'll make all the difference.'

'You don't really believe that, do you? That he's going to pull through?'

'Of course I mean it,' Enoch lied. 'I know his daughter, remember? And sheer guts and determination are more than half the battle in something like this.' He had already warned the doctor who was dealing with her father to gloss over the extent of his injuries, after the man had told him it would be a miracle if John survived the next few days. The doctor had agreed to play ball, adding that of course miracles did happen now and then that defied medical science, so there was always hope. Just the tone of the man's voice had confirmed to Enoch that Bonnie's father was a goner.

For the next twenty-four hours, apart from dealing with bodily necessities, Bonnie didn't leave her father's side. The officer who had been looking after them found her a wicker chair from somewhere, and she dozed in that when John slept, waking immediately if he began to stir. She sang softly once or twice for him and the patient with the injured face, and when one of the two men lying so still and unresponsive was quietly taken away, it made her pray all the harder for her father. Life seemed so frighteningly fragile in this little tent, so easily snuffed out. This was what war was about and it was madness.

When John was awake, they tried to fill in the lost years as best they could, each hungry for a picture of the other's life. John cried twice. Once when he told Bonnie of how he had come into his right mind, only to realize what he had done and that he couldn't return home because she would be better off without him. And again when he spoke of Robert's death. His friend had been killed in a booby trap with grenades set by the Japanese. He didn't go into details, but Bonnie got the impression Robert hadn't died quickly and cleanly.

'I wrote to his mother, of course,' John said quietly. 'I told her Robert died instantly and that he wouldn't have known anything about it, lies that any mother would want to hear. It's what Rob would have expected me to do. But I tell you, Bonnie, I still see him when I close my eyes. The British Army forbids booby traps but them devils make the most of them, and of course it scares our lads to death. Which is what the Japs want, I suppose. To create fear and uncertainty and ruin morale. You under-estimate them to your cost, that's for sure.'

He fought for breath with the effort of saying so much, and Bonnie said quickly, 'No more talking, Da. Rest a little.'

'I don't want to rest. You'll have to go soon and I can rest all I want then.'

Nevertheless, in spite of himself, he drifted off into one of the morphine-induced slumbers within the next moment or two. Bonnie sat looking at him while he slept, his words about the Japanese ringing in her ears. Before the war, Japan had just been the name of a dis-tant country to her, but not now. It was well known the

Japanese held their enemies in overwhelming contempt; their predilection for looting, rape and wanton bombing had been reported on the radio and in the newspapers, along with their cruelty to POWs. She had read what she could about Japan when she knew she was coming to Burma, and the Japanese belief in Yamoto dameshii, the Japanese spirit, that sees death in battle as man's finest destiny, was so at odds with the Western world that she had realized very quickly there was no meeting point between the two sides. Japanese values were unique to Japan, it was as simple as that, and things like seppuku – ritual self-disembowelling – were alien to the European mind. If the Japanese took over this camp they would kill her father and other injured men without a second thought.

She felt a moment's panic, as though it was already happening, and then told herself not to be so silly. But she didn't want to leave him here, so close to a ruthless enemy and in conditions that would be unthinkable for such an ill man in England. But Enoch had said the doctors had made it quite clear that to move him would kill him, and so she had no choice.

She wrestled with herself for some minutes before becoming aware that her father was awake and looking at her.

John stared at his daughter. Her face had always been the window to her soul – she was like Louisa in that way – and he knew she was fearful of leaving him. Nor did he want her to go. If there was any way she could have stayed with him, he would have welcomed it whole-heartedly. But there wasn't. And so he had to make this as easy for her as he could. Pretend. Lie, and lie well. He reached out his hand and when she took his, he turned it over in his fingers. Her hand wasn't the hand of a show-business star. It was grimy, the nails dirty, because that's what happened when you were deep in the Burma jungle, you got grimy and damp and all the niceties of civilization disappeared. No, this hand was the hand of a warrior, someone who had guts and courage enough for ten women, and he couldn't be more proud of her if he tried.

'It'll be all right, lass.' He smiled. 'I'm not going to meet my Maker for many a year, it's not my time. I know I'm not going to die, so once you get home you get a bed ready for me, is that a deal? We'll have Christmas together, I promise.'

He saw her face lighten a little and it enabled him to lie some more.

'I intend to be around for when you and your Art have a bairn and make me a granda. And if the first one's a boy then John is as good a name as any, don't you think? Good strong name, John, and I'm strong, lass. You know that. Always have been. It'll take more than the Japanese to finish me off before me time. I won't let them devils win, not me.'

Bonnie held his hand tighter. 'I can't bear to think I might lose you again. I don't know what I'd do.'

'So don't think it. Trust in your old da, all right? I have something to get better for now, don't I?'

'I'd love you to know Art. And Nelly will be pleased that I've found you.' It was the understatement of the year but intentionally so. She had told her father only that Nelly was a widow with a young son because that had seemed the right thing to do. If they met – *when* they met, she corrected herself – it was up to Nelly how much she said.

'I'm glad Nelly found someone even if they didn't have long together, and at least she has the lad,' John said now. 'She's a grand woman. And I'm not surprised her family is gentry. She always was a cut above. He's a nice lad, her Thomas, you say? Looks after his mam. That's good, that's good.'

They talked some more about Nelly and Thomas and other things before John slept again, and all the time Bonnie was aware that time was ticking away.

Chapter Twenty-Three

Bonnie had told herself she wouldn't cry and John had done the same, but, as it was, they both failed when the parting came. John cursed himself because he had wanted to make it as easy for her as he could, and here he was blubbering like a bairn. Bonnie just fell apart. In a twist of fate more extraordinary than anything she could have imagined she had found her da alive, and now they were being forced apart again. She was angry and frightened and heartbroken, and although she wanted to be strong it was beyond her.

Enoch had to almost carry her out of the tent and he was at a loss to know what to do, but after a few minutes Bonnie managed to compose herself. 'I have to go back and see him one last time.' They were sitting in the truck, ready to go, and when Enoch went to protest, she said, 'I can't leave him like that, I just can't. Give me five minutes, Enoch.'

When she walked back into the tent John was lying with his eyes closed. The other bed in the ward had been filled during the night and the man in it was moaning in pain like an injured animal. Bonnie swallowed hard. She wanted to scream and shout and cry and rail against the circumstances, but that would do her father no good. He was stuck here for the time being.

She knelt down beside the bed much as she had done when she had first come to him, and as he opened his eyes, she whispered, 'I had to come back, Da. Just to say I love you. And thinking about it, I know I was drawn to Burma and was meant to find you. I can't explain it, but I know it. And I don't believe God would do that and then let you die. So get well. Get well and come home. All right?'

John smiled. 'That's me girl,' he whispered as softly as she'd done. 'That's me bairn.'

By the time she left the tent once more, Bonnie was feeling – not exactly better – but more at peace.

She climbed into the truck and Enoch said nothing but put one of his hands over hers, pretending not to see the tears streaming down her face now she didn't have to be strong for her father any longer.

The rain had been pouring down for an hour or more, branches dripping either side of the track they were following, and Bonnie wondered how it could rain so hard and yet bring no relief from the heat and humidity. But at least while it was raining the flies were kept away to some extent. Of all the inconveniences in the jungle, she felt it was the flies and mosquitoes that bothered her the most. While she had been sitting with her father she had fanned them off him as much as possible, but who would do that now? No one.

She was still thinking of her father when Enoch said, 'What's that?' to their driver, and as she came back to the present she heard what he'd heard.

'It's the noise of the battle,' the man said impassively, 'but don't worry, you're not in any danger. In a short while you won't hear it any more.'

'Right.' Enoch sounded unconvinced. 'So we're pretty near the front line then?'

'Depends how you look at it.'

Enoch wriggled in his seat. 'Japanese jumping out in front of us and bombs landing on us was how *I* was looking at it.'

The driver smiled. 'Ninety-nine per cent sure you needn't worry about that.'

'Right. That leaves one per cent to worry about, though.'

'Hey, what can I say? You're bang smack in the middle of a war zone. Nothing is a hundred per cent, stuff happens.'

Enoch was clearly far from reassured, but funnily enough his anxiety made Bonnie feel better. This was normal; she was used to Enoch's panic attacks and knew her role in them. She patted his arm. 'It'll be fine. Listen, You can hardly hear the guns going off now. And look, the rain's stopping.'

They bumped and jolted along the road, stopping for

over an hour when a couple of wild oxen flatly refused to move out of their path, and being entertained by a woodpecker rattling its beak against a tree trunk as it fed off some ants. When poor Enoch had first heard the sound he'd been sure it was the enemy about to spring out at them. Again, their driver's comments, spoken in a matter-of-fact voice, did nothing to settle Enoch's nerves. 'This is a constant problem in Burma,' he drawled easily, 'knowing exactly where the Japs are. We find our maps are unreliable and air photographs are no good in revealing their position. The main method of relaying information is from the local natives but that can be suspect. You never really know who's on our side. Having said that, I owe my life to a Burman.'

'What happened?' asked Enoch, as the woodpecker continued its tapping and the oxen munched slowly.

'We were seventy-odd miles behind enemy lines in the middle of the night so we couldn't see a hand in front of us and we were ambushed, not the best scenario. Mules were cantering about throwing their loads, grenades were going off, machine guns firing, men screaming. Chaos. You get the picture? And all the time you're very aware the enemy are the Japanese who don't play by the Geneva Convention when it comes to POWs.'

Enoch glanced nervously around the green walls either side of the road, but Bonnie found that the driver's story was taking her mind off leaving her father. 'Go on,' she murmured.

'It was pitch black as only a tropical night can be, so

there was no way to distinguish friend or foe. The platoon scattered and before we knew it me and a pal of mine were on our own with Japs all around. At that point we didn't think we'd got a chance and our only resolve was to take as many Japs down with us as we could. And then this old Burman appeared. I nearly did for him before I realized he wasn't a Jap. Anyway, he took us to his house which was on stilts and there were his wife and kids and an old grandmother looking every bit as terrified as us, and we stayed there for the night. Worst few hours of my life. Any minute we expected the Japs to storm the place. You wouldn't believe how many noises there are at night in the jungle.'

'I would. Oh, I would,' Enoch said with feeling.

'The next morning he fed us and then led us umpteen miles through the jungle to where the platoon had been making for before the Japs had ambushed us. He was one of the good guys all right. We were the only ones who survived that ambush. And you know, we tried to give him some money and he wouldn't take it. No, he wouldn't take it,' he added, as though to himself.

'Did you ever see him again?' asked Bonnie.

The driver shook his head. They sat in silence for a while and Bonnie must have dozed off – she'd only had cat naps over the last forty-eight hours or so – because she was suddenly aware of the engine starting again and the oxen had disappeared into the jungle.

They arrived at the camp where Bonnie was due to perform an evening concert later that day, and after a meal of the inevitable nondescript stew and plain boiled rice, she mounted the makeshift 'stage' – a number of planks nailed together on two wooden pallets – and sang as though she didn't have a care in the world. No one hearing her would have dreamed her heart was some miles back in the jungle in a tent where a man was fighting for his life.

They slept that night in a large bamboo hut with several rooms. Bonnie hadn't expected to fall asleep quickly – her mind was taken up with her father as she lay under her mosquito net watching the bush rats that ran about in the roof of the shelter – but exhaustion must have played its part because when she felt her arm being shaken and Enoch saying, 'Wake up, sleepyhead,' it was ten o'clock in the morning.

She was due to visit two hospitals that afternoon before doing a show at another camp. More travelling along bumpy tracks, and for a moment, full of aches and pains from lying on the makeshift bed that was identical to so many others she'd slept on during the trip, and her mind full of her father now she was awake, she wanted nothing more than to sink back into oblivion. She was so tired, in mind, soul and body, and felt cut off from everything and everyone back home. She had been able to write letters to Art although she knew some would get lost, and had received one back at the beginning of May, but it wasn't like hearing his voice.

Because she was so worn out, she didn't register the excitement in Enoch's voice at first. Not until he said,

'Come on, Bonnie, wake up properly. There's great news,' did she sit up, moving her mosquito net aside as she asked, 'What news?'

'The Allies have landed in Normandy, the invasion of Europe has begun. The tide's turning, Bonnie. At last the tide's turning.'

'Are you sure?'

'The CO here told everyone this morning that Eisenhower's made an announcement so there's no doubt. It's the biggest combined land, sea and air operation of all time.' Enoch was fairly bubbling with excitement. 'Rome's been liberated by the Allies too. They say the Italians are wild with excitement – women are throwing flowers at the troops and men are handing out bottles of wine and shouting *Viva the English* and *Viva the Americans*.'

His excitement was infectious. Suddenly she didn't feel tired any more. There had been rumours for months about an Allied invasion but now it had actually happened. Her thoughts went immediately to Art fighting in Italy. Since he had rejoined his unit abroad there had been months of harsh and bloody battles against crack German troops, and her fear for him was always there in the back of her mind. Dampened down most of the time, because she had found early on in the war that no one could live in a state of heightened anxiety all the time, but always ready to spring into sharp terror, like now.

Her face must have betrayed her thoughts, because Enoch said, 'Art'll be fine, Bonnie. Don't worry.'

'Don't worry.' How many times had she had that said

to her, and how many times had she said the same thing to others worrying about their loved ones? They all knew the words were pointless but what else could you say?

After Enoch had told her all he knew, she tidied herself and then joined him outside the hut on a kind of narrow verandah that ran the length of it. One of the army cooks had brought over their morning meal – sausage-shaped soya links that had been seasoned with something or other but still tasted of very little, and white boiled rice with an indistinguishable green vegetable mixed in with it. The camp was going about its daily business, but even from where Bonnie and Enoch were sitting they sensed a different atmosphere from that of the day before. The news of the invasion had lifted everyone.

Bonnie forced down the food – she always ate everything she was given, conscious that she couldn't afford to fall ill. They were on the last leg of the tour now and it wouldn't be long before they did the outward journey in reverse. But for leaving her father, she would have been relieved she had nearly accomplished what she'd set out to do and could go home. As it was, she felt as though she was abandoning him to his fate and would have given anything to be able to remain in Burma and nurse him herself. But the war machine said otherwise.

She sighed, fending off the flies as she finished her meal and feeling totally helpless. She wanted to jump up and run back down the track they'd travelled the day before and not stop until she reached her father's side. The knot in her stomach that had been there since the day before tightened as she thought about his injuries. Losing his leg would have been bad enough, but she knew it was the wound in his stomach that was the main concern. And accepting that there was nothing she could do was the hardest thing. It seemed such a cruel twist of fate that having found him, they'd had such a short time together.

Their driver walked across to them in the next moment and she knew it was time to go. Every stage of the journey from now on would take her further away from her da and there wasn't a thing she could do about it.

It was another week or so and many more shows and hospital visits before they reached Jorhat and the little airport from where they would fly to Calcutta. For the first time in weeks the bed was soft and comfortable that night, and Bonnie enjoyed the luxury of a bath.

They were delayed in Jorhat for some days due to the weather being too bad for planes to fly, and it was there that Bonnie and Enoch heard that US bombers had reached the Japanese mainland. According to the District Commissioner, the long-prepared-for air offensive against the heartland of Japanese imperialism had finally begun in earnest, and as he put it, the beggars would now have a taste of their own medicine. The strategy of heavy bombing, used so effectively against Nazi Germany, was now being adapted to destroy the Japanese war industry and weaken morale.

'Even their Emperor must see they are going to lose the war,' one officer said to Bonnie and Enoch over dinner, the talk at the table inevitably about strategies and counter-strategies. 'But whether they'll admit defeat easily is another question. What possessed them to take on the United States of America in the first place is beyond me. Talk about catching a tiger by the tail. But it's this Emperor-worship thing that makes them so formidable. It produces a desperate form of courage that is beyond the European mind. Bushido, the way of the warrior, is everything to them. Did you know that words such as "surrender", "retreat" and "defence" were removed from the language of the revised 1928 Field Service Regulations in Japan, because their negative connotations might adversely influence morale? I mean, what can you say? What is going to have to happen to make such a nation surrender when losing face is worse than death itself?'

'You think they'll fight on no matter what?' said Bonnie, thinking of her father and all the men she had sung to and visited in the camps and hospitals over the last weeks.

'I fear so, yes. If fifty Japanese are holding a position, forty-five of them will have to be killed before the last five kill themselves rather than be taken prisoner. It's self-destructive bravery on a scale I've never seen before. If it wasn't for a supreme lack of grasping tactics by their officers that starts right at the top of the tree, they'd be invincible. As it is, they make the most elementary mistakes and become easy targets for our boys. You'll find this hard to believe, but one of our patrols climbed a low escarpment a few weeks ago and surprised two Japanese machine-gunners, capturing them and their weapon. These two Japs had been told by their officer that no one could climb to where they were, and so they hadn't resisted our boys when they did just that even though it was happening right in front of their eyes.'

The officer shook his head, clearly still finding such behaviour unbelievable. Bonnie found it terrifying. Such blind obedience was unnerving.

She went to bed that night with the officer's words ringing in her ears and wondering how many of the men she had sung to on this trip would make it out of the jungle. The officer had wound up their conversation by stating that of course the Allies would win the war and Japan would be defeated, but it would take time.

Time, she thought as she lay listening to the mosquitoes buzzing outside the net surrounding her bed. In the jungle a day seemed like a week, and a week, a month to the men so far away from home. Time was perhaps the greatest enemy of all . . .

Chapter Twenty-Four

The journey home took longer than the one out. The air over Europe was thick with aircraft as the Allies continued their offensive. They were delayed for some days in Gibraltar, and the talk there was about the Nazis' terrible new weapon that was targeting England, the pilotless, jet-propelled aircraft that carried nearly a ton of explosive and fell indiscriminately wherever they liked.

'They're calling them doodlebugs,' Enoch said grimly, passing Bonnie a newspaper he had been reading. They were sitting in a café drinking coffee, hoping they would be able to leave Gibraltar that day. Bonnie had visited a hospital that morning, and no one watching her would have thought she was counting the minutes until she could leave for home. 'Apparently you're all right if you can hear the engine – it's when it stops you have to worry.'

The newspaper article was full of the fact that Londoners were bracing themselves for another blitz, having been free of bombs and air battles for a while, warning that Goebbels's use of the phrase 'V-1' when describing the weapon hinted that the bombs were just the first of several such secret weapons Britain would have to face. Apparently anti-aircraft guns were proving to be in-effective against the remote-controlled weapon although hundreds were being rushed to the south coast, and RAF fighter pilots were seeking new techniques to counter the high-speed menace that was purposely bombing civilians.

'They're not even pretending to be targeting munition factories or docks or military camps,' Enoch said as Bon-nie finished reading the article. 'This is just plain murder of as many men, women and children as possible.'

Bonnie nodded. Art had been worried to death about her going to Burma, but in reality, especially with this new terror, it was just as dangerous at home. Nowhere was safe. You simply had to get on with your life and do what you wanted to do, Hitler or no Hitler.

She knew Enoch was aching to get home to Gladys and she was longing to crawl into her own bed and sleep for a week. She had hoped that there might be a letter from Art waiting for her somewhere on the route home, or some notification as to how her father was, but there had been nothing. And in truth she was so exhausted that she couldn't think straight which was perhaps a blessing in a way. She didn't have a moment's regret on embarking on the Burma trip, but it had taxed her body, soul and spirit. She had lost over a stone in weight and she had been slim to begin with; her clothes were hanging on her and her skin was a funny colour, but thanks to a hairdresser in Gibraltar who had soaked her hair in some oil or other before cutting and shaping it, at least it felt as though it belonged on her head again.

They flew home the next day, and when Bonnie's feet landed on British soil she felt quite emotional. The first thing Enoch did was to call Gladys, his relief palpable when she answered the phone and said all was well.

Once home in the little cottage in Kingston upon Thames and being fussed over by Annie, Bonnie did nothing but eat and sleep for a few days. But when she was rested, and before she started in the new show at the Empire which was opening after the weekend, she was determined to pay a visit to Manchester. She wanted to tell Nelly face to face about her father, not write or telephone her. Nelly deserved that at least. And Bonnie wanted to do it discreetly when Thomas wasn't around in case Nelly got upset. It troubled her that she had no way of finding out how her father was before she spoke to Nelly, but in spite of that she felt she couldn't delay putting her friend in the picture. She could wait for weeks, months, before she heard anything. Enoch had seen to it that the army had her full particulars as next of kin, and everyone in the hospital in Burma had been very kind, but the situation was what it was. Her father was lying desperately ill in the middle of enemy-occupied jungle, and she had seen for herself how stretched resources were for the doctors and nurses in the hospital. The medical staff didn't have time to write to her on her father's behalf, she understood that. But it left her not knowing. And that was worse than anything.

It was even worse than the scourge of the doodlebugs that were now falling day and night on the south-east. The second mass exodus of children was under way, many of the little ones returning to their former billets in the country, and more purpose-built deep shelters were opening to cope with the new threat. But terrifying though the bombs were, Bonnie and Annie had made the decision that they were going to sleep out raids in their steel-built Morrison shelter that had replaced the dining-room table at the beginning of the war.

'I'm too long in the tooth to go dashing about in the middle of the night,' Annie had said when they'd discussed it. 'Freddy –' as she had called their Morrison shelter – 'got us through the Blitz, and he'll get us through this.' And so they retired to Freddy when the sirens began to whine, snuggling down on the thick mattress under a thin sheet because the weather was so warm, and managing to sleep very well, considering everything.

Bonnie did wonder at times if she and Annie and lots of other Londoners like them had become hardened to bombing through the Blitz, and she supposed there was an element of that in their decision to stay put through this new attack by Hitler. But she didn't want to die, and she didn't think she was foolhardy, it was just that enough was enough. Hitler had instigated a war that had taken the lives of millions of men, women and children and caused untold suffering, and she was blowed if she was going to be reduced to running underground like a rat in a sewer every time the sirens sounded. And just as she'd told herself during the first Blitz, if a bomb had her name on it then it would find her wherever she was. But she had to admit that when the doodlebugs whizzed overhead she prayed the noise wouldn't stop, and that made her feel guilty because she was wishing them on someone else.

Selina and Cyril were expecting their first baby in September, and Bonnie knew the arrival of the doodle-bugs had affected her friend's nerves badly. Cyril had been invalided out of the navy in the autumn of the previous year so at least he was with her most of the time, but during one raid in broad daylight in a crowded shopping street Selina had been by herself and had arrived home terribly shaken.

'It's not me I'm bothered about,' Selina told Bonnie, the night before Bonnie was going to Manchester to see Nelly. 'It's the baby. If anything happened to it I don't know what I'd do.' She put her hands on her rounded stomach, her face pensive. She had confided in Bonnie months ago that the baby hadn't been planned, but once they had known it was on the way Selina had been thrilled even though previously she and Cyril had decided to wait until the war was over before considering bringing a child into such an uncertain world.

'Nothing is going to happen to you or the baby.' Bonnie hugged her friend. She had popped round to see

Selina and Cyril and give them some bananas she had bought in Gibraltar before they had flown home. No one in Britain had seen bananas since the war had begun, and Selina had been delighted, peeling one and eating it immediately while Bonnie and Cyril had laughed at her expression of ecstasy.

'I try to keep telling myself that but then I think of Betty and Cyril's mum and dad. They were having a sing-song that night, the night they died, you know how they were, and then within an hour or so of us leaving they were all dead. And you hear such horrible things, people killed or maimed or blinded—'

'Stop it.' Bonnie took Selina by the shoulders. 'You're all worked up because of the baby and that's understan-dable, but you can't worry yourself like this. It'll be all right, I know it will.'

'I keep regretting that we fell for a baby and then I feel guilty. It's not that I don't want it, not really, and I already love it more than anything in the world.'

'Of course you do.'

'But what if everyone's wrong and we don't win the war? I mean, no one knew about the doodlebugs, did they? What else have the Nazis got up their sleeve? And what if it drags on and on for years – what sort of life will my baby have?'

'Selina, we *are* going to win the war, and soon, and your baby will have a wonderful life with parents who love it to bits. And that's all that counts in the long run.'

Bonnie had said a lot more and by the time she left the

house Selina was more cheerful, but Bonnie was worried about her. Cyril had told her his wife cried for hours at a time some days and no matter what he said or did, she wouldn't be comforted. That wasn't like Selina. She had continued in her post as a schoolmistress right through the war until she had become pregnant, and at one point she had marshalled all her small charges out of the school playground when an unexploded bomb had been discovered, not leaving until she was sure every child was out of the school and safely away. She had received a commendation from the School Board for that and had been in the local newspaper.

Annie was waiting up for Bonnie with a mug of cocoa when she got home, and as soon as she told her about Selina, Annie nodded. 'Baby blues,' she said sagely. 'Some get it before and some after, but that's what it is, all right. You won't get any doctor tell you that, mind you, but you ask any woman who's suffered from it and they'll tell you it's real. An' of course with the war and all, that don't help.'

'Baby blues?'

'I had it real bad with my first all the time I was carrying him, but the minute he was born I was as right as rain, thank goodness, and a friend of mine had it after. Months before she was her old self, poor thing. Look, if you're going to Nelly's tomorrow, I'll nip round and see Selina and take Hilda with me. We'll put her right. It's never so bad if you know what you're dealing with, is it, and I don't expect Cyril's much help. Worse than useless at a time like this, a man.'

Bonnie blinked. She had never wondered why Annie and Hilda hit it off so well. They were two of a kind. 'She'd appreciate that, I know she would.'

'And I'll have a quiet word with Cyril and put him to the wise. My husband, God rest his soul, just used to tell me how fortunate I was and that I should pull myself together and count my blessings. It was my old mum who got me through.'

'Right.' Bonnie stared at Annie. It was the first time she had heard of the baby blues. 'Does every woman suffer with it then?'

'Good gracious, no. But for them as do, it's no picnic. A cousin of mine, nice girl, quiet, refined, drowned herself in the Thames after her doctor told her there was nothing wrong with her except in her mind and if she didn't make an effort she'd end up in an asylum. Her little girl was three months old when she did herself in. And they wouldn't give her a proper funeral because she was a suicide. Wicked, I call it. Her husband had been as bad as the doctor, she told me that herself before she died, but after she'd gone he got all the sympathy you could wish for.'

Annie sighed, finishing her cocoa before she said, 'There's them that keep on about how the war's changing how women are, what with them going out and doing men's jobs and drinking in pubs and the rest of it, but I tell you, Bonnie, I'm all for it.

'If women are good enough to be called up by the government in this war, then they're good enough for equal pay and the rest of it, but I can't see that happening and it's a crying shame. I can remember the fight for the vote and the day Emily Davison was buried after she fell under the King's horse at the Derby.

'Huge procession across London there was. I went with me mum and sisters, and everyone was saying that terrible though her sacrifice was, it would cause change. And it has to some extent, but not enough. No, not enough.'

'I never knew you were a suffragette, Annie.' Bonnie was amazed.

'I don't suppose I was, not a proper one anyway, but I believed in what they were fighting for. It was like in the First War when the government appealed for women to sign up for work in trade and industry and agriculture and making shells in the factories. All of a sudden the government was saying that women were capable of being employed in any capacity of physical or intellectual work, where a few years before they were claiming our minds didn't work as well as men's and our bodies were weak and we couldn't be trusted with the vote. That made me, and not just me – thousands of women – think long and hard, I tell you. They couldn't have it both ways. And look at you, going out to Burma and coping with goodness knows what as well as any man, better than some, I dare say. No, we're not weak, and this baby-blues thing is a definite affliction, not something imagined by a woman's "inferior" mind as that doctor told my poor cousin.'

They talked some more, and once Annie had gone up to bed Bonnie sat for a while longer thinking about their conversation. She had never really thought about equal pay for men and women or some of the other things Annie had brought up, but one thing was for sure, she had known plenty of strong women in her life. Nelly, Betty, Hilda, Selina, not to mention Annie herself. And her grandma had been strong too. She hadn't liked her grandma – she'd been a wicked woman, truth be told – but no one could have accused Margarita of being weak. She had led her life the way she had wanted to, the same as she – her granddaughter – was doing now.

It was a new thought that she had something in common with her grandmother, and not altogether a welcome one, but the more she considered it, the more Bonnie came to the conclusion that it was their similarities in certain respects that had made her and her grandmother clash so violently from when she was a little girl. One of her first memories was of herself standing outside her father's wagon while her grandmother yelled at her, and of herself yelling back. She could even picture the little red dress she'd been wearing – she couldn't have been more than four or five years old – and the way her grandmother had towered over her, her face red with temper.

Oh, dear. Bonnie shook her head at herself. This was awful. She didn't want to be like her grandma. But everyone had said how gentle and sweet and pliable her mother had been, so her fiery side didn't come from her. There was her da, of course, but the fire that ran in her genes couldn't altogether be put down to him.

For a little while Bonnie didn't know if she wanted to laugh or cry. It was one thing to be proud of her Spanish heritage – and she was, she always had been, the same as she was proud of being northern – but quite another to recognize characteristics in herself that could be attributed to her grandmother. The more she thought about it, however, the more she told herself that the things that had come from Margarita – strength, determination, passion and intensity of spirit – were good in themselves, they'd just got twisted and distorted in her grandmother. She would never know quite why Margarita had been the way she was, but there was no reason for her to be the same. Bitterness had wrapped her grandmother around like a shroud; she had *chosen* to become the woman she had been. Just as she'd chosen to marry Franco, and to hate her only daughter's husband with a hate that had burned her up and which had destroyed any possible relationship with her daughter's daughter, chosen to make her son-in-law's life so impossible that he had risked everything in a bid to leave the fair.

It was sad, it was actually sad to waste your life in such a way, Bonnie told herself, and but for the fact that her grandmother had hurt so many people along the way, she would feel sorry for her right now. Perhaps she did a little, even so. She had forgiven Franco for what he had done to her, but then he had asked for forgiveness in his letter and shown remorse. Her grandmother never would have done that, it hadn't been in her to do so. But did she forgive her?

She sat with her arms crossed round her waist as though she was hugging herself, rocking gently as a child rocks itself in a cot when in need of comfort. And into her mind came a picture of her father lying desperately ill and in pain so far away from home.

She stopped rocking and her chin lifted. She knew the answer. Maybe one day she would find it in herself to forgive her grandmother for her part in ruining her father's life, for all the years that she and her father had lost, but not now. No, not now. Her grandmother had been a spiteful, cruel and manipulative woman and she hated her, and she was glad that she was dead. And if that meant that her grandmother didn't have the mono-poly on bitterness, then so be it.

Chapter Twenty-Five

Bonnie arrived outside Nelly's house in Manchester at four o'clock in the afternoon. Although the street had suffered no bomb damage, unlike some in the surrounding area, the consequences of war were apparent in the absence of the iron railings which had previously separated the few yards of front garden from the pavement. Nelly's lovely profusion of sweet-smelling flowers had gone too, and now the small plot of earth held vegetables around which a home-made-looking picket fence had been cobbled together.

As Bonnie looked around, she saw that most of Nelly's neighbours had done the same sort of thing. Clearly the Ministry of Food's exhortation for folk to make the most of even the tiniest bit of earth had been well heeded. The terraced houses only had a very small yard at the rear of each, barely enough to swing a cat, but if she wasn't mistaken there was parsley and mint in Nelly's window boxes too.

Bonnie knew Nelly probably wouldn't be home from

her job in a munitions factory yet, and sure enough there was no answer to her knock on the blue front door. She walked along the street and turned into the back lane that ran between the terraces. It was dusty and dry underfoot with clumps of yellowing grass here and there. Some of the houses still had functioning outside lavatories in the backyards, and Bonnie caught a whiff to confirm this as she passed one gate. Others, like Nelly's house, had been modernized with indoor plumbing and the outside lavatory had become redundant, often being turned into a storage area for coal.

The high brick walls either side of the lane made it something of a sun trap on a hot summer's day such as this one, and as Bonnie counted off the houses before she came to Nelly's backyard gate, she found herself thinking that you would barely know there was a war on in this quiet little oasis. A group of children were playing some game or other further down the lane; a big tabby cat sat cleaning itself on top of a wall, and through one open gate, Bonnie caught a glimpse of two grey-haired matrons chatting over a cup of tea while three or four toddlers – presumably their grandchildren – played in an old tin bath full of water.

The timelessness of it all gripped Bonnie and brought a lump into her throat. After all the devastation of the last few years, the bombed-out buildings and mountains of rubble and terrible loss of life, and Burma, where man's inhumanity to man had been ever present, this peaceful back lane was so different. This was how life should be lived.

She lifted her face up to the blue sky in which the odd cotton-wool cloud floated and shut her eyes for a moment so that the sun beat orange against her closed lids. She had almost forgotten that the sky could be something other than an expanse in which enemy aircraft travelled, bent on destruction. But it had been a benign and beautiful thing in the past and it would be so again, she believed that. The Allies would win the war, they had to, and Art would come back to her. They would have a family together, fat little babies who would grow up in a world that had been made safe again. She had to hold on to that. *And please God, let my father come home . . .*

It was a minute or two before she walked on and reached Nelly's gate. The small paved backyard was neat and clean, a row of pots holding tomato plants along one wall and a big wooden trough made from what looked like planks of wood and filled with earth along the other side. This was full of potato plants if she wasn't mistaken.

Nelly's back door was locked, but Bonnie had no sooner sat down on the step to wait than the gate opened and Thomas walked into the yard. Thomas was now fifteen years old and somewhat lanky, his golden-brown curly hair and dark eyes ensuring that the girls were after him already, according to Nelly. And Bonnie could see why. It wasn't just Thomas's good looks that were charming but his whole manner. It was the first time she had seen him for some months, and she noticed straight away that he looked even more like his father. She wondered why it didn't make her feel a little odd, but it didn't. Perhaps it was because in nature Thomas was very much his mother's son, and his innate gentleness and kindness shone out of his face.

He grinned at her now, his hug almost lifting her off her feet as he said, 'Auntie Bonnie, what a great surprise. Does Mother know you're coming? How was Burma? My school friends were well impressed when I told them what you were doing. They all have your records, you know. I get a lot of reflected glory, having a famous auntie.'

'Go on with you.' She kissed him on the cheek. 'You and your soft soap.'

'It's true.' He was opening the back door as he spoke, and when he stood aside for her to enter before him and Bonnie walked into Nelly's bright, welcoming kitchen, she reflected not for the first time that her friend had given Thomas a wonderful home in which to grow up. He had only known love and security in spite of not having a father in his life.

Thomas put the kettle on for a cup of tea and Bonnie told him all about her trip, leaving out the part about finding her father, as they sat at the kitchen table drinking and eating a slice of the eggless sponge in Nelly's cake tin. It was during a pause in the conversation that Thomas asked a question that caused Bonnie to nearly choke on her cake. 'Did you know my father, Auntie Bonnie?' he asked very quietly.

Thomas had never mentioned his father before, not to her. Nelly had told her that Thomas had asked about him a few times, and she had parried his questions as best she could. She had stuck to her story that Thomas's father, her husband, had been killed in a motor-car accident not long after Thomas was born, and had made excuses about the lack of any photographs by saying that there had been a fire and that documents and photographs had been lost. Thomas knew his mother had travelled with the fair with her performing dogs and that was where she had met Bonnie, but Nelly had told him that was after her parents had died and before she had met Thomas's father. An interlude in her life, was how she had described it.

Bonnie was thinking about all this as she looked at Thomas and wondered how to reply. That was the trouble with lies, you could trip yourself up so easily.

But before she could say anything, Thomas added, 'I found my birth certificate the other day, you see, the one that was supposed to have been destroyed along with my mother's marriage certificate and so on. And I confess I didn't stumble across it by accident, I went looking for it – or at least for something to explain the mystery I feel surrounds my birth and my mother's life before she had me.'

Bonnie stared at him. She didn't ask what the birth certificate had said – she could guess from the look on his face. Gently, she reached across the table and placed her hand on his. 'Have you spoken to your mother about this?'

'I want to but . . .' He shook his head. 'She gets so upset if I ever mention my father. When I was younger I used to think it was because she loved him so much and had lost him so early in their marriage, so I tried not to ask questions. But now . . .'

'Now you don't think that?'

'No, I don't.' He looked at her, a straight look, and in that moment Bonnie realized that some time during the last months the boy had become a man. 'And I want to know the truth.'

Softly she said, 'You have to talk to your mother, Thomas. Tell her that you've seen your birth certificate. You can't pretend everything is the same when it's not and I know she wouldn't want that. Anything your mother has said or done, she has done for your sake, I do know that. From the moment you were conceived you've been her whole life and she would sacrifice anything or anyone for you. You do understand?'

'It's all right, Auntie Bonnie.' He put his other hand over the one she'd placed on his. And now he confirmed what she had thought earlier, when he said, 'I'm not a child and I've got a pretty good idea of what happened, but I need to know the facts, the details, you know? It won't make me love Mother any the less but I won't be lied to any longer.' And when Bonnie would have protested, he said, 'I know, I know, she did it for my own good, that's what you're going to say, aren't you? The world can be cruel with its labels, I'm aware of that. But sooner or later the truth will out and I'm not ashamed of who I am.'

'I should hope not,' said Bonnie, somewhat helplessly. He was clearly upset but trying not to show it, and her heart went out to him.

'So, I come back to my original question. Did you know my father?'

She removed her hand from his and stood up. 'Thomas, I'll tell you anything I can but only after you have spoken to your mother. I'm going to go for a walk now as she'll be home soon, and you need to speak of this together without anyone else present. Tell her I'll buy myself a meal somewhere and be back before dark, all right?'

Thomas looked disconcerted. 'No, you don't have to do that. You've only just got here.'

'Don't worry, I'll be fine and I'll see you later. Just be honest with her. Tell her about the birth certificate and why you looked for it and she will understand it's time for you to know. Your mother only ever has your best interests at heart.'

He nodded, looking as though he was going to cry for a moment before making a visible effort to pull himself together. 'Things have been a bit strained lately,' he admitted as he walked with her out of the kitchen and into the hall. As Bonnie opened the front door, he added, 'Sometimes I've felt so angry and yet I still couldn't bring myself to say anything because I knew it would upset her, but you're right, we can't carry on like this.' He squared his bony shoulders that looked too wide for his thin, gangling frame. 'I don't want us to end up hating each other.'

'That would never happen.' She stepped down into the street that was hot after Nelly's cool kitchen, and turned to look up at him and say, 'See you later,' before walking purposefully along the pavement without any idea where she was going. And as she walked, she went over their conversation in her mind, worrying at it like a dog with a bone until she was panic-stricken she had done the wrong thing in encouraging Thomas to have it out with his mother. But then what else could she have done? she asked herself miserably, passing a huge bombsite that took in half a street and in which children were playing in the rubble. Thomas had seen his birth certificate and he had made it plain he needed some answers. The longer he left talking to Nelly, the longer things would fester.

Eventually she found a little café that was open and bought a cup of tea and a sticky bun, sitting at a table by the window and moving her chair so that her back was to the rest of the room. She sat fretting about what was happening back at Nelly's, and half listening to a conversation between two lorry drivers about the recent assassination attempt on Hitler at his Wolf's Lair HQ in East Prussia. The suitcase bomb under the conference table had apparently been planted by one of his own officers, but although three men had died, Hitler had escaped with only minor burns and cuts.

'I tell you, Harry,' one of the men was saying, 'the Devil looks after his own. Old Hitler's saying that Providence was preserving him to continue his life's work. Old Nick, more like. Wicked so-an'-so.'

'Aye, but don't forget what this really means,' the man called Harry answered. 'Hitler's own officers are turning against him. There's been rumours before but this is living proof. Nazi Germany's nearing collapse, all the papers are saying so, and once we finish them off it'll be time to do the same to the Japanese in the Far East. They're as bad as the Nazis any day, to my mind.'

'I agree with you there, Harry. Aye, I do. My poor old Phyllis is worried to death about her brother if the Japs know they've lost the war and I can't say I blame her. I reckon they'll do for our lads in their POW camps and then top themselves rather than surrender. Mind, poor old Joe might be six foot under already, she hasn't heard from him in months.'

The two men talked on but Bonnie wasn't listening any more, fear for her father spiralling through her. These men were right and they had voiced the fear that continued to haunt her day and night. She finished her tea, her hand trembling so that it slopped in the saucer.

One day at a time. It was a resolution she'd made at the beginning of the war because to look into the future was weakening. She couldn't help her father, not today, but she could be here for Nelly, and this was going to be a difficult day for her friend, however it went with Thomas.

The lorry drivers left the café after a few more minutes and Bonnie ordered another cup of tea, making it last as long as she could before she walked out into the street. It was still light and a beautiful evening, the relative quietness so different from London where the V-1s continued their deadly assault. Nevertheless, the ravages of war were reflected in the bombsites and burned-out buildings that were everywhere, as in all the major cities of Britain. The government were already talking about plans to build three or four million houses in the first decade after the war, stating that houses would be bigger, with three bedrooms, well-equipped kitchens, better heating arrangements and constant hot water, but as Annie had said when she'd read the report about the Ministry of Health's 'Design of Dwellings' in the newspaper, let's concentrate on winning the war and getting the men and women in the forces home first.

Bonnie took her time walking back to Nelly's. She got lost once or twice and had to ask her way, but it didn't matter. She was in no hurry, after all. She wanted to give Nelly and Thomas plenty of time.

Twilight was falling as she walked into the back lane for the second time that day, and as she looked down the length of it she saw Nelly standing at her gate. Nelly came towards her the moment she saw her, calling, 'I've been so worried, it's getting late. Thomas is out looking for you on his bike.' And as she reached Bonnie, she hugged her hard, saying, 'I'm so glad to see you.'

'I wanted to give you and Thomas time.'

'I know, he said. Oh, Bonnie.' Nelly hugged her again. 'I'm glad you told him to talk to me. He's been so different lately, withdrawn and snappy, not like my Thomas at all. I put it down to the pressure of his schoolwork, I must admit.' Thomas was in the top five per cent at the private school Nelly sent him to but he didn't enjoy school life or being stuck in a classroom.

They had started to walk on but now Nelly stopped. 'We've talked things through, Bonnie, and I've told him everything.' She swallowed hard. 'I think it was the most difficult thing I've ever done. I felt . . . Well, you can imagine how I felt.'

'How did he take it?' Bonnie asked gently.

'He'd guessed some of it already and he said it was a relief to know at last. I think he was disappointed Franco was dead. He said he would have liked to meet his father, even if it was only once.' Nelly's eyes filled up and she swallowed again. 'I hope he'll forgive me for that in time. We cried together and we're all right, sort of.' She dabbed at her eyes with her handkerchief. 'I suppose I always knew this day would come and perhaps I should have told him the truth a long time ago. I hate to think he was so troubled that he went hunting for information secretly.' She heaved a sigh. 'I feel like the worst mother in the world tonight.'

'Well, you're not. You're one of the best, believe me.

And Thomas loves you very much, Nelly. You know that.'

'But I'm no longer on the pedestal where every little boy puts his mother. I've got to learn to live with that.'

'Thomas isn't a little boy any more, Nelly. But knowing how much he loves you, he'll work this through. It won't crush him – he's strong, like you. When you knew you were expecting a baby you didn't try to get rid of it like lots of women would have done, and when he was born there was no question about giving him up so you could pretend it had never happened. He came home to a warm, safe, loving environment and a mother who has devoted her life to him. There are lots of bairns with two parents who don't have a quarter of the security and love Thomas has had, so keep this in perspective. I know it's hard but there are a lot worse things than growing up without a father.'

'Thank you.' Nelly smiled weakly. 'I can't tell you how glad I am you're here today. What made you come, by the way? You've got a season starting at the Empire after the weekend, haven't you?'

For a moment Bonnie wondered whether to tell her. Nelly had enough to cope with at the moment. But then it might help take her mind off Thomas to some extent, and if she was Nelly, she'd want to be told. 'Let's go inside and have a cup of tea and I'll explain,' she said quietly, hoping Thomas wouldn't come home for a while. 'I've got some news and it might be a shock.'

Once in the kitchen, Nelly plumped down on a chair

and waved her hand for Bonnie to do the same. 'I'll get the tea in a minute. Tell me. You're worrying me now.'

So Bonnie told her. And if she had ever been in any doubt that her father still held Nelly's heart as irrevocably as ever, her friend's reaction to the news that he was still alive would have put paid to it. They had cried and talked and cried some more when Nelly murmured, 'Did – did he say anything about me?'

Bonnie had thought she might ask this, and she could say in all honesty, 'Of course he did. In fact, you were the first person he asked after, Nelly, and he was so pleased we had found each other again when I explained. I told him you're a widow with one child and that you had made a good life for yourself. He asked to be remembered to you, Nelly.'

Nelly stared at her, tears still welling up as she whispered, 'To be so badly injured and so far from home. Oh, Bonnie, if you hear anything let me know at once, won't you?'

'The very minute, I promise.'

They talked some more until Thomas came home, and then the three of them ate a supper of fishcakes – salted cod that Nelly had mashed up with plenty of potato, vegetables and Worcester sauce – and the inevitable coarse brown bread with a scraping of margarine. They chatted about inconsequential things, each one aware that the atmosphere was a little strained.

Once ensconced in Nelly's spare bedroom, Bonnie lay awake for a long time. It had been an emotional day all round, and she would have given the world to have Art lying at the side of her, to hear his deep, steady breathing, to be able to reach out and know he was there. Strangely, now that there was all this talk about the Allies taking ground and the end of the war being in sight, she felt more panicky about him being at the front line. To be so close to the possible end of fighting and constant danger and then for him to be badly hurt or worse would be the ultimate heartache. But there was nothing she could do about it and so she had to wait. Her life seemed to be all about waiting.

Nelly was thinking much the same thing in her room. She hadn't bothered to get undressed because she knew she wouldn't sleep a wink; her head was buzzing. She needed to sit quietly and think about what had happened today – about Thomas certainly, but mainly the news that John was alive. Terribly injured, and Bonnie had stressed the fact that her father might have lost his fight to live even before she had left Burma, but for all the endless years that she had been inwardly mourning John, he had been in the world. Eating, drinking, sleeping, laughing, *living*.

She looked down at her hands that were clenched in her lap and realized that, ecstatic as she was that he was alive, she was angry too. With him, with John. How could he have just decided to cast off his old life the way he had? How *dared* he? Bonnie had explained about his loss of memory in the first months he'd disappeared, and she understood about that, but once he'd been restored to his right mind, why hadn't he swallowed his pride and feelings of shame and guilt and made himself known to his daughter? Poor Bonnie – she didn't deserve to have suffered the way she had, thinking he was dead.

Poor Bonnie? her mind probed. *Don't you mean, poor you? You're angry because he didn't come back to you but he was never going to do that.*

Nelly slid off the bed and began to pace. The room was hot and stuffy. The window was open but the thick, heavy blackout curtains let little of the night air through and she felt as though she was suffocating. She picked up her shoes and tiptoed onto the landing and down the stairs. Slipping her shoes on in the kitchen, she opened the back door and stepped outside. It was still warm, but there was a slight breeze, and she sat down on the edge of the container Thomas had built for their crop of potatoes, lifting her face to the sky.

It was a clear night. The stars twinkled like so many diamonds and the moon shone brightly in the darkness. A night for lovers to whisper sweet nothings. She sighed. She loved John, she always would. There'd been more than one man over the years who'd made it plain they were interested and would be prepared to take Thomas on too, but she had never even had a drink with any of them. She had been desperately lonely at times, even with her darling Thomas and the dogs when they were alive, but lonely for John, not simply for someone to love her and look after her. And as Bonnie had talked to her and explained why her father had taken the jewellery and got mixed up with ne'er-do-wells, she had felt such sorrow that he couldn't have fallen in love with her and told her what he wanted for Bonnie. She would have been able to set the three of them up in a little house together if they'd been married; Bonnie would have had a stepmother who adored her, and she and John might have had a little Thomas of their own. All their lives would have been so different.

She sat there in the warm night for more than a couple of hours battling her demons and working through a host of emotions. Rage, regret, humiliation, feelings of failure as a mother, remorse over her decision to keep Thomas from Franco and in the same breath fierce relief that she had, and overall the intense longing to see John again that had her bowing her head as scalding tears poured down her face. She wrestled with it all, and by the time she stood up and walked back into the house she was more at peace with herself. John would never love her. If, as she prayed, he survived his injuries and came back to England, she knew Bonnie wanted to provide a home for her father which meant that she might be able to feature in his life in some small way. But that was all. And it would be enough. To be able to talk to him occasionally, look into his eyes, see him smile and know he was happy, it would be enough. It might appear as crumbs from a rich man's table to some, and maybe it was, but she had no pride where John was concerned.

For Thomas, all she could do was to show him the

same love and devotion she always had and hope one day he would forgive her for the lies and deceit. She had offered him no excuses, nor would she; she was just so bitterly sorry that her son, her beloved son, was paying for what had been one night of madness.

In the kitchen, she looked to where the dogs' baskets used to be and would have given everything she owned to have them back with her for one hour; to be able to cuddle them on her lap, see the adoration in their canine eyes and know that their love was unconditional. But they had long since gone and she had to face life in the present, even though tonight it tasted like ashes in her mouth.

Chapter Twenty-Six

Bonnie spent the weekend with Nelly and Thomas, returning to London on the Monday morning and starting work at the Empire that afternoon. Somehow, after her time in Manchester, the capital seemed noisier and more dangerous than ever, but it was where home was and that was that. And so she did the show at the Empire every evening along with matinees at the weekend, fitted in broadcasts and recording and visits to hospitals and army camps and the rest of it when she could, and found herself without a minute to brood which was just as well. Keeping busy helped to keep the fear for Art and her father at bay to some extent. She had received no news from Burma, but neither had she heard from Art for weeks, and by the time a further attack on London began with a new and terrible weapon that was far worse than the V-ls, terrifying the capital in September, she was convinced something bad had happened to Art.

The new weapon, V-2s, were long-range rockets carrying one-ton warheads; they added to the chaos and devastation caused by the flying bombs, giving no warning of their arrival except for a tearing sound like an express train as they landed vertically from heights of fifty miles or more. The first, which hit Chiswick in West London, caused a blast wave that could be felt for miles, and Annie, who had happened to be visiting a member of her family in the area at the time, had been blown clean off her feet and had returned to Kingston upon Thames covered in cuts and bruises but as defiant about Hitler and his Nazis as ever.

Amid reports that the Allies had swept across Belgium after liberating Paris and Marseilles, along with Florence in Italy in August, came news that Mr Churchill and President Roosevelt had resolved to shift the war effort to the Far East. This occurred a week after the first V-2s fell on London. The newspapers were full of the proposed destruction of the 'barbarians of the Pacific' and that Nazi Germany was nearing collapse, but with death raining down from the skies in London, Bonnie didn't know what to believe. Everyone was aware that the power of propaganda had been used by both sides in the war, and like Annie said, if the Germans were doing so badly why were these 'gaswork explosions', as the government were maintaining the V-2s were, killing so many men, women and children?

She and Bonnie had been discussing the present situation one morning before Bonnie left for a radio broadcast, and as ever Annie put her finger on the pulse of the bewilderment felt by a lot of Londoners. 'Daft as brushes, half of 'em in government are,' she said with feeling. 'They say all these explosions are down to gas to confuse the Germans, but them blighters know full well it's what they're sending over that's causing them. And it just makes us ordinary folk at sixes and sevens, and wondering what other lies the government are telling. Gas explosions, my backside.'

Bonnie nodded her agreement as she finished her breakfast. The V-2s were much more frightening than the doodlebugs because you couldn't hear them at all until it was too late, and the blind bombing of civilians by an invisible enemy was unnerving. As, she supposed, it was meant to be. But she agreed with Annie about the government and their stories; it didn't exactly inspire confidence about anything that was in the newspapers or reported on the radio. She wanted to believe that the Germans were on the run throughout Europe and that knocking out Japan was the next job, but who really knew? One minute you heard one thing and then something else entirely the next. But one positive and undeniable fact was that the government had decided to relax the stringent blackout regulations and allow modified street lighting, along with railway stations being lit again, and trains and buses and trams. Some small children were seeing street lights for the first time in their lives. That had to be hopeful, didn't it, after five years of darkness?

She said as much to Annie, who lowered her chin into her neck and made a noise in her throat that could have meant anything. Annie had been born in the roughest part of the East End and had her own opinion about the government and the police and any other authority, and it wasn't commendatory.

It was drizzling with rain later, when Bonnie finished the radio broadcast and drove to the theatre. The matinee was at one o'clock, and she arrived in her dressing room with half an hour to spare. She sat applying her stage make-up which she preferred to do herself, but thinking about Art. She had a heaviness on her about him, that was the only way she could describe it, and she knew Annie was worried too. The fighting in Europe was so vicious and desperate. Thank goodness she had Annie to talk to.

Dear Annie, Bonnie thought fondly. And Hilda too. The pair of them had done as Annie had said and called in to see Selina and Cyril while she was in Manchester with Nelly, and since then had visited two or three times a week, giving Selina the motherly support and advice she needed. A sudden desire to see Selina herself came over her. She would pop to her little house for a cup of tea and a chat in between performances today, she decided. She'd have time as long as she didn't stay too long and she wouldn't bother to take off her stage make-up before she left the theatre, so all that would be needed would be a quick touch-up when she got back.

So it was, at just after four o'clock, Bonnie drew up outside Selina and Cyril's terraced house, parking half on the pavement as the street was so narrow. She'd stopped to buy a little gift for the baby on the way; each time she called she took something, and this time it was a pair of beautifully soft cot blankets in primrose yellow with a white teddy bear embroidered in one corner.

Selina and Cyril had to keep to a tight budget, especially because his injuries meant it was unlikely he would be able to return to his old job at the docks. Some weeks ago Bonnie had arranged for a lovely new cot, highchair and Silver Cross pram to be delivered to the house, with a note saying that as the baby's godmother – Selina and Cyril had already asked her and Art to be godparents – she hoped they wouldn't mind her taking such a liberty. The pair had been overcome, but as she had said to them, it was little enough to do. Her own bank balance was beyond healthy and Art was a rich man in his own right. It was easy for her to be open-handed, but true generosity, in Bonnie's opinion, was when folk gave out of the little they had rather than a bounty of wealth.

Selina opened the door to her knock, Cyril standing just behind her on his crutches. His legs had been smashed up when his boat had been torpedoed, but if determination was anything to do with it he would be walking unaided in time.

The baby was due any day and Selina was huge; she fairly waddled ahead of Bonnie into the kitchen to make the tea. 'I just want it out now,' she grumbled once the three of them were sitting round the kitchen table – another Morrison shelter in disguise – with a cup of tea and a slice of Selina's carrot cake in front of them. 'I mean, how much bigger can I get before I burst?'

'At least the weather's a bit cooler now,' Bonnie said comfortingly. The first half of September had been something of an Indian summer and had tried Selina sorely, but over the last days the temperature had dropped dramatically; there was a bite to the air even in the day and the nights were cold.

Selina nodded, swallowing a mouthful of carrot cake before she said, 'I was just saying to Cyril this morning—'

Bonnie never did hear what Selina had said to Cyril. The next moment the house shuddered as an unimaginable noise ripped right through it, and as Cyril shouted, 'Get down,' the three of them slid off their chairs and scrambled into the Morrison shelter at which they'd been sitting. Cyril flung himself over his wife as the world seemed to explode, bricks and dust and glass covering the shelter as most of the upper part of the house collapsed on top of them. Through the deafening ringing in her ears Bonnie was conscious of Selina screaming, of the pounding noise on the shelter and Cyril shouting something she couldn't make out, but her overall feeling was one of furious disbelief. To think she had driven her car here and there through the Blitz and come through unscathed, and travelled to Burma and back with all the dangers that entailed, only to be buried alive when the end of the war was in sight. It wasn't *fair*. And Selina's baby, it hadn't even drawn breath, poor little mite. Instead of the terror she had expected to feel if anything like this happened, she felt murderously angry. With Hitler, with the Nazis, and with the Germans at the launch sites who were sending over the V-2s so indiscriminately.

It was as the noise began to lessen that all three of them realized that, miraculously, the Morrison shelter had done its job. They were alive. And the meshed steel sides had so far prevented the piled-up rubble and bricks from spilling into the shelter and crushing them, although the thick dust was making them cough and splutter. Sensing that the initial danger was over, Cyril wriggled off his wife and to the side of her so that Selina was in the middle of them, his voice shaking as he said, 'I'll never complain about the space this thing takes up again.'

They were in complete darkness, but because the Morrison shelter had been designed like a double bed with a lid, it was comfortable enough. Selina and Cyril had fitted it out like the one at Bonnie's with a mattress and other bedding; unfortunately though, however accommodating a tomb is, it remains just that, a tomb, and Selina's voice reflected this when she muttered, 'It's like we're in a coffin under the ground. I – I don't think I can stand this.'

'It's all right, it's all right.' Cyril's voice was soothing. 'They'll get us out, love, you know they will.'

'But how soon? What if the roof gives in?'

'It's not going to buckle now. These things are built to withstand just this very thing.'

'I can't breathe . . .'

'Yes, you can, Selina,' said Bonnie sharply, sensing that Cyril's softly-softly approach wasn't working. 'But you have to take control of yourself like you did when they found that unexploded bomb. You got all the children out, remember? So this is nothing in comparison.'

There was a moment's silence and then Selina's voice came small and trembling when she whispered, 'I've never been able to cope with confined spaces. It's – it's a thing of mine. I've had it since I was little. I'd been naughty one day and Mother told Mrs Eden to lock me in a cupboard to teach me a lesson. I screamed and screamed in there until I was sick and – and wet myself, but they still didn't let me out. It was dark and small and the smell . . .'

'Oh, Selina.' Bonnie heard rustling and surmised that Cyril had put his arms round his wife. 'I wish you'd let me go round there years ago and give them a taste of their own medicine, the evil so-an'-sos.'

'And have you taken away and locked up? Because that's what would have happened, you know it would, if you'd come face to face with my father. Anyway, it doesn't matter now.' Selina's parents' house had received a direct hit during the Blitz and not even the Anderson shelter in their garden had saved them. Her father, mother and Mrs Eden had been found in pieces, and at first Selina had been terribly upset. It had been when she had discovered that in a final act of cruelty the pair had left everything in their will to a nephew that she had mastered her grief and finally come to terms with the past. They had disowned her and, in doing so, any last lingering feelings of guilt which she had harboured had been extinguished.

'Selina, you can do this, I know you can.' Bonnie felt for her friend's hand. 'You're not that unhappy, helpless, hurt little girl any more, you're a woman, soon to become a mother. And right now you're with Cyril who loves you to distraction, and me, who only loves you a little less than he does. You and Cyril will give your baby a wonderful life with a mam and da who love it as a child should be loved.'

Selina's fingers wrapped more tightly round Bonnie's. 'I love that northern terminology, mam and da,' she said softly. 'It's so much warmer than mother and father which is what I was brought up with. And we will be a mam and da.'

'Of course you will.'

'Oh, Bonnie, the cot and pram and everything.'

'Don't worry about all that, we'll get new ones. And you and Cyril must move in with us until you get another place – Art would want that too. Now stop worrying and relax.'

Selina was still gripping her hand with all her might and Bonnie knew her panic hadn't subsided. Hoping Selina's parents and Mrs Eden were somewhere very hot and very final, Bonnie began to talk about the baby – about what it would look like, how big it would be, names, its first Christmas – and gradually Selina's fingers slackened. Cyril guessed what she was doing and joined in, even making Selina giggle when Bonnie said he would be on hand to change nappies, and Cyril commented that when he had promised to love, honour and cherish, no mention of changing dirty nappies had been included. 'Men don't know how to change nappies,' Cyril said very solemnly. 'It's one of the rare things we can't do, no matter how much we would like to. Shame, really.'

Selina giggled again, but then it was cut short in a little gasp that ended in a moan.

'Selina?' They both spoke at the same time.

'I – I think the baby's coming.'

'It can't.' Cyril's composure went out the window.

Bonnie tried not to let her own panic come through in her voice as she said, 'Have you had a pain?'

'I've had what I thought was backache since we were first in here. Actually, I think I woke up with it this morning, but now it's moved to the front and – oh, oh . . .' They didn't have to see her face to know the pain she was in. 'Oh, Bonnie,' she gasped when she could speak again. 'The pains are really strong.'

'Selina, cross your legs.' This was from Cyril and not meant to be funny, as the appalled tone of his voice confirmed.

Ignoring him, Bonnie said, 'All right, you've had what you put down to just backache since when exactly? What time did you wake up?'

'*It* woke me. About five o'clock.'

'Why didn't you tell me?' Cyril practically shouted.

'Shut up, Cyril.' It wasn't the time for niceties, Bonnie had decided. 'And did the backache get worse after the bomb?'

'Much, but I thought it was because we were cramped in here and – oh, oh, ohhh . . .'

There was no doubt about it, the baby was coming. Bonnie broke out in a cold sweat, so terror-stricken she was glad she didn't have to speak for a few moments as Selina's groans filled the air. She had pulled herself together by the time they subsided, trying to remember everything she had ever heard about the process of giving birth, which wasn't much. One thing she did know was that it wasn't meant to be in the pitch black in a steel box. Cyril had begun to shout for help at the top of his voice, clearly frightened out of his wits, but his hysteria wasn't going to inspire confidence in Selina, and again Bonnie said, 'Shut *up*, Cyril.'

'Don't tell me to shut up, my wife's having a baby, damn it. We need to get out of here.'

'I know that but they'll get to us as soon as they can,' Bonnie said quietly. 'The neighbours will know you're here.' Any neighbours who had survived, that is, she thought grimly. They didn't know where the bomb had landed, after all. It wouldn't have been a direct hit on Selina's house or else they wouldn't have known anything about it, Morrison shelter or no Morrison shelter. A fifteen-ton rocket carrying a one-ton warhead took no prisoners, as Annie had remarked the other day.

She couldn't see him, but she wouldn't have been

surprised if Cyril was wringing his hands when he said, 'How do you stop it happening?'

'You can't.' Selina's voice was remarkably calm and if she had been able, Bonnie would have fallen on her knees and given thanks. 'If it's coming, it's coming, and that's that.'

'It'll be fine, Selina.' Bonnie knelt as best she could. 'We'll manage this between us.'

'I know.'

'First thing, all right, Cyril? Help me turn over the dusty side of the eiderdown so that when the baby's born it's as clean as we can make it.'

Cyril groaned, but did as he was told, swearing under his breath as another contraction brought more moans from Selina. Somehow they managed it in the confined space and once that was done, Bonnie took a pillowcase off one of the two pillows in the shelter, turning it inside out so again it was something relatively clean to wrap the baby in. Cyril's injuries meant he could only prop himself on one arm, but as the minutes went by and Selina's groans became more animal-like, he seemed to have gained more of his self-control. Bonnie had told him to hold Selina's hand, and now with each contraction he murmured encouragement.

If only there was even a chink of light, Bonnie fretted, as she bent over her friend. They had pulled Selina's knickers off and hoisted her dress up over her thighs, but feeling in the dark as she was, Bonnie wouldn't be able to see the baby's head when it crowned, as Selina said the term was. Selina was trying to remember all that her midwife had told her but as the possibility of the birth taking place without the midwife and in pitch-black darkness in a Morrison shelter hadn't been on the cards, most of it was irrelevant.

Bonnie counted to herself and the contractions seemed to be coming every couple of minutes after what must have been half an hour or so, but then suddenly the nature of Selina's groans changed, becoming more guttural as time went on. 'I feel I have to push . . .'

'No, Selina, don't push.' Cyril's precarious composure faltered and died, and Bonnie was as surprised as him when Selina hissed a swear word they never dreamed she knew, before telling him to shut up the way Bonnie had done.

This time Cyril didn't protest, muttering, 'I'm sorry. I'm sorry, love,' before falling silent.

At one point Bonnie became aware that her friend was crying as Selina sobbed, 'I can't do this, I can't, I'm going to die.'

She felt for Selina's brow, stroking back damp hair as she whispered, 'You're not going to die and you can do this. You can do anything, Selina. You're strong and courageous and wonderful,' praying silently all the time that the baby would be safely delivered. Selina couldn't lose the baby now, she couldn't. God wouldn't be so cruel, would He? After everything her friend had been through, it had been a new beginning for her with Cyril. And then the war had come and he had gone away to fight the Nazis and got injured, but against all the odds he had survived and come back to her. And then they'd found out Selina was expecting a baby . . .

'Oh, it's coming out,' Selina screamed a little while later, and as Bonnie felt between Selina's legs there was a sudden rush of liquid and the baby slid into her hands.

Feeling as though she was in the middle of a nightmare she couldn't wake up from, Bonnie grasped the baby to her, feeling what was the head and what was the bottom as she prayed for it to cry. Babies always cried when they were born, didn't they? It had to cry. Please, God, it had to cry.

And then she heard the most beautiful sound she'd ever experienced. An indignant, lusty 'wah-wah' filled their small space and the baby moved tiny arms and legs in her hands. Weak with relief that it was breathing, Bonnie wrapped the pillowcase round the small shape as best she could with the umbilical cord still attached to Selina, saying, 'Can you take it, Selina? Are you able?'

'Yes, yes.' Selina was sobbing again, but this time with joy, and Cyril's voice was choked up when he muttered, 'Thank God, thank God . . .'

Bonnie settled the baby in its mother's arms, telling Selina to lie still while she tried to sort out the eiderdown so that Selina wasn't lying on wet material. She was unutterably relieved, on feeling around, that the liquid that had gushed out wasn't sticky or smelling strongly of blood, assuming, rightly, that it must be the fluid surrounding the baby in the womb as Selina said she hadn't been aware of her waters breaking before. Once Selina was as dry and comfortable as she could make her, she helped her friend unbutton her dress and pull her bra aside so that they could position the baby at her breast. It took a few moments but then Selina whispered, 'It's feeding, it's sucking, I can feel it.'

Bonnie sank back on her heels, light-headed now the immediate danger was over. Keeping her voice calm, she said, 'Keep it wrapped up and warm and everything will be fine now. They'll get us out in a little while and we're safe in here till then,' hoping desperately she was right. She had no idea how long it would take for them to be dug out or whether the air would last. Thus far the Morrison shelter had kept them alive, but what if, when the rescuers started digging, it was the final straw for the steel keeping the bricks and rubble from crushing them to death?

She didn't know if Cyril was thinking along the same lines; he had moved to take Selina and his child into his arms but, apart from telling his wife she was the most amazing woman in the world, had said little else. He was in shock, they all were, Bonnie thought tiredly, although actually, now the baby was here, Selina was billing and cooing to it and seemed in a world of her own. Such was the power of motherhood, Bonnie reflected, smiling to herself. Selina didn't know what her child looked like or even if it was a boy or a girl, but from the sweet nothings that she was murmuring it didn't matter.

It was totally inappropriate considering the circumstances, but suddenly a great rush of maternal longing swept over Bonnie. She wanted her own baby and soon, war or no war. Reason and logic had nothing to do with it; she loved Art with every fibre of her being and she wanted his child, and at this moment in time she didn't know if he was dead or alive.

How long they sat in the darkness before hearing the faint sound of voices shouting, Bonnie didn't know, but immediately Cyril bellowed at the top of his voice, waking the baby who added its cries to its father's, causing Selina to reprimand her husband. 'Don't be daft, woman, we need to let them know we're alive,' muttered Cyril, before yelling again for all he was worth.

Within minutes there were other sounds above them and they knew the rescuers had heard Cyril, but it seemed a long time until the first chink of light appeared and someone said quite clearly now, 'How many of you are there?'

'Three adults and a newborn baby. My wife's had it in here.'

Someone swore and then apologized, and Cyril shouted back, 'Don't worry, mate, I felt the same.'

It was a slow, laborious process clearing the rubble and bricks and other debris. Cyril had watched other rescues; he had even assisted in one when he had been home on leave once before he was injured, and so he knew how precarious it could be. It became clear that rather than attempt to clear the wreckage on top of them the rescue team had come in from the side in a kind of tunnel, but eventually the first chink of light had expanded so they could see each other again.

It was a fireman who reached them first with another man just behind him, and he said, 'We're going to get you out of here right now, all right? One at a time, nice and easy. Mother and baby first. We've got a midwife waiting and she'll go with you to the hospital, love. This one is going to have a story to tell when it grows up, eh? That's it, that's it. You're doing fine, love.'

Because the umbilical cord was still attached to mother and child, getting Selina and the baby out was far from straightforward but somehow, with Selina protecting the precious bundle in her arms and the help of the fireman, and Bonnie and Cyril, they managed it. It was then, once it was just her and Cyril, that Bonnie saw the state of Selina's husband. His trousers were drenched in blood. 'Cyril?' She stared at him in horror. Even under the coating of dust she could see that his face was as white as a sheet. 'What's the matter? Are you hurt?'

'It's all right, don't panic. It's just one of me legs. I didn't get inside here quick enough and I think it might have opened up the damage again.'

'Can you move?' There was so much blood . . .

'I told you, it'll be all right. You get ready to get out.'

'There is absolutely no way I'm going first and leaving you in here. You're going next.'

'I'm damn well not. Art'd never forgive me.'

'Art isn't here and I'm not arguing, Cyril.'

The fireman was back in the hole, bringing a shower of dust and rubble with him. Bonnie called to him, 'We've got a badly injured man here.' And as Cyril protested, she said grimly, 'You *are*, and I told you, I'm not arguing. You go next or we both stay here indefinitely.'

The fireman grinned, showing white teeth through the dust coating his face. 'I wouldn't argue with the lady, pal. Seems like she knows her own mind and you'll never win.'

Cyril gave in with bad grace, but once they began to try and get him out, it took all of the rescuers' expertise, and Bonnie helping to manoeuvre and assist from behind, to move him out of the shelter and into position. Cyril passed out once with the pain and any movement was clearly excruciating. Bonnie found herself marvelling at his resolve to keep his injury concealed from Selina so she didn't worry.

Finally it was her turn, and it was then, as she wriggled partway out of the shelter, that there came a kind of rumbling sound. She twisted over, trying to see above her, and heard the fireman say, 'Hold on, love,' but that was the last thing that registered before the debris shifted and came thundering down on top of her. She felt as though her breath was being squeezed out of her body by a mighty fist as a terrible weight descended, and then there was nothing but choking darkness and finally oblivion.

Chapter Twenty-Seven

Bonnie didn't know how much time had elapsed before she realized that what she was hearing was in the real world and not the sometimes pleasant, sometimes not so pleasant, dream existence she'd been trapped in for what seemed for ever.

A woman's voice, brisk and authorative, said, 'She's beginning to come out of it, Doctor, I'm sure of it. The signs are there.'

'Good, good.' There was a moment's pause and Bonnie felt cool fingers at her wrist. 'The wife's quite a fan of hers, you know. Got all her records.'

'I'm the same. She entertained the troops overseas, and I always think that takes courage, to go far afield and into goodness knows what.'

'Yes, Burma, wasn't it? Charlotte's got newspaper clippings.'

Bonnie took a deep breath – she wanted to speak, to tell them she could hear the conversation, but as she did so pain so intense as to be unbearable took her into the darkness once more.

The next time she surfaced it was quiet but through the layers of heaviness holding her down she forced her eyes open. And then she realized she must still be asleep because she was looking up into Art's face. She tried to keep her eyes open even when the mirage said very softly, 'Everything's all right, my sweet, go to sleep now,' but she couldn't. She was too tired, deathly tired. So again she went to sleep.

The third time she awoke she knew it must be daytime because of the white glare that met her tired eyes. Her head ached and her limbs felt leaden, but it was when she tried to take a deeper breath that the pain reared itself again. She must have moaned because there was a movement to the side of her and then a nurse bent over her, saying, 'Mrs Franklin, you're awake. That's wonderful,' as she pressed a bell on a wire hanging to one side of the bed. The next moment another nurse, middle-aged and far more officious, was there, and it was the voice Bonnie remembered from before that said, 'Don't try to move, Mrs Franklin, not just yet.'

'I – I can't breathe.'

'Yes, you can breathe, dear, but just not too deeply, all right? You've got a few broken ribs and other injuries, but nothing that won't heal in time. All you've got to do for now is to concentrate on getting better and not worry about anything.'

She fell asleep even as the Sister talked on.

It was Art's voice she heard next and this time when she opened her eyes her head felt clearer. It still ached but the dazed fuzziness had lifted and suddenly she remembered. She moved her head and instantly Art leaned over her, and for a moment she didn't question how he was there because of the urgency of what she'd remembered. 'Selina and the baby?'

'Both well, darling. You did a fine job as a midwife.'

'And Cyril?'

There was the slightest hesitation before Art said, 'He's doing all right but has had to stay in hospital.'

'And you? How . . .' She wanted to ask how he was here, with her, but it was too much effort to get the words out.

He must have known what she was thinking. 'I'm home with you for good, sweetheart.' He kissed her tenderly. 'I'm never going to leave you again, I promise. Caught some shrapnel in the shoulder and the quack made a bit of a mess of digging it out. It's going to take time to heal.'

Her gaze moved from his face and she saw that his arm was in a sling. 'I knew something was wrong.' She was sinking again and she didn't want to go to sleep – there was so much she needed to ask him.

It was another few days before Bonnie was well enough to sit up, and she was horrified to find that she had been in hospital for well over a month. She remembered nothing of the first week or so when apparently it had been touch and go, the injuries to her head and chest taking her to the brink and back more than once.

According to the pretty little nurse who took care of her most of the time, it was when Art arrived at the hospital that the doctors had noticed a change in her condition. 'He wouldn't leave you to start with,' Tessa, the nurse, whispered confidentially. 'Had a right hoo-ha with Sister Croft, but he wouldn't budge. He's very masterful, isn't he?' she added wistfully. 'Anyway, as you're in a side room he told Sister he was staying and that was the end of it. She's not had anyone stand up to her like that.'

Bonnie smiled. That sounded like Art. Once she was properly conscious she had persuaded him to go home and sleep in a proper bed each night, arguing that he wasn't well himself, but he had been reluctant.

'I think you knew he was there even though you couldn't respond or anything,' Tessa continued, obviously taken up with the romance of it all. 'He'd sit and talk to you for hours. I said to my Edward, if ever I'm at death's door and they try and keep you away, you do what Mrs Franklin's husband's done.' Edward was Tessa's intended and a junior doctor at the hospital. 'And do you know what he said?'

Bonnie said she didn't but she was hoping Edward had been supportive as Tessa was a sweet girl and clearly loved him to bits. Given half a chance she would rattle on about him for hours.

'He said he was sure that people in a coma, like you

were, Mrs Franklin, can hear far more than we think. They might not even remember it when they come to properly, but he thinks it helps them fight to get better. He wants to be a brain surgeon eventually, so this sort of thing interests him no end.'

Bonnie nodded, but she knew she was drifting off to sleep again against the propped pillows. That was the trouble, she was always going to sleep. She had mentioned it to her doctor and he had smiled. 'Better medicine than any I can prescribe, Mrs Franklin. Nature's own.' Which was all very well, but there were times when she didn't *want* to sleep. Like when Selina had come in to see her with the baby, a beautiful little girl who was as bald as a coot but with the biggest pair of blue-grey eyes Bonnie had ever seen in a baby.

That had been a few days ago, and it was when Selina had told her Cyril had had to have his leg amputated. The damage it had sustained during the recent attack, when added to the previous injuries, had been too much. But, Selina had added, Cyril had taken it amazingly well. 'He just keeps looking at Violet and saying we must count our blessings,' she'd confided, a little tearfully. 'And I do, truly, but I feel so sorry for him, you know?'

Bonnie did know. This war was leaving so many broken and damaged lives in its wake, and she still had heard nothing from Burma.

But like Cyril had said, she had to count her blessings. Art was home; against all the odds Selina's baby, little Violet, had been born safely; and she herself was going to get well. No matter what it took, she was going to get well. It was something she told herself every day, especially when the doubts came. She could hardly believe how exhausted she was, like now. All she'd done was to sit up in bed, and she hadn't even managed that herself. Tessa and Sister Croft had lifted her between them.

But it was no good; as Tessa chatted on, sleep overtook her and she couldn't fight it. But then she didn't want to. Sleep provided a rest from the questions buzzing in her mind that she didn't dare ask. Questions like how long would she have to remain in hospital; would she be able to sing again once she was well, with the damage her chest had sustained; how soon would the weakness in her arms that had her barely able to lift a cup of tea to her lips diminish; but, most importantly of all and terrifying in its significance for the rest of her life with Art, would she still be able to have children? Her upper torso and arms had been worst affected – she'd been told she had instinctively thrown her arms over her head as the debris had crushed her which had probably saved her life – but her stomach had been hurt too. She could move her legs and wriggle her toes, and the doctors had said there was no reason why she wouldn't be able to walk again once she was strong enough, but that still didn't mean she could become a mother. A mam. And she knew now that more than anything else, she wanted to carry Art's baby inside her, to feel it grow and kick and move, to give birth to a little being that was part of her and part of Art.

Her life was such a battle, she told herself as she sank into oblivion. It had always been that way from when she was a little girl with her grandma right through to now. And she was tired of it. But from what the doctors and nurses and even Art *hadn't* said, rather than what they had, she sensed the battle to get well was perhaps going to be the biggest fight of all. And she didn't know if she had it in her to struggle on. She wanted to rest. She wanted to go on resting for ever and ever.

She couldn't have slept for long and when she next opened her eyes it was to see Art sitting by the bed, a smile splitting his face from ear to ear. 'Look at you, sitting up,' he said softly, but in spite of himself he couldn't hide the relief in his voice. 'I didn't expect this when I came today.'

Tessa had washed and dried her hair for her that morning before pulling it into two little bunches either side of her head, and now he touched one gently. 'You look about ten years old with your hair like that,' he said with a catch in his voice.

She felt like an old, old woman. It took an enormous effort to lift her hand and reach for him, and he immediately took it between his own. Her eyes looked into his as she whispered, 'How are you feeling? How's the shoulder?'

'Good. It's good.' He lifted the arm in the sling.

'Art?'

'Yes, sweetheart? What is it, my love?'

431

'I – I need to know.' It barely hurt to breathe now – the pain was all in the core of her, in her emotions.

'What, my love? What do you need to know?' His voice was soothing but she saw his expression change and become guarded.

'Will I get better? Better enough to leave here and live a normal life with you and Annie?'

The relief was in his face now when he said, 'Of course you will. Of course. The doctors are amazed at your progress.'

'And sing again?' she asked softly. 'Like before?'

The hesitation was brief but it was there. 'Of course, darling.' And the closed look was back.

'Please, Art, I want the truth. Don't humour me. I'm ill but I'm not stupid.'

It was so like the old Bonnie he almost smiled. But this was no laughing matter. The doctors had told him that on no account was he to tell her that they suspected she would never sing again, not as she had, at least. The damage to her chest and throat had been life-threatening and severe, and even now they were worried that something might happen to jeopardize her recovery. Like telling her that her career as a singer was over. But he knew his Bonnie better than they did and furthermore they had promised never to lie to each other, however difficult that might prove. And as she'd said, she wasn't stupid.

He moistened his lips, his gaze holding hers for a long, long moment. 'The truth is that they don't know for sure but there's a possibility that that stage of your life is over.'

Bonnie nodded. Two down and one to go. The hardest of all. 'And – and my stomach?'

He stared at her, his brow wrinkling. 'Your stomach?'

'The injuries to my stomach. How – how bad are they?'

'They've healed fine, darling. Why, are you in pain? Shall I get Tessa to give you some painkillers?'

'Can I still have children, Art?'

'Can you . . .' And then the confusion cleared. 'Hell, baby, is that what you've been worrying about? Of course you can have children, darling. They were just minor injuries and – oh, Bonnie, don't cry, don't cry. Oh, darling.'

'You're sure? You're *sure* we can still have babies?'

'One hundred per cent.' He put his arms round her. 'I promise. How long have you been torturing yourself like this? Why didn't you ask me before? Oh, love, love.'

'I didn't dare ask in case the answer was no.'

'Look, sweetheart.' He sat carefully on the side of the bed with a glance at the glass panel in the door. If Sister Croft caught him sitting on her patient's pristine bed she'd have his guts for garters. 'Your chest and arms took the load, not your stomach, all right? According to the men who got you out, you were still partly protected by the shelter, thank God, when they pulled you free. That's the truth, darling. I swear it.'

'So we can have babies?' she said again.

433

'Dozens.'

Bonnie relaxed in his arms. If her singing career was over she could come to terms with that. It would be hard, and she wouldn't like it, because she had always imagined that in the future when she and Art started a family she would still perform now and again when the circumstances were right, as much for her own satisfaction as anything else. But she could let it go. If she had to, she could let it go.

The important thing now was to begin to battle again . . .

It was December, and now there was no doubt in people's minds that the war would soon be over. It had moved into its final stages and the Allies were unbeatable. Even in the hospital the atmosphere had changed, an air of expectancy pervading the corridors. The week before, Bonnie had read in the newspaper that the Queen had thanked women for their war work, praising the 'magnificent' efforts of those who worked for the Civil Defence, the fire, ambulance and police services, the WVS, and ordinary housewives who had all contributed to winning the war. She had spoken as though it was already a done deal and Bonnie and countless others had been heartened and reassured.

'It may well be that all which we women have endured in the war may indirectly save our children and our grandchildren from another,' the Queen had said, and Bonnie had nodded to herself as she'd read that. She hoped so, oh, she did so hope so. It would help to make some sense of the obscene madness that had taken over certain nations. Nations that had committed atrocities only now beginning to come to light as the Allies liberated concentration camps on their march against the enemy. It must never happen again.

She and Selina had discussed the Queen's speech one day as Violet had slept in her mother's arms, and they'd both been thinking of those other mothers who'd loved their children just as passionately as Selina loved Violet, and who'd had to endure the unspeakable. But as Selina had said, you couldn't dwell on such horrors for long or else you'd go stark staring mad.

Selina and the baby had stayed in Bonnie and Art's spare room while Cyril remained in hospital. Art had arranged for a pram and cot and anything else they needed to be delivered to the house, but after a few weeks when talk of Cyril being discharged was mentioned, Hilda had come up with a suggestion that had surprised them all. 'There's only me rattling about in my house now,' she'd said to Selina one day. Verity had gone to live with her mother after Larry had been killed the year before. 'And I don't want new lodgers, people I've got to get used to. Why don't you and Cyril take over the top two floors and turn it into a kind of flat for yourselves? There's the two bedrooms on the second floor as you know, and you could make one of the bedrooms on the first floor into a nice sitting room easy enough. The son of one of the neighbours is a handy lad and he'd turn what used to be my bedroom into a kitchen for you, so you'd be independent of me. I don't hold with two women sharing a kitchen, it never works. I'll get myself a nice sofa bed for my front room and make some changes in there. It's about time it was actually lived in, and I'll be as snug as a bug in a rug downstairs, especially now I'm feeling my age a bit. And I'd like the company, tell you the truth.'

Selina had been thrilled by the offer and the chance of her own home again, and between her, Hilda and Hilda's neighbour, the work had been done and Selina and Violet had moved in just in time for Cyril to be allowed home. The sitting room had been furnished with a second-hand suite at one end and a small table and four chairs at the other, and the kitchen boasted a gas cooker, a sink, built-in cupboards and little else, but Selina was thrilled, and that was all that mattered. Violet had her own bedroom, and the upstairs 'house' was even bigger, square foot for square foot, than the house Selina and Cyril had lived in before. What with the lights being switched on in Piccadilly, the Strand and Fleet Street, and Britain's Home Guardsmen hanging up their guns after four and a half years' service, everything was on the up and up, Selina assured Bonnie every time she visited the hospital.

And whilst Bonnie was glad for her friend and for the signs that Britain was nearing the end of the war, these occurrences – wonderful though they were – weren't so important as achieving her goal to go home. She didn't want to listen when the doctors encouraged her to be patient, and Art and her friends told her not to fret. She wanted to get well, she wanted to be *normal* and out in the real world. She wanted to *see* the lights in Piccadilly, not hear about them second-hand, but without really realizing it she used her frustration and impatience to push herself to the maximum and the doctors were amazed at her progress.

The Allies had made good on their promise to shift the war effort to the Far East and the tide was being turned on the Japs, but this had prompted the enemy to use a new and alarming weapon – human suicide bombs – and this further added to Bonnie's sense of helplessness. When she read about the Japanese deliberately diving their planes into the decks of American ships and calling the tactic a kamikaze or 'divine wind', she got herself into such a state that Art refused to let a newspaper into her room, but it was too late.

The reports had already revived her fear and anxiety about what the Japanese would do to POWs or American and British hospitals where men were too sick to flee, now that the enemy were worried they might lose the war. 'My da's a sitting duck,' she fretted to Art. 'If he's still alive, of course.' For all their obsession with honour and saving face, the Japanese thought nothing of slaughtering unarmed prisoners or sick and dying men. It didn't make sense, not to the Western mind.

Art tried to reassure her every time Bonnie brought it up, which was almost every time he visited, but in truth he had little hope that Bonnie's father had survived his injuries, let alone the Japanese. Unbeknown to her he had tried to find out anything he could about John Lindsay, or Abe Turner as he called himself, but with the renewed onslaught in the Far East and communication there being fraught with difficulties at the best of times, he'd drawn a blank.

Nelly had come to see Bonnie several times since she had been hospitalized and she told him she had made enquiries too. 'I know Bonnie is down as next of kin now,' she said to Art one evening on their return from the hospital when they sat having a glass of wine together. 'But I've told them I'm John's sister.' Art had raised his eyebrows and Nelly had smiled, a sad smile. 'It's as near as makes no odds,' she said quietly. 'I thought just in case they couldn't contact Bonnie at any time it'd give us a second string to our bow, you know?'

Art didn't, not really. Surely Bonnie being John/Abe's daughter was sufficient for any information, but he liked Nelly and Bonnie had confided that she had been fond of her father once, and so he'd just nodded and smiled. Nelly had had a rough deal, in Art's opinion. He knew the circumstances surrounding Thomas's birth – Nelly had told him about it herself when they had sat by Bonnie's hospital bed one evening whilst she slept. He had got the impression she had expected him to be shocked or to look at her differently as she had spoken, and when he had told her that he wished all mothers loved their children the way she loved Thomas and that her son was a very fortunate boy to have her, it had cemented their friendship in a way nothing else could have done.

Art was thinking of Nelly and Thomas as he walked into the hospital one bitterly cold afternoon in the middle of December. He knew it still wasn't all plain sailing between the two and he thought it would do both of them good to spend Christmas in London where there was plenty for Thomas to see and do. He'd suggest it to Bonnie and see what she thought, he decided, as he made his way to her room. She could help him plan where to take the boy, and he could perhaps spend some time with Thomas on a man-to-man basis while Nelly came to see Bonnie. If nothing else, it might take Bonnie's mind off the tragedy of Glenn Miller being lost at sea – she'd been terribly upset the day before. Miller had gone missing over the Channel a couple of days ago on a routine flight to France where his band was due to play. Bonnie had met him, singing with the Miller Orchestra once when the band had come to the UK on a visit the year before, but now it looked as though the man who had given the world 'In the Mood' and 'Moonlight Serenade' was no more.

He opened the door to Bonnie's room quietly – sometimes she was sleeping if she'd had a bad night – but he needn't have bothered. She was sitting in the big easy chair by her window and immediately she saw him her face lit up. 'I can come home.' She beamed at him and then stood up and flung her arms round his neck. 'Tomorrow I can come home. Oh, Art, I'll be home for Christmas.'

Chapter Twenty-Eight

It was Christmas Eve, and as Nelly stood waiting at the train station with Art and Thomas, her heart was thudding fit to burst. For the umpteenth time, she turned to Art and said, 'You're sure we're doing the right thing – in not telling Bonnie, I mean? You're sure the surprise won't be too much for her?'

'I'm sure.' Or rather he had been, Art told himself. And he still was sure the surprise wouldn't be too much for her – it was just keeping the news secret for the last five days that Bonnie might give him gyp for. But it was too late now. He had made the decision not to get her hopes up in case something went wrong at the last minute and that was that. He'd have to take the consequences, and if she was angry with him, so be it.

The train was pulling into the station and now he winced as Nelly clutched at his arm so tightly it hurt. Her eyes were wide and staring as the train rumbled to a stop and the carriage doors began to open, passengers alighting and being greeted by waiting loved ones. In a few moments it was all noise and clamour and activity, and Nelly stood on tiptoe, oblivious to Art and Thomas as she searched frantically for one face among the happy crowd full of festive cheer.

The number of passengers descending onto the platform had lessened and gradually dwindled to just the last few. Now Nelly was holding her breath, terrified it wasn't going to happen. It had been by no means certain, after all.

And then she saw two soldiers in uniform helping another man on crutches down onto the platform. She couldn't see the injured man clearly – one of the others was in the way – but she heard the soldier who was obscuring her view say, 'You sure you're gonna be all right, mate? We can wait a while with you if you want?' as a third soldier jumped down from the train with a holdall.

It was then that the man moved, just as John raised his head and stared straight at her. All her senses came together in an acuteness nearing ecstasy and for a moment she couldn't speak. She was supposed to tell Art when she saw Bonnie's father – Art had never met him which was one of the reasons he had asked her along – but instead she found herself going forward although she wasn't aware of walking at all. *He's here, he's here, he's here* . . . It was her only thought, and in the seconds it took her to reach him she saw his expression lift from one of exhaustion into a smile.

As she reached him one of the soldiers said, half-laughing, 'Well, I can see you're gonna be well looked after, pal. We'll leave you to it then,' and she heard John answer, while still continuing to look at her, 'Yes, thank you. Thank you for your help,' but that was on the perimeter of her mind. She had long ago given up hope that he was alive, even before she had become reacquainted with Bonnie and learned that she'd never heard from her father again. But her subconscious, that part of her that had been unable to let go of him, had brought him to her in her dreams. And now this was dreamlike and for a moment she was terrified that was all it was, a dream, and that she would wake up and be in the real world again.

'Nelly.'

His voice was the same but that was all. His hair was grey, almost white, and his face was unnaturally pale, and he was nothing but skin and bone. The empty trouser leg had been folded up and secured, and she was weeping inside at the brokenness of him, but it was still John. Somehow a miracle had happened and she could still hardly believe it. Softly, very softly, she said, 'Hello, John.' Such inadequate words when she wanted to fling her arms round his neck and press her lips to his.

'Oh, Nelly, I'm so sorry.'

She didn't know exactly what he was apologizing for and it didn't matter as she was choked by her love for him. All the hurt and disappointment and loneliness and agony of loss were wiped away by those few words, melted into nothingness. And even though she knew she couldn't express her love for him it didn't matter. It was enough that she would be able to see him, to talk to him, be near him, even if only as a friend. With that she would be content. She had made herself that promise when Art had told her John was safely out of Burma and the army had sent notification – which he had intercepted before Bonnie had seen it – that he would be home for Christmas. Art had immediately rung someone high up in officialdom that he knew who had been able to glean a few more details. Apparently the army doctors had wanted to hospitalize John for a while once he reached England's shores, but he was having none of it. Nelly had smiled when Art had told her that. It seemed that John's spirit was intact even if his body wasn't. She'd said as much to Art who had nodded, saying it boded well for the future.

And it did, it did bode well, Nelly thought, as she stood aside and said, 'This is Bonnie's husband, Art Franklin. Art, John Lindsay.' But now that she could see just how frail John was, she knew the road to recovery was going to be a long one.

The two men shook hands, both a little awkward, and then John turned to Thomas. Before he could speak, Thomas held out his hand, saying, 'Hello, Mr Lindsay, it's nice to meet you. I'm Thomas.'

Nelly saw John's eyes widen for an infinitesimal moment, and she knew he had seen Franco in the boy when his gaze flashed to her and then back to Thomas. 'Call

me John,' he said warmly. 'I'm such an old friend of your
mother's we can't stand on ceremony.'

Art had picked up the holdall. 'You must be wondering why Bonnie isn't here to meet you, John, but that's
my fault. It's like this . . .'

By the time he had finished explaining they were in
the taxi and on their way to Kingston upon Thames. It
had been a little difficult getting John into the cab; he
had been clumsy but had refused any help even when
he had floundered and nearly fallen as one of the crutches
had gone off at an angle. It was clear his helplessness and
what he perceived as his inadequacy didn't sit well, and
mixed in with Nelly's love and desire was such a strong
compassion that her chest ached with it. She purposely
kept the conversation away from the war and on inconsequential things during the journey, Art doing his bit
when he realized what she was about. John said little,
and as he leaned back in his seat, his acute thinness
struck Nelly anew. She'd heard the expression 'a shell
of the former man' and that's what he was. He looked
brittle, breakable, and it frightened her.

When the taxi reached the house they all got out but
after Nelly had assisted John with his crutches and Art
had the holdall, she said, 'Thomas and I aren't coming
in,' and motioned for her son to climb back into the taxi.
'We'll see you tomorrow for Christmas dinner.' Selina
had moved Violet into her and Cyril's room and Nelly
and Thomas were sleeping at Fairview.

Art made to protest, but Nelly said softly, 'No, please,

we'd prefer to go now. Bonnie needs some time with her father and I'd feel we were intruding.'

Which was true, but not the total truth. She had seen the glances John had made Thomas's way and she knew at some point she was going to have to explain about Franco, but for now she couldn't answer any questions about her supposed 'marriage'. She knew Bonnie had told her father that she was a widow with a son, and she'd always imagined that should John survive his injuries and come home, one day she would tell him how Thomas had been conceived, but, stupidly, it hadn't occurred to her that John would see Thomas and *know*. When she looked at Thomas she just saw Thomas, her beautiful, handsome, wonderful son, but seeing him afresh with John's eyes, of *course* the similarity in looks to Franco was unmistakable.

She had seated herself beside Thomas when John came to the open window of the taxi. 'Thank you for coming today,' he said quietly. 'I'm not a one for words, never have been, but you know that.' He smiled. 'It's lovely to see you again, Nelly.'

Her smile was a little shaky. 'Lovely' didn't even begin to describe how she felt about seeing him. Keeping hold of the iron control she was exerting was taking every ounce of willpower. 'Likewise,' she said weakly.

'Till tomorrow.' His eyes held hers for another moment before he said to Thomas, 'It was good to meet you, Thomas.'

As the taxi drew away Nelly wanted to resist the

impulse to turn and look back but failed miserably. John was still standing looking after them. In the rapidly deepening twilight he looked a lonely, solitary figure and the poignancy of the crutches and the space where his leg should have been tore at her heart. She didn't want to cry; things between her and Thomas were still not right, and whatever would he think?

And then she felt her son's arms go round her. 'It's all right, Mum,' he murmured, the use of 'Mum' rather than the 'Mother' he usually favoured touching her even more than the hug. 'He's the one, isn't he? The one who broke your heart and caused you to seek comfort from my father that one night?'

'I never said anyone broke my heart,' she whispered, tears wetting her face.

'I worked that out for myself. I've been doing a lot of thinking lately – you could call it growing up – and I know what a good person you are. I love you. I love you very much and I don't care about my father, all right? It's you who brought me up and loved and cared for me, not some philanderer who bedded you when you were at your most vulnerable.'

'Thomas, it wasn't altogether his fault, he wasn't a bad man—'

'Mum, I'm not stupid. I know I'm only fifteen but already some of my friends think that girls are there for one thing only, like – like he did. I asked Auntie Bonnie about him when we were in the hospital one day and you'd gone out for a breath of fresh air, and she didn't pull her punches. She said he'd been after you for a long time and that there had always been women; even though he was married. She said you would never have gone with him if it hadn't been for something that happened, something that rocked you to your core. And then he pounced. But she wouldn't say what had happened, only that you had been terribly hurt and lost and alone.'

'Oh, Thomas.' His understanding was too much on top of seeing John again, and now she wept unrestrainedly.

'I'm not like my father, Mum. I'm like you.'

'Oh, I know you are, I know.'

'And I'm sorry for how I've been.'

'No, no, it's my fault. I should have told you. Of course you had a right to be upset.' She was making his coat damp and now she sat up, blowing her nose on her handkerchief before she said, 'But Bonnie was right – I would never have succumbed to your father but for the fact that John had disappeared and we all thought the worst.'

Thomas nodded. He knew John's story. 'And you loved him.'

'From the first moment I saw him. And we were friends, we still are, I hope. But – but he loved his dead wife. He never gave me any encouragement, you mustn't think that. He's a good man, an honourable man. In spite of all that's happened and the mistakes he's made, I am sure of that.'

'You still feel the same about him.' It was a statement, not a question, and said very gently.

'I can't help it.' She turned her head and met his eyes. 'Was – was it obvious?' She would hate that, for John to know.

Because he loved her, Thomas lied. 'Of course it wasn't, but I'm your son, you can't keep anything from me.' He grinned at her and Nelly felt a flood of overwhelming relief that she had him back again. They had weathered the storm.

He had kept one arm round her shoulders and now she settled back in the seat, a peace coming over her. She might have lost Thomas for ever, she knew that, and it would have broken her. Even John coming back into her life wouldn't have compensated for the loss of her son. But he had forgiven her and he loved her still, and she would thank God all her days for it. She was a blessed woman.

Bonnie heard the taxi draw up outside but she didn't get out of her armchair near the roaring fire. It wasn't so much that she was tired, although she was – she hadn't realized just how draining it would be when she left the comfortable womb of the hospital room – but it was more that she was feeling extremely hard done by.

It was Christmas Eve; the yule log was on the fire, the smell of Annie's cooking pervaded the house and carols were playing on the radio, and here she was sitting by herself while Art took Nelly and Thomas shopping. She didn't mind that, or at least she hadn't earlier on, but they had been gone for such a long while now. And she didn't understand why Nelly hadn't wanted to stay with her and Art this Christmas either. It had all been arranged weeks ago, and then Nelly had suddenly decided she was going to Hilda's and nothing she had been able to say had changed her mind. Nelly's excuse had been that it would be too much with her just coming out of hospital, but that was ridiculous. Thomas loved staying here; Annie treated him like one of her grandsons and spoiled him rotten and Thomas loved every moment.

Bonnie bit hard on her lip, telling herself not to be so grumpy. If Nelly wanted to stay with Hilda, that was up to her. She shouldn't mind. But she did. She had thought this Christmas was going to be so special but now she felt almost . . . abandoned. And then she checked herself again. Abandoned. How dramatic. She was feeling sorry for herself, that was all, and it wasn't a very attractive characteristic at the best of times.

The front door opened and closed and she heard voices in the hall, and determining that she would be bright and happy no matter what, she stitched a smile on her face. The door to the sitting room opened and the light, laughing remark she was about to make died on her lips as she took in the gaunt figure standing there. She was out of her chair like a shot, her cry of 'Da' torn from her, the note it contained so full of an inexpressible joy that it made Art shut his eyes and wrinkle his face against the shaft of emotion it caused in him.

Laughing and crying and utterly beside herself, Bonnie helped her father to the chair she had been sitting in, and once he was seated she knelt on the floor at his feet, her arms round him as he strained her to him. There were no words, but their tears mingled as she rested her cheek against his, carols playing in the background and outside the first starry flakes of snow beginning to fall.

It was much later that night, and the rest of the household were asleep when Bonnie carefully climbed out of bed, moving cautiously to avoid disturbing Art who was snoring softly at her side. She had lain awake for a couple of hours watching the flickering shadows from the fire in the little black-leaded grate, her heart so full of wonder and thankfulness it made sleep impossible. Pulling on her dressing gown and slippers, she made her way downstairs and into the kitchen, intending to make a drink of hot milk. But as her hand reached for the light switch, she paused. The little courtyard garden had been transformed into a winter wonderland; fat, feathery flakes of snow still falling from a laden sky.

Walking to the back door, she opened it and stood breathing in the icy cold air. For once the city was still and hushed, not a sound disturbing the enchantment that wrapped itself around her. *Her da was home, he was safe.* Her chest felt as though it could burst with the emotion filling it, an emotion similar to the one she'd always experienced when she'd begun to sing. As the feeling caused her throat to ache she shut her eyes and softly, very softly because her voice had lost its power and volume, the words of 'A Song at Sunrise' trembled on her lips. But now she was singing a love song to her father . . .

She stood lost in the words and melody, her voice tremulous and sweet, and for the first time since she had come round in the hospital she truly felt like herself again.

How long she stood on the doorstep in the quiet of the night Bonnie didn't know, but when she finally turned back into the warmth of the house and shut the door, a deep peace had enveloped her. She might never sing professionally again, but this song, a winter love song, would be the first of many she could sing down the years for her family, she told herself.

She sat down at the kitchen table, her legs trembling as though she had run a great distance, which in a way she felt she had.

She'd sing to the babies she and Art would have, gentle lullabies to soothe them to sleep and to let them know how precious they were and how much she loved them. She pictured it in her mind and smiled, even as the tears slid down her cheeks. Her children wouldn't mind that her voice had no strength or vigour to it, that it wasn't the voice of the famous artiste, Bonnie May. It would be their mam singing and that was all that mattered. The rest, wonderful though it had been, was just tinsel and glitter . . .

She brushed her hand across her damp face and stood up. It was Christmas, her da was home and Art was sleeping upstairs. What more could she ask for?

When Nelly and Thomas arrived for Christmas dinner at midday on Christmas Day, they found a radiant Bonnie waiting for them. She flung her arms round Nelly, saying, 'Thank you, thank you,' as she hugged her, putting Nelly's mind at rest that they'd done the right thing in it all. 'I didn't understand why you wouldn't stay here,' Bonnie said a little while later as they sat in the sitting room sipping a pre-dinner sherry, 'and then you and Art and Thomas disappeared for most of the afternoon. I was feeling a bit put out, I have to confess.'

Nelly smiled. 'I don't blame you. But has Art explained why he didn't tell you? He thought he was doing it for the best in case something went wrong at the last minute.'

'I know.' Bonnie's smile dimmed. 'And it could have. He's so poorly, Nelly.'

John was upstairs taking a nap, Annie was in the kitchen and Art and Thomas were outside clearing snow, so it was just the two of them, and Nelly put her hand on Bonnie's. 'Take each day and be thankful for it,' she said softly. 'He'll improve no end now he's home, you'll see. Being with you is the best tonic he could have. He'll get better, Bonnie. We'll will him to between us.'

'Art is going to see about getting him an artificial leg now he's back in England. If Da had stayed in hospital here like the army wanted, that would have happened in the normal course of things, but Art said we'll see that he gets the best one money can buy. He hates the crutches, Nelly. Hates not being independent and able to move about freely.'

'But that's good in a way, it means it'll motivate him. And they've made wonderful advances in artificial limbs since the war began. Everything will be all right now, Bonnie. I know it will.'

'Oh, Nelly, what would I do without you?'

They talked a little more before John came downstairs, and once she had given her father a glass of sherry, Bonnie left him and Nelly together, saying she was going to set the table, or rather the Morrison shelter that masqueraded as a table. 'It's one of the few things Annie lets me do at the moment,' she said ruefully. 'If she could wrap me up in cotton wool, she would.'

John smiled at his daughter. It had shocked him to the core to hear how badly injured she had been and that she might never sing again, but she seemed to be taking that well, unless she was putting on a brave face, of course. When Bonnie had left the room, he turned to Nelly, his voice low as he said, 'How cut up is she about the possibility of not singing again?'

Nelly looked into the dear face that was so pale and thin, the bones prominent under the skin, and her voice was soft when she said, 'Don't worry about her, John. She really has settled that in her mind. She was much more concerned that she might not be able to have children, but the doctors have assured her that's not an issue. She has the right perspective on things, on life.'

John nodded. He turned his gaze to the crackling fire; it was almost hurting him to look into Nelly's heart-shaped face. She was just the same as he remembered; she didn't seem to have aged at all apart from the faint touch of silver here and there in the sandy gold hair. But her skin was still clear and unlined, her deep-green eyes wide and heavily lashed and she was as slim as someone half her age. A beautiful woman. But she had always been lovely. 'The right perspective on life,' he murmured. 'She doesn't take after me then.'

'Don't say that.'

'It's true though, isn't it?' He continued to look into the fire. 'Through my stupidity she was left at the mercy of Louisa's mother and grew up without me to take care of her. Nothing I can do or say will change that.'

'We all make mistakes, John, and you were trying to find a way to make a better life for her.'

'A flawed way. I was a fool. I've been a fool most of my life, one way or another.'

Again she said, 'Don't say that.'

Once, years ago, this woman had been his for the taking. He had known he only had to say the word and she would have married him and been a good mother to Bonnie, but he had clung to the belief that to do so would have been a betrayal of what he'd felt for Louisa. It had taken Skelton's thugs and the years since then for him to understand that loving Nelly – and he had, although he'd fought against admitting it to himself for a long time – didn't lessen what he'd felt for Bonnie's mother one iota. But none of that mattered, not really. He hadn't been good enough for Nelly then, and he was even less so now. Once he would have been able to give her his strength and virility, children of her own, but now . . . look at him. He made himself sick.

Quietly, he said, 'Thomas's father?' He didn't say Franco. That had to come from her and if she wanted to pretend the boy was her husband's, then that was her right. 'Were you happy with him, this – this Mr Harper?'

'We both know who the father of Thomas was, John.'

Her quiet reply brought his gaze swinging to her face but now Nelly was staring into the flames. She had made the decision some time during the night when she had lain awake tossing and turning, that should he enquire about Thomas she would tell him the truth. About Franco, about her supposed marriage, everything.

'After you left the fair we thought you were dead. Everyone thought you were dead, even the police. I – I was upset.' The understatement of the year, Nelly thought painfully. 'Franco had always wanted me and one night . . . Well, you can guess. That once – and it was only once – gave me my beautiful boy, so in all honesty I can't say I completely regret it. Does that shock you?' She raised her eyes for a moment.

'Of course it doesn't shock me, Nelly.'

'And there was no husband. Harper is my real name. I was born Eleanor Harper and my parents were wealthy, but we never got on. I rebelled against them and used the money that my grandmother had given me to make a new life for myself. When – when I discovered Thomas was on the way I left the fair, took up my real name and bought a house, and began yet another new life as a widow with a small son. That's it, really.'

She looked fully at him. There was no condemnation in his face, only astonishment and admiration. 'You're an amazing woman.'

'Not really. You talk about mistakes, and mine with Franco meant my lovely son has had to grow up without a father. He didn't deserve that. It's my biggest regret, I suppose.'

'Like I said, I was a fool back then, Nelly.'

Something quivered deep in her stomach. His words could have meant anything; she mustn't read more into them. She'd loved this man for twenty-five years and for most of that time her love had brought her nothing but agony of mind. It was only in the last little while that she had come to terms with the fact that he would never see her as more than a friend and learned to be content with that. And with the acceptance had come a quietening of spirit and even a kind of happiness. She couldn't go back to the uncertainty, the longing, the sheer pain of before, she couldn't. She'd endured enough. It would break her. And she wouldn't allow anyone, even John, to do that.

'I want to say something, to set the record straight, and once I've said it I'll never mention it again. Never embarrass you again. And I'm not saying it because I think anything could ever come of it, that we could . . . No, I only have to look in the mirror to see what I am, and you – you're as beautiful as you were back in the days at the fair. More beautiful, if anything.'

'John, don't—'

'I loved you back then, Nelly, but like the fool I am, I had the idea I'd be letting Louisa down if I admitted it, to myself as much as anyone else. You were a cut above then and you still are, and I don't mean just because you come from a different class and all that. It's you, your beauty and your goodness, everything about you. But like I said, I was all knotted up inside then, still am, I suppose, but not about you, not any more. I just wanted you to know how it was, that's all. And I suppose at the heart of me, while I'm being honest, I thought if we got together you'd find out very quickly that I wasn't what you wanted and I'd be a laughing stock. That sort of thing mattered then, before the war. So I'm just saying this once, while it's the two of us, that it was never you. That's all. It was me being a lily-livered coward. I promised myself years ago that if I ever got to see you again I would tell you how it was, so I have.'

The strength was draining from her; she had no defence against the wonder of what she was hearing. In a dream, once in a while, she would hear him say he loved her, that he'd got it all wrong and that he wanted her. But it had only been a dream. Her head was sunk on her chest and her shoulders were hunched, her eyes closed, but his name was wrenched up from the depths of her, 'John, oh, John.'

He went to get up and comfort her, still unsure if her love for him had survived the years and what he had put her through, because it seemed impossible that she could want him as he was now. It was a clumsy and hasty effort to rise and before he could steady himself one of his crutches had clattered to the floor and he almost went sprawling before floundering back into the chair. And then Nelly was kneeling beside him, much as Bonnie had done the evening before, saying, 'It's all right, it's all right,' as he swore his deprecation of himself.

'I just wanted you to know, that's all. I don't expect anything—'

She cut short his words by placing her lips on his, and as she kissed him he realized he'd never been kissed by a woman like this before. Louisa had loved him, and there had been women in the years since he had left the fair – fleeting encounters, mostly, along with one or two who had professed love with the idea of him putting a ring on their fingers – but none of them, even Louisa, had wanted him like this, needed him, loved him with such a naked passion.

He took her face in his hands and now he was kissing her until they were both breathless and gasping, but even then his lips continued to move over her face, kissing her eyes, her brow, her nose and catching the tears on her cheeks. 'I never expected—' he began again, but Nelly put her finger to his lips.

'*Expect*,' she said fiercely. 'Do you hear me, John? Expect, and go on expecting for the rest of our lives. This is the beginning – all that's gone before doesn't matter now.'

'But you could have anyone, you're so beautiful, so lovely.'

'I've only ever wanted you.'

'Even as I am now?' He still couldn't quite believe it.

She kissed him again in answer, and then, as they heard voices approaching, the sitting-room door opened and she rose to her feet. 'Happy Christmas,' she whispered in the moment before the others came into the room, and they were both laughing, albeit with a touch of hysteria, as they turned to face Bonnie and Art and Thomas.

It was going to be a wonderful Christmas.

Epilogue

1950

It was John's sixtieth birthday, and he and Nelly, along with Thomas and his girlfriend and a whole host of friends, were gathered at Bonnie and Art's house to celebrate the occasion. Bonnie and Art, along with Annie, had left London for the coast at Newhaven shortly after the war was over, once it became apparent that the doctors were right and Bonnie would never be able to take up her singing career again. They had bought an old and decrepit but once-grand house set in some fifty acres of land, a view across rolling fields to the back of it that eventually led to a coastal path and down to the beach if you were prepared for a very long walk. The grounds had a wonderful five-acre orchard containing productive fruit trees, a huge vegetable garden and several greenhouses, and most important of all a separate three-bedroomed cottage that was actually in better condition than the house when they saw it. It was here that John and Nelly, who had married within weeks of John coming back to England, set up home together, along with Thomas.

Bonnie had decided that if her career in the limelight was over then she wanted more of an outdoor life, and a smallholding with a bit of market gardening thrown in was the answer. It had taken nearly a year to get the house in order, but they had managed to furnish the six-bedroomed property fairly cheaply. It seemed that people didn't want big houses after the war and large places were being subdivided into smaller units with the result that more and more items were finding their way into junk shops and auction rooms – huge old pieces of furniture that were nevertheless beautiful with an ageless charm. They fitted well into the somewhat baronial rooms of Westwinds.

And it was here, in the master bedroom, exactly a year to the day after the country had celebrated VJ Day, that John Arthur Franklin made his way into the world, followed sixteen months later by his twin sisters, Daisy Louisa and Rose Bonnie, in the middle of the coldest winter in living memory. Relentless snowstorms, six-foot drifts and sub-zero temperatures for weeks on end brought Britain to its knees, but the huge roaring fires that were kept going twenty-four hours a day in Westwinds' cavernous fireplaces, and the self-sufficiency that Bonnie's smallholding-cum-market-garden was already well on the way to providing, meant everyone was warm and snug and well fed.

Thomas had made it clear to Nelly and John after the move that further education was not for him, despite his academic prowess, and John wisely persuaded Nelly not to force the issue in spite of her disappointment. Thomas agreed to take a couple of courses on farm management and accountancy, however, with a view to developing and running the business side of the enterprise at Westwinds under Bonnie's overall control. Along with Thomas, Bonnie employed two gardeners, a woman who came each day to assist Nelly in the dairy that was attached to the main house – they had a small herd of five gentle dairy cows – and two general hands, big burly village lads who worked, as Art put it, like the dickens and were worth their weight in gold.

John would never be the man he was before the war – his injuries had been too severe for that – but over time he'd learned to walk very well on his new artificial leg and function independently which meant the world to him. He was in charge of their flock of chickens, and his care was reflected in the huge quantities of eggs the birds laid regularly. Like the cows, he knew each of the fowls by name and swore they all had personalities of their own, which effectively put paid to the idea of any of his charges ending up as a roast dinner.

Art had continued to keep on his nightclub in London when they had moved to Newhaven, unable to let go of his old life completely. Most weekends he joined the band he employed there, and often Annie would make the journey to London with him and visit her children and grandchildren, staying overnight with one or another of them.

Bonnie completely understood her husband's need to

continue to perform. The band members, on the whole, were the old crew Art had played with before the war, with a few new faces replacing the ones who hadn't made it home. She knew Art came into his own when he played in front of a live audience and she would never have dreamed of denying him that, or asked him not to fulfil the record contracts that continued to come his way. Music and performing were in his blood, as singing had been in hers, and but for the accident that had put paid to her career she knew she would have continued to sing occasionally. But she didn't brood about that. If, now and again, she became a little sad, she would look into the faces of her precious children and know that she had been given much more than she had lost. And she would be content.

Westwinds and its little community was a happy, blessed place, the peacefulness, the breathtaking views, the clean, clear air and the proximity of the animals and birds providing healing to her father in a way that nothing else could have done. And they all needed healing in their different ways after the war. The price of victory and defeat had been fifty-five million men, women and children dead, countries facing years of rebuilding and inevitable political turmoil, and memories that would scar many more millions for the rest of their days – because lives lost can never be recaptured and those who grieve will never forget.

Bonnie looked down at the baby in her arms. She had left the celebrations for her father downstairs, and escaped to the quiet of her bedroom for a little while to feed her newborn baby in peace. Little Betty was only two weeks old, a bonny nine-pound baby with a shock of blonde hair like her namesake. 'Bonnie and Betty once again,' Bonnie whispered, stroking the soft downy brow with the tip of one finger as the baby snuffled in her feeding. 'And I'll tell you all about your lovely Auntie Betty, my darling. She won't be forgotten.'

She lifted her head and sat gazing out of the open window, drinking in the mellow September afternoon. The high sky was a deep cornflower blue, and the smell of woodsmoke drifted on the warm breeze.

Betty should have been here today. She should be laughing and celebrating downstairs with the others, with Selina and Cyril and Violet and little baby Cyril, with Hilda and Annie, Enoch and Gladys, Ralph and Mary, Nelly and Thomas, and all their other friends. She was so glad that Verity had come today with her new husband, but it should have been Larry down there. Poor Larry, who'd driven Hilda mad half the time but who'd given his life for what he believed in, as so many others had done.

She heard Thomas's voice below her window, and in the next moment he and his girlfriend, a local girl, came into sight, strolling arm in arm. Thomas was twenty-one years old now, and he had been courting his Esme for nearly two years. He had never even looked at another girl, in spite of the lassies buzzing around him like bees round a honeypot. And Esme adored him. But then why wouldn't she? Bonnie thought with a smile. He was a lovely lad, inside and out.

She watched them as they walked, and as he turned his head, laughing at something Esme had said, the resemblance to Franco was so strong it caused Bonnie to inhale sharply. She hadn't thought about it for years, but like this, from a distance, the similarity was striking.

She sat up straighter, causing little Betty to give a loud squawk of protest as the baby momentarily lost her grip on the nipple, before once more taking it into her mouth and sucking greedily.

Along with the thought of Franco came her grandmother. Bonnie pictured Margarita in her mind, waiting for the curdling in her stomach of hate and resentment that always accompanied thoughts of her grandmother. And then one of the baby's soft little hands opened and shut on her breast like a warm flower, and she gazed down at the new life in her arms. Outside in the vast open sky a flock of starlings were swooping and whirling, the sun touching their wings as they flew, free and living in the moment, and suddenly Bonnie realized this was her moment. Her moment to let the past go, to let the bitterness and hate and anger seep out of her. She didn't want to hold on to it any more – that wasn't the person she was now.

'I forgive you, Grandma,' she whispered softly. 'Whether you want it or not, I forgive you.'

Her gaze followed the birds in their joyful elation and she felt she was one with them. She had her life and it was precious, a life full of love. From somewhere outside the room she heard her name being called and her mouth lifted in a smile . . .

Dancing in the Moonlight

By Rita Bradshaw

As her mother lies dying, twelve-year-old Lucy Fallow promises to look after her younger siblings and keep house for her father and two older brothers.

Over the following years the Depression tightens its grip. Times are hard and Lucy's situation is made more difficult by the ominous presence of Tom Crawford, the eldest son of her mother's lifelong friend, who lives next door.

Lucy's growing friendship with Tom's younger brother, Jacob, only fuels Tom's obsession with her. He persuades Lucy's father and brothers to work for him on the wrong side of the law as part of his plan to force Lucy to marry him.

Tom sees Lucy and Jacob dancing together one night and a chain of heartbreaking events is set in motion. Torn apart from the boy she loves, Lucy wonders if she and Jacob will ever dance in the moonlight again . . .

Beyond the Veil of Tears

By Rita Bradshaw

Fifteen-year-old Angeline Stewart is heartbroken when her beloved parents are killed in a coaching accident, leaving her an only child in the care of her uncle.

Naive and innocent, Angeline is easy prey for the handsome and ruthless Oswald Golding. He is looking for a rich heiress to solve the money troubles his gambling and womanizing have caused.

On her wedding night, Angeline enters a nightmare from which there is no awakening. Oswald proves to be more sadistic and violent than she could ever have imagined. When she finds out she is expecting a child, Angeline makes plans to run away and decides to take her chances fending for herself and her baby. But then tragedy strikes again . . .

The Colours of Love

By Rita Bradshaw

England is at war, but nothing can dim land girl Esther Wynford's happiness at marrying the love of her life – fighter pilot Monty Grant. But months later, on the birth of her daughter Joy, Esther's world falls apart.

Esther's dying mother confesses to a dark secret that she has kept to herself for twenty years: Esther is not her natural daughter. Esther's real mother was forced to give up her baby to an orphanage – and now Joy's birth makes the reason for this clear, as Esther's true parentage is revealed.

Harshly rejected by Monty, and with the man Esther believed was her father breathing fire and damnation, she takes her precious baby and leaves everything and everyone she's ever known, determined to fend for herself and her child. But her fight is just beginning . . .

Snowflakes in the Wind

By Rita Bradshaw

It's Christmas Eve 1920 when nine-year-old Abby Kirby's family is ripped apart by a terrible tragedy. Leaving everything she's ever known, Abby takes her younger brother and runs away to the tough existence of the Border farming community.

Years pass. Abby becomes a beautiful young woman and falls in love, but her past haunts her, casting dark shadows. Furthermore, in the very place she's taken refuge is someone who wishes her harm.

With her heart broken, Abby decides to make a new life as a nurse. When the Second World War breaks out, she volunteers as a QA nurse and is sent overseas. However, life takes another unexpected and dangerous turn when she becomes a prisoner of the Japanese. It is then that Abby realizes that whatever has gone before is nothing compared to what lies ahead . . .

FOR MORE ON

RITA BRADSHAW

sign up to receive our

SAGA NEWSLETTER

Packed with features, competitions, authors'
and readers' letters and news of exclusive events,
it's a must-read for every Rita Bradshaw fan!

Simply fill in your details below and tick to confirm that you would
like to receive saga-related news and promotions and return to us at
Pan Macmillan, Saga Newsletter, 20 New Wharf Road, London N1 9RR.

NAME

ADDRESS

POSTCODE

EMAIL

☐ *I would like to receive saga-related news and promotions (please tick)*

*You can unsubscribe at any time in writing or through our website where you can also
see our privacy policy which explains how we will store and use your data.*

The People's Friend

If you enjoy quality fiction, you'll love
The People's Friend magazine. Every weekly issue
contains seven original short stories and
two exclusively written serial instalments.

On sale every Wednesday, the *Friend* also includes
travel, puzzles, health advice, knitting and craft
projects and recipes.

It's the magazine for women who love reading!

For great subscription offers, call 0800 318846.

twitter.com/@TheFriendMag
www.facebook.com/PeoplesFriendMagazine
www.thepeoplesfriend.co.uk